Susan Stephens was ⟨...⟩
meeting her husband ⟨...⟩
of Malta. In true Mills & Boon style, ⟨...⟩
Monday, became engaged on Friday and married
three months later. Susan enjoys entertaining, travel
and going to the theatre. To relax she reads, cooks
and plays the piano, and when she's had enough of
relaxing she throws herself off mountains on skis or
gallops through the countryside, singing loudly.

Born and raised in the Australian bush, **Miranda Lee**
was boarding-school-educated, and briefly pursued
a career in classical music before moving to Sydney
and embracing the world of computers. Happily
married, with three daughters, she began writing
when family commitments kept her at home. She
likes to create stories that are believable, modern,
fast-paced and sexy. Her interests include meaty
sagas, doing word puzzles, gambling and going to
the movies.

Also by Susan Stephens

The Sheikh's Shock Child
Pregnant by the Desert King
The Greek's Virgin Temptation

Passion in Paradise collection

A Scandalous Midnight in Madrid

Also by Miranda Lee

Taken Over by the Billionaire
The Italian's Unexpected Love-Child

Marrying a Tycoon miniseries

The Magnate's Tempestuous Marriage
The Tycoon's Outrageous Proposal
The Tycoon's Scandalous Proposition

Discover more at millsandboon.co.uk.

SNOWBOUND WITH HIS FORBIDDEN INNOCENT

SUSAN STEPHENS

MAID FOR THE UNTAMED BILLIONAIRE

MIRANDA LEE

MILLS & BOON

All rights reserved including the right of reproduction
in whole or in part in any form. This edition is published
by arrangement with Harlequin Books S.A.

This is a work of fiction. Names, characters, places, locations
and incidents are purely fictional and bear no relationship to
any real life individuals, living or dead, or to any actual places,
business establishments, locations, events or incidents.
Any resemblance is entirely coincidental.

This book is sold subject to the condition that it shall not,
by way of trade or otherwise, be lent, resold, hired out
or otherwise circulated without the prior consent of the publisher
in any form of binding or cover other than that in which it is published
and without a similar condition including this condition
being imposed on the subsequent purchaser.

® and TM are trademarks owned and used by the trademark owner
and/or its licensee. Trademarks marked with ® are registered with the
United Kingdom Patent Office and/or the Office for Harmonisation
in the Internal Market and in other countries.

First Published in Great Britain 2019
by Mills & Boon, an imprint of HarperCollins*Publishers*
1 London Bridge Street, London, SE1 9GF

Snowbound with His Forbidden Innocent © 2019 by Susan Stephens

Maid for the Untamed Billionaire © 2019 by Miranda Lee

ISBN: 978-0-263-27368-7

This book is produced from independently certified FSC™ paper
to ensure responsible forest management.
For more information visit www.harpercollins.co.uk/green.

Printed and bound in Spain
by CPI, Barcelona

SNOWBOUND WITH HIS FORBIDDEN INNOCENT

SUSAN STEPHENS

For Vic,
editor extraordinaire,
who makes the compulsion of writing
such an absolute pleasure.

CHAPTER ONE

PARTIES BORED HIM. He didn't want to go to tonight's jamboree, but his guests expected it. Ambassadors, celebrities, and royalty who craved the Da Silva glitter expected to see the head of the company and to feast at his table.

He took the short route to the ballroom via his private elevator. Senses firing on full alert, he was on his way to check every single element organised by the company he'd hired to run the event, and woe betide Party Planners if anything fell short of his expectations.

Why should it? Party Planners was reputed to be the best in the business or he wouldn't have signed off on his people hiring them. There was just one fly in that very expensive ointment. Having assumed responsibility for the event last minute when the principal of the company, Lady Sarah, had been taken ill, his best friend Niahl's kid sister, Stacey, had taken over responsibility for running his banquet in Barcelona. And, in the biggest surprise of all, his people had assured him that Stacey was now considered to be the best party planner in the business.

It was five years since he'd last seen Niahl's sister at another Party Planners event, where she hadn't exactly filled him with confidence. In fairness, she'd just started work for the company and a lot could happen in five years. On that particular occasion she'd been rushing around trying to help, spilling drinks left right and centre, in what to him, back then, had been typical Stacey. But of course his memories were of a young teenager whom he'd first met when Niahl had invited him home from university to visit their family stud farm. Niahl, Stacey and he had lived and breathed horses, and when he'd seen the quality of the animals their father was breeding, he'd determined to have his own string one day. Today he was lucky enough to be one of the foremost owners of racehorses and polo ponies in the world.

His thoughts soon strayed back to Stacey. He was curious about her, and how the change in her had occurred. She'd always tried to help, and had been slapped down for it at home, so it wasn't a surprise to him when he heard she'd gravitated towards the hospitality industry. He hoped she'd found happiness and guessed she had. She'd found none at home, where her father and his new wife had treated her like an indentured servant. No matter how hard she'd tried to please, Stacey had always been blamed, and in anyone's hearing, for the death of her mother in childbirth when she was born. No child should suffer that.

Niahl had told him that as soon as she'd been old enough and the opportunity had presented itself, Stacey had left home. All she'd ever wanted, Niahl added, was to care for people and make them happy, no doubt in the hope that one day someone might appreciate her, as her father never had.

He shrugged as the elevator descended from the penthouse floor and his thoughts continued to run over the past five years. Stacey had obviously gone quite a way in her career, but he wondered about her personal life. He didn't want to ponder it too deeply. She'd been so fresh and innocent and he couldn't bring himself to think about her with men. He smiled, remembering her teenage crush on him. He'd never let on that he knew, but it was hard to forget that kiss in the stable when she'd lunged at him, wrapping her arms around his neck like a vice. Touching his lips where stubble was already springing sharp and black, he found the memory was as strong now as it ever had been. The yielding softness of her breasts pressing against the hard planes of his chest had never left his mind. Thinking back on it made him hard. Which was wrong. Stacey Winner was forbidden fruit. Too young, too gauche, too close to home, and a royal argumentative pain in the ass.

Stacey was the reason he'd visited the farm. Supposedly he'd been there to look at the horses he'd longed to buy one day when he'd made some money, but once he'd met her he hadn't been able to stay away. She'd kept throwing down the gauntlet, and he'd kept picking it up. She'd invigorated him, kept him alive, when the grief that had threatened to overwhelm him had become unbearable. He'd never shared his feelings with her—never shared his feelings with anyone. Nobody had suspected the battle going on inside Lucas except perhaps for Niahl, but Niahl was a good friend whereas Stacey had just liked to torment him.

He wasn't short of cash now, and could buy all the horses he liked. Some had come from their farm—whatever else he was, Stacey's father knew his horse-flesh—and had gone on to become winners, or to earn fortunes at stud. The tech company Luc had founded in his bedroom as a desperate measure to pay off his parents' debts went from strength to strength. Money kept pouring in. He couldn't stop it if he tried.

Determined to support his siblings when their parents had been killed in a tragic accident and the bank had called in his parents' loans, he'd used an ancient computer to put together a program that traced bloodlines of horses across the world. One programme had led to another until Da Silva Inc had offices in every major capital, but his first love remained horses and the wild foothills of the Sierra Nevada where the animals thrived on his *estancia*.

As the elevator slowed to a halt, and the steel door slid open with a muted hiss, he stepped out on the ballroom level. He couldn't help but be aware of the interest he provoked. Da Silva Inc was now a top company. Thanks to his talent for tech, and with desperation driving him forwards, he was the owner of all he surveyed, including this hotel. But it was not his natural habitat. Staring at the glittering scene beyond the grand double doors leading into the ballroom, he wished he were riding the trail, but this lavish banquet was an opportunity for him to thank his staff, and to raise money from the great and good for an array of well-deserving charities. No matter that he was already uncomfortable in his custom-made suit, with the stiff white collar of his shirt cutting into his neck and the black tie he'd fastened while snarling into the mirror strangling him, he would move heaven and earth to make tonight a success. Untying the bow tie, he opened the top button of his shirt and cracked his neck with pleasure. There had to be some compensations for running the show, though he longed for the freedom of the trail and a flat-out gallop.

He scanned the bustling space, but while his eyes clocked mundane details, his mind was fixed on finding Stacey. What differences would five years have made? His people had dealt with the minutiae of the contract and briefing meetings so there'd been no reason for him to get involved. He hoped she was happy. She was certainly successful. But how would she behave towards him? Would she be reserved now she was older and presumably wiser, or would that demon glint still flare in her eyes? Part of him hoped for the latter, but his guests deserved a calm, well-run evening with no drama to ruffle their expensive feathers. He'd called her room, but there'd been no answer. The party was almost due to begin. She should be here... So where was she?

He quartered the ballroom, pacing like a hunting wolf with its senses raw and flaring. Guests were starting to arrive. Curious glances came his way. Some women took an involuntary step back, fearing his reputation, while others, attracted to danger, gave him signals as old as time. They meant nothing to him. His only ambition had ever been to blank his mind to the horror of his parents' death, and then to care for his siblings. He had no time for romance, and no need of it, either. His business had brought him wealth beyond imagining, which made any and all distractions available, though horses remained the love of his life. A string of high-profile, though ultimately meaningless, affairs were useful in that they allowed him not to dwell too deeply on himself.

As he passed the bar he remembered the last time he and Stacey had met. She'd knocked a drink over his companion by accident, costing him a replacement couture gown. He hadn't troubled her with the detail, as Stacey had very kindly offered to have the dress cleaned. Naturally that hadn't suited the woman on his arm at the time, who had seen the incident as an opportunity to add to her greedy haul. It had certainly proved a necessary wake-up call for him. He'd arranged for his

PA to deliver the usual pay-off to the woman in the form of an expensive jewel, delivered the next morning, together with a new, far more expensive dress.

Why had fate chosen to put Stacey in his way again?

Or had he put her in his way? His people worked on the finer details of an event, but it was up to him to okay the contract. With a short cynical laugh, he acknowledged that he missed their verbal jousting. No one stood up to him as Stacey did, and he was weary of being fawned over. He craved her stimulating presence, even though she used to drive him crazy with the tricks she played on him at the farm. He missed the looks that passed between them and the electricity that sparked whenever they were close. It was ironic that a man who could buy anything couldn't buy the one thing he wanted: a few moments of her time.

Money meant nothing to Stacey. She'd proved that on the day he'd bought her favourite horse. He hadn't realised when her father had offered him the promising colt that the animal had meant so much to Stacey. When transport had arrived to take the horse to his *estancia* in Spain, he'd offered Stacey the same money he'd paid her father if she would just stop crying. He couldn't have said anything to annoy her more, and she'd flung everything she could get her hands on at him. It had done him no good at all to point out that the money would pay her college fees.

'I hate you!' she'd screamed. 'You don't know anything about love. All you care about is money!' That had hurt because he did know about love. The pain of losing his parents never left him, though he rarely examined that grief, knowing it might swamp him if he did. 'If you hurt Ludo, I'll kill you!' she'd vowed. Staring into Stacey's wounded green eyes, he'd understood the anguish of someone who relied on a madcap brother and a horse for affection; she was losing one of them, when she couldn't afford to lose either.

'Is everything to your satisfaction, Señor Da Silva?'

He swung around to find the hotel manager hovering anxiously behind him. Such was the power Da Silva Inc wielded that however he tried to make things easy for people they literally trembled at the thought of letting him down.

'If anything falls short in your eyes, Señor Da Silva—' the manager wrung his hands at the thought '—my staff will quickly make it right for you, though I have to say Party Planners has excelled itself. I can't remember any big event we've held here running quite so smoothly.'

'Thank you for the reassurance, *señor*,' Lucas returned politely. 'I was just thinking the same thing.' As there was still no sign of Stacey, he asked, 'The team leader of Party Planners—have you seen her?'

'Ah, yes, *señor*. Señorita Winner is in the kitchen checking last-minute details.'

The manager looked relieved that he had finally been of help, and Lucas gave his arm a reassuring pat. 'You and your staff are top class, and I know you will give the party planners every assistance.'

Why hadn't she come to find him? He ground his jaw as the manager hurried away. Surely the client was important too?

So thinks a man who hasn't given Stacey's whereabouts or well-being a passing thought for the past five years, he mused. *And yet now I expect her to dance attendance on me?*

Frankly, yes. Da Silva Inc was everyone's most valuable account. To be associated with his company was considered a seal of quality, as well as a guarantee of future success. She should be thanking him, not avoiding him.

Was that his problem? Or was it picturing Stacey as she might be now, a worldly and experienced woman, socially and sexually confident in any setting?

That might be grating on his tetchy psyche, he conceded grudgingly. She'd always had her own mind, and would no doubt appear when she was ready, and not a moment before. And if he didn't know what to expect, at least he knew what he wanted.

He wanted the wild child Stacey had been as a teenager, the woman who could be infuriating one minute and then caring and tender the next. He wanted all of her and he wanted her now, for, as frustratingly defiant as Stacey was, she could light up a room. Every other woman present would fall short because of her.

Irritating, impossible to ignore, beautiful, *vulnerable* Stacey...

And that vulnerability was the very reason he couldn't have her. She'd been through enough. He was no saint. No comfort blanket, either. He was a hard-bitten businessman with ice where his heart used to live, who only cared for his siblings, his staff, and the charities he supported. Beyond that was a vast, uncharted region he had no intention of exploring.

By the time he reached the kitchen he had convinced himself that it would be better if he didn't see Stacey. There'd be no chance to stand and chat, and a man of his appetite shouldn't contemplate toying with the sister of his friend. Instead, he sought distraction in the winter wonderland she had created in the ballroom. A champagne fountain, its glasses seemingly precariously balanced, reached all the way to the mezzanine floor. Ice carvers were putting the finishing touches to their life-sized sculptures of horses and riders, while in another corner there was an ice bar—which perfectly suited his mood—where cocktail waiters defied gravity as they practised tossing their bottles about. Turning, he viewed the circular dance floor around which tables were dressed for a lavish banquet. The best chefs in the world would cook for his guests, and had competed for the honour of being chosen for this privilege. Heavy carved crystal glasses sat atop crisp white linen waiting to be filled with vintage wines and champagne, while a forest of candles lit the scene. His chosen colour scheme of green and white had been executed to perfection. The floral displays were both extravagant and stylish. Wait staff had assembled, and the orchestra was tuning up. An excited tension filled the ballroom, promising a night to remember.

Like a finely bred horse held on a short rein, everything around him was on the point of leaping into action. Except his libido, he conceded with a twist of his lips, which he would stamp on tonight.

Everything was on the point of being ready. Stacey loved this moment just before the starting gun went off. She was still dressed in jeans and a tee shirt, ready to help out wherever she could, but she wanted to be showered and dressed as elegantly as she could to witness the excitement of the guests when they saw the room for the first time, and feel the tension of the hard-working chefs and staff as they waited for service to begin. She found this early atmosphere at any event infectious. It always sent a frisson of anticipation rippling down her spine, though tonight that frisson was more of an earthquake at the thought of seeing Lucas again. She couldn't wait to prove herself, and show what the team could do. She wanted him to know that she'd made it—perhaps not to his level in the financial sense, but she could *do* this and, more importantly, she loved doing this. What the Da Silva people couldn't know was that Lady Sarah, the owner of Party Planners, had been taken ill and the bank was threatening to foreclose, but if Stacey could keep things on an even keel tonight, and secure the next contract with Da Silva, the bank had promised to back off. They wouldn't lose the Da Silva account, of that she was grimly determined. The team had worked too hard. If anything did go wrong, she would take responsibility.

Coming face to face with the man who'd given her so many sleepless nights when she was a teenager was something else. It should have been easy, as she'd kept track of Lucas through Niahl and through the press. Lucas was frequently pictured with this princess or that celebrity, always looking glorious but elegantly bored. He'd never had much time for glitz, she remembered. Would he be with someone tonight? She tensed at the thought.

She couldn't bear it.

She had to bear it.

Lucas didn't belong to her and never had. He was her brother's friend, and he and Niahl moved in very different circles. Stacey had always been happiest on the ground floor, grafting alongside her co-workers, while Lucas preferred an ivory tower—just so long as there was a stable close by.

Spirits were high when the Party Planners team assembled for a last-minute briefing in the office adjacent to the ballroom. This was a glamorous and exciting occasion, and, even in a packed diary of similar glamorous and exciting occasions, the Da Silva party stood out, mainly because the owner and founder of the company was in the building. There wasn't a single member of the team who hadn't heard about Lucas Da Silva, or wondered what he was like in person. His prowess in business was common knowledge, as was his blistering talent on the polo field, together with his uncanny ability to train and bring on winning racehorses. Everyone was buzzing at the thought of seeing him, even from a distance, and that included Stacey.

Would she stand up to him as she had in the past?

Would she toss a drink over his date if he had one?

Resist! That's just nerves talking.

Or would their client relationship get in the way of all that? The only thing that mattered, she reminded herself firmly, was proving to Lucas that she and the team were the best people for this job.

Her first sight of Lucas Da Silva sucked the air from her lungs. At least he was alone, with no companion in sight. *Yet.* Whatever she'd been expecting, pictured or imagined, nothing came close to how Luc looked now. Hot back in the day in breeches or a pair of old jeans he was unbelievably attractive in a formal dinner suit. And five years had done him favours. Taller than average, he was even more compelling. Age had added gravitas to his quiver of assets. Dressed impeccably with black diamonds glittering at his cuffs, he'd left one button open on his shirt and wore his bow tie slung around his neck. Only Lucas, she mused with a short, rueful laugh. Built like a gladiator, with shoulders wide enough to hoist an ox, he exuded the type of dangerous glamour that had every woman present attempting to attract his attention. With the exception of Stacey, for whom familiarity had bred frustrated acceptance that Lucas probably still thought of her as the annoying younger sister of his friend.

She recognised the expression of tolerance mixed with tamped-down fire on his face, and knew what had caused it. Lucas was happiest mounted on the strongest stallion, testing the animal, testing himself. This easy life of unsurpassed luxury and entitlement was not for him, not really—he paid lip service to the world into which his tech savvy had launched him. Having said that, he'd look amazing no matter whether his bow tie was neatly tied or hanging loose—probably best wearing nothing at all, though she would be wise not to allow her thoughts to stray in that direction. It was enough to say the pictures in magazines didn't come close to doing him justice. Power emanated from him. As she watched him work the room, she could imagine sparks of testosterone firing off him like rockets on the fourth of July.

Yes, he was formidable, but she had a job to do. She would welcome him to the event, and be ready to take any criticism he might care to offer, and then act on it immediately. She had to secure that next contract. The annual Da Silva event in the mountains was even bigger than this banquet but when news leaked, as it surely would, that Lady Sarah was ill, would Lucas trust Stacey to take her place?

He had to. She'd make sure of it any way she could.

As the team left to complete their various tasks, Stacey had a moment to think. Her thoughts turned to the man her gaze was following around the ballroom. Forget five years ago when she'd been a blundering intern, trying her best and achieving her worst by spilling a drink down his date, all she could think about was that kiss…that *almost* kiss, when her feelings had triumphed over her rational mind. Teenage hormones had played a part, but that couldn't be the whole story or why would she feel now that if she had Lucas boxed in a corner she'd do exactly the same thing? She was a woman, not a flush-faced teen, and she had appetites like everyone else.

She broke off there to go and check that there was enough champagne on ice, with more crates waiting to fill the spaces in the chiller as soon as the first batch had left for the tables. It was inevitable as she worked that she thought about Lucas. He'd been there the day she'd decided to leave home, and had played a large part in her decision. She'd felt very differently about him on that occasion, and tightened her mouth now at the memory. He'd found her in the stable saying goodbye to the colt she'd cared for all its lively, spirited, magical life. She could even remember looking around, heart racing, thinking Lucas had come to tell her that he'd changed his mind and that she could keep Ludo, but instead he'd offered her money. What had hurt even more was that he'd understood so little about her. If he'd thought cold cash could replace a beloved animal, he hadn't known her at all. Her father had promised he would never sell Ludo. They'd breed from him, he'd said. But he'd lied.

She'd learned later that Lucas hadn't realised Ludo was her horse when he'd made the offer, but her father had sold him on without even telling her. That had been the straw that broke the camel's back. She'd been thinking about leaving the restrictions of the farm, and after that there had been no reason to stay. The only way she could ever keep an animal was by funding it herself, and to do that she had to study and gain qualifications. A career was the only route to independence.

She gave those members of the team dealing with the supply of drinks the go-ahead to stack the extra cases of champagne out of the way but close by the chiller ready to reload, and joined them in moving the heavy boxes. Lucas wasn't to blame for her decision to leave home, she reflected as she got into the rhythm of lift, carry and lower. Actually, she should thank him. This was a great job, and she had fantastic co-workers. Even out of sight of the ballroom the atmosphere was upbeat and positive.

What a contrast to life on the farm, she reflected as she gave everyone their official half-hour notice to the doors opening to the Da Silva guests. Everyone here supported each other and remained upbeat. Whatever challenges they might face, they faced together. She was happy here amongst friends. Her father had never liked her, and his new wife liked Stacey even less. With Ludo gone there had been no reason not to leave the isolated farm. It had been a chance to test herself in the big city, and now she was a professional woman with a job to do, Stacey reminded herself as she hurried back to the ballroom on another mission. She'd do everything she could to keep Lucas happy tonight and Party Planners in business. She'd prove herself to him, in the business sense, that was—not that Lucas had ever shown the slightest interest in any other kind of relationship with her, she reflected wryly.

She was halfway across the dance floor when a member of the team stopped her to say that some of the guests were swapping around the place cards on the tables so they could sit closer to Señor Da Silva.

'Right,' Stacey said, firming her jaw. 'Leave this to me.' They'd spent hours on the seating plan. A strict order of hierarchy had to be observed at these events, as it was all too easy to cause offence. Her guess was that Lucas wouldn't care where he sat, but his guests would.

By the time she had set things to rights there was no sign of him. Her stomach clenched with tension, requiring her to silently reinforce the message that when they met she would assume her customary cool, professional persona. It was important to keep on his right side to make sure he didn't pull the next contract.

Which didn't mean the right side of his bed, she informed her disappointed body firmly.

CHAPTER TWO

HE BROODED WITH irritation as he caught sight of Stacey hurrying around the ballroom without once glancing his way. Dressed casually, with no make-up on her face and her hair scraped back, she still looked punch-in-the-gut beautiful to him. The run-up to any event was hectic, but that didn't excuse her not seeking him out. *Am I the client, or am I not?*

She's busy. Isn't that what you want and expect of a party planner in the hour before your guests arrive?

He drew a steadying breath. For once in his charmed life what he wanted and what he could have were facing each other across a great divide. He shrugged. So he'd close that gap.

At last she was back in her room, safe in the knowledge that she and the team had every aspect of the night ahead covered between them. With very little time to review her choice of gown it was lucky she'd made her decision earlier. Seeing Lucas again had shaken her to the core. When he wasn't in her life she thought about him constantly, and now he was here, a real physical presence in this same building, she couldn't think of anything else, and she had to, she *must*. The *only* thing she must think about tonight was the work she loved.

Closing her eyes, she blew out a shaky breath. She had a phone call to make, and needed her wits about her to do that. Since Lady Sarah had put her in charge of running the Da Silva account, Stacey had established an excellent working relationship with the top people at Da Silva and wanted to give them a heads-up to make sure she wasn't treading on any toes when she told Lucas she'd also be running his party in the mountains. It was no use burying her head in the sand. He had to know, and she had to be the one to tell him, and the sooner the better.

Her counterpart greeted her warmly, and listened carefully before admitting that, just as Stacey had suspected, they'd seen no reason to trouble Lucas with the fact that Stacey was in charge of his big annual event in the mountains. Lady Sarah's word was good enough for them. 'We haven't kept it a secret,' the woman explained. 'He doesn't appreciate gossip, and expects us to get on with things, so there was no reason to trouble him with the fact that Lady Sarah is unwell, and you're taking over.'

'That's what I thought,' Stacey admitted. 'Don't worry. I'll handle it.'

'No other problems?'

'None,' she confirmed, wishing that were true. She could pretend to other people, but not to herself, and Lucas coming back into her world had changed everything.

The outfit she'd put together was stylish enough to blend into the sophisticated crowd, yet discreet, so it wouldn't clash in colour or style with anything one of the high-profile guests might choose to wear. A limited budget had confined her choices to the high street, but she'd been lucky enough to find some great buys on the sale rails of a famous store, including this simple column of lightweight cream silk. Ankle length, the gown reached just above the nude pumps she'd chosen to take her through the night, knowing she'd be on her feet for most if not all of the evening. The neckline was discreet, and boasted a collar and lapel that gave the elegant sheath a passing nod to a business suit. Having tamed her wild red curls into a simple updo, she tucked a slim radio into her understated evening clutch, swung a lanyard around her neck to make sure she was easily identifiable, and, having checked her lip gloss, she spritzed on some scent and headed out.

She checked her watch as she stepped into the elevator. Perfect timing. Her heart was racing—and not just with excitement at the thought of the impending party. Would Lucas feel anything when he saw her? No, she concluded with a wry, accepting curve of her mouth. He'd be as smoulderingly unconcerned as ever. But that didn't stop her pulse spiking at the thought of seeing him again.

His first meet with Stacey did not go as he had expected. He cut her off in the ballroom, where, typically, she was rushing about.

'I'm sorry, Lucas, but I can't stop to talk now—'

'I beg your pardon?' He jerked his head back with surprise. 'Is that all I get?'

She stood poised for flight. 'After five long years?' she suggested, her eyes searching his. Professional or not, she'd always been a participant, never afraid to take on a challenge, rather than a person content to laze on the benches. He took some consolation from the fact that those beautiful green eyes had darkened, and her breath was both audible and fast. 'Are you run off your feet?' he suggested dryly as she snatched a breath.

She was smart and knew at once what he meant. 'I'm quite calm,' she assured him with the lift of one elegant brow, as if to say, *You don't faze me*, and swiftly following on with, *Not everyone falls at your feet.* Then professionalism kicked in. Fully aware that she was speaking to a client, she hit him with an old memory. 'You don't need to worry about drinks going flying tonight.'

'Do I need to worry about anything else?' he queried, staring down into her crystal-clear gaze.

She held her breath and then released it. 'No,' she said with confidence. 'Good to see you, Lucas,' she added as a prelude to dashing off. 'You look well.'

'You look flushed.'

'The heat in here—'

He pinned a frown to his face. 'If the air con isn't up to the job—'

'It is,' she flashed.

'Then…?'

'Then, I have to get on.'

He smiled faintly. 'Don't let me stop you…'

'You won't,' she assured him, and was he imagining it, or were her shoulders tense with awareness as she hurried away?

A member of staff attracted her attention and Stacey moved on to sort out another problem, leaving him in the unusual position of standing watching the action, rather than directing it. And he wanted more. A lot more. Those scant few minutes hadn't been enough. Had they been enough for Stacey? Her eyes suggested not, but dedication to her job clearly overruled her personal feelings, leaving him more frustrated than he could remember. Did she feel the same? She didn't glance back once.

She couldn't just walk away.

But she had.

The last time he'd looked in the mirror Lucas Da Silva had stared back. *He* was supposed to give the rain check, not Stacey. He huffed with grim amusement. She clearly hadn't read the rulebook. That must have gone out of the window when she left the farm—not that she'd been easy then. Stacey Winner had always been a piece of work. And looked amazing, he conceded as he followed her progress around the ballroom, trying not to think of her moaning in his arms and begging for more. Her carefully arranged hair was still damp from the shower and her make-up was simple, but she'd undergone a complete transformation from casual tee shirt and jeans into an elegant, ankle-length gown of cream silk that moulded her lush form with loving attention to detail. He watched as she stopped to reassure a member of staff with her arm around the woman's shoulders. As soon as the team member returned to her duties he made his move. There was no reason why Stacey couldn't speak to him now.

She had survived the first encounter with Lucas. Doing a little happy dance inside, she was a little breathless and a lot shaken up, but… *I survived!* And felt a little proud at the thought that she had managed to revive the old banter they used to share on the farm, yet had maintained a reasonable balance between her personal and her professional persona. At least, she hoped she had, Stacey reflected as she glanced across at Lucas, who was speaking to members of the band. Seeing him from a distance like this was bad enough, she mused, moving on. Standing close enough to touch him was a torment with no parole. He was like a force field, threatening to suck her in and turn her brain to jelly and she couldn't afford to have that happen tonight.

'Stacey.'

'Lucas!'

He was right behind her. And it happened again. Her brain turned to mush, while her feet appeared to be welded to the spot. Forcing herself into a professional frame of mind, she focused on the job in hand. 'The doors will open in a few minutes,' she exclaimed brightly as he opened his mouth to say something, and then she slipped away.

Cursing beneath his breath, he determined they would spend time together. Admittedly that was difficult for her now, but it wouldn't always be so.

He was too used to everything being easy, he supposed, to women staring at him with lust in their eyes and dollar signs. Stacey was different. She was a novelty. *Novelty was the most valuable possession a wealthy man could have.*

Hard luck, he reflected with grim amusement. As far as he could tell, there was nothing in Stacey's expression but passion for her work, and determination to make tonight a success.

Left to stand and stare as she moved around the glittering ballroom like a rather glamorous automaton on wheels, he ground his jaw and, with an exclamation born of pure frustration, he left to take up his role as host. Seeing Stacey again had roused feelings inside him he wouldn't have believed himself capable of, and there was only one thing to cure that. And then she turned to stare at him, still with no hint of lust or dollar signs in her eyes, but instead they seemed to say,

'What do you think of this fabulous setting? Hasn't the team worked hard?'

Infuriating woman. This wasn't the farm, and she was no longer the teenager playing tricks on her brother's friend. Had she forgotten that he was the client, and it was he who was paying the bill? Then, right out of the blue, there it was, the flash of mischief in her eyes, the demon glint he remembered. Shaking his head, he returned that look with a dark, warning glance, but his irritation had melted away.

She rewarded him with a smile so engaging he wanted to have her on the spot. His timing was definitely out. The grand double doors had just opened and his guests were pouring in. Forced to banish his physical reaction to Stacey by sheer force of will, he gave himself a sharp reminder that she had never been in awe of him. He could stand on his dignity as much as he liked and all she would do was smile back.

From the first time Niahl had brought him home to trial the ponies on the farm, Stacey had tested him. Daring him to ride their wildest horse, she would jump down from the fence where she was perched, seemingly uninterested, and walk away when the animal responded to his firm, yet sympathetic hand. She was fearless on horseback, and had often attempted to outride him. 'Anything's possible,' she'd tell him stubbornly as she trotted into the yard after him. 'I'll get you next time.' She never gave up, and became increasingly ingenious when it came to stopping him buying her favourite ponies. 'You'll be far too demanding,' she'd say, blushing because she knew this was a lie. 'You'll break their spirit.' The ponies in question, according to Stacey, were variously winded or lame, and would almost certainly disappoint him in every way.

These supposed facts she would state with her big green eyes wide open, and as soon as she got the chance she'd free the animals from their stable and shoo them into the wild, forcing him and her brother to round them up again. Everyone but him had been surprised when she left home. He suspected her father had been relieved. His new wife had made no secret of her relief. She'd never liked Stacey. Perhaps only Lucas and Niahl had appreciated the courage it had taken for Stacey to seek out a new life in the big city when she'd barely travelled more than five miles from the farm.

She'd always loved a challenge. So did he, he reflected as he watched Stacey greet the first of his guests. He leaned back against the wall as she guided the various luminaries to their places. She did this with charm and grace, making his high-tone guests look clumsy. Stacey Winner was as intriguing as the wild ponies he loved to ride. It didn't hurt that she looked fabulous tonight. Simplicity was everything in his eyes. True glamour meant appreciating what nature had bestowed and making the most of it, and she'd done this to perfection. Compared to Stacey, every woman in the place appeared contrived, overdressed, shrill. They failed to hold his attention, while Stacey, with her gleaming hair and can-do attitude, was everything he'd been waiting for.

And couldn't have, he reminded himself as his tightening groin ached a warning. Stacey Winner was forbidden fruit. His life was fast-moving with no room for passengers. She was Niahl's beloved kid sister, and he had no intention of risking his friendship with Niahl.

As if she knew the path his thoughts were taking, Stacey glanced his way, then swung away fast. Was she blushing? Did he affect her as she affected him? Should he care? Only one thing was certain: beneath the professional shell she had developed over the past five years, the same fire burned. She was just better at hiding it.

But uncovering that passion and watching it break free was a pleasure he would never know.

While he'd been studying Stacey, the ballroom had filled up. The smiles on the faces of his guests confirmed what he already knew. Party Planners had done a great job. He returned Stacey's glance with a shrug and a stare full of irony that said, *Well done.*

Watch me, the demon glint insisted. *I'm not done yet.*

Oh, he would. How could he not, when the gown she was wearing displayed every luscious curve, and though her flamboyant red hair had been tamed for the evening it wouldn't take much to pull out those pins to fist a hank and kiss her neck? The hairstyle flaunted cheekbones he hadn't even realised existed. Maybe they hadn't existed five years ago. *Maybe a lot of things had changed in five years.* He felt a spear of jealousy to think of some man—maybe men—touching her. Which was ridiculous when she would never be his.

Smoothing his hackles back down again, he continued his inspection. It was Stacey's quiet confidence that impressed him the most, he decided. That and the glaringly obvious—that she was classy and stylish with a particular brand of humour that appealed to him.

Avoiding close contact with Stacey was a must, he accepted with a grim twist to his mouth. His party in the mountains was a no-go if he wanted to keep things platonic between them. He was a man, not a saint.

A fact that was proved the very next moment when he noticed an elderly ambassador place his wizened paw on Stacey's back. The urge to knock him away was overwhelming, which was ridiculous. He was more in control than that, surely?

Apparently not, he accepted as he strode across the ballroom? *She was his.* To protect, he amended swiftly, as he would protect any woman in the same situation.

By the time he reached Stacey, she had skilfully evaded the aging satyr and moved on, but no sooner had she extricated herself from one difficult situation than she was confronted by another in the form of a notoriously difficult film star. The prima donna had already laid waste to several junior members of the Party Planners team by the time Stacey reached the tense group. With a quick kind word to her co-workers, she took over, making it clear that anything the woman wanted would be provided. The diva was already seated in the prized central spot where everyone could see and admire her, but there appeared to be something on the table that displeased her. Curious as to what this might be, he drew closer.

'Remove that disgusting greenery,' the woman instructed. 'My people should have informed you that I'm allergic to foliage, and only white roses are acceptable on my table.'

Where exactly would she get white roses at this late stage? he wondered as Stacey soothed the woman, while discreetly giving instructions to a member of her team. Clearly determined to keep everything under control and to protect his other guests, she showed a steely front as she moved quickly into action.

'Nothing is too much trouble for a VIP everyone is honoured to welcome,' she assured the star. 'I will personally ensure that this unfortunate error is put right immediately. In the meantime,' she added, calling a waiter, 'a magnum of vintage champagne for our guest. And perhaps you would like to meet Prince Albert of

Villebourg sur Mer?' she suggested to the now somewhat mollified celebrity.

As the diva's eyes gleamed, he thought, *Bravo, Stacey.* And *bravo* a second time, he concluded wryly as an assistant hurried into the ballroom with a florist in tow. Stacey had not only arranged an exclusive photo shoot with the prince for her difficult guest, but had arranged for the orchestra to play the theme tune from the diva's latest film, and while this was happening the original centrepiece was being replaced by one composed entirely of white roses.

A triumph, Señorita Winner! He was pleased for her. But—was he imagining it or had Stacey just stared at him with a 'Now what have you got to say for yourself?' smile? Whatever he thought he knew about Stacey, he realised he had a lot to learn, and she had made him impatient to fill in the gaps.

There would always be hitches, Stacey accepted as she continued with her duties. Solving those hitches was half the fun of the job. It pleased her to find answers, and to make people happy. And not just because Señor Iron Britches was in the room, though Luc rocked her world and made her body yearn each time their stares clashed. Formal wear suited him. Emphasising his height and the width of his shoulders, it gilded the darkly glittering glamour he was famous for. Though Luc looked just as good in a pair of banged-up jeans… or those shots of him in polo magazines wearing tight-fitting breeches… Better not think about tight-fitting breeches, or she wouldn't get any work done. She had better things to do than admire a client's butt.

In her defence, not every client had a butt like Lucas Da Silva.

CHAPTER THREE

SHE WASN'T GETTING away from him this time. He stepped in front of Stacey the first time their paths crossed. 'Señorita Winner, I'm beginning to think you're avoiding me.'

She looked at him wide-eyed. 'Why would I do that?'

Her manner was as direct as ever, and held nothing more than professional interest. Opening her arms wide, she explained, 'Forgive me. We've been very busy tonight, but I hope you're pleased with what we've achieved so far?'

'I am pleased,' he admitted. 'You've dealt with some difficult guests, defusing situations that could have disrupted other people's enjoyment of the evening.'

Stacey shrugged. 'I want everyone to enjoy themselves whoever they are. We all have different expectations.'

'Indeed,' he agreed, staring deep into her eyes.

She searched his as if expecting to find mockery there, and, finding none, she smiled. 'Anyway, thank you for the compliment. I'll accept it on behalf of the team. But now, if you'll excuse me, I have one more thing to check before the banquet begins.'

'Which is?' he queried.

'I want to make sure that no one else has swapped around their place card to sit closer to you.'

He laughed. 'Am I so much in demand?'

'You know you are,' she said with one of her classic withering looks.

'But not with you, I take it?'

'I don't know what you mean,' she said, but she couldn't meet his eyes.

'Forget it.' He made her a mock bow. 'And thank you for protecting me.'

'My pleasure,' she assured him, on the point of hurrying away.

'So, where *am* I sitting?' he asked to keep her close a little longer.

'Next to me.' She held his surprised stare in an amused look of her own. 'I thought you'd like that. You don't have a companion tonight, and I've seated the princess on your other side. I'll be on hand to run errands.'

'You? Run errands?' he queried suspiciously.

'Yes. Like a PA, or an assistant,' she said in a matter-of-fact tone.

'And you don't mind that?'

'Why should I? I'm here to work. If you'd rather I sat somewhere else—'

'No,' he said so fast he startled both of them. 'I'm happy with the arrangements as they are.'

'Then...' She looked at him questioningly. 'If you'll excuse me?'

'Of course,' he said with a slight dip of his head. 'Don't let me keep you.'

She didn't see Lucas again until everyone was seated for the banquet and she finally took her place beside him. 'I was only joking about sitting down,' she explained as a waiter settled a napkin on her lap with a flourish. 'I wasn't sure if you had someone in mind to take this place, and now I don't want to leave an empty seat beside you.'

'That wouldn't look good,' Luc agreed. 'Is that the only reason you came to sit next to me?' He gave her a long, sideways look.

'I can't think of any other reason,' she said, though she knew she had to broach the subject of Lady Sarah's leave of absence.

'You impressed me tonight.'

'You mean the team impressed you tonight,' she prompted.

'I mean you.'

Luc's tone was soft and husky and he held her gaze several beats too long. She took advantage of the moment to ask him, 'Does that mean the next contract's secure?'

He frowned. 'Is there something you'd like to tell me?'

He'd already heard, she guessed. Lucas hadn't climbed the greasy pole of success without doing his research. She guessed he'd brought up her CV to check on her rise through the company, and would know the latest news on Party Planners, including the fact that Lady Sarah was ill. If she knew anything at all about Lucas Da Silva, she was prepared to bet he was on the case. 'Only that Lady Sarah is unwell and has asked me to run this function as well as the next for you. Do you have a problem with that?'

'A problem?' Luc dipped his chin to fix her with a questioning stare.

'The team has turned itself inside out for you, and will happily do so again.'

'And I will thank them,' he said.

'But?'

'You want assurances here and now?'

Before she could answer, a member of her team made a discreet gesture that would take Stacey away from the table. 'If you'll excuse me, I have to go.'

'You're not even going to stay long enough to test the food?'

'I trust your chefs.'

'That's very good of you,' Lucas commented dryly.

'I trust you,' she said, touching his arm to drive the point home.

Immediately, she wished she hadn't done that. It was as if she'd plugged her hand into an electric socket. Her fingers were actually tingling. What she should be asking herself was whether Lucas would trust her enough to let her run an event as important to his company as the annual escape to the mountains. To make matters worse, it now seemed their old connection was as strong as ever, and she couldn't resist teasing him before leaving the table. 'Would you like me to deliver the happy news to one of the placecard-swapping starlets that a seat has become available next to their host?'

'You'll do no such—!'

Damn the woman! She'd gone! And with a smile on her mouth that promised she could still give as good as she got. This was like being back on the farm, where for every trick Stacey played on him he paid her back. His hackles were bristling. And his groin was in torment. He huffed a humourless laugh. Perhaps he deserved this, deserved the demon glint in her eyes, deserved Stacey.

He was still mulling this over when a young woman he vaguely recognised from the polo circuit approached the empty seat next to him, and, with what she must have imagined was a winsome expression on her avaricious face, commented, 'You look lonely.'

'Do I?' Standing as good manners demanded, he waited until she'd sat down and he'd introduced her to a handsome young diplomat in the next chair. 'I was distracted,' he explained, swiping a hand across his forehead. 'And unfortunately, I've just been called away. Please forgive me.' He summoned a waiter. 'Champagne for my guests.'

He left the table with relief. Whatever kind of spin he'd put on saving Stacey from the excesses playing on a loop in his mind had evaporated. They couldn't leave things here. Confrontation between them was a given. Why try to avoid it? He knew when to pull back, didn't he? Maybe not, he reflected as he crossed the dance floor in search of the one woman he would consider dancing with tonight. His primal self had roared to the surface of his outwardly civilised veneer, and it wouldn't take much to tip that over into passion. Stacey had given him more than enough reason. He wouldn't sleep until they'd had it out.

Lucas had left the table. There was no sign of him. Had she offended him, thereby ruining Party Planners' chances of securing the next contract? She would never forgive herself if that were the case. The couples on the dance floor were thinning out, but it would be a long time until she was off duty, because Stacey would stay until the last member of staff had left. There were always stragglers amongst the guests who couldn't take the hint that the people who had worked so hard to give them a wonderful time would like to go home at some point. The band had been hired to play for as long as people wanted to dance and, while both wait staff and musicians looked exhausted, none of the guests had taken the hint. There was only one thing for it. Politely and firmly, she told those who seemed hardly to know where they were any longer that the next shift would soon be arriving to set up for breakfast, and that the cleaners needed to come in first, and then she stood by ready to shepherd every last partygoer out of the room.

That done, she returned. She'd helped to tidy up the kitchen, and now she made herself useful by checking beneath tables for forgotten items. A surprising number of things were left behind at well-lubricated parties.

Another job completed, she crawled out backwards from the last table. Straightening up, still on hands and knees, she groaned as she placed her hands in the small of her back.

'Can I help you?'

She jerked around so fast at the sound of Lucas's voice she almost fell over.

'You all right?' he asked, lunging forward to catch her before she hit the ground. Shaking him off, she gave him one of her looks. 'I see nothing has changed. Still the same accident-prone Stacey,' he suggested as she staggered to her feet.

'Only when you're around. You jinx me.'

'Can I help?'

'No, thank you. Just put a safe distance between us and I'll be fine.'

'As always,' he observed. 'The status quo must be maintained—Stacey is fine.'

'I *am* fine,' she insisted with an edge of tiredness in her tone.

'Too tired to keep your professional mask on?'

'Something like that,' she admitted with a sigh.

He laughed, and maybe she was overtired, because the sight of that sexy mouth slanting attractively made her want to stop fighting and be friends.

'You've done enough tonight,' he stated firmly as she looked around for something else to do.

'It's my job.'

'Your job is to dance with me,' Luc argued to her astonishment. 'Unless you decide to blatantly ignore a client request, in which case I'll have no alternative other than to report you for being uncooperative.'

'You are joking?'

'Am I? Are you willing to take that risk?'

If this had been ten years ago, she would have challenged him all the way down the line, but she was sure she could see a glint of amusement in his eyes. And why was she fighting anyway? 'You're going to report me because I won't dance with you?' she suggested in a very different tone.

One sweeping ebony brow lifted. 'Sounds fair to me.'

'Everything you say sounds fair to you,' she pointed out, but she was smiling. Luc did that to her. He warmed her when she was in her grumpiest mood, and tonight, looking at him, grumpy was the furthest thing from her mind. 'You are definitely the most annoying man in the world,' she told him.

As well as the most exciting.

'And, thanks for the offer, but I have a lovely placid life and I intend to keep it that way.'

'Boring, do you mean?' Luc suggested, thumbing a chin shaded with stubble as if it were morning and he'd just got out of bed.

'I do not mean boring,' she countered, thoroughly thrown by the way her mind was working. 'I like things just the way they are.'

Luc sucked in his cheeks and the expression in his eyes turned from lightly mocking to openly disbelieving. 'You don't stay still long enough to know what placid means.' And then he shrugged and half turned, as if he meant to go.

She felt like a hunted doe granted an unexpected reprieve. Badly wanting to prolong the encounter, she was forced to admit that Luc scared her. They'd always had a love-hate relationship: love when they were with the animals they both cared so deeply for, and hate when she saw the easy way Luc wound everyone around his little finger, especially women, forcing teenage Stacey to grit her teeth and burn. How could she not appear gauche compared to the type of sophisticated woman he dated? If she took her clothes off, would she measure up, or would Luc mock her as he used to when she tried to outride him? She couldn't bear it. And…*if* they had sex—heaven help her for even thinking that thought— she would surely make a fool of herself. Having made it her business to be clued up where most things were concerned, short of doing it, it wasn't possible to be clued up about sex, especially with a six-foot-six rugby-playing brother standing in the wings to make sure no half-decent man got near her. When she'd left home for college she hadn't found anyone to match up to Lucas, and the few dates she'd been on had put her off sex for life. Who knew that not everyone showered frequently, or had feet as sexy as she had discovered Luc's were when the three of them used to go swimming in the river? And he wouldn't have patience with a novice. Why should he, when the women she'd seen him with were so confident and knowing? Was it likely he'd give lessons? Hardly, she reflected as she followed his gaze around the room.

'Staff shouldn't be working this late,' he said, turning to her. 'That goes for you too. I'm going to send everyone home.'

'Even me?' she challenged lightly.

'No. You're going to stay and dance. Don't move,' he warned as he went to give the order.

Stacey had done her research and knew Lucas owned this hotel together with several more. He gave the word and came back to her. Everyone apart from a lone guitarist left the ballroom. When Luc returned, he explained that the musician had asked if he could stay on, as he had a flight to catch, and there was no point in going to bed.

'He told me that he'd rather unwind by playing the melodies he loved than spending a few hours in his room, and I get that.' Lucas shrugged. 'I told him to stay as long as he likes. He's not disturbing anyone. Certainly not us,' he added with a long, penetrating look.

Us?

Okay. Get over that. Had she forgotten Luc's love of music? He used to stream music for her to work to at the farmhouse. Maybe she'd added a special significance to the lyrics of the tunes he chose, but the music had helped her escape into another world where there were no grimy floors and dirty dishes. 'I'd welcome anything that drowns out the sound of men's voices,' she would say.

And now?

'Do you always get your way?' she asked, biting her lip to curb a smile.

'Invariably,' Luc admitted, straight-faced. And then he laughed. They both laughed, and what they shared in those few unguarded moments was everything she could wish for: warmth, a past that needed no explanation, and acceptance that they'd both changed, and that life was better now.

'So, why aren't you in bed?' she asked cheekily as the guitarist ended one tune and segued into another.

'I should be,' Luc agreed, but in a way that made her

cheeks warm, and suddenly all she could think about was that thwarted kiss all those years ago. Would he push her away if she kissed him now?

'Come on—tell me why you're here.'

'To see you,' he admitted with a wicked look.

'Me?' She laughed, a little nervously now. It always amazed her how the old, uncertain Stacey could return to haunt her at emotionally charged moments like this.

'Why are you so surprised?' Luc asked, bursting her bubble. 'I'm the host of a party you planned. Don't you usually have a debriefing session?'

'Not over a dance,' she said.

He shrugged. 'Why not?'

'We've never danced together before.'

'Let's start a new tradition.'

His eyes were dark and smouldering, while she was most certainly not looking her best after the busiest of evenings. Was he mocking her? It wouldn't be the first time. They'd mocked each other constantly when she was younger. 'Me dance with you?' she queried suspiciously.

Luc's black stare swept the ballroom. 'Do you see anyone else asking?'

'This had better not be a pity dance,' she warned.

'A pity dance?' he queried.

'Yes, you know, when Niahl used to dance with me whenever I attended those balls you two used to rip up together?'

'The cattle markets?' Lucas frowned as he thumbed his stubble.

'That's what you called them back then,' Stacey agreed.

'What would you call groups of hopefuls with one end in sight?'

'Sheep to the slaughter'

He laughed. 'Of course you would.'

'I was a poor little wallflower,' she insisted, pulling a tragic face. 'No one ever asked me to dance.'

'I wouldn't call you a wallflower. You were more of a thistle. No one wanted to dance with you because you scowled all the time. People want happy partners to have fun with.'

'The type of fun it's better to avoid,' she suggested.

Lucas didn't answer but his expression said that was a matter of opinion.

'Anyway, I didn't scowl,' she insisted, 'and if I had smiled as you suggest, Niahl would have gone ballistic. He never let anyone near me.'

'Quite right,' Lucas agreed, pretending to be stern while the corner of his mouth was twitching. 'Your brother never liked to see you sitting at a loss, so he danced with you. I don't see anything wrong with that.'

Stacey rolled her eyes. 'Every girl's dream is to dance with her brother, while he scans the room looking for someone he really wants to be with.'

'You're not at a loss now,' Lucas said as he drew her to her feet.

'It appears not,' Stacey answered. She was amazed by how calm she could sound while her senses were rioting from Lucas's firm grip alone. And now their faces were very close. She turned away. 'I'm sure there must be something I should be doing instead of dancing.'

'Yes,' Lucas agreed. His wicked black eyes smiled a challenge deep into hers. 'I plan to discuss that as we dance.'

CHAPTER FOUR

SHE WOULD DANCE and keep a sensible distance.

Lucas was so big, was that even possible?

Even his mouth was sexy, and, like a magnet, was drawing her in. And then there was his scent: warm, clean man, laced with citrus and sandalwood. Damn him for making her feel as if anything he had to say or do was fine by her. She should have stayed until she'd checked every table for lost items, made sure the staff had all gone to bed, and then departed for her room, too tired to think about Lucas.

Where she would continue her lonely existence? She'd made lots of friends since leaving home, but they had their own lives, and carving a village out of a city as big and diverse as London wasn't easy. She had achieved her goal in maintaining her independence and progressing her career, but there was a price to pay for everything, and romance had passed her by. It would have been safer not to dance with Lucas, but he was an anchor who reminded her of good things in her past. Teasing and tormenting him, laughing with him, caring for the animals they loved side by side, had bred an intimacy between them went beyond sex. There was a time when she'd rather have had Lucas tell her that he admired her horsemanship than her breasts, and that was still partly true today. In her fantasies, being held safe in his arms was always the best option, but this wasn't safe. His hands on her body as they danced and his breath on her cheek couldn't remotely be called safe. It was a particular type of torture that made her want more.

Thankfully, she was stronger than that. 'So we've danced,' she declared as if her body wasn't shouting hallelujah, while her sensible mind begged her to leave. 'It's time for me to go to bed.'

'No,' he argued flatly. 'You can't leave now. It would be rude to the musician. He might think we don't like his music.'

She glanced at the guitarist, who was absorbed in his own world. 'Do you think he'd notice?'

Luc's lips pressed down as he followed her gaze. 'I'm sure he would. Do you want to risk it?'

'No,' Stacey admitted. The man had played non-stop during the banquet. Who could deny him his downtime?

'Good,' Lucas murmured, bringing her close.

He'd turned her insides to molten honey with nothing more than an intimate tone in his voice, and the lightest touch of his hands. The sultry Spanish music clawed at her soul, forcing her to relax, and, as so often happened when she relaxed, she thought about the mother she'd lost before even knowing her, and those long, lonely nights of uncertainty when she was a child, asking herself what her mother would have advised Stacey to do to please everyone the following day. She'd failed so miserably on that front, and had begun to wonder if she would ever get it right.

'You're crying.' Drawing his head back, Lucas stared at her with surprise. 'Have I upset you?'

'No. Of course you haven't.' Blinking hard, she shook her head and pasted on a smile.

He captured a tear from her cheek and stared at it as if he'd never seen one before. 'Perhaps you hate dancing with me,' he suggested in what was an obvious attempt to lighten the mood.

'I don't hate it at all,' she said quickly, wishing her mouth would stop trembling. This wasn't like her. She always had her deepest feelings well under control.

'Then what is the matter, Stacey?'

When Lucas talked to her with compassion in his tone he made things worse. She badly wanted to sob out loud now, give vent to all those tears she'd held back as a child. 'I really need to go to bed,' she said, sounding tetchy, which was infinitely better than sounding pathetic. 'I'm tired.'

'You really need to dance,' Lucas argued, tightening his grip around her waist. 'You know what they say about all work and no play?'

'Success?' she suggested with bite.

He refused to be drawn into an argument and huffed a laugh. 'Even I take time out from work, and so should you.'

Perhaps he was right, she conceded. Being in his arms was so different from what she'd expected that the urge to make the moment last was stronger than ever. She'd been waiting for this all her adult life, and even if the guitarist was doing his best to make her cry, perhaps she needed that too. But not tonight. Tonight was a time for celebration, not tears.

'I'm sorry,' she said. 'It's just that this tune makes me sad.'

'It's good to let your feelings out,' Lucas observed, 'and I'm glad you feel you can do that with me.'

'I do,' she murmured.

He must have given the guitarist a subtle directive, as the mood of the music had changed from unbearably affecting to a passionate, earthy rhythm. They fell into step and began to dance in a way that was far more intimate than before, and as the music climbed to a crescendo it seemed only one outcome was possible. Enjoying Lucas was dangerous because it was addictive. It made her want him in a way that was wholly inappropriate for someone hoping to make an impression on a client.

'I should go.' She pulled away while she still had the strength to do so.

'You should stay,' Lucas argued, and as the guitarist continued to weave his spell, Lucas brought her close enough for their two bodies to become one. She nestled her face against his chest as if she belonged there, as if there had never been any conflict between them, no gulf at all, as if this was how it should be, as if it was right and good.

Dancing with Stacey was harder than he'd thought. Not because she couldn't dance, but because she could; because she was intuitive and could second-guess his every move. Stacey was no longer a vulnerable tomboy on the brink of entering an adult world, but a woman who knew her own mind. She'd looked exhausted when she'd finished work, but there was no sign of tiredness now. If anything, she seemed energised as she moved to the music like a gypsy queen. Though she'd looked close to tears when the music had affected her, determination had since returned to her eyes. And fire. She wanted him, and she wasn't afraid to let him know it.

The ache in his groin was unsustainable. He was see-

ing her as she was, not as she had been. The urge to feel
her naked body under his, to drown in her wildflower
scent, and to fist her thick, silky hair as he buried his
face in her neck, her breasts—

'Why don't you do it?' she challenged softly.

'Why don't I do what?'

'Kiss me?' she stated bluntly.

She was hyped up on success and impending exhaus-
tion, which meant treating what she said with restraint.
In the morning she'd be his friend's little sister again,
and would wake up with regrets. 'I've got more sense—'

He hadn't expected such a violent reaction. Springing from his arms, she speared him with a glance, then
stalked away. Halfway across the ballroom her stride
faltered. Turning to face him, she surprised him even
more with an expression that was pure invitation.

Lucas was following and she knew that look on his face.
It was the same look as when he chased down a ball
in polo, or when a shot of him appeared in the broad-
sheets after he'd closed some mammoth deal. He was a
man on a mission and she was that mission. But they'd
meet on her terms and on a ground of her choosing.
She'd waited so long for this that her mind was made
up. If they only had one night together, she was going
to make it the best night of her life. Her body was on
fire. He'd done that. Her senses had never been keener.
Where Lucas was concerned, she'd been honing them
for years. Each erogenous zone she possessed had been
teased into the highest state of awareness.

Walking into the now-deserted office that she and
the team had been using during the banquet, she left
the door ajar. Luc walked in behind her and closed the
door securely, before leaning back with a brooding ex-

pression on his dangerously shadowed face. 'It's been a long time,' he observed in a drawl as lazy as treacle dripping off a spoon. 'And now this?'

She started to say something but thought better of it. No explanations. No excuses. No regrets. The tension in the room was rising. Their gazes were locked. There could be no turning back. The room was so quiet she could hear them breathing. It was as if, having waited all this time, they were balanced on the edge of an abyss, and when they plummeted over that edge they'd both be changed for ever.

'It has been a long time,' she agreed, starting to walk towards him. 'Far too long, Lucas.'

There was an answering spark in Luc's eyes. She was no longer a teenager, or a red-faced intern crushed with embarrassment because she'd ruined his date's dress, or a tomboy arguing the toss with her brother's friend; she was a woman and he was a man. On that level, at least, there was no divide between them.

'Are you sure you know what you're doing?' he said as she stood on tiptoe to cup his face.

'In some ways yes, and in others no,' she admitted truthfully. 'Some might say I'm seducing you.'

'Some?' he queried. 'I'm only interested in what you have to say.'

Black eyes plumbed her soul. 'I want you,' she admitted, as if her whole life had been leading up to this moment. 'For one night.'

'One whole night,' he said, staring down with a glint of humour colouring his black stare. 'Half an hour ago you were determined to go to bed.'

'I still want to go to bed,' she whispered.

Luc hummed as he glanced around the office. 'But not here, surely?'

'Why not?' All the old doubts came crowding in. Was that a genuine comment, or was Lucas looking for a way out?

'Because I don't see a bed,' he suggested dryly.

He made her decision easy when he brushed her lips with his. 'A nightcap?' she suggested. 'Somewhere a little more comfortable than this?'

He didn't answer right away. Stacey's intention was clear. If he accepted there could only be one outcome. He'd resisted temptation where Stacey was concerned for so long he craved sex like a man craving water in a desert. But there was the added complication of his upcoming mountain event. Working side by side would bring them closer still and Stacey could never be some casual fling.

His hunger combined with Stacey's intention to move things forward fast, and in a very different direction, triumphed over any hesitation he might have had. There was nothing safe about entering into the type of situation she was proposing, since he was a man who would happily entertain risk on the polo field, and sometimes even in business, but who would never risk his heart.

Without another word they headed for his penthouse with Stacey in the lead. If she'd been holding his hand, she'd be dragging him. Linking their fingers, he ushered her into his private elevator, which, conveniently, they found waiting on the ballroom level. The instant the doors slid open he backed her inside. Boxing her into a corner, he linked fingers with her other hand. Raising both hands above her head, he pinned her with the weight of his body so he could tease her lips and torment them both as the small steel cocoon rocketed skywards.

Her hands felt wonderfully responsive in his as she made sounds in her throat like a kitten. There was nothing juvenile about her body. That was all woman.

Teasing her lips until she parted them, he kissed her with the pent-up hunger of years. He'd seen this woman grow and endure, survive, and eventually thrive, so this kiss was more than a kiss, it was a rite of passage for both of them.

She whimpered as he mapped her cheeks, her neck, her shoulders, and finally her breasts with his hands, and when he tormented her erect nipples with his thumbnails, she cried out, 'Yes… Oh, yes, please…'

'Soon,' he promised as the elevator sighed to a halt.

He swung her into his arms the moment the doors slid open. It felt so good. She felt so good. Warm and scented with the wildflower perfume he would always associate with Stacey, she was so much smaller than he was, and yet strong in every way. She was perfect, and he had never felt more exhilarated than when he dropped kisses on her face and neck for the sheer pleasure of feeling her tremble in his arms, and hearing her moan with impatience to be one with him.

He pressed his thumb against the recognition pad at the entrance to the penthouse suite and the door swung open.

'Crazy,' she exclaimed as he carried her into the steel, glass and pale wood hallway. 'How the other half lives,' she added, glancing around.

There was barely a chance to lower her to her feet in his bedroom before the storm. He couldn't wait a moment longer and yanked her close as she reached for him. It was like two titans clashing, both equally fierce. The urgent need for physical satisfaction clawed at their senses, demanding they do something about it fast. Stacey growled with impatience as he unzipped her dress and let it drop to the floor in a pool of silk.

They both tugged at her thong.

'Let me,' she insisted.

He answered the argument by ripping the flimsy lace and casting the remains aside. As he carried her to the bed she was still kicking off her shoes. Papers and files littered the cover so he swept it clear, before laying her down. Discarded jeans, files, a laptop, and a briefcase tumbled to the floor, but he cared for nothing beyond the fact that Stacey's eyes were black, and her lips were swollen from his kisses.

'I want you,' she gasped as he shrugged off his jacket. 'Be quick,' she insisted.

Hooking a thumb into the back collar of his shirt, he tugged it over his head. Her sweeping glance took in his torso and he could only suppose it passed her test as she moistened her lips and reached for him. 'Don't make me wait,' she warned.

Stacey didn't wait. Even he couldn't have freed his belt buckle that fast.

Whipping Luc's belt out of its loops, she exclaimed with triumph. With another growl, she freed the top button of his trousers and attended to his zipper. That didn't take much persuasion. It flew down as he exploded out of it. Curbing the exclamation of shock that sprang to her lips, she recognised what she'd been missing.

Having never seen anything on this scale before, she took a moment to recalibrate her thinking. Her previous experience was confined to fumbling in the back of a car, or unsuccessful student couplings where both parties were clueless, so this was very different—but then Luc was very different. He was the only man she'd ever really wanted, and here they were.

Wild with need, she drew her knees up and before he had a chance to react she had wrapped them around his waist.

'*Yes! Please! Now!*' she commanded fiercely, her fingers biting into his shoulders.

'But gently,' Luc insisted.

'No!' she fired back, fighting against him trying to dial down the rush. The reality of being hugely inexperienced compared to Luc wasn't relevant. All that mattered was that he wanted her, *really* wanted her, and if that only lasted for a few moments, a minute or an hour, she'd take it.

'Yes. Gently,' he said on a steady breath that she was sure was intended to soothe her. 'I don't want to hurt you. I'm…big.'

A cry flew from her throat. *Big?* Luc wasn't big, he was enormous, but as he dipped and stroked, and then retreated, her confidence grew. 'I'm okay…o*kay*!' she gasped when he pulled back to check she was all right, but it was too late; Luc already had his suspicions.

'Are you a virgin?' He frowned.

'Why?' Her fingers tightened on his shoulders. There were so many emotions colliding inside her, she didn't know what she was, only that Luc was holding her close and she wanted the moment to last a little longer. 'Why do you ask?'

His look was enough. They knew each other too well for her to lie to him. 'I'm not a virgin. Technically,' she added, red-faced.

Luc's eyes narrowed in suspicion. 'Technically? What does that mean?'

'I'm not intact down there,' she blurted.

'Are you sure you want to go ahead with this?'

'Are *you* sure?' she countered, and, with desperation driving her, she tilted forward to make the outcome inevitable. 'You see,' she said in a tone to make light of things, while her mind was spinning as her body battled to accept a new and very different feeling of being occupied, 'I'm in charge.'

'I don't think so, princess.'

A cry of sheer surprise escaped her as Luc cupped her buttocks in his big hands, lifting her into an even more receptive position. Was she ready for this? Could she take him? Could she take all of him?

Encouraging her with husky words in his own language, Luc rotated his hips to tease her with the promise if not the pressure where she needed it most. Alarm manifested itself in a cry as he sank a little deeper, but then he pulled back. Luc knew exactly what he was doing, and gradually she began to relax. Teasing made her pleasure grow until it became indescribably extreme. Her doubts and fears had disappeared by this time, and all she felt was hunger for more, and then his hands worked some magic, and another type of alarm struck her. 'I can't—'

'You don't have to, princess...'

The word 'wait' was lost in her screams of shocked delight. Release came so suddenly she wasn't ready for it. If it hadn't been for Luc keeping her still to make sure she enjoyed every single beat of pleasure, the cataclysmic waves racking her body might have been less intense. As it was, all she could do was allow them to consume her.

'You've waited a long time for that,' he remarked, dropping kisses on her mouth as her outburst slowly quietened to rhythmical moans of satisfaction.

'Perhaps I have,' she agreed groggily, 'but I won't admit as much to you.'

'And now you want more?' he guessed.

'I'll admit that much,' she agreed. 'But what about you?'

'I can wait.' He frowned. 'And shouldn't you be safely asleep by now?'

'I warned you not to tease.' Summoning up what little strength remained, she balled her hand into a fist and pummelled it weakly against his shoulder.

'You're going to delay that sleep and make time for me?' Luc suggested with a wicked grin tugging at one corner of his mouth.

'I suppose that depends on how efficient you are,' she gasped out, as if she could ever pretend that this feeling of being one was an everyday experience.

Throwing his head back, Luc laughed. 'I can be efficient. Shall I prove it?'

'What do you think?'

'Right now? I prefer actions to thinking.'

She felt warmth flood her veins, knowing they could lie together in perfect harmony, talking and trusting, and—

She must not get too heavily involved. Past experience of trying to give love where it wasn't wanted had not gone well.

'Relax,' he murmured, staring into her eyes to gauge her pleasure in a way that made her feel as if she was the most important thing in the world to him in those moments. It was as if she were standing on the top of a mountain, and no one but him could push her off.

Drawing back, Luc stared down, as though he had to be sure, and then, seeming to have made his decision, he firmed his jaw in a way that made her shudder with desire. He took her slowly and deeply to the hilt. He was so big it was shocking, but wonderful too, and all he had to do was rotate his hips for her to lose control again.

Her pleasure was short-lived, because this time when her screams had quietened Luc said the one thing that could bring her round as fast as if he'd dashed a bucket of ice-cold water in her face. 'I only wish I could make more time for you,' he observed with a concerned look.

The bottomless pit that opened up in front of her this time had nothing to do with the promise of pleasure. It held only the prospect of being alone again. Of course her rational mind accepted that Lucas led a very busy life, but what had been rational between them up to now? Somehow in the throes of passion she'd forgotten he had a job to do and so did she, and that their paths through life were very different.

Sensing the drop in her mood, he did everything he could to reassure her. Kissing her, he soothed her with long, caring strokes. 'I'll see you later…'

'Perhaps you will,' she agreed as he withdrew carefully.

Regret was a double-edged sword. Whatever Stacey felt now or in the future, this was her first time, so he couldn't begrudge a defensive comment. He'd taken the experience with a pleasure so deep and strong, it would fight bitterly, possibly for the rest of his life, with the knowledge that he had nothing to offer her long-term.

Stacey doubted Lucas would make a point of seeing her later. His last glance in her direction might have been one of conflicted regret, or maybe he'd just given her her marching orders. Which hurt like hell when she had given him the only part of her she had never wanted to give to another living soul. But the facts could not be disputed. 'I'll see you later' was the type of thing people said to each other when they didn't want to firm up a date, let alone set a time for another meeting. She'd see him again in the mountains, where it would be all business.

Maybe if she'd been a different person she would have come straight out with it and asked him, *Do you want to see me again?* But the old doubts were never far away.

What made her think Luc wanted anything more than a pleasurable tussle in bed to relax and prepare him for sleep after the banquet? Did she flatter herself that she could hold anyone's interest for longer than it took to give them what they wanted?

Everything had changed, and nothing, she reflected as images of her father and stepmother mocking her attempts to please them slipped unbidden into her mind.

CHAPTER FIVE

STEPPING INTO THE empty elevator on the penthouse level before dawn on the night after the banquet, which she had spent with Luca, was an eerie experience. She'd left him glued to his monitor as he responded to emails from across the world. He had an early-morning meeting, he'd told her, so she should get on.

'Oh, okay, then,' she'd said, realising she'd expected something more—a peck on the cheek… Something… Anything.

Pulling herself together, she'd headed out.

It was a special time in the hotel before the morning rush began. The building seemed empty, but that was an illusion as deceptive as Stacey's belief that Luc must feel something after they'd spent the night together. She had no regrets. It had seemed fated somehow. There was no one in the world she would rather have shared that experience with, but Luc had barely looked up when she'd left.

As the elevator dropped like a stone, thinking about how much she believed she'd shared with him, made her throat tighten. Gritting her jaw, she resolved to pull herself together. She had to get over it, and get over him. When she arrived in the mountains she wanted everything to run smoothly, which meant showing no sign of personal distress. She was his party organiser and Luc was the host. And that was all they were to each other.

Thinking back over the night it was fair to say Luc had given no indication that he wanted to see her again, and neither had she. She'd taken a shower. He'd taken a shower. Separately. He'd dressed. She'd prepared for the walk of shame, donning her evening gown, and shunning Luc's offer of a robe before heading back to her room to change. The choice between towelling and silk was easy when she no longer cared.

Tears came when she least expected them. Her emotions were all over the place, Stacey accepted as she braced her balled fists against cold, unyielding steel and willed the doors to open so she could step out into a new day and make a better job of it. Squeezing her eyes tightly shut, she tried to understand why, after getting everything she'd ever wanted with Luc last night—everything she had *thought* she wanted—it still wasn't nearly enough.

His penthouse had never felt empty before, but lacking Stacey's vibrant presence it was just another hotel room. Having showered, he slipped into sweats, and began pacing the sleek, Scandi-style sitting room overlooking Barcelona. The astonishing sights were lost on him. Even the sun shooting its rays above a distant horizon meant nothing to him. He'd never felt like this after making love to a woman. Truthfully, he'd never felt anything. Animal instinct was a powerful driver, and knowing that, he should have slowed things down with Stacey, but his first sight of her after a space of five years had tilted his world on its axis.

What the hell was happening to him?

Staring into the mirror, he raked his hair and growled

as he shook his head like an angry wolf. Stubble blackened his face. His hard, unyielding face. Beneath her professional shell, Stacey was still as soft and vulnerable as ever, and damaged by the past. He, of all people, should understand that. But he'd never felt like this before. It was as if everything that had been missing from his life had come pouring in, but too fast, so that instead of tender, protective thoughts, wild, animal passion consumed him.

Planting his fists against cold granite on the breakfast bar, he dipped his head and tightened his jaw. He'd seen too much of Stacey's early life not to care. She'd used him for satisfaction, but he'd hardly been a passive bystander and had never known pleasure like it. Stacey had well and truly turned the tables, and when they met again...*if* they met again...

When they met again, he determined fiercely. For her sake, he'd be cool and distant so as not to mislead her. But was that the best he could do to save her from another cold, unfeeling man? Her father had done enough damage, and he could not bear to do more.

Did she feel anything for him?

Damage from the past cut deep in both of them. Doubt and mistrust were never far away. Lifting his head, he smiled in acknowledgement of this.

But they could change. He could change.

Could he?

The real question was, did he want to?

She was looking forward to the big event in the mountains, and it had to stay that way. How Luc would feel when he saw her again, remained to be seen. Her feelings were unchanged. From day one she had felt something for him—a lot, she admitted—so if he ignored her or, worse, if he was unemotional, and confined their dealings solely to business, it would mean putting on the act of her life.

And she would, she determined as she said good-bye to the team. 'See you in the mountains!' she exclaimed brightly as she wondered why life had to be so complicated.

Because life was tough for everyone, she concluded when she was alone in the room, gathering up her things. Nothing was straightforward for anyone, and, short of locking herself away and never doing anything, there *would* be hurt and disappointment, and pain, but there would be moments of happiness too, so she'd cling to those and get through it. Dreaming of a life with Luc was not only unrealistic, it would be like walking into pain with her eyes wide open. Any thoughts of a long-term relationship between them was a fantasy too far. Luc was a high-flyer while she had barely tested her wings. As far as business was concerned, she was confident he couldn't have any complaints, but when it came to personal feelings... Maybe she'd never know what he felt. Luc had always kept personal matters close to his chest. Niahl's theory was that Luc would never open up, because that would mean confronting the grief of losing his parents. The stresses of business and people who depended on him for their livelihoods, together with concern for his siblings, had robbed him of the chance to grieve.

Niahl was probably right, and Luc had spent so many years regarding her as nothing more than Niahl's annoying little sister that he probably couldn't conceive of her being anything more.

Except for last night.

Which was already behind her.

What happened to your confidence?

She'd left it in his penthouse suite. Luc had restored her confidence in being someone worth spending time with, but one night of passion did not a romance make. Better one fabulous night, she concluded, gritting her jaw. It was more than some people had. Instead of dwelling on what she couldn't make happen, she should concentrate on what she could, which, with the aid of her team, was to create the most fabulous party of the year.

After a tense breakfast meeting during which he could hardly concentrate long enough to sign a multimillion-dollar contract to upgrade the tech for the government of a small country, his thoughts turned back with relief to Stacey. Anything that had happened between them was his fault. He could have resisted and had chosen not to.

Calling the elevator, he stepped into the cab and, leaning back against the wall, closed his eyes. This was the same Stacey who used to wear her hair in braids and give him a hard time at the farm. He smiled as he pictured her at the banquet last night, so determined to make everyone's night a success, including his. A little tired and frazzled around the edges, but definitely all grown up, as she'd proved later in his bed. As far as business went, early reports from his team said the banquet was the best yet.

As he stepped out into the lobby of the glass and steel monument to his success, she consumed his thoughts. His hunger to chart every change in Stacey from gauche ingénue to the professional woman she was today was eating him alive. And he'd never know, because he wouldn't risk getting closer to her. He'd seen enough of her home life to know the journey she'd taken to this point. With no intention of adding to her woes, he'd put distance between them.

His Lamborghini was waiting at the kerb. Tipping the valet, he folded his athletic frame into the car and eased into the morning traffic. His thoughts turned to the day Niahl had left home. Stacey had been too young to follow her brother, and had made such a lonely figure standing at the farm gate waving them off. She'd looked broken. He'd watched in the wing mirror until they'd turned a corner and he hadn't been able to see her any more. It had been a desperate end to an unhappy visit, during which he'd seen her run ragged as she'd tried to care for everyone. It had seemed to him that no one cared for Stacey but her brother, Niahl.

As soon as she'd been old enough, she'd changed her life. A scholarship to a college specialising in the hospitality industry in London had resulted in her graduating as the top student in her year. How could he risk destroying the confidence that had given her by embarking on some ultimately doomed affair? Stacey deserved more than a man who walked away if emotion ever threatened to cloud his rational mind.

Almost four hectic weeks had passed since the memorable encounter with Luc in Barcelona. Planning any party could be a logistical nightmare, but when the venue was in a challenging location Stacey and her team had to work flat out to make sure that everything was delivered well in advance. She'd barely had a moment to breathe, let alone consider what memories Luc had been left with after their passionate night.

After the clamour of the city the serene peace of the mountains was nothing short of a dream come true. The air was cool and clean. Crisp white snow crunched underfoot, and the sky was a flawless, cerulean blue. The small village with its backdrop of towering mountains was like the best picture postcard in the world. The slopes were teeming with skiers, all of whom moved to their own sure, rhythmical pattern, while beginners on the nursery slopes made shakier and more uncertain figures. One thing, however, was common to all. Everyone was smiling.

'What a fabulous atmosphere! What a place to hold a party!' she exclaimed to her companions in the team. 'We're going to have the best time ever here. It's going to be the party of the year.'

Only the final tweaks remained and Stacey was as certain as she could be that Lucas would love what they had planned. *Lucas.* She was desperate to see him, and dreading it too. What if he—?

No. Don't think that way. Only positive thoughts from now on.

They had to meet, and she'd take it from there. It wouldn't be easy with the brand of his lips on her mouth and the memory of his hands on her body, but what was easy? Nothing worth having, that was for sure.

'We'll make this event something the Da Silva guests never forget, and for all the right reasons,' she told the team. 'How beautiful is this?' she exclaimed, turning full circle. 'Let's get settled in, and then we can make a start.'

The success of any team depended on its leadership. That was something Lady Sarah had drummed into her right at the start, so, whatever Stacey's personal feelings about Lucas, she had to get on with things for the sake of the team.

'There will be a few more hurdles to cross here than we had in the city,' Stacey observed later when she and the team were seated around a boardroom table in an office the hotel had made available for them. 'The weather, for one thing,' she said, glancing out of the window. The quaint, pitched-roofed buildings had been covered in deep mantles of snow when they'd arrived, but now they were gradually fading out of sight. A drift of snowflakes falling like a veil was growing heavier by the minute, while the flawless blue sky that had so impressed her was rapidly turning to unrelieved grey. 'I should get out and scout the various locations while I still can,' she said, drawing the meeting to a close. 'Take the night off. I'm going to need everyone firing on all cylinders tomorrow.'

'What about you?' a colleague piped up.

'I'll rest when I'm reassured about our venues. Until then...?' She shrugged.

'Keep in touch.'

'I will,' she promised.

The village proved to be a fascinating place with its glitter and sparkle, but what struck Stacey more was the resilience of visitors and residents alike as they crowded the pavements in what were undeniably extreme weather conditions.

Still, everyone was dressed for it, Stacey reasoned, admiring the beautifully decorated shop windows as she strode past in her snow boots and Party Planners padded jacket. She was heading for the gondola station as, not only was there to be a party down here, but a reception higher up the mountain at Luc's ski lodge, as well as a firework display and a torchlit procession down the mountain. Pausing briefly to adjust her snow goggles, she studied the statue of a miniature couple in one of the windows. Placed outside the model of a typical chalet, both figures were wearing skis and staring up at each other in apparent rapture.

I should have learned to ski, she mused silently. Too late now. But the gondola would take her where she needed to be. She could just step in and out, no problem.

Craning her neck when she reached the station, she tried to spot Luc's eyrie. It was supposed to be the biggest chalet on the mountain. She thought of it as his castle, his fortress, his ivory tower. But she couldn't see anything as low cloud and the misting of snow had blotted out the upper reaches of the route the gondola would take.

What if the gondola stopped running? How would they transport the guests?

There was time, Stacey reasoned. They had a good few days before the party. Surely the weather would have improved by then?

The hotel manager had told her that Lucas had arrived by helicopter that same morning. Her heart went crazy all over again, just as it had the first time she'd heard it. 'Nothing deters him,' the hotel manager had said. 'Bad weather has been forecast, but Señor Da Silva is an expert pilot, so he knows all about timing to escape the worst of any oncoming storm.'

Yes, he would, she'd thought then. Niahl had warned her that the weather could be unpredictable but that this resort had some of the most challenging slopes in the world, which was what had attracted Lucas to the village in the first place. It would, she mused.

Would Luc be thinking about her, as she was thinking about him?

Only in as much as he might wonder if she and the team had arrived before the weather closed in, she concluded. She hadn't heard from him since Barcelona, confirming her belief that their night together meant more to her than it did to him. Of course he'd take for granted the fact that she'd get on with things. And why shouldn't he? She wanted him to know he could rely on her, and that Party Planners would give him the event of the year.

She paused at the foot of the steps leading up to the gondola station. Her pulse jagged at the thought of seeing Luc again. Dragging deep on the ice-cold air, she hunched her shoulders into her jacket and drove forward into the wind. Behind her, vehicles with snow chains were crawling along. Even they were having difficulty negotiating the road. But what she'd started, she would finish. All she needed was a quick look-see so she could brief the team, and then she'd head straight back down the mountain to take a hot bath and have a good sleep before the real work began tomorrow.

CHAPTER SIX

STACEY ONLY REALISED what she'd taken on as the packed gondola transporting skiers to their chalets on the higher levels left its berth on the lower station. It was one thing agreeing to what had seemed a perfectly reasonable request by the Da Silva team, to hold a party in the main village before transporting guests up the mountain for the grand finale of fireworks and a torchlit descent. There was no doubt that the infrastructure was here to support that. But when the weather closed in as it had done today, she could only be grateful that she'd taken the precaution of having everything delivered in good time for the party. She doubted anything else would get through.

Luc had intimated through the head of his team that he had a novel idea for ferrying guests up the mountain for the champagne reception. Stacey had yet to learn what that was, and had put in an urgent request for more information so she could plan for whatever needed to be done.

Firming her jaw, she stared out of the window. There were always challenges, but this took things to the wire. As the ground dropped away the wind picked up and whistled around the swaying car. None of her companions seemed concerned, so she made herself relax and wait until that blissful moment when she was back on solid ground.

Snow was falling steadily when she joined the crowds streaming out of the station. She had a map but it wasn't much use now the street had disappeared beneath a thick white carpet. Seeing a ticket booth, she stopped to ask directions and was told that she couldn't miss the Da Silva chalet as it was the largest private structure in town. 'Will the gondola continue to run?' she asked, staring up at the leaden sky.

'Of course,' she was told. 'Only a white-out or heavy winds could stop the service, and this weather system is supposed to move on.' A glance at the sky seemed to confirm this. A big patch of blue had broken through the cloud. Thanking the clerk, she took the precaution of donning a pair of high-performance ski goggles to prevent snow-blindness and set off, but she had barely made it out of the station before a strong wind kicked up. The patch of blue she'd been so relieved to see soon disappeared behind a fresh bank of cloud and these clouds were thicker and darker than before.

Weather in the mountains was known to be unpredictable. Could anyone accurately predict the capricious path of Mother Nature? Somehow, she doubted it.

A heavy silence gathered around her as she trudged along. Everyone else seemed to have retreated into their houses or hotels, and even those buildings had turned ghostly in the half-light. Her heart was racing. The snow was falling so heavily now, it was like a thick white curtain in front of her face. Her heart was racing. She'd heard enough horror stories to know she should be concerned. She couldn't even be sure if she was walking in a straight line or going around in circles. Luc's chalet was supposed to be close to the station, and, though it might be the largest private home in the area, if she couldn't see the other buildings, what hope did she have of finding it?

Adjusting her neck warmer so it covered her mouth and nose, she bent her head into the wind and slogged on. Going back wasn't an option. When she stopped and turned to try and get her bearings, the gondola station had disappeared. Tugging off a thick ski glove with her teeth, she located her phone and tried to call her colleagues in the village. No signal. There was only one option left, and that was to keep on walking in the hope that something would come into view, though that didn't seem likely in this all-encompassing sea of white.

'Hello! *Hello!*' she called out, panic-stricken. 'Can anyone hear me?'

Silence answered her call.

'Hello! *Hello!*' she repeated at the top of her lungs. 'Is anyone out here?'

She stood motionless in the snow with her arms crossed over her chest as she tried to slap some life into her frozen limbs. There was not a sound to be heard other than the wailing of the wind and the deceptively silky whisper of deadly snowflakes.

And then...

Was she dreaming?

'Hello!' she cried out wildly, feeling certain she'd heard a faint sound in the distance. 'Hello?' she called again.

She tried to locate the source of the sound, but it seemed to come from everywhere and nowhere at once. 'I'm over here!' she bellowed tensely.

'Stay where you are! Don't move. I'm coming to get you.'

'Luc?' Relief engulfed her.

'I said, stay where you are.'

His voice was harsh, imperative, quashing her relief, and turning it to exasperation that of course it had to be Luc who found her.

'Stacey? You have to keep shouting so I can find you.'

The wind tossed his voice around so it was impossible to tell which direction he was calling from. 'Hello! Hello!' she called out in desperation. 'I'm over here.'

'Don't move. I can hear you. Keep shouting…'

But his voice sounded fainter as he was walking away from her. 'I'm over *here*,' she yelled, frantic with fear that he might walk straight past her. 'Please…' Her voice broke with sheer terror that, having been found, she might be abandoned again. And then, quite suddenly, they were standing face to face. Regardless of anything that had gone before, she catapulted herself into his arms. 'Thank God you found me!'

'*Dios!* Thank God I did. What on earth are you doing up here?'

'Researching.'

'Couldn't that have waited until tomorrow?'

'I like to be prepared.'

'But you've only just arrived,' Luc pointed out. 'My people gave me your schedule,' he explained.

'The team is resting,' she confirmed, 'but I want to be informed, ready to brief them in the morning.'

Luc frowned down at her. 'There's dedication to duty, and then there's obsession,' he observed. 'Didn't it occur to you that you should be resting too?'

'Pot, kettle, black?' she suggested. 'Do you hang around when an important deal is on the table? No. I didn't think so. And I wouldn't be here at all if I hadn't checked first that the gondolas would be running in spite of the weather.'

'In fairness, no one could have predicted this,' Luc agreed, driving forward. 'The gondola station has only just closed.'

'Closed?' Stacey exclaimed. 'How do I get down the mountain?'

'You won't—not tonight, at least.'

'A hotel, then,' she said hopefully, looking about.

'All the hotels are full of people who are stranded,' Luc explained.

'So where *are* you taking me?'

'Does it matter?' Grabbing hold of her arm, he urged her along. 'Come on, we'll freeze if we stay here.'

Against her better judgement where Luc was concerned, she felt safe for the first time since coming up the mountain. And optimistic for some reason. She felt way too much of everything, Stacey concluded as she admitted, 'This is not how I expected us to meet.'

'I'm sure not,' Luc agreed, forced to shout as he drove them both on against the battering snow. 'You're lucky I was checking the progress of evacuating skiers, and making sure the slopes were clear, or we wouldn't be here.'

'Where exactly *are* we?' she asked. 'How do you even know where we're going?' Having stared about, she couldn't be sure of anything but an unrelieved vista of white.

'I just know where I am,' Luc said with confidence. 'In-built GPS, I guess.'

She wouldn't put anything past him. 'I'm sorry to have caused you so much trouble.'

'Not your fault,' he said brusquely. 'It's been called the freak storm of the century. No one saw this coming.'

Reassured that he didn't think her completely reckless in venturing up the mountain, she asked another question. 'Do you have a phone signal at your chalet? I need to reassure the team I'm okay.'

'I have a landline,' Luc confirmed, 'though mobile lines are dead. You can ring the hotel and leave a message.'

'Sure?'

'Of course.'

'That's very kind of you.'

This was too polite, she mused as Luc steered her away to the left; a bit like the calm before the storm.

'My chalet's over here.'

'So close,' she exclaimed with surprise.

'As close as the black ski run where I found you.' Luc's voice held irony and humour in matching amounts. 'You might have had a shock if you'd gone that way.'

'Terrifying,' she agreed. 'Particularly as I can't ski.'

'Nor can I without skis,' Luc pointed out dryly.

In all probability, Luc had saved her life. 'I can never thank you enough for finding me.'

'We'll find a way.'

Her heart almost leapt out of her chest. Her brain said it was a throwaway remark, but it was still Luc speaking. She hoped he'd say more. He didn't. Locking an arm around her waist, he steered her until finally he half carried her up a slope that had probably been steps to his chalet before the snows came.

'Thank you,' she said as he steadied her on the ground as the impressive entrance door swung open.

'You'll have plenty of chances to thank me,' he observed with some irony. 'You won't be going anywhere tonight. Neither of us will. You'll have to stay in the chalet with me.'

Left with that alarming thought, she smiled as obliging staff gathered on the doorstep to greet them. Without exception, they were relieved to see Lucas return safely. He introduced Stacey to his housekeeper, a rosy-cheeked older woman called Maria, who wanted nothing more than to take Stacey under her wing, but they all paused in the same instant as a thin wail cut through their greeting.

'Did you hear that?' Stacey asked.

'Go inside while I take a look around,' Luc instructed.

'No way. I'm coming with you. It isn't safe to be out on your own tonight.'

'Says you?' he countered with a devastating smile. 'Do you think two of us will be safer?'

'Two will stand more chance of finding someone stranded.'

'No.' He shook his head. 'You're freezing. Go inside.'

'I can last a little longer, and if there is someone out there, we have to find them.'

'You have to call your team,' he reminded her.

'And I will, just as soon as I get back.'

Luc frowned. 'That sounds like an animal in distress...'

'Let's go,' Stacey insisted, tugging on his arm.

An hour later, she and Maria were tending a cat after a most astonishing encounter in Luc's boot room. Two calls later, and Stacey had informed her team that she was safe and they should stay where they were. 'I'll give you an update tomorrow,' she promised.

'Bath. Now,' Luc instructed from the doorway. 'I won't be answerable for your well-being if you don't take my advice.'

'I didn't ask you to be answerable.' She couldn't bring herself to add, *I'm fine. I can look after myself*, as the blizzard had clearly proved her wrong about that.

'Lucky for you, I'm still going to care about your welfare,' Luc said in a tone that made her think he was speaking as her brother's friend, rather than as her lover. 'Just remember—you're in my house and I'm in charge. No arguments,' he added in a mock-stern tone. 'And when you take a shower be sure to run it cold, or you'll burn yourself. Even on the coldest setting the water's going to feel warm to you. It's only safe to increase the temperature when the water starts to feel chilly to you. When you're confident everything's back to normal you can take a bath. Don't rush. I'll be doing the same thing.'

He was almost out of the door when he thought better of it and turned around. 'You did well tonight. That could have been a person, and a cat is no less deserving of our care. Mountain rescue will be on the case by now. They're a lot better equipped than I am for this sort of thing, so you can relax. I'll call them to let them know the area we covered, and then we can safely leave them to it. I'll join in later if they need me.'

'Then so will I,' Stacey insisted.

'No, you won't. You can't ski, and you don't know the mountains. You'll only get in the way. Stay here. You were brave tonight. Don't be foolish now.'

'I wasn't brave, I was scared to death,' she admitted. 'That's why I had to go out again, in case there were others trapped like me.'

'You're very honest,' he observed.

She shrugged. 'I try to be.'

Stacey, Stacey, Stacey! What was she doing to him? Lucas reflected as he paced the great room, attempting not to think of her naked beneath the shower. He'd passed the time while she'd been warming up, making calls to reunite the cat with its owner, and to alert the mountain rescue team to their actions. The search chief had praised Stacey for her bravery. Any visitor who, having found safety, set out again in such terrible conditions to help others was worthy of a commendation, he'd said. 'I'll pass that on to her,' Luc had promised.

No one got through to him like Stacey, who had made a mockery of his intentions to save her from him. Saving her *for* him made more sense right now—especially when, in a moment of complete madness, he had felt moved to enclose her face in his hands in the boot room to give her a brief, reassuring kiss—on the cheek, but still… What the hell had he been thinking? It was bad enough they were here, trapped together in his chalet overnight, without him making things worse. So much for good intentions! She'd ridden roughshod over his control.

What alternative did he have? With many of his guests having arrived early to make the most of their trip, he could use all the people he could get, both up here and down at the hotel. Stacey's team was in place in the village while she was here, ready to act on any changes to her plans for the party brought on by the weather.

At least she appeared to be following orders for once. *For now.* Maria had reported back that warm clothes had been delivered to Stacey's suite of rooms, and she was enjoying a bath. She could stay one night, but no longer. His libido couldn't take it. He had nothing to offer Stacey that she'd be interested in. Money, jewels, fashion meant nothing to her. Her practical nature was fulfilled by her rigorous working regime, but when it came to the personal side of things, she was a dreamer, a romantic, who, now they'd had sex, would expect more than he could give.

A beautiful woman had sought refuge under his roof, but all he could think about was keeping his thoughts and feelings locked up tight.

That wasn't strictly true, was it? However many times he told himself that this was Stacey, the imp who used to plague him at her father's farm, his straining groin begged to differ. Rearranging his over-packed jeans, he grimaced. He couldn't even trust himself to guide Stacey to her bedroom, and had left that task to Maria. Having known her intimately, he wanted her again, and that want was like a fury drilling away inside him to the point where he found it impossible to concentrate on anything else.

He had to have her. It was as simple as that.

Would it be so simple for Stacey?

A humourless laugh escaped him at the thought that she was quite capable of turning him down. Stacey wasn't like anyone else he'd ever known. She lived life by her own rules, and his gut instinct warned him that obeying him would figure nowhere in her plans, a thought that only sharpened his appetite.

He glanced at the thick fur rug in front of the hearth, longing to hear her moan beneath him as her eyes and mouth begged him to take her again. To feel her hips straining to meet his; to have her until she couldn't stand; to bring her more pleasure than she'd ever known—

Stop! Get over this obsession with Stacey and accept that she's here to work!

How was he supposed to forget the telling signs of arousal in her darkening eyes when she looked at him?

Or his desire to kiss every inch of her body? The disappointment on her face when he'd passed her over to Maria had told him everything: Stacey wanted him as much as he wanted her.

Get over it. Forget it.

Pouring a stiff drink, he gulped it down. Discarding the glass, he gave a roar of frustration as he planted his fist into the wall.

CHAPTER SEVEN

BACK TO SQUARE one with Lucas?

Possibly, Stacey accepted as Maria showed her to her room. She touched her lips. Having returned with relief to the chalet, Luc had seemed almost eager to hand her over to someone else, while she was still obsessing over the ice crystals outlining his mouth, and the frosting of snow dampening the thick whorls of pitch-black hair escaping his ski hat. Having so recently been familiar with every naked inch of him, she found it strange now to think how awkward she would have felt if she'd reached up to push back his hair. She touched her mouth again, remembering.

As if she could forget.

The heated racks made the boot room a cosy space to strip off outer clothes, but Luc had shown no interest in conversation. Appearing lost in thought, he'd tugged off his gloves and tossed them on a chair. His boots had gone onto the racks, and he'd grunted at her to do the same with hers. Then he'd stilled and turned to look at her.

'Well done, you,' he'd murmured, frowning as if he couldn't quite believe she'd insisted on going with him into the snow.

'And you,' she'd said. 'Thank you…'

Another few long moments had gone by as they had stared into each other's eyes, and then, enclosing her cheeks in his big, strong hands, Luc had kissed her, but not as Luc the lover, more as a caring friend, which had almost been worse than not being kissed at all.

'And this will be your room while you're staying with us, Señorita Winner.'

'Thank you so much. It's beautiful,' she said, jolting back to the present as she realised Maria was waiting for a reaction to a most beautiful suite of rooms.

'Please do remember what Señor Da Silva told you about the shower,' Maria cautioned as she opened the door on a fabulous marble-lined bathroom.

'I won't forget anything Señor Da Silva said,' Stacey promised, which was the absolute truth. Memories were almost certainly all she'd have to take away from here.

Climbing out of a deliciously warm scented bath some time later, she swathed herself in towels, and began to pace her room. Like everything else she'd seen in the chalet so far, the guest suite was the last word in luxury. Everything was operated from a central console by the bed. She would expect nothing less of a tech billionaire. Exactly like his expert kisses—kisses that conveyed so much, whether that be kisses of reassurance, or kisses in the height of passion—Luc was a genius. It was as simple as that.

She'd rather have that genius here at her side, celebrating life, than be raising the bed with the flick of a switch, and lowering it again, just because she could. It wasn't enough to *try* and stop thinking about Lucas when he occupied every corner of her mind. It was all too easy to picture them both on the bed—intimate, close, loving, kissing. Turning her back on the offending mattress, with its lush dressing of crisp linen sheets and cashmere throws, she wished fervently he could open up enough for her to know if this ache in her heart was futile.

Had she given up?

She stared into the mirror. That wasn't the question.

This was the question: Was she wasting her time pining for a man who might never reveal himself to anyone?

There's only one thing for it...

Seduce him?

Honestly, sometimes her reckless inner self came up with some extraordinary ideas.

Why not? that same inner voice demanded. *You've got the tools, now go to work!*

She laughed as she pushed away from the console table beneath the mirror. Seducing Lucas Da Silva would certainly be a first.

Maria was as good as her word and had dropped off a set of sweats for Stacey to wear. Fortunately, they fitted, along with the underwear, which was still in a pack from the store. She took her time going downstairs to join Lucas, as she wanted to have a proper look around. Everything she'd imagined about Lucas Da Silva's mountaintop eyrie was improved upon. She'd seen a lot of fabulous homes with the team, but nothing close to approaching this. Floodlights were on outside, revealing the smooth carpet of snow with its shadowy mountain peaks beyond. The sky had cleared and the moon was shining brightly, adding to the illumination that revealed a heated outdoor swimming pool with steam rising, and a veranda overlooking the ski slopes where the torchlit procession would take place.

'Wow,' she murmured.

'You approve?'

She swung around. 'You spying on me?'

Luc's low growl came from a shady corner of the room. 'I'm having a drink.'

Now she saw him properly, firelight flickering off the harsh planes of his face as he lounged back in a big, comfortable chair.

'Come and join me,' he suggested. 'Unless you've got something better to do?'

She hummed, and then said lightly, 'You're in luck. I can't think of anything better to do right now. Give me enough time, and maybe I will.'

'Come over here. I've got a message for you.'

'For me?' She couldn't resist crossing the room to sit by Lucas anyway. Hadn't she vowed to bring matters between them to some sort of conclusion?

Padding barefoot over luxurious rugs that made the mellow wooden floor seem even homelier, she couldn't help but marvel at the easy mix of tech and comfort he'd achieved in this house. In spite of the emotional turmoil raging inside her, there was a good feeling in the building. It was easy to see why Luc loved his mountain retreat. He could relax here.

'Drink?' he suggested.

'Water, please.' She needed her wits about her.

'As you wish. I'll open champagne, if you prefer?'

'Perhaps after the party, when, hopefully, I'll have something to celebrate.'

'Hopefully?' he probed with a keen look.

'When we'll *both* have something to celebrate,' she amended in answer to his question. 'You mentioned a message to pass on to me?' she prompted.

'Ah, yes. I spoke to mountain rescue and the team

was full of praise for you. They wanted you to know, that's all.'

'Thank you.' She couldn't pretend that didn't light a glow inside her. It was always good to be appreciated. 'I hope you told them why I did it, and how scared I was.'

'I didn't need to.' He shrugged. 'Only fools don't feel fear.'

'If you can't experience emotion, what do you have?'

'You're asking the wrong person,' Luc assured her.

There was an ironic twist to his mouth as she went to warm her hands in front of the blazing log fire while he fixed their drinks.

'I love your photographs,' she said in an attempt to break the sudden tension. They showed Luc and his brothers playing polo, and there was another photograph of him and his siblings, though not one single image of his parents. She knew their death had been a tragic accident, but found it strange that he wouldn't want to be reminded of happier days.

'Water?' he prompted.

'Thank you.' A glance into shuttered eyes warned against asking too many personal questions about Luc's photographs, or any that she might perceive as missing.

'I think hot chocolate would be better than water, don't you?'

She knew him well enough to suspect that this was a ploy to change the subject completely, rather than to provide her with an alternative drink.

'That would be good,' she agreed. 'I'd love one. Thank you.'

How prim she sounded, when all she could think about was his hands on her body and his mouth on her lips, and the pleasure they'd shared. She must be a better actress than she'd thought.

Would she ever get used to the sight of him? Stacey wondered as Luc picked up the phone to call Maria. Freshly showered with his thick hair still damp and catching on his stubble, Luc was a magnificent sight. Her heart pounded with bottled-up emotion, while her body was more forthright when it came to aching with lust.

But how did he feel about her? Could anyone read the thoughts behind those enigmatic black eyes? Somehow, she doubted it.

'Your wish is my command,' Luc assured her in the same soft drawl as Maria tapped lightly on the door.

His faint smile sent shivers coursing down her spine, and the moment Maria had left them she felt compelled to ask, 'Is my every wish really your command?'

'What do you think?' Luc asked.

She shrugged and smiled with pure disbelief.

'But of course it is,' he assured her wickedly.

A few moments later they were seated in front of the fire, each with an aromatic mug of cocoa in their hands. To any onlooker, it was a cosy scene, a safe scene, with two people who knew each other well. Stacey had relaxed, and in doing so had decided to forget her reckless plan to show Lucas how much she wanted him. Why set herself up for failure, when things were going so well? Did she always have to stick her chin out? Couldn't she for once keep quiet and say nothing? Hadn't she vowed on the day she left home that she would never be pushed aside again? Her intention was to be useful and to help people, and wasn't that better? Didn't it give her a warm feeling inside? Why lay her heart on the line now? Her reckless self could take a hike, she concluded. With a career to foster, and a life to live long after tonight was over, she had safer things to do with her time than seduce Lucas.

'What about supplies in the village?' she asked, determined to turn her mind back to business. 'Does everyone have what they need? I've ordered in enough to withstand a siege, so please tell me if I can help.'

'I will,' Luc assured her, 'but I doubt it will be necessary.' Relaxing back, he explained. 'All the mountain villages are self-sufficient. They have to be prepared for weather like this, but I'll let them know of your offer,' he promised.

As Luc sipped hot chocolate thick enough to stand a spoon in, she dwelt on him. It was inevitable. Thoughts about business were vital to her peace of mind, but with each minute that passed he was becoming increasingly vital to her existence.

Warm chocolate was slipping down her throat like a delicious promise of more pleasure to come, and Luc was a big source of pleasure.

'What are you smiling about?' he asked.

'Me? Just relaxing. Okay, the party,' she admitted when he raised a brow. Just not the type of party Luc was imagining.

And from there the fantasies came thick and strong. He'd showered and changed into banged-up jeans with frayed edges brushing his naked feet—how could feet be so sexy? she asked herself—and a soft black cashmere sweater that clung to his powerful shoulders, emphasising his strength and musculature like a second skin, and she wanted to stroke him, smell him, touch him, taste him. The scent of something citrusy he'd used in the shower was clearly discernible above the tang of wood smoke and the sugary smell of chocolate.

He'd pushed his sleeves back, revealing deeply tanned forearms like iron girders, shaded with just the right amount of dark hair. He was a magnificent sight and she wanted him. The fact that Lucas had always been completely unaware of his staggering appeal only made him all the more attractive to Stacey.

'I'd better take that mug before you drop it,' he said.

Realising it had tipped at a perilous angle while she was lost in her thoughts, she laughed. 'I'm going to lick out every last drop first.' When she passed it over to him their fingers touched, and Luc's heat seeped into her. Who was seducing whom here? Her nipples responded on cue, as did the rest of her aching body.

'Now we eat,' he said, which snapped her back to reality. 'You need food.'

So much for reality! Being free from consequences, fantasies were more enjoyable. And, yes, she was playing with fire sitting close to Luc when she could be safely asleep in the guest wing, but she preferred playing with fire to kicking around cold embers in the morning.

When she stretched and grimaced, he commented. 'You could use a massage. Cold does that to your muscles.'

'Are you offering?' She gave him a sideways look while her heart started banging in her chest.

'If you like,' Luc said matter-of-factly. 'A good rub down,' he suggested.

'I'm not your horse.'

'Clearly,' he observed.

She laughed. They both laughed, and she had to tell herself that the attractive curve on Luc's mouth was just his way, and, though she was staying here overnight, she was as safe from him as she would be in a convent.

'Penny for them?' he probed, shooting a smouldering look her way.

She drew herself up. 'You can't know all my secrets.'

'Let's start with one.'

'Says the man who never reveals a single detail about his life?'

Luc shrugged. 'I asked first.'

'Okay,' she agreed. 'You asked for it, so here's one. What happened to my horse? What happened to Ludo?'

He sat back.

'Don't pretend you don't know. And don't keep me waiting for your answer, or I'll know it's bad news. That horse meant the world to me. He was the only friend I—' She broke off. 'Well?' she demanded after a few seconds of silence had passed. 'Tell me.' She braced herself.

'Ludo,' Luc murmured.

'Well, at least you remember his name.'

He frowned. 'Of course I remember his name.'

'So?' she pressed.

'Your pony is having a very happy retirement.'

Tension flooded out of her. 'Go on…' She sat forward eagerly.

'He's at stud siring some of the finest foals in the world. You don't need to worry about Ludo. If you asked him, I doubt he'd want to be anywhere but with his harem on my *estancia*.'

'I'll ask him to confirm that the next time I see him,' she teased, and then she thought of something else. 'Do you still ride him?'

'All the time,' Luc confirmed.

'Good. I can imagine the two of you together.' One so fiery, and one so deep. They belonged together; deserved each other for all the right reasons, and she could see now that something that had hurt her at the time had done Luc and her beloved horse the world of good. 'Ludo would be lost without regular exercise.'

'As would I,' Luc assured her, not troubling to hide the wicked glint in his eyes.

'I wouldn't know about that,' she said, and before he had the chance to speak she put her hand up to stop him. 'And I don't want to know. Just so long as Ludo's happy, that's okay with me.'

They fell silent after that, reminding Stacey that, however much she longed for things to be easier between them, Lucas would always be intractably welded to honour and dignity, and, though he would quite happily talk about the horses they both loved, or the parties Stacey arranged for him, their encounter in Barcelona had been a one-off that he almost certainly regretted.

And yet...

When their glances clashed and he didn't look away, she got the feeling that he would like to kiss her. Whether it was another of her fantasies, she couldn't tell. And if he did kiss her, she guessed it would be a reassuring kiss and not the way he'd kissed her in Barcelona.

'Food,' he reminded her. 'You must be hungry by now?'

'Starving,' she confirmed.

The tension between them released as he asked what she'd like and they talked easily about what to eat. 'When we've finished you can go straight to bed.'

'Yes, sir.' She gave him a mock salute. 'Any more instructions?'

'That covers it,' he said.

And...was she mistaken, or was that a glint of humour in his eyes? Either that or a reflection of the fire.

Why couldn't Luc get it through his head that she was a grown woman with feelings and emotions? Just because he was an emotion-free zone… Or was he? Sometimes she suspected that his feelings, long since bottled up inside him, were longing for a trigger to let them out.

CHAPTER EIGHT

DIOS! EACH TIME he saw her he wanted to do a lot more than kiss her. When he'd found her in the snow his world had tilted on its axis. The thought of losing her was insupportable.

'Lucas?'

'What?' Her voice held a concerned note that made him feel bad for locking her out. If there was one person who could undo him it was Stacey, and those memories were better where they were, buried deep. Easing back on the sofa, he spread his arms across the back in an attitude of apparent unconcern.

'You looked so tense,' she remarked, frowning. 'You were actually scowling—not that I haven't seen that expression before. Is something wrong?'

Yes, you're *wrong*, he thought. He should be looking to settle down and start a dynasty to perpetuate Da Silva Inc, but when that time came he'd choose a woman bred for the role, someone sparkling and superficial who he couldn't hurt.

'I'm hungry,' he said with a shrug. 'And you know what I'm like when I'm hungry.'

'Bear? Sore head?' she suggested. And then, without warning, she sprang off the sofa. 'Come on, then...'

She held out her hand to take his. 'Let's eat. I'll get no sense out of you until we do.'

He stood, but he didn't make any attempt to hold her outstretched hand. Any contact between them was dangerous. He'd learned there was no such thing as an innocent kiss between him and Stacey, and she deserved a lot more than he could offer.

It was a relief to find himself at the breakfast bar where he could occupy himself with the business of eating rather than dwell on the prospect of sex with Stacey. She helped by chatting about details for the upcoming party, but every now and then she'd look at him with eyes full of compassion, and that wasn't very helpful. She was waiting for him to confide in her, tell her things he'd never told anyone, things he hadn't even confronted himself. Neither of them made any reference to their recent kiss, though, while she might have found it easy to put that behind her, he still brooded on it.

Eventually she sighed, as if she'd given up on him. 'Sorry, but I have to get some sleep,' she said, standing up to go. 'You've been amazing. You saved my life.' And before he knew what she was doing, she leaned forward to brush a kiss against his cheek. It was such a little thing, but long-hidden feelings squirmed inside him. No one kissed him like that. No one had for a long time.

'Okay, goodnight,' she said. 'Try and get some sleep.'

'You too,' he encouraged. *Before I yank you close and kiss the breath out of your body.* 'You've had quite an ordeal today.'

'Not as bad as the cat,' she said dryly.

'Ah, the cat,' he murmured, remembering how tender she'd been with the animal. That memory dredged up more. His parents, his siblings. It was definitely time for Stacey to go. Carrying their plates to the counter, he kept his back turned. 'We both need sleep,' he agreed, but more sharply than he had intended. He felt bad for snapping, but memories were dangerous things. His were better left undisturbed.

When her footsteps faded, he stood in the great room surveying what he could see of the village. Snow had stopped falling, though it had left everything cloaked in white. His best guess was that they would be cut off from the village for a few days. A lot could happen in that time. Yes, a party could be held, and guests entertained. Anything beyond that he would put from his mind.

Rest? Rest was unlikely with Stacey in the next room. If the hotels hadn't been full he'd have shipped her out, but they were where they were. He'd be shovelling snow in the morning, too busy to think of anything else, he reassured himself. Then he would liaise with his people to make sure they had everything covered for the party. The last he'd heard there were no more supplies getting through to the village. He could only be glad Stacey was so well organised.

Stacey...

There she was again. Each time he thought it was possible to stop thinking about her, she invaded his mind. He just had to face facts. The woman she had become was not simply more of a challenge than the tomboy she used to be, but a damn sight more attractive too.

Stacey's usual upbeat mood was flagging as she flopped into bed. Why would Lucas never open up? Instinct told her he'd never move on until he did. And though building a monstrous business was huge credit to him, where was his personal life? Did he have one? Didn't he want one? Or wasn't he capable of building something requiring feelings and giving his all, and risking his heart?

You're a fine one to talk.

Yup. That was a fair accusation. But this was about Lucas, not about Stacey.

Even with all the complications, she loved being with him. The rescue spoke volumes about him. He was a very special individual, and their relationship, such as it was, was very special to her. Sex had been extraordinary; far more pleasure, and infinitely more emotional investment than she had expected.

She smiled, remembering the moment they'd found the cat. Cradling the small, half-frozen animal had woken her heart. Maybe she should get a cat. However fabulous this accommodation and however successful her life, it didn't make up for the stark fact that she was alone.

So change things.

Change things? Her mouth tilted at a disbelieving angle as her inner voice had its say. It wasn't that easy to change things, as proved by the fact that it was midnight and she was out of bed pacing the room. She glanced at the huge, comfortable bed. There was nothing wrong with it, it was just too big for one person.

Luc's room was only a little way down the corridor.

That's a crazy idea, her sensible self warned.

Crazy or not, he had to get things off his chest.

Pardon me if I stay out of the way when he shoots you down in flames.

When you cared about someone that was a chance you had to take.

She smiled as she glanced at the door…the door she'd left a little bit open, as if Luc would take that sort of hint! He was far too worldly-wise to fall for her clumsy ruses these days. If he did notice her door was open, he'd close it as he walked past. Bottom line. If she didn't do something, nothing would change. Reviewing occasions of being proactive in the past, she could only conclude they'd all worked out well. There was no rule that said she had to wait around for things to happen, and she had no intention of revisiting that wallflower on the bench. It was time the wallflower took matters into her own hands. And there was no time like the present.

Sucking in a deep, steadying breath, she tiptoed out of the room. Padding down the corridor, as she had expected she found Luc's door firmly closed. Turning the handle carefully, she opened the door without a noise. Cautiously peering in, she was rewarded by the sight of Lucas sprawled face down on the bed in all his naked splendour. She took a moment to admire him as she might admire a sculpture in a gallery. Built on a heroic scale, he was a magnificent sight.

She curbed a smile at the thought that her crazy plan was to slip into bed beside him. *And when he woke they'd have a chat?* Fantasies like that were dangerous. But how she longed for him…longed to feel his arms around her, and to make love quietly, deeply, tenderly—

In practical terms, there were two things wrong with that plan. She hadn't expected to find him naked or in full starfish position, so there wasn't an inch of bed to be had.

'Just leave, will you?'

She yelped with shock at the sound of his voice. 'I thought you were asleep.'

'Clearly not.' He shifted position, muscles rippling, but he kept his head turned away from her. 'I mean it, Stacey. Please leave. Now.'

She remained frozen in place by the door, trying

to decide how best to rejig her plan. Slipping into bed beside him without waking him until they yawned, stretched, and reached for each other in the morning, according to the natural flow of things, clearly wasn't possible now.

Surprisingly, coming to a decision proved easier to navigate than she'd thought.

He'd heard her padding down the corridor, and was already on full alert when she entered the room. Having suspected something like this might happen, he hadn't even tried to sleep. She usually did as he asked in the end. That was his only comfort. Would she this time?

'I'm serious, Stacey. Say what you've got to say and then leave.'

In the shadows of the darkened room he couldn't see her expression clearly, and she remained silent, which forced him to prompt, 'Whatever it is you've got to say, just spit it out and go.'

'Make me.'

'I beg your pardon?'

'I'm not going anywhere unless you make me,' she said again.

'That's ridiculous.'

In the ghostly light her shoulders lifted and fell again. 'Ridiculous or not, I'm not going anywhere.'

'Until I eject you by force?'

'That's up to you.'

'This is wrong, Stacey. What happened between us in Barcelona was a mistake—'

'A mistake?' she interrupted in a voice full of raw wounds from the past. 'Is that what you think of me?'

'No,' he bit out. 'It's just that you don't belong here. I don't have anything to offer you, other than in a business sense, so please don't make this harder than it has to be.'

Undaunted, she walked towards the bed. Her face was rigid and pale. But then, just as he should have expected, she firmed her jaw to confront him head-on. 'Isn't that for me to decide?' she asked. 'I know what I want, and I'm fully aware of what I'm doing.'

'You think you are,' he argued. 'But really, you've got no idea.'

'About you? I'd like to know you better, but you don't show yourself to anyone, do you, Luc? At least, I know some part of you,' she conceded, 'but that's only the part you've had the courage to show.'

'You're calling me a coward now?'

'I'm saying we're not so different. I don't find it any easier than you to show my feelings.'

'So you thought if we made love again it would all sort itself out?'

'I'm not that naïve. Pain that's taken years to build won't vanish with the first orgasm.'

Burying his hands in his hair, he said nothing.

'But if I've learned one thing, it's this,' she went on. 'If I want something, I know it won't fall into my lap. I have to get out there and make things happen.'

He raised his head. 'And that's what you're doing now?'

She smiled and shrugged.

'You're an intelligent and successful woman who has proved herself ten times over, which is exactly why you don't need me. There's no space for you in my life.'

'Nor you in mine,' she agreed. 'So must that consign us both to solitude for ever?'

What she was suggesting appeared to be a relationship of convenience, into which they would dip in and out as it suited them. Normally, he might applaud that sort of thing, but when Stacey was involved, the idea appalled him. He would not agree to flirting with her feelings. She'd get hurt.

Wouldn't he too?

So what? He doubted he was capable of feeling anything.

'Think what you like, but my answer's still no. I won't do anything to stop you moving forward.'

'Nice speech, but I'll stay here all night if I have to.'

'Please yourself,' he said, turning over in bed.

She didn't move.

'Go to bed, Stacey, before you get in any deeper.'

'But I want to be in deep. I want to experience life to the full. I *want* to feel. I don't want to be an onlooker. That only makes the ache inside me worse.'

'Oh, for goodness' sake!' Shooting up in bed, he glared at her.

She shrugged and smiled. 'There you are,' she whispered. 'Now, can I thank you for finding me?'

'You already did.'

'I don't mean when I was lost in the snow.'

'What do you mean?'

'Can I explain?' Before he could answer she was sitting on the bed. 'I just want to talk.'

Dipping his head, he gave her a disbelieving look. 'We can talk in the morning.'

'I don't want to wait that long.'

'Okay, so what do you want?'

'I want to have sex with you.'

His body responded immediately. 'Be very careful,' he warned.

'Why? Will you pounce on me?'

Swinging out of bed, he grabbed his jeans. 'Does this answer your question?'

'If you go you'll regret it.'

'I'll regret it if I don't go,' he assured her.

'Then, I guess it's up to me to stop you.'

'I'd like to see you try.'

Slipping off the bed, she knelt in front of him. 'Oh, I'm going to try all right,' she assured him.

Before he had the chance to stop her she drew her tee shirt over her head, revealing lush breasts. He could still remember the scent of them, and the taste of her skin. Her nipples were erect, and he grew harder in response. He didn't push her away; instead, he dragged her close. The ache, the need, the pain inside him could no longer be sustained.

'What the hell do you think you're doing now?' he asked sharply, throwing his head back to drag in some much-needed air as she made her intentions clear.

'Pleasuring you,' she informed him. 'Stay still, or I'll bite.'

Dios! What? The kitten had become a tigress. Lacing his fingers through her hair, he kept her close. A groan of pleasure escaped him. He needed this, needed Stacey, and she knew exactly what to do. Using her tongue, her teeth, and her lips, she made sure the outcome was inevitable. 'No!' he exclaimed at the very last minute. Control was everything. Here, in dodging the questions she asked him, in business, in everything. Fisting his erection, he pulled back.

Her eyes were wide and bewildered as she stared up at him. 'Did I do something wrong?'

'You did nothing wrong. *This* is wrong. *We're* wrong. This just cannot be.'

'Who says? We're not related. You're not very much

older than I am. Is it because I'm not rich, not good enough for you? Or are you frightened of my brother?'

'Your brother?' He shook his head and smiled. 'As for you not being good enough—'

'Don't bother,' she said, putting a crack in the stone wall of his heart as she stumbled to her feet. 'I don't want to hear your excuses. I don't have the patience to stick around while you find yourself.'

'Says you?' Grabbing her by the shoulders, he brought her to her feet in front of him. 'Don't you understand? I just can't think of you this way.'

'Still lying to yourself?' she countered tensely. 'Still hiding your feelings, Lucas? Is that why you've got an erection? We're both consenting adults, and however determined you are to banish emotion from your life, you can't hide that.'

'Don't make this harder than it has to be.' He stared pointedly at the door, but she refused to take the hint, and instead made a cradle of her hands to offer her breasts like a gift. This cut straight through his desire to protect her from him, and made him see the sensual woman he'd made love to in Barcelona. As if that weren't enough, she dipped down to capture his straining erection between her luscious curves.

'You like that, don't you?' she whispered. 'You don't want me to go now...'

As she began to move rhythmically to and fro, her question was redundant. Eventually, he managed to grind out, 'This does not mean I will allow you to seduce me.'

'Allow?' she said, angling her chin to one side as she stared up at him. 'I'd say you don't have any choice. Unless I decide otherwise, of course...'

CHAPTER NINE

SHE LET HIM go suddenly, which left him in an agony of frustration. Shaking his head, he barked an incredulous laugh at the incongruity of the situation. 'I suppose it's no use my telling you to go?'

'None at all,' she agreed.

'Then, for your sake, I must.'

'For my sake?' she said, moving quickly to stand between him and the door. 'If you were doing something for my sake you'd make love to me. You wouldn't walk out.'

'This is not a battle of wills,' he said, spearing a glance into her eyes as he fastened his jeans. 'It's about me caring for you.'

'Twaddle. It's about you reinforcing your barricades, leaving me feeling like a fool.'

Backing her into a shaft of moonlight that had unwittingly trespassed on the drama, he bit out, '*You* did nothing wrong. It's me. I'm wrong for you, and no amount of sex can make that right.'

'Try me,' she challenged.

He wanted to say a lot of things as he headed for the door, but prolonging this served no purpose.

Stacey flinched as the door closed behind Luc. Deep down she'd known this was a daft idea, and had been

primed for disappointment. But she hadn't expected it
to go quite so badly. Lucas was too sophisticated to fall
for her clumsy ploys, and all she'd managed to prove
tonight was that fantasies never played out as you expected them to. Only one thing was certain, and that
was that she couldn't leave it here.

Scooping up her discarded pyjama top, she dressed
and left the room. She found Luc downstairs in front of
a guttering fire with shadows flickering around him,
head back, eyes closed, jaw set, like a dark angel sitting on the steps of hell.

She wouldn't let him go through those gates. Somehow she was going to save him. And however *ridiculous* that sounded—a word he liked to use—she was a
very determined woman.

He didn't say anything as she came closer, but she'd
put money on him knowing she was there.

'Go away, Stace.'

'You haven't called me that for years.'

'I haven't *felt* this way for years.'

'Have you felt anything for years?'

Too deep, too intrusive a question, she thought when
he remained silent. She tried again. 'How do you feel?'

'Conflicted,' he admitted. 'Contrary to what you
think, I want you more than you know, but if you expect hearts and flowers, you'll be disappointed.'

Of course she was disappointed. Didn't every woman
want the dream? 'Did I say that was what I expect?'

'You didn't have to.'

Firming her jaw, she crossed the room and sat down
on the sofa facing his.

'Believe me, Stace,' Luc said with a touch of warmth
in his tone as he opened his eyes. 'You don't need me
in your life.'

'Don't tell me what I need.'

'You have so little experience.'

'Of sex?' she queried. 'I'd agree with you where that's concerned, but I'm not inexperienced when it comes to life, and I know when someone's hurting.'

'That's your strength,' he agreed. 'One of them.'

'So…?'

'So, don't waste your time on me. I'm a lost cause, and there are plenty of people who could benefit from the kind of thoughtfulness and compassion you want to give.'

'You make me sound like a saint and I'm far from it.'

'Me too,' he confirmed dryly.

'Don't you think it's time to confront the demons from your past?'

'While I'm having sex with you?' he suggested in that same ironic tone.

Stacey shrugged. 'It's an outlet—yes.'

Luc's mouth tugged in a wry sort of smile. 'Who knows what you might release.'

'You, I hope,' she said. 'I do know that you'll continue to hurt until you allow yourself to feel something.'

'And I can't ask what you know about that, can I?'

'I don't pretend my situation was anything like yours,' she assured him. 'I can't even begin to imagine how you feel, but isn't that when we need our friends the most?'

'Friends?' he challenged. 'I thought we were talking about sex. That's certainly the impression you gave me upstairs.'

'Don't,' she said softly. 'I don't want to argue with you. I just want to help.'

'You always want to help.' Getting up, he stoked the fire. 'I don't need *help*, not from anyone, and especially not from you.'

Luc's words were like a slap across the face, and it took a little time before she could do much more than watch the flames rise and dance in the hearth.

'Okay,' she said at last, getting to her feet. 'I guess even I can take a hint.'

'Maybe we can talk some other time,' he suggested.

'Is there any point?'

'You were lucky tonight that it was me and not some other man,' Luc called after her as she headed for the stairs.

She stopped dead. 'There's no chance of there ever being another man.'

'Then, you're a fool, Stacey,' Luc said coldly. 'For your own sake, accept that we don't belong together. You deserve someone far—'

'Oh, please,' she interrupted, 'spare me the gentle let-down. If I'm hopeless in bed and turn you right off, you only have to say so.'

'What the hell?' Luc was on his feet and grabbing hold of her within a second. Cupping her chin, he made her look at him. 'You're not hopeless. In fact, that's the problem.'

'I'm too good,' she suggested with a mocking huff as she braced to hear the truth.

'Yes,' Luc confirmed flatly. 'This is my fault. I shouldn't have let things go so far.'

'It takes two to tango. And as for consequences, I'll handle whatever comes around.'

'But can you do that?' His expression was sceptical. 'You're hunting for a fairy tale and what I'm looking for is sex. I devote most of my time to work and the rest of my time to polo. I travel constantly, and wherever I am—' he shrugged '—is home.'

'You don't have a home. You have a number of fabulous properties across the world, but when it comes to a home you don't know the meaning of the word.'

'I can remember,' he said quietly.

She could have ripped out her tongue. 'Of course you do. Luc, I'm so sorry. I don't think sometimes.'

'And you're not thinking now,' Luc warned.

'Oh, I am,' she assured him. 'What makes you think I want more than you? I'm a normal woman with normal, healthy appetites. Men aren't the only animals on the planet who want sex with no consequences or long-term complications. I'm not the clinging-vine type,' she added while her heart screamed that she was a liar, and that she did want Luc long-term. For as long as she could remember he'd been part of her life, and life going forward without him, especially now they'd been so close, was unthinkable. But if one night was all she could have she'd take it.

'Neither of us has the type of lifestyle that allows for a long-term relationship,' she said matter-of-factly, as desperation to have Luc kiss her, embrace her, make love to her, drummed relentlessly in her brain.

His lips pressed down attractively as he considered this. 'If you can accept reality, then I suppose…'

She jumped on the opening. 'Do you mean accepting the pace of your life means you snatch up a woman like you snatch up a meal, and when you've both had enough you walk away?'

Luc's head shot back. '*Dios*, Stacey! That's a little harsh, even for me. I could never think of you that way. I've watched you grow up.'

'Then you should know I'm no fool and I know my own mind. Please don't pity me, or make a joke of this, either. I know what I want, and I know what you need. What's wrong with that?'

He shrugged. 'Everything?'

Cocking her chin to one side, she demanded, 'Doesn't that make it irresistible…for both of us?'

No. It did not. *Dios!* What was he going to do with this woman—with himself? The fire they created between them was unreal. One minute they were arguing, and the next passion of a very different kind was threatening. Any challenge, or something forbidden to him, had always proved irresistible in the past, but this was Stacey. This was wrong. With no reprieve in sight, the best he could do was put space between them. What a joke talking about consequences where Stacey was concerned. He'd taken her into his home and it was *he* who had to live with those consequences. According to the latest weather forecast it would be three or four days at least before the roads to the village were passable, so, like it or not, they were stuck together.

'Lucas?' she prompted. 'Don't you have anything to say?'

'Irresistible is a dangerous word.'

'Thank you for your input, Señor Da Silva. I shall bear that in mind.'

He had plenty more to say on the subject, but thought it better now to stare out of the window, beyond which snow was falling again. The hotel across the road had become a vague, insubstantial shadow, a reminder that he'd called every hotel in the village, but they were all full with people who'd been stranded. No one had any room for Stacey except him. 'Haven't you gone to bed yet?' he asked without turning to face her.

'I'm waiting for you,' she said.

When he swung around, she gave him one of her looks, and he knew then that even if they went to their separate beds she'd still be on his mind. 'You should rest and so should I.'

'I'll let you rest…in between making love to me.'

'This isn't funny, Stace.'

'You're telling me.'

To his horror, there were tears in her eyes. 'Just let it go,' he advised. 'I'm a lost cause,' he added wryly.

'Okay,' she agreed with a jerk of her head. 'That should be easy.' But instead of moving away, she moved closer. 'Wow. We really are snowed in…what a cliché. Now I have to share your bed.'

Not so much a cliché as a challenge, he thought as he attempted to ignore Stacey's appeal, her scent, her vulnerability. 'Your bed,' he emphasised.

'I can take a hint.'

He doubted it. 'Thanks for your help tonight.'

'I was pleased to help.'

They stood staring out at the snow, which had started banking up thanks to a strong wind, and was collecting in even deeper drifts around the chalet. He'd dig them out in the morning and ski her down to the lower part of the village, rather than sit around waiting for the weather to change. That was the safest thing to do, plus he had a party to think about. They both did. He laughed inwardly at the irony of trying to avoid someone for their own good, only to have fate bind them together.

'We're stranded on a desert island of snow,' Stacey murmured beside him.

'No more fantasies, please,' he begged.

Needless to say, she ignored him. 'It's like a different world, isn't it? No rules, and nothing beyond us and this moment.'

'It doesn't take long for your imagination to start rolling, does it?' he commented.

'Well, how do you see it?'

'As a task tomorrow morning when I dig us both out.'

'Practical to the last,' she remarked with a laugh.

'I'm practical,' he agreed. 'As you can be.'

'I do have some good qualities, then?'

'Stop fishing,' he warned, but she'd made him smile, which made him want her more than ever. He'd be the first to admit that years of guarding his siblings had made him overprotective. That was what his brothers and sister told him, anyway. 'You're no fun any more,' was a frequent complaint that he supposed might be true, but it hadn't stopped him enjoying Stacey.

Did he really have to stop?

For her sake, yes.

'It's beautiful, isn't it?' she whispered, and then he felt her hand on his back… Her tiny hand on flesh he hadn't troubled to cover since leaving his bed. The sensation was incredible. 'Get out of here,' he said lightly, hoping she would, because his willpower had taken just about all it could.

'No,' she said flatly, and, rather than obey him, she ran the tips of her nails down his supersensitive skin, sending his moral compass into a spin.

Swinging around, he stared at her. 'No?' he queried.

She glanced down. Instantly hard, he was incapable of hiding his physical reactions; thoughts were much easier.

They stared at each other for a good few moments, then he reached out to hook his fingers into the waistband of her pyjamas. As he pulled them down she observed, 'So you're not entirely made of ice.'

'Try me,' he suggested.

'I intend to.'

A cry of triumph shot from her throat as he knelt between her thighs.

'Oh…please,' she begged as he began to explore her body as if he had never encountered it before. By bending her knees she increased the pressure from his tongue. Working her hips to and fro lazily, she was all too soon wailing, 'I can't hold on.'

'You're not supposed to, princess.'

And then she screamed out wildly, *'Yes! Yes… Yes!'* before exhaling noisily in time to each violent spasm as it washed over her.

'Oh, Lucas,' she moaned contentedly when the pleasure began to fade. 'That was amazing.'

Catching her as she collapsed, sated for the moment, he knew he had never wanted a woman more, had never wanted to pleasure a woman more. With all the barriers finally removed between them he swung her into his arms, and carried her to the deep fur rug in front of the fire. Arranging her to his liking, he parted her legs wide and allowed them to rest on his shoulders as he dipped his head and parted her lips to lave her with his tongue.

'I can't—not again—not so soon,' she insisted on a gasping breath.

'And I say you can,' he argued quietly, 'and not once, but many times.'

He proved it by delicately agitating the tiny bud at the heart of her pleasure. It didn't take much encouragement for it to spring back to life.

Exhaling with excitement, Stacey wound her fingers through his hair to keep him close. He knew what she wanted, and he gave it to her until she was thrusting her hips towards him, crying out, 'More… *More!* Don't stop!' Seconds later, she called out his name and fell noisily into release.

He held her firmly in place to make sure that she enjoyed every last pulse of pleasure. 'I had no idea it

could be so good,' she groaned when the initial vio-
lence of her climax had begun to subside into a series
of rhythmical pulses.

That was the problem, he reflected as he gradually
brought her down again with soothing words in his own
language and long, gentle strokes of his hand. Stacey
was beginning to understand what was possible, and
from there it was only a small step to feral lust, and
when that point was reached, there'd be no turning back.

What was he talking about? They'd already crossed
the Rubicon, he realised as she gripped his arms fiercely
to state baldly, 'I want you inside me.'

She had no idea how much he wanted her closing
around him, holding him in place as she drew him deep
and sucked him dry. 'Please,' she whispered, 'tease me
like you did before.'

Reaching for his belt, she unbuckled it and snapped
it out of its loops. Then she popped the button at the
top of his zipper. The moment that came down he exploded out of the placket.

'Is this what you want?' he asked, bracing himself
above her.

'Exactly that,' she agreed.

'Like this,' he suggested, stroking the tip of his erection down the apex of her thighs.

'Oh, yes,' she confirmed.

'And this?' he suggested, watching her closely as he
gave her the tip.

'Oh, yes…yes, *yes*!'

Capturing her wrists in one fist, he pinned them
above her head. 'Just one thing…'

'What?' she gasped.

'I say we take this slowly.'

'At first,' she agreed.

CHAPTER TEN

FANTASIES ABOUT MASTERFUL Lucas were nothing compared to this. She could dream of making love until the lights went out and the world ended and this would still be on another scale.

Luc was so much more than she remembered. That first time was nothing like this, because now she was ready and she welcomed his size and the way he stretched her. All her inhibitions had dropped away, so by the time he had protected them both, pressed her down and taken her as firmly as she could have wished, she was ready to respond with matching fire.

She'd dreamed for so long that one day Lucas would see her as a woman, rather than as an annoying nuisance who cropped up in his life now and then, that she refused to be responsible for the sounds and words leaving her throat. They were wild for each other. And while she was consumed by a ravenous hunger, the urge to be one with him was even stronger.

She was eager for more, but Luc refused to be hurried. He would take care of her, he insisted as he began a leisurely tour of her body that required him to kiss every part of her.

'Stop, stop,' she begged when he nuzzled the sensitive nape of her neck with his sharp black stubble.

Sensation overload. 'I can't stand it,' she gasped out, thrashing about.

'But you can,' he said.

Turning her, he proved this by kissing the back of her knees, where she hadn't even known she was sensitive, and then he kissed his way up her thighs, and on across her buttocks until she was trembling with anticipation. Next, he kissed the sway of her back until she groaned with contentment. He knew what he was doing. With every passing second she was becoming more sensitive. Her pulse was going crazy and her body craved him like never before.

'Again?' he suggested.

She smiled up as he eased her legs apart and moved between them. Grasping his erection, he teased her with the tip.

'Yes! *Yes!*' she groaned, arcing her hips instinctively to receive him. 'Don't stop now,' she begged. 'Don't you dare stop.'

And to some extent, he obeyed her, stroking and teasing as before, then entering a little way before pulling back again. It was a game she loved. Their game.

Grabbing Luc's shoulders, she drew her knees back and took the chance, brief as it was, to admire the magnificent power of the body looming over her. He was so careful with her, sinking a little deeper each time, until finally he was engaged to the hilt.

'Soon,' he murmured in reply to her gasping protests when he stopped moving.

'You okay?' he asked as she gasped with pleasure.

She couldn't speak for fear of breaking the spell. They were one, and that was all she cared about.

Dropping kisses on her lips, he began to move, not back and forth as he had before, but in a circular, massaging movement until her body could do nothing but respond. 'Oh!' she cried out in wonder as she drew closer to the abyss. *'Again...!'*

Luc obliged by slamming into her, so that this time when the waves hit they were stronger and fiercer, and what was almost better than that was when she closed her inner muscles around him and he groaned. Seeing him lost in pleasure of her making made her feel powerful and strong, while the discovery that by tensing and relaxing her inner muscles she could bring him pleasure thrilled her beyond belief.

They made love in front of the fire for hours, fiercely at first, and then tenderly, which she found almost unbearably poignant. When Lucas brushed her hair back from her glowing face, she knew without question that if nothing good ever happened again she'd cling to tonight and never forget it. What more could she want than this closeness, this oneness as they stared deep into each other's eyes? It required a special sort of trust to give herself to a man so completely.

'I don't know if you want to sleep, but I think you will sleep now,' Luc observed, smiling down. 'It's been a long day. You must be exhausted.'

'And a very long night,' she reminded him, 'though, surprisingly, I don't feel tired at all. You, on the other hand, must be exhausted?'

'I've never worked so hard,' he agreed dryly, grinning with pleasure as she tightened her muscles around him. 'Always a contest with you,' he added as she enticed him to do more than drop kisses on her lips.

They breathed in unison, with every part of them in full accord, and every part of their naked bodies touching. She'd never felt so safe, so cared for...*so loved?*

No. Don't kid yourself like that, Stacey's inner voice

recommended. *It's too cruel. You won't be able to bear it in the morning when you see everything through the lens of a bright new day.*

'I'd like to go to bed and sleep in your arms,' she said honestly.

'Sleep?' Lucas queried.

'Yes. Sleep,' she confirmed. 'For whatever remains of the night.'

'Not much,' he observed with a glance out of the window to where dawn's first frail rays were already silvering the mountain peaks.

'Whatever's left of the night, I'll take it.'

Luc's answer was to lift her into his arms so he could carry her to the bed.

There was no greater peace, he mused as he watched Stacey sleeping. No greater satisfaction than making love to a woman that he…

That he what?

Loved? Cherished? Had used?

Not used. Never used.

They'd come together because, short of swearing a vow of chastity, there was no other way for them. It was inevitable, and had always been inevitable since the first moment they met. Stacey had imprinted her unique and infuriating qualities on him in a way he couldn't have imagined possible, and now could never forget. She'd slept in his arms, giving him the gift of peace for the first time in years. Her breathing, so gentle and even, had soothed his. She looked so innocent and that soothed him too. He needed some uncomplicated goodness in his life, but that was selfish when he had nothing to offer Stacey long-term. It would be disingenuous to say he regretted that his darker side ruled his caring instinct. When she woke, Stacey would surely have come to her senses, and know that what they'd shared was over.

Even an ice-cold shower failed to subdue his libido. He'd never known another woman like her. Stacey had been wild when she was younger, but in his bed she'd been a revelation. Niahl's little sister was all grown up. Still cloaked in innocence perhaps, but beneath that cloak her sexual appetite matched his.

And Niahl? How would he square this with Niahl? This need, this lust inside him blurred the edges of right and wrong, making it hard to move on. The bottom line didn't include Niahl, he determined as he turned off the water and shook hair out of his eyes. The bottom line was Stacey. He didn't want to hurt her. Reaching for a towel, he secured it around his waist. He only had to think of her and he was hard.

Dropping the towel, he glanced out of the window at snow banked up high in drifts. *Avoid her if you can*, his inner critic challenged. He and Stacey had been thrown together and now they were stranded together. The only sensible answer to that problem was to clear a path in the snow to the black slope and ski her back to the village.

Donning work clothes, he congratulated himself on the fact that he'd always been able to identify the right moment to part. He'd known with his siblings when it was time for them to leave home, and he knew with Stacey. She needed a man who would have time for her, and dote on her, and provide her with a safe and cosy home. History suggested he could never do that. As soon as his siblings were fledged, he'd cast off, a ship without an anchor. After his parents' death nothing had remained the same. Life was a river continually moving on. This chalet wasn't his home. Stacey was right.

It was just one of many properties he owned across the world. The next acquisition was always more attractive. And in each there was something vital missing. If he could just put his finger on what it was…he'd buy it, Luc concluded as he headed downstairs.

Stacey woke in a state of deep contentment, instantly aware of a body well used. It took her a moment longer to realise where she was. *Luc's room!* And then the events of the previous night came flooding in. Reaching out to touch him in the big, wide bed, she found the other side empty. Where was he?

'Luc…?'

The silence that greeted her question had a particular quality that told her she was alone. Slipping out of bed, she grabbed a robe. Putting it on, she belted it. Crossing to the window, she exclaimed softly with relief to see Luc outside, clearing a path through the snow. Turning, she retired to the bathroom, where she took the fastest shower ever. She frowned as she put on the only clothes she had with her. There was a suspicion tugging at the back of her mind.

She'd examine it later, she decided as she hurried downstairs to put on her jacket and boots. There were all sorts of useful implements hanging on the wall of the boot room alongside the skis, so she grabbed a shovel and went outside to join him. 'Morning…'

'Hey.' Luc glanced up briefly before stabbing his shovel back in the snow.

She could feel his eyes burning beneath wrap-around sunglasses—a necessary precaution when the sun was low and bright. Whether the sky would remain blue like this remained to be seen, but while it did…

'Shot!' She'd got him square on the head with a snowball.

Shaking his unruly mop of black hair like an irritated wolf, Luc dug his shovel into the snow again and acted as if he hadn't noticed.

She tried again, and then again with mounting success, until, with a roar, he straightened up.

'You don't frighten me, Luc Da Silva,' she assured him.

'Then it's time I did,' he said, and in a couple of strides he was transformed from cool and aloof to the infuriating guy she remembered from her youth. Yanking her close, he plonked her down and dropped great handfuls of snow on her face, rubbing still more into her hair.

'Don't you—'

'Dare?' he suggested. '*Dios*, Stacey! You make me want to have you right here in the snow.'

'I don't see anyone stopping you…'

With a husky exclamation, he tossed his gloves aside. 'What are you doing to me?'

'And you to me,' she gasped as they began to fight with each other's clothes.

'Is this even possible?' Thermals stood in their way.

'Of course,' Luc confirmed as he freed himself.

Swinging her up so she could wrap her legs around his waist, he took her with a deep thrust. No foreplay, none needed. An exclamation of shocked delight flew from her throat. Nothing had ever felt this good. She was more than ready for him, and Luc was so caring, so careful of his size and her much smaller body. He held her as if she weighed nothing, and pounded into her until she could do no more than hang suspended in his arms. 'So good… I need this…'

'Me too,' Lucas admitted in an edgy growl.

'Harder! Faster!' They were wild for each other. She couldn't get enough. How could she ever live without this…without him?

'Again,' she insisted throatily when the first bout of pleasure started to fade. 'I need more.'

Luc laughed. 'Me too,' he assured her.

'Yes!' she hissed in triumph as he thrust rhythmically the way she liked.

'How strong are you?' she said some time later. 'Don't your arms ache?'

'I hadn't even thought about it. I was somewhat distracted.'

'And now?'

'And now… I want to have you in the snow.'

Beneath a bright blue sky with snow hillocks all around them, they made love again, and this time when Luc pinned her arms above her head, they stared into each other's eyes, and saw more than the fever of passion.

'I guess we'd better get to work,' he said reluctantly some time later.

'I guess we better had,' she agreed.

Arranging their clothes took less than a few seconds, and soon they were attacking the snow with real gusto.

'Something wrong?' she asked Luc, shooting a glance his way when he stopped shovelling and leaned on the handle. 'Have I exhausted you?'

He huffed a laugh and gathered her close. 'What do you think?'

'I think you're facing a decision between clearing the path, and visiting that sauna over there.'

'Could be,' he confirmed with a grin.

'Let's investigate. I don't want to leave you in agony.'

Planting their shovels, they ran to the sauna. Closing the door, they stripped off each other's clothes. The small log cabin was already warm, but Luc raised the temperature even more, both with water on the embers and with his unique take on lovemaking on scorching wooden benches. 'We have to be quick,' he explained, laughing against her mouth.

'I can be quick.'

'When you want to,' he agreed.

'I like to make you work.'

'I noticed.'

His grin was infectious, a slash of strong white teeth against his deep tan and sharp black stubble. There was only one problem. Their enthusiasm combined with the extreme heat inside the sauna sent the logistics of sex haywire. 'I'm sliding off you!'

'Time to cool down,' Luc agreed.

Who knew they could be so close? There was a lot of laughter involved as he carried her outside and dumped her in the snow, where they proved conclusively that heating up before rolling in ice crystals was a great aphrodisiac. Luc's strength and potency was glaring her in the face. His naked body, challenging the elements, had never looked more magnificent. 'On top of me,' he instructed, arranging her so she could mount him. 'Can't risk you catching cold.'

'No chance of that!' She gasped out her pleasure as he entered her in one thrust, and when she was quiet again and snuggled into his chest, she remarked groggily, 'No wonder this caught on.'

'Making love in the snow?'

'The whole sauna thing.' Had they ever been so close? she wondered.

'Come on.' Luc dragged her to her feet. 'Before we both freeze. Heat. Clothes. Then back to work.'

They talked as they worked, giving her hope that Luc might finally open up. He didn't. Instead he directed a barrage of questions her way, so she told him about her life and friends in London, and the fact that she missed the farm. 'I miss the horses terribly,' she admitted. 'And I miss Niahl, but he's so busy these days.' She stopped as a shadow crossed Luc's face. *Luc* was so busy these days. This snowbound interlude was a rare break for him. *That* was what he'd been trying to tell her, that she shouldn't expect anything beyond this, because he didn't have the time. That was okay. On the personal front, she could deal with it. She'd have to. But where Luc was concerned, if she could unlock even just a little bit of his angst, her job was done, and so she asked the question: 'How about you, Lucas?'

'Me?' His lips pressed down as he shrugged. 'You can learn anything you want to know about me from the press.'

'Can I?' she said disbelievingly. 'I can only learn what sensational journalism wants me to know, and I'd rather hear it from you.'

'Hear what from me?'

Okay. She got the message. This was going nowhere. If she pressed him he'd clam up even more. Why spoil the short time they had together?

'No.' Planting her shovel, she admitted, 'Whatever I read in the press, I see you as amazing. Always have.' She huffed a laugh. 'Pity me.'

'No faults?' Luc enquired, spreading his arms wide.

Stacey hummed as she pretended to consider this, but she was thinking, *This is my chance to let Luc know I'm there for him.*

'You're a little controlling, but only because responsibility came along in such a tragic way. However wild you were, there was no option but to rein in fast. Perhaps you overcompensated. Your parents' death happened when others your age were free to do as they pleased, so I think it's amazing that you not only built a business empire, but mended a family that had been so badly fractured.'

What she didn't add was her deeply held belief that Luc could have done with someone to mend him.

He hummed and raised a brow. 'I'm not sure I deserve that level of praise. You make me sound far more impressive than I am.'

'Do I?' She held his gaze steadily. 'Or do I say these things because they're true?'

'You haven't done too badly yourself,' he said, shifting the spotlight with effortless ease. 'You were also bound by duty, but you found an opportunity to try something new and forge your own path, which you've done very successfully, it seems to me.'

Disappointment welled inside her. She should have known better than to expect Luc to open up after so many years for no better reason than because she'd asked a question. Deciding to keep things light and try another time, she smiled. 'So you've finally accepted I've changed in five years.'

'I wouldn't go that far,' he growled, pretending to be fierce.

'Just a little?' she suggested.

He dragged her close. 'Quite a lot. Seems to me you've grown up in a very short time.'

'Are you surprised?' she said softly, smiling happily against his mouth. 'One night with you is enough to make anyone grow up. My initiation ceremony was spectacular. I can't recommend it enough.'

'I suggest you keep it to yourself.'

'Oh, I will,' she promised fervently. 'And please don't let this be the last time,' she whispered before she could stop herself.

'Let's finish the dig,' he said, easing out of their embrace.

'We'll feel much better for completing the task,' she said, packing away her feelings.

'Time will tell,' Luc agreed.

'And when time has done its job?'

He shrugged. 'We'll know.'

She didn't ask him what they'd know. The answer was clear to both of them. Time would push them apart, but there was no point in thinking about that now.

CHAPTER ELEVEN

THEY MET UP in the great room, having taken a shower after their marathon snow-shovelling endeavours. 'You look great,' Luc told her with a wicked smile. 'Exercise suits you.'

'You too,' she said a little distractedly, though Luc had never looked better than he did right now. Barefoot in a pair of old jeans, unshaven with his thick, wavy hair damp and clinging to his stubble, powerful torso clad in a faded tee shirt that had definitely seen better days, he could play the role of gypsy king to perfection. A very handsome, rugged, and extremely virile gypsy king, she amended as their stares clashed and locked.

'You've changed,' he said, frowning.

'For the better, I hope?'

'Hmm. I can't quite put my finger on it.'

But she could. He was right saying she'd changed. She'd changed more than he knew. She was late and she was never late. And there was more evidence that she might be pregnant, though this was something that other people might find hard to believe. Call it instinct, but she felt very different in a deep and fundamental way. She was as sure as she could be that she was no longer alone in her body, but was the nurturing home of a new young life. Her heart had expanded to embrace this new love, though where she went from here remained a mystery. She could only be confident about one thing, and that was that she would approach everything as she always did, head-on. She didn't sit on those thoughts, but came straight out with them. 'What if I seem different to you because I'm pregnant?'

Lucas stilled. 'I'm sorry? What did you say?'

'What if I'm pregnant?' she repeated. 'What if I'm having your baby?'

'That isn't possible.' Luc shook his head confidently. 'I made sure of it.'

'No one can make absolutely sure of that, not even you, Luc.'

'All right,' he conceded grudgingly. 'So how can you be absolutely sure that you are pregnant without undergoing the usual tests?'

'I'm as sure as I can be. It can happen the first time you make love.'

Luc frowned. 'Barcelona?'

'Almost a month ago,' she confirmed.

Thoughts flickered fast behind his eyes, and she was sure those thoughts said that a child didn't figure on Luc's agenda. He didn't even think of her long-term, let alone a child. So? So she'd manage on her own. She'd done it before and she'd do it again. She wouldn't be the only single mother in the world. And one thing was certain, no baby of hers would suffer rejection as she had. It would be loved unconditionally. A career and motherhood were compatible. It would take some organising, but she was good at that—

'Stacey? You do know we can't leave this here?'

'Of course I do.'

'Then…?'

'May I make a suggestion?'

'Of course.'

They had both turned stiff and businesslike. Pushing away regret and every other emotion, she concentrated on the facts. 'Let's wait until we're no longer snowbound and I can have a test. Then get the party out of the way before we discuss the particulars.'

'The *particulars*?' Lucas drew his head back with surprise. 'We *are* still talking about a child?'

Stacey's face flamed red. Of course they were. The expression in Luc's eyes shamed her. It was that of a man who had only ever known love from his parents, and who couldn't fathom Stacey's deeply held fear. Not having known her own mother, she worried that she might know nothing about mothering and mess up. It wouldn't be for want of trying. Now the seed of suspicion was planted in her brain, she wanted to be pregnant, already loved the thought of a child with all her heart.

'We're discussing the most precious gift in the world,' she stated firmly. Whatever else he thought of her, she couldn't bear to have Luc think she took after her father.

'Come here,' he murmured.

She hesitated, knowing that with each show of affection it was harder to accept that they couldn't do this together. Luc had no reason to change his life. Just as she wouldn't be the first single mother, he wouldn't be the first man with a love child, but that didn't mean they would become a family.

But she did go to him. And they did kiss. Enveloping her in a tender bear hug as if she were suddenly made of rice paper, he whispered against her hair, 'I shouldn't have let you dig the snow.'

She gazed up. 'I might be pregnant, but I'm not sick, and I'd like to have seen you stop me.'

'Still,' he said in a serious tone, pulling back to stare into her face. 'Take it easy from now on until you know.'

When people cared for her it brought tears to her eyes. Having Luc care for her was catastrophic, and these were tears she could do without, so she turned away before he'd seen them, in case he thought her weak.

'I've not finished with you yet,' he murmured.

The tone of his voice made her look at him. He pulled her close. Their mouths collided. They kissed as if tomorrow would never come.

Luc took some time for reflection alone in his study while Maria prepared a light lunch for him and Stacey. His experience of family life had been positive until the accident, when he had vowed never to risk his heart again. The pain of losing his parents had been indescribable. It still was. The wound cut deep and he had thought himself incapable of loving again.

A child changed everything.

Now he'd have to risk his heart. Anticipation and dread fought inside him at the thought. Where was he supposed to find time in his busy schedule for a child? Would he be any use as a father? He'd been lucky enough to have brilliant parents. Love had been in full supply, though their grasp of life and economics had been sadly lacking, as he had discovered when he took over the responsibility of running the family home. These days he could mastermind the biggest deals, and buy anything he wanted, but he still remembered the restrictions placed on him when he was caring for his brothers and sisters. It was a responsibility he'd taken on gladly, but he couldn't deny it was a relief when they were old enough to make their own way in life. Of course, they didn't know yet if Stacey was pregnant, but if she was, with her background, she'd need support too. He'd make time, Luc concluded.

First things first. For Stacey's peace of mind, he had to get her down to the village where she could take a pregnancy test, see a doctor, and get up to speed with the arrangements for the party. She'd start climbing the walls if she couldn't do that soon. With transport to the village suspended there was only one way to get her down safely, and he was confident he could do it. He wouldn't take risks with Stacey. The thought of anything happening to her—

Nothing would happen to her. He must put the past behind him. There were more important things to consider. His parents' death had been a tragic accident. That was what the police had told him afterwards, and only he knew the truth. Nothing Stacey could say or do would deter him from caring for her. And, if she proved to be pregnant, caring for their child. It was a surprise, but a good surprise, he reflected with a smile. They had certainly put enough work into it! He'd taken precautions, but precautions were never guaranteed one hundred per cent. So his duty now was to take care of her…and, quite incredibly, but undeniably possible, his unborn child. Whatever else happened from here on in he was determined that their baby, if there proved to be one, would know the loving upbringing he'd had, and not the tragically lonely home life that Stacey had known.

Decision made, he called Maria on the house phone. 'Hold lunch. I'm going to ski down to the village to check on the arrangements for the party.'

'Will Señorita Winner stay here?'

'Señorita Winner is coming with me.'

'No way!' Stacey exclaimed when Luc told her what he planned. 'Are you kidding me?'

'Don't you trust me?'

'You know I do.'

'But…?' he prompted.

'But if I'm pregnant…'

'You're not sick, as you put it,' he reminded her, 'and there's a smaller risk of having an accident if I take you back to the village, than if I leave you to your own devices up here. The frustration of not knowing where the plans are for the party will kill you…if the roof doesn't cave in from the weight of snow first.'

She glanced up to the exposed rafters with concern. 'Is there a danger of that?'

'No,' Luc admitted. 'But for the sake of the party and my guests, as well as getting you checked out, we need to get down to the village asap. The gondolas aren't running yet, so what I'm proposing is the safest way.'

'You're that good a skier? Of course you are,' she commented dryly. 'Is there anything you can't do?'

'I don't know.' He shrugged. 'Let's find out. You haven't eaten anything, so I'll take you for lunch.'

Stacey's eyes widened. 'Let me get this straight. You're proposing to take me to the village on *your* skis?'

'On my skis,' Luc confirmed.

'You are joking, I hope?' Stacey stared down the dizzying drop. 'This is a cliff edge. You can't possibly ski down it.'

She let out a yelp as Luc proved her wrong. With his arm locked around her waist, he kept her securely in place on the front of his skis as he dropped from the edge like a stone. Just when she thought they would continue like that to the bottom of the mountain, he made a big sweeping turn, before heading sideways at a much slower pace, until finally he stopped at the side of the slope. 'See? I told you that you can trust me to keep you safe.'

'Just warn me when you're going to do something like that again,' she begged through ice-cold lips.

'I won't let you fall,' he promised. 'I could lift you off the ground in front of me and still take us both down the mountain safely, but if you stand on my skis it's easier for me to put my arms around you to keep you in place.'

'I wish you joy of that,' she said, laughing tensely at her hopeless joke.

'True,' Lucas agreed. His lips pressed down attractively. 'I've been trying to keep you in place for years and haven't succeeded, so I have no idea what makes me think I can do it now.'

'You trust me?' she suggested.

He huffed a laugh, then coaxed, 'Come on. Let's try another run. Just a short one until you get used to it.'

'Won't my boots crack your skis?'

'You're wearing snow boots, and you've only got little feet.'

'You've got slim skis,' she pointed out.

'But big feet,' Luc countered.

'Very big feet,' she agreed, tensing as they started to move again.

Stacey's throat dried as she stared down the abyss. Her job had taken her to some surprising places, but nothing like this. Only desperation to know if she was pregnant, and to see the team again so she could get the final plans for the party under way, could make her grit her teeth and carry on. Was this her preferred method of descending a mountain? If Luc hadn't been involved, her answer would be a firm no.

Nothing about being with Lucas is normal. Get used to it, her inner voice advised.

And she did. After the first few frightening drops, shimmies and turns, Luc tracked across the entire width of the slope, before stopping to make sure she was okay to continue. 'Enjoy it,' he urged. 'This is the closest you'll come to flight without leaving the ground.'

She forced a laugh. 'Please don't leave the ground. I saw those drops from the gondola before the storm closed in.'

'Don't worry. I ski this slope several times a day when I'm here, so I know it like the back of my hand.'

'How often do you look at the back of your hand?'

He laughed and they were off again, though not straight down as she had feared, but swooping from side to side in a rhythmical pattern she could almost get used to, if she could only close her mind to the fear of what seemed to her to be a controlled fall down the mountain.

'Relax,' Luc murmured against her cheek the next time he brought them to a halt. His mouth was so close they shared the same crisp champagne air.

'I want to trust you. Honestly I do. I trusted you with my body, so it should only be a small step to trust you with my life, shouldn't it?' Her laugh sounded tense, even to her, and Luc's expression was unreadable.

'There are no small steps up here,' she observed with a twist of her mouth. 'It's all giant leaps and furious speed, and I don't get how you do it while I'm standing on the front of your skis. It's a miracle I don't quite believe in yet.'

'Just believe I'll keep you safe. That's all you need to do,' Luc told her with an easy shrug. And with that they were off again, skimming down the slope.

Surprising herself, Stacey found her confidence gradually growing as she got used to the speed. It helped that Luc made regular stops 'to check she was still breathing', as he jokingly put it.

'I'm tougher than I look,' she assured him.

'No mistaking that,' he said.

No mistake at all. With Luc's body moulded tightly to hers, she wasn't skiing, she was flying, and with the wind in her face and his heat behind her, the experience was wonderful, magical. There was silence all around, apart from the swish of skis on snow, and not one other person on the mountain to disturb the solitude. It was just the two of them, equally dependent on the cooperation of the other. 'I can see the houses in the village,' she called out at last.

Luc cruised to a halt. The mist had cleared, and the snow had stopped falling, leaving the sky above an improbable shade of unrelieved blue. 'Suddenly, I feel optimistic,' she exclaimed excitedly, turning to look at him.

'Me too,' Luc agreed in more considered tone. 'This is perfect weather for the party.'

The party. Something went flat inside her. She didn't want to be reminded that her whole purpose in being here was to arrange a party for Luc. But those were the bald facts. He was thinking ahead, while she was guilty of living in the moment.

'If only the gondolas were running,' she remarked, staring up in a failed attempt to distract herself from the hurt inside her. They were halfway down the mountain, but there was no sign of any small cabins bobbing along.

'I would have thought that with the return of reasonably good weather they'd be running by now.'

'Wind damage,' Luc explained, following her gaze before tightening his grip around her waist and setting off again. 'Each part of the system will have to be thoroughly checked before they're operational,' he yelled in her ear.

'But your guests...'

'Don't worry,' he shouted back. 'I've got an idea to transport them up the mountain.'

'I'm intrigued.'

'And I'm hungry. Are you up for going a bit faster with no stops until we reach the village?'

'Yes!' Stacey surprised herself with how much she wanted this. Testing herself with Luc at her back was easy. She felt so safe with him, and happier than she had been in a long time. Whatever the future held they'd have much to celebrate. And if that future didn't promise to be exactly conventional, the prospect of maybe having a child to crown that happiness was a precious gift she looked forward to, no matter what.

There was no point thinking *if only*, Luc reflected as he slowed at the approach to the nursery slopes bordering the village. He'd done too much of that. *If only* his parents had lived to see how successful his brothers and sister had become. *If only* they could share his good fortune. And now, *if only* they had lived to see their first grandchild. Wherever he was in life, and whatever the circumstances, the guilt he bore sat on his shoulder like an ugly crow waiting to peck out his happiness.

Stacey whooped with exhilaration as he slowed to a stop, then she noticed his expression and asked with concern, 'You okay?'

'Me? Fine.'

'That's my line,' she scolded.

He huffed a laugh that held no humour. Steadying her as she stepped off his skis, he freed the bindings, stepped out of them, paired the skis, and swung them over his shoulder.

As she glanced back up the mountain and shook her head in wonder at what she'd accomplished, he remarked, 'If I told you at the top that we were about to ski the World Cup course, would you have come with me?'

Her jaw dropped as she stared at him. 'Really?'

'Really,' he confirmed. 'Well done.'

She grinned. 'Maybe not,' she admitted, 'but I'm glad I did. You never had any doubt we'd get down safely, did you?'

'If I had you wouldn't be here. I would never take risks with your safety, especially not now. Anyway, congratulations again. You can tell your friends what you've done.'

Oddly, she felt flat. Maybe because Luc had made it sound like a holiday adventure, Stacey reflected as they walked along. Perhaps that was all it was to him. It made her wonder if the possibility that she might be pregnant had made any impact on him. Was he really so unfeeling, and if so why? Once the party was over they would speed off in opposite directions. Would Luc keep her at a distance? Surely a child was an everlasting link between them? Whether he wanted that link, however, was another matter. She trusted him completely, and yet she didn't know him at all, Stacey concluded as they walked along. As always, her concern for Luc won through over any other concerns she might have had. 'How will you get back to the chalet when you've finished your business in the village?'

'I won't be going back to the chalet.'

'Oh… I see.' She didn't see, but Luc didn't offer any more information, and she didn't feel it was her place to cross-question him. The last thing she wanted was for him to think her a clinging vine before she even knew if she was pregnant.

Everything about him suggested Luc was back in work mode. As she should be, Stacey reminded herself. They weren't lovers of long standing, let alone close friends, and when it came to his party in the mountains Lucas was the boss and she worked for him. She'd always known this had to end at some point. She just hadn't expected it to end so abruptly at the bottom of a ski slope after such an amazing run, when she'd been so sure the shared experience had brought them closer.

'I might stay over in the village,' he revealed in an offhand tone.

There was no invitation to join him, and why should there be? That said, it didn't make it any easier to accept how loving and caring he could be one minute, and how distant the next.

Of course you understand why he's this way, her inner voice insisted. The ability to love had died inside Luc on the day his parents were killed. Everyone but Niahl and Stacey had been surprised by the intensity of his grief. It had almost seemed Luc held himself responsible for his parents' death, but they'd been such a close family, loving and caring for each other, no wonder he'd been devastated. Many times she'd longed to tell him that he couldn't be everywhere at once, working up a business, and caring for parents who, however lovely they'd been, had struck Stacey as being unrealistic, even irresponsible, when it came to money. They were always chasing the next new idea, leaving Luc to bail them out on many occasions. The true extent of their debt had only come to light after the funeral, which Stacey believed had been the driver for Luc believing it was down to him to support his siblings and to pay off those debts. He had nothing to regret, and she only wished she could tell him so, but doubted in his present mood he'd appreciate it.

She flashed up a glance into his harsh, unyielding face. Loving might be beyond Luc, but caring was instinctive, having been bred into him by those same wacky, but deeply loving parents. He'd done so much for her already, she mused as they crossed the road, giving her confidence she'd never had in her body, and a sense of being wanted, which was entirely new. For however short a time, he'd made her believe she was worth wanting, and if whatever it was they had between them ended today, she would always be grateful for what Luc had taught her. Now it was up to her to accept this short time together for what it was: a brief reunion; amazing sex; care for each other and a renewal of friendship, as well as all the support she could wish for when it came to personal concerns, as well as in her professional life. It would be a mistake to read more into it. Luc was a realist, she was a dreamer, and if she mixed up the two she'd be heading for disappointment.

'We'll have lunch here,' Luc said as they approached a busy café with steamed-up windows. 'Then you can call by the pharmacy on your way to meet up with your team, and book an appointment with the local doctor for a check-up.'

He barely drew breath before adding, 'I'll speak to

my people, while you see yours, and then we'll have a joint meeting.'

To discuss the party, and clearly not the results of a pregnancy test or her visit to the local doctor. Shouldn't they be discussing their future?

Their future? *Touch base with reality*, Stacey's inner voice recommended.

Luc's only interest at this precise moment was the vastly elaborate and hugely expensive party he'd paid for. Other things could wait. That was how he operated. Luc prioritised. He was a process-driven man. She was the dreamer, or had she forgotten that?

'Of course,' she confirmed in the same business-like tone. She had filled a space in Luc's life, and now he was done with her. 'Actually, I'd like to eat with my team, if that's okay with you?'

He looked at her with surprise. 'Whatever you want.'

'Forgive me—and thank you for your hospitality—but I've been away long enough.' One sweeping ebony brow lifted as Luc stared at her and frowned. 'Everything should be ready for the party,' she hurried on, 'but I need to check that all we have to do is light the touchpaper and stand back.' She was gabbling now, talking nonsense, eager to get away before he realised how upset she was. Luc's ability to close himself off was notorious, but it hurt when he raised those same barricades to her. 'I'll keep in touch,' she promised. 'I'll bring you and your people into a team meeting, if you like?'

'Of course,' he insisted. 'And let me know the result of the test right away, and what the doctor says. And if you need anything—'

'I'll let you know,' she cut across him as her heart threatened to shatter into tiny pieces.

CHAPTER TWELVE

She had to close her mind to Luc and that wasn't easy. Thankfully her forward planning had borne fruit. The Party Planners team was ready to roll. Everything was in place. They could hold the event this very minute without a hitch. The biggest and most glamorous party of the season had taken over everyone's thinking, and now it must take over hers, Stacey determined.

She hadn't even asked where to find him. Luc hadn't asked her—

Her throat dried as she remembered that she had his contact details safely logged in her file, where Luc and everything else to do with him should have remained.

Caressing her stomach, she thought, *Not everything.*

Lucas was a vitally important client, and she and the team had this chance to build on their success in Barcelona. She couldn't allow her personal concerns to get in the way of that. 'Go, team!' she said as their meeting broke up. 'This is going to be the most amazing event yet.'

He stowed his skis at a local hotel he owned, then had a meeting with his people, who confirmed arrangements for the party were well under way, and there was nothing for him to worry about. *Except Stacey.* His guts were in knots. News of a possible pregnancy had bull-dozed every thought from his head. It was a relief to know that the business side of things was going well. He doubted he could sort a problem with the party in his current state of mind.

Leaving the hotel to pace the streets to eat up time until he could reasonably call Stacey for the promised meeting, he spotted her leaving the pharmacy. Jogging across the road, he caught up with her. 'Coffee. Now,' he prescribed, glancing across the road at a café with steamed-up windows.

'Don't we have a meeting?'

She seemed pale to him. 'You need warming up. Business can wait.'

'Isn't the café a bit public for you?' she asked with concern.

'Aren't you exposed out here on your own with a pregnancy test clutched in your hand?' he countered.

'Don't,' she bit out tensely. 'Don't do this to me, Luc.'

'Don't do what?' he asked, uncomprehending.

'Just stop it, okay?'

Her voice was tight, and, though she kept her face turned away from him, he cursed himself for being a fool. Stacey could never handle kindness. Aside from her brother's care it was out of her ken. 'Okay. I'll back off,' he agreed. 'What you do and when you do it is up to you. All I ask is that you keep me informed. We could be starting a dynasty here.' His last remark was a failed attempt to lighten the mood, and the look she gave him could strip paint. He deserved it and stuck out his chin. 'Go on. Hit me,' he offered. 'You'll feel better if you do.'

'No. That's a man thing, Luc.' And then she smiled faintly. 'Coffee sounds good to me. And then I've got some more work to do,' she hurried to add.

'Of course,' he said, dipping his head in apparent meek submission. 'Whatever you say, *señorita*.'

Her look now said as clearly as if she'd spoken the words out loud: *But it's always whatever you say, Luc.* Swiftly followed by defiant eyes that warned him to get ready for a change of regime. If anything could persuade him she was pregnant, it was that, and not the test she'd bought at the pharmacy. Stacey remembered his mother's care for her children; she would have died for them. And she had.

Luc looked as wound up as she felt, which was why she had agreed to a coffee before their meeting. And so here they were in a cosy café, sipping hot drinks, surrounded by happy people on holiday, and even some of Luc's guests, whom he greeted with enthusiasm, as if he and they shouldn't and didn't have a care in the world. However incongruous it seemed to Stacey with a pregnancy test stuffed securely in the zip-up pocket of her snowsuit, she was the lover of this man, his possibly pregnant lover...

What was she? What was she really? Was she Luc's friend? His lover? His girlfriend?

Or did she merely work for him, and had been his 'bit on the side'?

None of the above, Stacey concluded as Luc shook his head as he stood talking to a group who knew him, causing his thick black hair to fly about his face. This exposed the gold hoop in his ear that glittered a warning to all and sundry—except to Stacey, who was blind to common sense when Luc was in the picture—that this was Lucas Da Silva, consummate lover, ruthless polo player, hard man of business, and a bona fide Spanish grandee who mixed in the most exalted circles, and who it sometimes seemed only resembled Stacey in as much as they both liked a good cup of coffee.

While they'd been stranded in his chalet she'd lost sight of the depth of his complexity. Luc didn't belong to her, he belonged to the world, to this world, to this sophisticated world, where she had never been comfortable. Being brought up on a farm hadn't given her airs and graces, it had given her grit. And now she could be having this man's child. It hardly seemed possible. Until her body throbbed a pleasurable reminder that it was.

'Okay?' he asked, coming to sit down again at their table. 'Excuse me for leaving you. As you could see, duty called.'

As it always would for both of them. What type of foundation was that for a child?

'You look cold,' he said. 'Come on, drink up that coffee. It will warm you.'

If only life were that simple. There was no offer to warm her from Luc, she noticed, but they were in public now. 'It's cold outside,' she commented lightly, looking out of the window.

'Understatement,' Luc agreed in the same disappointingly neutral tone. 'They're saying it might snow again.'

When he'd held her in his arms, she'd been warm enough. It was only when they'd reached the village that a chill had started creeping through her veins. It was the chill of anticipated loss of Luc when they parted, rather than anything she could blame on the weather. Though snow had started falling again, she noted with concern.

'Weather conditions will impact everything,' she observed. 'Where possible, I've accounted for every eventuality.'

'And where it's not possible?' he probed.

'I'm still worried about getting people up the mountain for your torchlit descent and the firework display.'

'Leave that to me.'

'Really?'

'I have an idea.'

'Let me know as soon as you can.'

'I will,' he promised, holding her gaze. 'And you let me know as soon as you can.'

'Of course.' Her heart lifted as she realised Luc hadn't forgotten anything. 'If we can get this right your guests will be talking about this party for the rest of their lives.'

'And you?' he pressed with a keen stare. 'What will you be talking about, Stacey?'

'Happy times.' She pressed her lips flat as her eyes smiled. 'I won't let you down,' she promised.

'Okay?'

'Not sure.' The strangest feeling had just swept over her. It was the same not-alone-in-her-body feeling she'd had before. First stop: a bathroom.

'I'm relying on you to get this right,' Lucas said, draining his cup.

She nodded, half in business mode, half planning to dash off right away to see the doctor at the drop-in clinic. 'I won't let you down. It's going to be the event of the year.' The event of *her life* if she was pregnant.

'What would you like to eat?'

'No time to eat. The bathroom?' she reminded him. 'Coffee's fine.'

'Soup,' he said. 'You must eat something.'

'Okay, soup,' she agreed. 'But this one's on me.'

Luc had relaxed a little over a bowl of soup, and now she was on her way to one of the last briefings with her team before the big event with a pregnancy test stuffed in her pocket.

As they'd parted, he'd said, 'Thank you for bringing me up to speed regarding the party, and now I must speak with my people.'

There'd been no mention of seeing each other again, but she'd taken that for granted, she supposed. Luc would obviously want to know the result of the test.

'Your global empire calling?' she'd teased.

'Well, I'm more concerned about the party right now,' he'd admitted, 'as it's only a couple of days away, but, yes, the global empire is always waiting in the wings. I never know from one day to the next when I'll be called away at a moment's notice.'

A cold wind had brushed her cheek when he'd said that but, keeping her promise to herself that she wouldn't become a clinging vine, she'd simply nodded her head in agreement.

They'd done a lot of reminiscing over lunch, leaving out details like how it felt to make love after wanting and caring and needing for so long. Or how safe she'd felt when Luc had steered her down the mountain. They hadn't mentioned taste, touch, or sensation, but it had been there all the time in their eyes—the glance that had lasted a beat too long, the small shrug of resignation that things couldn't be different between them, because of who they were, and the very different paths they trod. Luc's first memory of Stacey at the farm had been waking up in the morning to discover she'd squirted shaving cream into his hand while he was asleep, so the minute he raked his hair, he was covered in the stuff. 'I remember your roar of fury,' she'd told him with relish.

He'd looked like a great angry bear when he'd stomped out of his room in search of the bathroom with foam all over his face. She'd suspected at the time that no one treated Lucas Da Silva with such scant regard for his position in life, for, though his parents had been impoverished, they'd been aristocrats with a lineage stretching back through the mists of time. 'And the chilli in my ice cream,' he'd reminded her.

'It was strawberry, so I thought you wouldn't notice. Clever, huh?' she'd said with a mischievous look over the rim of her coffee cup.

'Deadly,' he'd agreed, and then they'd laughed together before falling silent again.

Would she never lose this yearning for Lucas? The more she saw of him, the more she liked him. She couldn't help herself.

And what was wrong with that?

Everything, Stacey concluded as she entered the hotel where the team was waiting. She was setting herself up to be hurt.

CHAPTER THIRTEEN

WHAT WAS SHE doing now? What was the result of the test? What was the doctor's view?

These were his thoughts as his jet soared into the sky, leaving the mountains and Stacey behind. An emergency call to return to London had necessitated an immediate change of plan. He'd ring her when he landed. No panic. She'd be busy with last-minute arrangements and he'd see her at the party. If anyone could cope, it was Stacey. He'd tried to call her several times, but her phone was always engaged. She occupied his thoughts in ways that left no room for anything else—not for business, for the all-important annual party to thank his best customers and staff, nor even his siblings and the fellow members of the Da Silva polo team.

What could be more important to him than the fact that he and Stacey might be expecting a child?

On that thought, he called her again.

Her phone rang out.

She would be busy, he reassured himself. He'd called in at the hotel where mammoth structures for his party were already being created, but no one had been able to find her. He'd guessed she was at the drop-in clinic. Her plans to delight and amaze his guests had exceeded even his jaundiced expectations, but now, instead of seeing towering structures mimicking an ice kingdom, or animatronic dragons breathing fire on demand over a banqueting hall of unsurpassed splendour, his mind was full of Stacey, and how beautiful she'd looked when they'd skied down the mountain. Cheeks flushed, eyes bright with excitement, snowflakes frosting soft auburn tendrils framing her face, she'd appeared lovelier to him than he'd ever seen her.

If he had a different life and could shake the guilt that haunted him, and Stacey weren't welded to her career, they might be planning a very different future. As it was, they must both be tense as they waited for the result of the pregnancy test, and he only wished he could be there to reassure her. But that was his life. That was his solitary life, and she was better out of it.

He called her again.

No reply.

So it was true. She wasn't going crazy, Stacey reflected as she left the walk-in clinic with a sheaf of leaflets advising on pregnancy and what to expect. Just as she'd suspected, the feeling inside her was a miraculous spark of new life. She was jubilant and terrified, as well as full of determination and purpose, all at once. Jubilant because it was a miracle she embraced with all her heart, and terrified because she didn't exactly have a pattern to follow, or a guidebook to help her, let alone a mother to advise and promise that it didn't have to be like the childhood Stacey remembered, full of mental anguish and regret. It could be a happy time. It *would* be a happy time, she determined as she pulled out her phone to call Lucas. Their child would be happy. She'd give her life to that cause.

No way!

Her phone was flat!

She'd been rather too busy over the past twenty-four hours to think about charging her phone. Exhaling noisily with frustration, she determined to call him as soon as she arrived at the hotel.

But as she crunched across the snow-covered pavement, the panic to call him subsided. Part of her wanted to tell him right away, while another part wanted to keep the news in a tight little kernel in her chest just a little while longer. Sharing things at home in the past had always got her shot down in flames. She knew Luc was a very different man from her father, but the past was a powerful enemy.

And she was stronger. Mothers had to be the strongest of all.

Once she had charged up her phone, she resolved to call him.

'He's been called away?' she repeated, bewildered, once she got through.

Luc's phone was on call divert and she was speaking to one of his PAs. The woman was to the point, rather than sympathetic. 'I'm afraid I can't give you any more information, but I will pass on the message that you called.'

'Thank y—'

The line was already dead.

You've never had any hand-holding, so why do you need it now?

Correct. She'd got this.

Those were Stacey's exact thoughts two days later as she stared into the mirror before heading off to the Da Silva party, where, regardless of how she felt inside, she couldn't wait to showcase the talents of her team.

The thought of seeing Luc again was a constant thrum of excitement that she was fully aware would play in the background of everything she did that night. She'd deal with that too.

This particular event was difficult to dress for, as there were so many elements to the night. First there would be a champagne reception, followed by a traditional banquet with dancing and an auction afterwards at the hotel in the village. Then a trip up the mountain to the balcony of Luc's chalet, which was the ideal vantage point for a firework display, and then later the famous torchlit procession of the most expert skiers in the area, who would descend a mountain floodlit by snow tractors. Thermals beneath a ball gown were a sensible precaution to cater for everything the weather could throw at her, and she had snow boots at the ready.

Luc had arranged an ingenious mode of transport to get guests up the mountain after the main party in the hotel. They made a great team, she mused as she checked her make-up in the mirror. Or might have done, if he'd troubled to speak to her. Everything was being conducted through their teams, so Luc had obviously made his decision regarding any possible future for them. If he had got in touch she could have told him the happy truth. Perhaps it was as well they kept things this way, though she couldn't deny his behaviour surprised her. Luc wasn't the type to turn his back on anything, but he had, and of all things, on the possibility of becoming a father. She didn't know whether to pity him for being more damaged than she'd thought, or whether she should regard herself as just another of his discards. Either way, it hurt. Once this party wrapped they wouldn't be part of each other's lives. Their amazing fling was over. There was no way anything could happen between them in the real world, their paths were too different, as were their dreams.

So...?

Swinging a lanyard around her neck, she blinked back tears. *So, go, team! Go, Stacey!* Make this the best party ever, adding another brick in the foundations you're building for your child.

His first sight of Stacey sucked the air from his lungs. The gown she'd chosen to wear was a deep shade of blue that contrasted beautifully with her rich auburn hair and Celtic colouring. She was wearing her hair up tonight, displaying those incredible cheekbones and her lush, generous mouth. She was easily the most attractive woman at the party, and it took an effort to drag his gaze away to concentrate on his guests.

This was quite literally an evening for the great and good. Some of the guests were undeniably pompous, and some were snobs he could have done without, but the various charities he supported needed their money. There were those who were fabulously rich and correspondingly stupid, and he could never understand how they held onto their wealth. He had also invited members of his staff from across the world, pearls beyond price without whom nothing would get done, as well as representatives from each of the charities.

And then there was Stacey.

His gaze kept stealing back to her, and each time he looked her way she was being equally gracious to everyone. Whether she was greeting a member of the aristocracy, one of the many ambassadors he'd invited, a group of cleaners from his London office, or a head of government, she behaved with the same gentle charm. His only regret was that her brother couldn't be here tonight to see her as he was seeing her, but Niahl was with the team playing polo. He hadn't told Niahl how far his relationship with his sister had progressed, but they knew each other too well for Niahl not to notice how many times Stacey had cropped up in conversation. 'Take care of her,' Niahl had said. 'That's all I ask. Above anyone I know my sister deserves to be happy.' A spear of regret hit him at the thought that he had pretty much allowed this unique woman to slip through his fingers without even putting up a fight. He'd allowed business to take precedence over Stacey, and even the possibility of a child.

One day he would have to confront his feelings, and could only pray that by the time he got around to doing so, it wouldn't be too late.

He watched her deal with more difficult guests, and felt anger on her behalf that she turned herself inside out for everyone, but who cared for Stacey? Who massaged her shoulders after an evening like this when she was exhausted? Who would kiss the nape of her neck, fix her a drink and bank up the fire to keep her warm?

'Señor Da Silva!'

He wheeled around to face an elderly Spanish duke.

'What a pleasure! What a party! You have quite a find in Señorita Winner. I'd hold onto her if I were you.'

'Don Alejandro,' he said, smiling warmly as he gripped his compatriot's hand. 'So delighted you could make it.'

'Not half as delighted as I am, Lucas. Take my advice for once and hold onto her.'

He didn't need advice to do that, Lucas reflected as his elegant friend went to join his companions at their table. But in all probability he'd already blown it.

He'd greeted all the guests, and now there was just one more thing to do.

He stood in Stacey's way as she patrolled the ballroom. 'Are you avoiding me?'

Seeing him, she tensed, but her eyes darkened as she looked up at him to ask coolly, 'Should I?'

'You are the most infuriating woman,' he said as he backed her into the shadows.

'Lucas, I'm busy.'

'Too busy to talk to your most important client?' But there was a lot more than business in his eyes. She knew what he wanted to know.

'You're here to talk business,' she said. 'Of course, I'm not too busy to speak to you, Señor Da Silva.'

'Luc, surely?'

'What can I do for you, Señor Da Silva?'

She was a cool one, but there was a flicker of sadness in her eyes.

'I want to congratulate you on a fabulous evening, of course.'

'It isn't over yet.'

He raised a brow and had the satisfaction of seeing her blush.

'Is there something I can get for you?'

'We'll talk about that later. I notice you plan to hold an auction after the banquet, and there are some truly spectacular prizes.'

'You have very generous friends.'

'And you can be very persuasive.'

She said nothing, refusing as always to take any praise. The tension between them was extraordinary.

'A silent auction,' he observed.

'Yes. It's less intrusive, and goes on longer—all night,' she explained. 'The prizes remain on view, either in here on tables at the far end of the ballroom, or in a photograph. To place a bid on a certain lot, all your guests have to do is place their offer in a sealed envelope. Competition is fierce, as no one has any idea what anyone else has bid.'

'Smart woman.'

'Did you think I was stupid?'

'No,' he said in the same easy, conversational tone she had used. 'I admire you.'

'It's my job,' she dismissed with a shrug. 'I promised to do my best for you, and I will. There's no chance to show off, but no one wants to miss out.' Her eyes bored into his. 'So the charities benefit far more from these secret bids than they would from a noisy auction.'

'Excellent.' He dipped his head in approval while every fibre of his body demanded that he claim her now. 'I approve. Well, you'd better get on.'

'Yes, sir.'

'Luc,' he reminded her through gritted teeth. 'We'll see each other at the end of the evening.'

Stacey's eyes flashed open. *Oh, will we?* she thought.

Her heart twisted into knots of confusion as Luc walked away. She hated that he could shake her professional persona to this extent, yet she longed for a glance that said he cared. She expected too much. Always had. Her father had told her that frequently, and he was right. She was needy inside and had to shrug it off and don her armour.

It wasn't easy to ignore Luc, and as she worked the room she watched him. With his easy stride and magnificent physique—a body she could undress in her mind at a moment's notice—he was outrageously hot, a fact she could see being logged by every sentient being in the room. It reminded her of when she'd been the wallflower on the bench and admirers had mobbed him. Would she see him after the party? She could be cynical all she liked, but her heart leapt at the thought.

Stacey's silent auction proved to be a brilliant idea, and was an incredible success. He wanted to congratulate her, but, as usual, she was impossible to find. Eventually, he almost crashed into him on her way to find an extra drum to hold all the bids. 'Kudos to you,' he called out as she rushed past. With every base covered at this, his most important event of the year, she had exceeded his expectations by a considerable amount.

There were so many bids to count he thought they'd never be finished, but when the final total was announced, the money raised for the various charities was a record amount. He'd tried celebrities and royalty before, but nothing had worked like this. Stacey should share the spotlight with him, he determined as he mounted the stage. He called for her but there was no answer from the crowd. Shrugging this off with a smile to reassure his audience, he told them she was probably hard at work on his next event and raised a laugh. Turning to his aide, he added in a very different tone, 'Find her.'

He strode from the stage to tumultuous applause that should have been Stacey's. 'On second thoughts,' he said, catching his aide's elbow before the man could leave, 'I'll find her.'

Stacey was sitting alone in the office her team was using as a temporary base in the hotel. She could hear cheers in the distance, and guessed the amount of money raised by the auction had just been announced, but this was one of the few opportunities she would have during the night to be alone, and she had just realised that she couldn't 'suck it up' as she'd thought, as Lucas remained resolutely centred in her mind. Anything he did or said affected her. However pathetic that was, it was a fact she had to deal with. There was no possibility of conveniently ejecting him from her mind. At the same time, she was alert for the end of this part of the evening. Transport was already waiting outside for the guests. She'd scheduled everyone's departure, so there was no need to show her face yet. The team had done its work, begging for prizes, and then organising and displaying them to best advantage, and she was more than happy to leave the glory to them and to Lucas. Raising money for good causes was something he did extremely well, and the auction was always a high point for Stacey. Tonight had seen a phenomenal result, mainly due to the fact that Lucas had an incredible array of wealthy friends. She'd noticed the sideways glances between the rich and famous as they'd attempted to outbid each other. In a silent auction no one knew what anyone else was bidding, so the temptation was always to add a little more, which was all to the good for the charities.

Leaning back in the chair, she closed her eyes and sighed with relief. Chalking up another success should have her buzzing with excitement. It would secure the immediate future of the company, and she was optimistic about requests for quotations flooding in once the press spread the word of another stunning Party Planners event. But it also heralded the end of working with Lucas.

A child should bring them together, if only for the occasional meeting, but would he want that? His attitude so far had been distant in the extreme, and she didn't want him dropping in and out of their lives. Their baby needed both its parents—not living together, necessarily, but both equally invested in its current and future well-being. So much for his talk of a dynasty, she reflected with a small sad laugh. If he took this much interest in his line going forward, it would die out.

She started with surprise as the door burst open and Luc walked in. 'There you are,' he exclaimed as if she'd been hiding. 'Come with me. I want to introduce you on stage so you can take credit for your success.'

It took her a moment to rejig her brain back into work mode. Luc was like a tornado who swept in and then out again with equal force. Taking a deep breath, she asked the only question that mattered where business was concerned. 'Has the team been on stage?'

'Of course,' he said impatiently. 'But you weren't there.'

You make it so inviting, she mused tensely.

'You're part of the team, aren't you?' he demanded.

'Yes, but—'

'No buts,' he said. 'This is your night. And if you won't take the praise for yourself, then at least take it for the team, and for the hotel staff that has supported them.'

Put like that she had no option.

CHAPTER FOURTEEN

THE CROWD IN the ballroom listened attentively as Stacey thanked them for their generous contributions. Then she invited key members of staff up on stage. 'Nothing would happen without these people,' she explained to a barrage of cheers and stamping feet. 'And now, if you would like to join us in the hotel lobby, your transport awaits! And please, dress up warmly. I'll meet you outside, where my team will show you where to go.'

She left the stage as people rushed to grab their coats and boots from the cloakroom. Luc was waiting at the foot of the steps. 'Thank you,' he said politely. 'I know this is your job and what you're paid for, but you've excelled yourself tonight, and I couldn't be more pleased.'

'Thank you,' she said with a tight smile, before hurrying away to join the growing crowd in the hotel lobby.

Was that it? Thank you? Was that all he had to say?

She felt sick inside.

Trying not to think too hard, she smilingly arranged the excited guests into travelling groups. If she dwelled on Luc's manner, she'd break down. She knew it was time to grow up—this was work—but if only he could be a little less distant, and maybe ask some intelligent questions about the baby. His disregard hurt so much, she had to believe there was a reason for it. He couldn't have changed so much, become so cold. She knew he had a problem with feelings, but taking it to these lengths? There had to be something wrong.

Get over it. It was probably all for the good, she decided as she started to muster guests into travelling groups. She would never belong in this sophisticated world. If they could return to the easy relationship they'd shared on the farm when they weren't fighting, chatting easily about horses, maybe there'd be a chance for them. She huffed a humourless laugh as she moved on to the next group of guests.

Operation Up the Mountain was a welcome distraction. Stacey's passion remained unchanged. Seeing people enjoy themselves at the events she organised was everything to her, and she never allowed personal feelings to get in the way. It was crucial that guests remained unaware of the mechanics behind an event, and it never felt like work to Stacey. But to be on the receiving end of this carousel of parties and lunches, banquets and fashion shows, rather than organising them? She couldn't do it. She had to get her hands dirty. She had to be real. False eyelashes wouldn't last five minutes in the country in a rainstorm, and, though she loved the city and all the glamorous occasions she helped to arrange, her long-term goal was to live on a small farm surrounded by ponies, where the only event she ever went to was the local county show.

The transport Luc had arranged was inspired. Nothing could stop the big snowploughs trundling up the mountain on their tank treads. Headlights blazing, music blaring, the party continued as they travelled up the slope. Stacey found herself seated next to Lucas, but this was business so she kept her distance and he kept his. The only comments they made were directed at their guests to make sure they were seated comfortably and well wrapped up in rugs.

When they arrived at Luc's impressive chalet, she'd made sure that champagne, mulled wine and soft drinks were waiting for his guests.

'You've thought of everything,' he commented as he helped her to climb down. 'And you look amazing.'

She blinked. Not that Luc's touch on her arm wasn't as electrifying as ever, or his face as wonderfully familiar, nor were the expressive eyes holding her own bemused stare any less darkly commanding and beautiful, but...compliments? Really? Was that the best way to start when they had so much more to say to each other?

So what would you say? She shrugged inwardly. He'd made a start. She should too. 'You don't look bad yourself. We'll talk later. Yes?'

Angling a strong chin already liberally shaded with stubble, Luc gave her a measured look. 'I think I can make time for you.'

'Make sure you do.' And with that she was off about her duties.

He tracked her down in an empty kitchen minutes before the fireworks and the torchlit descent were due to start. 'I sent Maria out to enjoy the show,' she explained in a neutral tone, swiping a cloth across the granite worktops without pausing to look up.

'Well?' he prompted, suffocated by tension he could cut with a knife. 'Do you have some news for me?'

She stilled and slowly raised her head. 'Are you saying you don't know?'

Of course he knew. He made it his business to know everything concerning him. His security team hadn't been hired for their pretty faces. But he wanted Stacey to tell him. Whether she could open up enough to do so remained to be seen. 'Just tell me.'

'Congratulations,' she said in the same emotion-free tone. 'You're going to be a daddy.'

He ground his jaw so hard he could have cracked some teeth. The way she'd told him, and, worse, the way this most marvellous news was overshadowed by concerns from his past, made him madder than hell, and saddened him equally.

'Don't you have anything to say?' she pressed.

'Congratulations,' he echoed with a brief, accepting smile.

'Wow. Your enthusiasm overwhelms me.'

'Not now,' he warned as Maria bustled back into the kitchen.

'When, then?' Stacey mouthed across the counter.

'When everyone else has left and we're alone.'

With a shrug she seemed to accept this, and they split, each attending to their duties, which left them both, he suspected, with a grinding impatience that wouldn't leave them until they'd talked.

The most spectacular firework display Stacey had ever seen was accompanied by classical music. The combination of fire in the sky and the passionate strains of a full orchestra turned a spectacular event into a spellbinding affair. She couldn't resist watching for a while, though tensed when Luc joined her. She didn't need to turn around to know he was there.

'Enjoying it?' he asked.

'It's amazing,' she confirmed. 'But shouldn't you be spending time with your guests?'

'Shouldn't you?' he countered softly.

'Of course, *señor*—'

'For goodness' sake, don't call me that. And no. Stay with me,' he commanded, catching hold of her arm when she started to move away. 'I want to watch the display with *you*. My guests won't care with all this going on.'

'I guess not,' Stacey agreed as a starburst of light exploded high in the night sky over their heads. Luc didn't speak as he came to stand close behind her. He made no attempt to touch her, but that didn't stop all the tiny hairs on the back of her neck standing to attention. She could almost imagine his heat warming her, and she found herself wanting to forget their differences and start again. More than anything she wanted them both to throw off the shackles of the past and express themselves freely to the extent that Luc took her in his arms and kissed her in front of everyone, and she kissed him back. But that was never going to happen when a muted 'Congratulations' was the best he could manage at the news of their child.

He wanted to drag her into his arms and kiss the breath from her lungs, but not with so many interested eyes on them. It hadn't been easy for Stacey to build a new life, and the last thing he wanted was to cast the shadow of his so-called celebrity over her, bringing her to the world's interest. Her childhood and early teens had largely been composed of fantasies, Niahl had told him, and that was to block out the fact that she felt invisible at home. Stacey's only fault was being a reminder of her mother. She'd tried hard to shake that off, but in doing so had ended up feeling disloyal to her mother's memory. She couldn't win. From the youngest age she hadn't been able to do right in her father's eyes, and that had stripped her confidence bare. She had worked hard when she left home to build up her self-belief, and he could so easily destroy it with a few misjudged words. Everything he said to Stacey had to be weighed carefully, and, unfortunately, like her, he was a man with a tendency to spit things out.

Deciding there was only one way around the problem, he knew that it wasn't enough to rejoice in the fact that they were having a baby, and that Stacey would always know he was holding something back. The only answer was to unlock the darkest secret from his past and confront it, but that would have to wait, as the torchlit descent in which he was taking part was about to begin.

'I'm sorry… I have to go,' he explained. 'My job is to ride shotgun and make sure no one falls or gets left behind.'

'I understand,' she said with a quick smile before glancing back at the chalet. 'And I need to make sure that everyone's glass is full to toast the parade as you start off.'

'You'll be okay if I leave you here?'

She shot him a look and smiled. 'I'll be okay,' she confirmed, but her gaze didn't linger on his face as it once had, and he knew that if he lost her trust it would be gone for ever. Stacey was a survivor who knew when to cut a hopeless cause loose. He ground his jaw at the thought that he was in real danger of falling into that category, and right now there was nothing he could do about it. The ski instructors and other advanced skiers were waiting for him on the slope. He was one of the stewards, and the torchlit descent couldn't begin until he was on his skis, ready to go with them. 'Don't get cold,' he warned Stacey.

She laughed. 'Don't worry. I won't. I'll be far too busy for that.'

* * *

After making sure all the guests had a drink, and a blanket if they needed one, Stacey chose a good vantage point. She had selected the music to accompany the skiers' decent in a sentimental moment, asking the guitarist from Barcelona, where she had so memorably danced with Luc, if he would agree to play live with a full orchestra, and he had agreed. Everyone around her commented on the passion and beauty with which he played, and as the other instruments swelled in a crescendo behind him her eyes filled with tears at the thought that special moments like these could never be recaptured.

But they would live on in the memory. Cling on to that...

She must not cry. This wasn't the time or the place, so she bit down hard on her bottom lip. Luc's guests relied on her to entertain them and their evening wasn't over yet. Personal feelings were unimportant. She'd be better off without them, and must certainly never show them. Maybe she had revealed too much to Lucas, because what had he shared with her? He kept more hidden than he revealed.

Her thoughts were abruptly cut short when everything was plunged into darkness, signalling the start of the descent. The murmur of anticipation around her died. Nothing was visible beyond the ghostly white peaks. Then the lights of the same snowploughs that had brought the guests up the mountain blazed into life and it was possible to see the skiers assembling with their torches like tiny dots of light. She wished Luc safe with all her heart. It reassured her to know that the chief mountain guide always led the procession, as no one knew the ever-changing nature of the trail better than he. Skiing at night at speed always held some risk, and there had been fallers. Not this year, she prayed fervently as she fixed her gaze on the top of the slope.

The long snake of light with its accompanying music was an unforgettable sight and Stacey was as spellbound as the rest. As if one party wasn't enough, there would be another in the village square to welcome everyone safely home. Transport was waiting for Luc's guests, and as she moved amongst them it was wonderful to feel their upbeat mood. The feedback so far suggested this was the most successful event Party Planners had ever arranged. It was just a shame the lights went out at the end of it, Stacey reflected, pressing her lips flat with regret.

The snowplough was approaching the village, where she could see that every shop and restaurant was ablaze with light. There were bunting and bands in the square and so many food kiosks they were banked up side by side. This was the first real fun people had been able to enjoy since the village had been snowbound, and everyone was determined to make the most of it. And it didn't take long, once they had been taken down, to learn that the roads were clear, and everything was on the move again.

She glanced around, but couldn't see Lucas. Quartering the square in the hope of finding him proved useless; there was no sign of him. None of the guests had seen their host and the torchlit descent had ended some time ago. So where was he?

'Some people peel away and ski home before they reach the village,' a ski guide still pumped with success and effort told her. 'Maybe Lucas is one of these. He's very popular...'

As the guys around him laughed Stacey walked

away, red-faced, but she couldn't give up. Maybe Lucas had gone home with another woman, but that was his business. She just wanted to know he was safe. And it didn't seem likely that he'd desert his guests. At last, she found someone who'd seen him.

'He stopped on the slopes to help a young woman who was trailing behind, and then she fell,' the elderly man informed her.

'Not badly hurt, I hope?' she exclaimed.

'The clinic's just over there,' he said, pointing it out. 'You could go and ask.'

'Thank you. I will.' She had to know for sure what was happening. If Lucas didn't show his face, she'd have to explain to his guests why their host had deserted them. Summoning reinforcements from the team on the radio to look after the guests milling about the square, she crossed the road to the clinic. Each small community in the mountains had a medical facility and a doctor on standby. She'd discovered this while she'd been researching the area for information to pass on to the guests.

The receptionist at the clinic explained that Lucas had stopped to help a young woman, but the young woman had turned out to be only thirteen years old, and skiing on the mountain without the consent of her parents. 'It isn't the first time and it won't be the last,' the smiling receptionist told Stacey. 'The mountain is like a magnet to local teenagers, and the annual parade is the biggest draw of all.'

'Can I help you?'

Breath shot from her lungs. '*Lucas!* Thank goodness you're safe!'

Regardless of anything that had gone before, she was just so relieved to see him.

Still dressed in dark ski wear, he looked exactly like the type of big, swarthy hero any young woman would dream of sweeping her off her feet on the slope. It was lucky she was Lucas-proof, Stacey reflected as he shot her a brooding look.

'Why are you here?' he demanded coolly.

'To find you, of course.'

'Shouldn't you be with my guests?'

'Shouldn't you?' She stared up at him, unblinking, while her heart shouted hallelujah to see him unharmed.

'Are you here to remind me of my manners?'

'If you need a nudge…?'

A glint of humour in his eyes greeted this remark.

'How is the girl you rescued?'

'A painful pulled ligament. Thankfully, nothing more.'

'And you're okay?' She searched his eyes.

'Obviously.'

Why didn't she believe him? Because the wounds Luc carried weren't visible, Stacey concluded as he glanced at the exit.

'I'm going to say goodnight to my guests,' he explained, 'and then I'm going to take you home. I've checked the girl's parents are on their way, so there's nothing more for me to do here except thank the staff and hold the door for you.'

'I can stay in the hotel in the village,' she protested. 'People are leaving now the roads are clear.'

'The gondolas are running too,' Luc commented as they left the building, ignoring her last comment, 'so no excuses. You're coming with me.'

They needed to talk, she reasoned, so why not? Just because Luc was unconventional and unpredictable didn't mean they couldn't communicate successfully.

Demanding clients were her stock in trade. How much harder could it be to discuss the future of their child with Luc?

After an extensive round of farewells, Stacey was able to wrap up the night with her team, and Luc led the way up the steps of the gondola station. 'Come on,' he encouraged. 'We can have a car to ourselves.'

Grabbing her hand, he pulled her into an empty car just as the doors were closing.

CHAPTER FIFTEEN

'Luc—' As the gondola started off she was thrown against him. Pressing her hands against his chest, she reminded him that they hadn't even talked about the baby.

'You're well,' he said, 'and that's all that matters.'

And then he closed off.

'And those guests you couldn't find to say goodnight to?' she pressed, wanting some reaction from him.

'I'll see them at the airport tomorrow. Tonight is for you.'

For sex, she assumed. Not that she didn't crave Luc's body, but she wanted more from him. She had other concerns on her mind, notably an unborn child.

'You're taking a lot for granted,' she observed, steadying herself on the hand rail.

'Yes,' he agreed. 'I want to spend the night with you.'

Her pulse went crazy, but she had to accept that nothing had changed. How many times had they been together without Luc opening up? And she had to know the father of her child. They could be so close in so many ways, and complete strangers in others. He shut her out when she needed to be sure that Luc bore no resemblance to her own father. She couldn't bear that. She wouldn't bear it, and neither would her child. No infant should be shunned, and if Luc was incapable of expressing his feelings, then perhaps she should keep him at a distance. What was it in his past that had made him so insular? She was bad enough, but he was gold standard when it came to hiding his feelings. If she couldn't find out tonight, what chance did she have?

'We will talk?' she pressed.

'Of course we will,' he promised.

'When?'

'Soon.'

'Should I be satisfied with that?'

He raised a brow and smiled down, forcing her to realise that she had underestimated his devastating appeal. Luc only had to look at her a certain way for her scruples to vanish. 'No, we can't,' she protested as he dragged her close.

'Where does it say that in the rule book?' he murmured. 'You carry around a very heavy rule book, Señorita Winner, but it's not one I care to read.'

'Seriously, Lucas…'

'I intend to be very serious indeed, as I'm dealing with an emergency situation.'

One more night with the man she loved. What could be wrong with that?

Everything, Stacey's cautious inner voice suggested. *You'll miss him even more when he's gone.*

So be it, she concluded as Luc drove his mouth down on hers.

Arranging her to his liking, with her legs around his waist, he supported her with his big hands wrapped around her buttocks.

'Are you sure I'm not too heavy?'

'What do you think?' he said, slowly sinking to the hilt.

She was thinking that she would never get used to this…to Luc wanting her, and to the feeling of completeness that gave her—or to the size of him. 'What do I think?' she asked on a gasp. 'Take me gently.'

'Gently?' he queried as he drew back to plunge again.

'The baby,' she reminded him.

'I can do gentle,' he murmured, proving this in the most effective way. 'Though you should know that babies are quite resilient.'

With a smile she shook her head. 'You did your research on that too?'

'Let's find out,' Luc suggested, and from that moment on he had her exclaiming rhythmically as she urged him on to take her repeatedly on the journey to the top station. It was long enough for several mind-shattering bouts of pleasure, and by the time they'd straightened their clothes and stepped out of the small cabin, she was committed to spending the rest of the night with Luc. Anything else would not only be wrong, it would be inconceivable. She wanted him too much to resist him. Pregnancy had made her mad for sex, and Luc was only too willing to help her with that.

They fell on each other the moment they entered his chalet. The inside of the front door proved a useful surface as he took her again, and while she was still whimpering in the aftershock of pleasure, he carried her over to the sofa in the living room and pressed her down. 'Again!' she demanded fiercely as he moved between her legs.

Luc gave her everything she needed and more, and it was only when she quietened that she thought to ask if they were alone.

'If we weren't to begin with, I imagine you've frightened everyone away by now with your screams.'

Balling her hands into fists, she pummelled him weakly. 'That's not funny, Lucas.'

'Oh, but it is,' he argued as he rolled her on top of him. 'I'm going to strip you, and make love to you again, and you can scream as loudly as you like.'

They moved from sofa to rug in front of a glowing fire where they made love until she fell back, exhausted. 'I'll never forget this trip…or you…us…' she whispered as Luc soothed her down.

'That sounds like goodbye,' he commented, frowning as he pulled back his head to stare into her eyes with concern.

'Not yet, but soon,' she whispered. It was inevitable.

'Not yet,' Luc agreed, brushing smiling kisses against her mouth, 'because first I'm going to take you to bed.'

'To sleep in each other's arms,' she murmured contentedly as he sprang up and lifted her.

'To sleep in each other's arms,' Luc confirmed.

He watched her sleep. This was fast becoming one of his favourite occupations, he had discovered. Was this caring warmth inside him a sign he was capable of feeling something and could master the guilt?

Was this love?

He huffed a cynical smile. He'd always liked Stacey. A lot. As a teenager she'd driven him crazy, and now he admired her like no one else. But love? Love was dangerous.

She's the mother of my child.

The warmth inside him grew at the thought. There was no one he'd rather choose for that role than Stacey. Brimful with character, integrity, intelligence and determination, she would make a wonderful mother.

On her own again?

If anyone was equal to that task, it was Stacey.

Could I really stand back and let her do that after everything I saw when she was younger? This woman who's been starved of affection will be abandoned again?

Not abandoned. He'd always care for Stacey and their child. She didn't need the additional burden of his guilt to carry around, so this was for the best.

She looked so peaceful he didn't want to wake her. Exhausted from working tirelessly on behalf of his guests and from making love for most of the night, she'd earned her rest. He'd speak to her later about future arrangements when everyone else had gone.

Slipping out of bed to take a shower, he shrugged off the memories crowding his mind of warmth and peace and happiness. They belonged to someone who deserved them...deserved Stacey. She could safely sleep on. The first departure for his guests wasn't due until noon, by which time she'd have a chance to don her professional face and head out with her usual sense of purpose to smooth everyone's passage home.

Her work rate pricked his conscience. He wanted to wake her and make love to her again, but instead he was heading out to make sure there were no hitches for her to face. Her charges were his guests and ultimately his responsibility. She'd done enough and more besides. He'd catch her later at the airport with a token of his appreciation to thank her for all she'd done.

She'd overslept. When did that ever happen? Never. And she was alone. Luc had gone. Of course he had. He had work to do.

Didn't she, also?

Everyone remembered the start of an event, and the event itself, if the planner had got things right, but what stayed with them was the end, when they must feel valued enough to hope they might be invited to another similar event.

Leaping out of bed, she snatched up her clothes and ran to the bathroom. A quick shower later and a scramble to put those same clothes on again, she headed out with a beanie tugged low over her still-damp hair. Glancing out of the window, she saw with relief that the gondolas were running as smoothly as if they'd never stopped.

She was alone in the chalet, no sign of Luc or Maria. She'd grab some breakfast in the village, then head straight for the hotel to make sure the departing guests had everything they needed.

The sky was blue and the skiing was good. As the small cabin swung high above the slopes she searched for him amongst the skiers. There was no sign of him. She longed to see him. They had to talk about the baby before she left for home. Surely he'd open up about that? He must. Whatever was holding him back, he had to put it behind him for the sake of their child. He couldn't be like her father.

She chose the same café where they had eaten before. There were booths where she could be private. She would eat first, settle her mind, and then set out to complete the business side of things. Breezy wait staff brought milky coffee and French toast. She suddenly realised she was ravenous and ordered more. Glancing at her watch, she confirmed that she could afford another few minutes, and her stomach insisted on it.

Her heart jolted when she noticed Luc at the counter, speaking on his phone. He was frowning, but not too preoccupied to thank the staff behind the counter as they loaded his tray. She put her head down as he approached the line of booths where she was sitting.

Phone tucked into his shoulder as he walked along, he was holding an intense conversation. She was no eavesdropper, but this was Luc. Whatever he had on his mind, she wanted to help. He looked so serious. What was it? What could it be?

He sat down in the adjoining booth. The seat backs were so high he hadn't seen her.

This wasn't right. She should make herself known.

Why? She wasn't doing any harm.

He was talking to Niahl!

They'd always been a tight unit, she reasoned, and she should have known it was only a matter of time before the bond between them closed her out, relegating her yet again to the tag-along benches; the kid sister to be endured and humoured. She might be older, but she was obviously no wiser, given that the hurt she felt now was so ridiculously intense. Luc was telling her brother they were close and Niahl was ranting. She could hear him…almost as clearly as she could hear Luc's placating reply. 'You're right. I overstepped. It was a huge error of judgement.'

She didn't need to hear more. Throwing some money down on the table, she rushed out. Luc was still talking on the phone as she ran past the window. He hadn't even noticed a woman in distress fleeing the café. That had to be a first for him. The knight in shining armour had clay feet after all.

'You're right, Niahl, and maybe I should have told you sooner, but I wasn't even sure of it myself.'

'Then why were you sleeping with my sister?'

'Stacey isn't like the others. This isn't a fling, Niahl. I love the woman she's become, and I think she loves me.'

'Has she told you this?' Niahl barked suspiciously.

'She doesn't need to.'

'Have you told Stacey that you love her?'

'I'll make it my mission to love and protect her for ever—'

'Have. You. Told. Her?' Niahl roared. 'For God's sake, and yours, don't you think you should?' A colourful curse followed this observation. 'The two of you are hopeless!'

'I love your sister and I'm going to marry her.'

'Maybe you should tell her that too?' Niahl suggested. 'Arrangements take time.'

'You can put your shotgun away. We're going to get married.'

'You hope!' Niahl exploded. 'If you're not too late!'

'I have to tell her something else first.'

There was a long silence, and then Niahl said quietly, 'Yes, you do.'

By sheer force of will, she ground her gears into work mode as she entered the hotel, where she now discovered that everyone was either sleeping, or just not picking up their phone. It had been one hell of a party. Requesting a discreet wake-up call to be delivered to those guests she knew should be leaving for the airport in time for early flights, she now needed something else to do… something to take her mind off what she'd overheard.

Luc had overstepped…

She was a huge error of judgement.

At least she knew where she stood.

Actually, why should he get away with that? Now she was angry. She tried his phone. No answer. With no intention of leaving a message, she headed for the hotel café. She got as far as the entrance when a group of guests saw her, and called her over to their table.

'You'll join us? It's the least we can do. We've had an amazing time, thanks to you.'

'It was a team effort,' she said, embarrassed by the praise.

'Sometimes it's enough to say thank you,' an older woman cautioned with a smile. 'Enjoy it when you're appreciated. You deserve it. You worked hard.'

Was the past responsible for the way she brushed off praise now? Maybe that was because she couldn't quite believe her life had turned around to the extent it had. Did that make her as guilty of hiding her feelings as Luc? Were they both to blame for this situation? She would have to speak to him at some point about their child, but not here, not now, while she was still stinging from what she'd overheard. Niahl used to warn her that she would never hear anything good about herself if she listened in—which she'd used to do when he and Luc were in a huddle discussing their latest adventure. Boy, was he right!

'I agree with my wife.'

Stacey refocused on the kindly face of a man who had spent more money at the charity auction than most people saw in their lifetime. 'I watched you last night and you never stopped. You deserve all the praise you can get. I'm going to tell that man of yours he's found a diamond and should hold onto you.'

'What—? I don't—'

'Understand when a man's madly in love with you?' his wife chipped in. 'Perhaps everyone sees it but you,' she suggested. 'It's obvious to anyone with half an oil field that Lucas Da Silva adores you.'

Stacey gave a fragile laugh. She didn't want to disillusion the couple. Her first and only task was to make sure they got safely on their way. And then the couple made a suggestion that at first she refused and then accepted. 'Thank you. I'd love to,' she said.

Somehow he'd missed her at the hotel, so he gunned the Lamborghini down the highway to the airport. He'd thought a lot about Stacey since speaking to Niahl. *When didn't he think a lot about her?* The thought of losing her was inconceivable, yet Niahl had made it seem a real possibility. It was time to face his demons and explain why he always held part of himself in reserve, and how that had stopped him expressing his feelings. If he got this right they had a lifetime ahead of them. If he failed...

He wouldn't fail.

That was inconceivable.

'She's gone?' For the first time in his life, he was dumbfounded.

'Yes,' his aide explained, unaware of the turmoil raging inside him. 'Your Texan guest offered Señorita Winner and her team a ride back in his jet. He said it was the least he could do to thank her for giving him and his wife such a wonderful evening.'

She would never have gone without her team. Stacey would never take credit for herself, or fail to share any bonus she might receive. He'd seen her own personal donation to the charity. Sealed bids, maybe, but her handwriting was unmistakeable. Stacey's tender heart had seen her give away the bonus he'd paid to each member of the Party Planners team, and she'd done so quietly, without fanfare. This was the woman he'd allowed to slip through his fingers, and all for want of facing up to his past.

CHAPTER SIXTEEN

'CONGRATULATIONS!' BEAMING WIDELY, the doctor leaned over the desk to shake Stacey's hand. 'You must feel reassured to be under the care of your local clinic. It's a shock to learn you're expecting a baby when you're far from home. Do you have anyone to support you?'

'Financially, I don't need it. Emotionally...?' She shrugged.

'It's a lot to take in at first, but I'm sure you'll get your head around it soon.'

Thanking the doctor, she left the room. As soon as she'd spoken to Lucas the mist would clear, she hoped. There was just one small problem. She had to find him first. Bolting wasn't the answer. She should have stayed to confront him, but she'd been so angry and hurt. Now she had no excuse.

There was only one foolproof way to track him down.

'Niahl? How am I supposed to get in touch with Lucas when he won't pick up his phone?'

'You too,' Niahl commented.

'What do you mean, me too?'

'I imagine Luc is in the air by now.'

'You've spoken to him?'

'You left without saying goodbye. What's that about?'

'Do I cross-examine you?'

'All the time.'

'Not this time, Niahl,' she warned in a tone that told her brother she meant it.

'Because this time it's serious?'

'You took the words right out of my mouth. I heard you talking to him.'

'You mean you *overheard* us talking about you?' Niahl corrected her. 'What have I told you about that?'

'No lectures, Niahl. I need to speak to him.'

'How much of our conversation did you hear?'

'Enough,' she insisted.

'So you heard the part about him loving you like no other woman in his life before?'

'What?' she said faintly. 'I heard him say he overstepped, and that getting together with me was a huge error of judgement on his part. How does that square up with him loving me?'

'Simple. It takes time for any normal person to come to terms with the depth of their feelings, and you and Luc are far from normal. He's damaged and you're crazy impulsive sometimes.'

'Damaged?'

'Give him a chance to explain.'

There was a long pause, and then she asked, 'So you're okay with this?'

'Does it matter?'

'Of course it matters. Who else do I have to confide in?'

'Luc,' he suggested. 'That's if either of you can open up enough to trust each other with the truth.'

When the line was cut she stared blindly ahead, hollowed out at the thought that if Luc's barricades were high, hers were even higher, to the point where he'd found it easier to confide in her brother.

* * *

Even taking the pilot's seat, it seemed to take longer to fly to London than it ever had. He'd never been so restless or felt in such danger of losing something so vital to his life. He had to get this right. He'd tried to stay away from Stacey to save her from him, and had failed spectacularly. He'd made to love to her, yet never once told her how he felt. *Was it too late now?* They shared equally in their love for an unborn child, so it had to be possible to save the situation.

He *would* save the situation.

He *must*.

'Luc!' She shot up from her office desk so fast, he worried for her safety and crossed the room in a couple of strides. Whatever had gone before, his relief at seeing Stacey was so overwhelming he dragged her into his arms and kissed her over and over again.

'I was just ringing you,' she gasped when he let her up for air. 'I wanted to say that I'm so sorry I left without speaking to you. I acted on the spur of the moment, thinking I'd heard something when I hadn't, and—'

'Don't worry about that now,' he soothed. 'I should have answered my phone but I didn't, because all I could think of was seeing you again. I flew straight here, then drove from the airport.'

'You didn't need to worry. I got an appointment with the doctor the moment I got back. The baby's fine. I'm fine.'

'And now I'm fine too,' he confirmed with a slanting grin as he echoed Stacey's familiar mantra. Though, that wasn't quite true.

'Luc?' She knew at once that he was holding something back. 'What aren't you telling me?'

Relaxing his grip, he stepped back and admitted, 'There is something I have to tell you, but not here. My house?'

'You have a house in London?'

'Not too far away,' he confirmed. 'My car's right outside. Can you come now?'

She searched his eyes and must have seen the urgency in them. 'Of course. I'll ask my secretary to clear my diary, and then I'm all yours.'

Luc's London house was amazing. It was one of those smart white town houses in an elegant Georgian square with a beautifully manicured garden for the exclusive use of residents at its heart. The interior was exquisite, but soulless, Stacey decided until Luc led the way into a library that smelled of old books and leather.

'This is lovely.' She gasped as she turned full circle to take it in. The walls appeared to be composed entirely of books, and there were several inviting armchairs, as well as a welcoming fire behind a padded brass fender.

'I chose each of these books myself,' Luc explained as he followed her interested gaze. 'I can't claim credit for the rest of the house. Apart from the tech, it was designed by a team.'

'We rely a lot on teams, you and I,' she observed with a crooked smile. 'I suppose that's how we keep ourselves isolated so successfully. There's always a buffer between us and the world, and that's the way we like it.'

'That's the way I used to like it,' Luc admitted.

'And now?'

'And now I want to tell you why I am as I am, and why I've never told you that I love you.'

She was so shocked by Luc's declaration she couldn't find a single word to say. As the old clock on the mantelpiece ticked away the seconds they stared at each other with so much in their eyes it would have taken a week to express it, anyway.

Taking both her hands in his, Luc led her to the window where light was shining in. 'I closed off my heart… to you…to everything. It was the only way I could come to terms with the love I destroyed.'

Stacey's heart lurched, but she didn't dare to interrupt. Luc was staring out of the window looking as fierce as she'd ever seen him. 'I must have told you about my parents?' He shot her a look of sheer agony.

'Niahl spoke of them with great affection…' She couldn't remember Luc mentioning them once. In fact, if the subject of mothers and fathers ever came up, however innocent the reference, Luc would always clam up.

'Yes…yes, Niahl met them,' he confirmed, frowning as he no doubt examined the memory. 'Perhaps he told you they were eccentric—reckless, even—always coming up with new ideas?'

'Not really. He said they were funny and warm, and that they adored you and your brothers and sister, and that, unlike the farm, your family house was a real home.'

'He didn't mention they were practically penniless?'

'No.' She shook her head decisively. 'He said they were the most generous people he'd ever known, and that he loved visiting, because they always made him so welcome. I remember him saying that everything was so relaxed and friendly.' And now it was time for the hard question. 'So what went wrong?'

'Their death was my fault.'

Luc rattled off the words as if they had to be said but he couldn't bear to say them.

'How was it your fault?' Stacey pressed. 'They were

killed in an air crash, weren't they? You weren't the pilot. You can't blame yourself for that.' Oh, yes, he could, she saw from Luc's expression.

'I'd just started to make some real money,' he said grimly, staring blindly out of the window. 'I was still working from my bedroom, but I was selling programs hand over fist. My parents had this new idea to make mobile buildings, of all things—it made perfect sense to them. My mother would design these portable homes, and my father would build them.'

'Niahl told me they were wonderful and so clever that he was always learning something from them, but I didn't realise they had those skills.'

'They didn't, and I told them so. They begged me to give them the chance to visit a factory a short flight away. I said of course, and gave them the money to book a ticket. I should have checked...'

'What should you have checked?' But Luc wasn't listening.

'How could I deny them when I had enough money to pay for the flight?' he murmured, narrowing his eyes as he thought back. 'I pointed out the difficulties they might encounter with this new business venture—the cash-flow problems, the complexities of hiring staff. The one thing I didn't think to insist on was that I booked the tickets, and so they went to a friend instead who'd built his own single-engine aircraft in the garage, and was always bragging about it, though he hadn't flown it for months—maybe never, for all I know. I guess my parents thought they could save me some money. They were never greedy. They didn't know what greed was, but they were...impressionable'

'Oh, Luc. You can't blame yourself for any of this.' He couldn't cry, either, Stacey realised. Luc was a man of iron, who ran a global enterprise that kept thousands of people in work, with brothers and a sister to whom he'd devoted a great part of his life. He'd had no time to grieve, and so he bottled it up, and when the anger became too great, he worked it off with physical exercise—polo, sex—anything would do, but as yet he'd found nothing to wipe out that pain.

He sighed. 'They just wanted a chance and I gave it to them. I killed them as surely as if I had been flying the plane.'

'No, you didn't,' she cut in fiercely. 'Their friend killed them and himself with his vanity. You're not to blame, any more than the child I used to be was to blame for my father's coldness towards me. My father suffered grief at the loss of my mother that he had no idea how to deal with. Don't be the same as him. Don't be like that with our child. Accept the pain and live with it, if you must, but promise me you'll never visit your suffering on our child.'

'*My* suffering?' Luc murmured, frowning.

'Yes. Your suffering, and the sooner you accept that and let me in, the sooner we can start to heal each other.'

There was silence for quite a time and then he said, 'When did you become so wise?'

She gave him a crooked smile. 'When I broke free of you and my brother?'

Luc laughed. He really laughed. Throwing back his head, he laughed until tears came to his eyes, and then she held him as he sobbed.

CHAPTER SEVENTEEN

A WEEK LATER Luc asked her to marry him.

'I can't think of anyone who'd be a better mother,' he mused as they lay in the bed they'd barely left for seven days. 'I love you, Stacey Winner. I should have told you years ago, but we are where we are.'

'And it's not too late to make amends,' she suggested.

'I was hoping you'd say that,' Luc agreed, turning his head lazily on the pillow so they could hold each other's gaze.

'I'd better marry you because I love you, and I can't think of anyone else who'd have you.'

'Or who'd put up with you,' he countered, smiling against her mouth.

'I just worry that there are dozens of women in the world better suited to your sophisticated life.'

'So change my life,' Luc insisted. 'Keep your job. Work. I'll never stop you. Whatever you want to do is fine by me, because that's who you are, the person I fell in love with, and I love you without reservation. I don't want a puppet I can bend to my will. I love the challenge of you being you, in case you hadn't noticed?'

'I might have done,' Stacey admitted with a grin as they paused the conversation for a kiss…several kisses, as it turned out.

More kisses later, Luc added, 'I love complex, vibrant, capable you, and the last thing I want is to change you. That would be defeating the object, don't you think? Having rediscovered the only woman I could ever love as completely as I love you, I've realised there's more to life than work and money, and that this is the man I want to be...the man I am with you.'

'Marry me,' she whispered. 'I love you so much.'

'I will,' Luc promised solemnly.

'When?'

'Now! Today!' he enthused, shooting up in bed.

'Special licence?' she suggested.

'You're the expert,' he said with a burst of sheer happiness.

'But I doubt it can be today. As soon as possible?'

'Sounds good to me,' Luc confirmed, drawing her back into his arms.

'You want to get married right away because of the baby,' Stacey reasoned out loud.

They still had a way to go, Luc realised. Stacey had set him free, and now it was his turn to heal her, and if that took the rest of his life it was fine by him. 'Because of you,' he stated firmly. 'I can't let you get away a second time.'

'Really?' Her eyes widened on the most important question she'd ever ask.

'Really,' he confirmed, and then he kissed her as a future full of love, care, happiness and laughter finally came within their reach.

'Trust me, love me,' he whispered. 'I need you more than you know.'

EPILOGUE

THEY WERE CALLING it the wedding of the year. True to her pledge, Stacey had arranged everything in record time, so a mere six weeks after Luc's proposal here they were, about to wear each other's ring.

Her wedding day was the culmination of almost an entire lifetime of love for one man. There was nothing imaginary about the splendour of the setting, or the man waiting for her at the altar. The scent of countless pink and white blossoms filled the air, and the abbey was full of her favourite people—notably her brother, her team, and Lady Sarah, who had thankfully recovered in time to be her matron of honour.

The organ thundered and the voices of the choir rose in heavenly chorus as she walked forward with confidence into the next chapter of her life.

The pews were filled with the great and the good, as well as her friends and Luc's polo team. There was even a sprinkling of royalty. Lucas Da Silva was still a Spanish grandee, after all. Her brother was giving her away, and she had to say Niahl did look stunning in an impeccably tailored dark suit. He'd even finger-combed his hair for the occasion, so it almost made him look less of a devil in a custom-made suit—though not quite…a fact that wasn't lost on the female members of the congregation, she noticed.

'Thank you for doing this,' she whispered as she attempted to glide alongside Niahl's giant footsteps.

'Don't thank me,' he whispered back, mischief brightening his sparkling green eyes. 'I thought I'd never get rid of you.'

'And now?'

'And now I couldn't be happier for you—or for Luc. You deserve each other.'

She hummed. 'Just when I thought you were being nice.'

'I was being nice,' Niahl insisted with a wicked grin as he stepped back to allow the ceremony to begin.

Lady Sarah, who was dressed beautifully for the occasion in a long, plain gown of soft lilac chiffon with a pink blush corsage of fresh flowers on her shoulder, took charge of Stacey's bouquet, and when Stacey whispered her thanks, she smiled.

'I think of you as the daughter I never had,' Lady Sarah had said as they got ready. 'There's no one I trust more than you, Stacey.' And then she'd cupped Stacey's cheek to elicit a promise. 'But I'll only do this for you on one condition. Now I'm back at the helm I expect you and Lucas to make the most of your lives, and not to spend all your time working.'

Lucas had come to the same conclusion, he told Stacey when she confided this to him. 'We're going to enjoy life together,' he'd stated, 'and I'm going to spoil you as you deserve to be spoiled. So if you receive a shipment from Paris, or a delivery from one of the foremost jewellers in the world, you'll just have to be brave.'

'I'll grit it out,' she'd promised, trying not to laugh.

This was a new chapter, and an entirely different

life, as it would be for anyone who wasn't a billionaire, or a member of the aristocracy. But all that mattered to Stacey was that this was the start of a new life of love, which she would spend with a man she trusted with all her heart. Lucas would be at her side, as she would be at his, organising the heck out of him, as he'd put it.

When he took her hand in his, she wanted nothing more than to melt into him, kiss him, and be one with him, and that was before the ceremony had even begun.

'Patience,' he murmured, reading her as he always had.

That wouldn't be easy, she accepted as the voices of the choir rose in a sublime anthem. Somehow Lucas had managed to look more devastating than ever today, in an austere black suit with his crimson sash of office pinned with a jewel on his chest.

'And don't forget, I have a very special present for you,' he added discreetly.

What could that be? Surely not another piece of jewellery? Lucas had given her so much already, and had refused to take it back when she'd said the jewellery box he'd given her, laden to the brim with precious gems, was far in excess of anything she could ever need. Could it be another dress? She glanced down at the fabulous couture gown he'd insisted on having made for her in Paris. The slim sheath of silk to accommodate the first hint that she was pregnant had a discreet slit at one side. 'For ease of movement,' he'd said.

So he can whip it off fast, she thought.

But it was a beautiful gown. Encrusted with crystals and pearl, it boasted a cathedral-length train in silk chiffon that floated around her as she walked.

As they stood beneath the stained-glass windows, she couldn't help but feel the echo of countless other couples who had brought their hopes and dreams to this place and turned them into reality. 'I love you,' she whispered as Luc put the circle of diamonds on her wedding finger.

'And I love you more,' he said.

Finally the ceremony was over and they were showered with rose petals as they left the fragrant interior of the abbey for the sunshine and fresh air of a happy new day. She looked for the limousine she'd booked. 'But I organised a car,' she exclaimed worriedly.

'Of course you did,' Luc said, smiling. 'But I arranged a different sort of transport for the love of my life.'

She followed his dangerous black stare to where two horses, plaited up and dressed in their finest regalia, were being brought up to the foot of the steps. 'Ludo?' she breathed. 'Is that really Ludo?' She gazed up at Luc.

'Are you pleased?'

'Pleased? I've never been so happy to have an arrangement go wrong!'

'I thought you wouldn't mind riding to our wedding breakfast if you two were reunited,' Luc said as he helped her into the saddle. 'You might have to hitch up your dress…'

'I might have to do a lot of things to get used to this new life with you.' Dipping down from the saddle, she took Luc's face between her hands and kissed him. 'Thank you.'

'Thank *you*,' he said, turning serious. 'You gave me my life back and now I'm going to do the same for you.'

* * * * *

MAID FOR THE UNTAMED BILLIONAIRE

MIRANDA LEE

Dedicated to my sister, Wendy.
A lovely lady and my best friend.

PROLOGUE

JAKE NEEDED A HOUSEKEEPER.

But not the live-in kind. The last thing he wanted was someone underfoot all the time, picking up after him, forcing him to make conversation and invading his space. The reason Jake had bought a house a few years ago was to have his own space.

After spending weeks in hospital and then another month at the rehabilitation clinic, he'd wanted nothing more than to be by himself. So he'd turned down the offers to live with relatives and bought this place in East Balmain, calling it a thirtieth birthday present to himself.

He'd thought he could make do with a cleaner coming in three times a week. And he *had* managed—in a fashion, even in the beginning when he'd been pretty useless, his leg still not totally healed. He'd shopped online and sent his laundry out, a routine he'd continued even after he was fully better and back working.

But it had finally become tedious, seeing to all the other chores which owning and maintaining a house involved. He loathed having to wait for tradespeople, who didn't always turn up on time. Patience was not his strong suit.

Jake could well afford to pay someone to do everything for him. He'd already been a wealthy man before the success of his television show, so it had never been a matter of money. More of privacy.

Not that he had much privacy any more, his star having risen over the last couple of years, his every move recorded on social media and in the gossip rags.

But not at home. His home was his sanctuary, as well as his castle. So it was imperative that Jake find the right kind of housekeeper, a task which had proven to be much more difficult than he'd assumed, mostly because he simply hadn't *liked* any of the women he'd interviewed for the position.

It was silly, really, given he wouldn't have to have anything much to do with the woman on a personal basis. His brief to the various employment agencies was for his housekeeper to work only during the week, not at the weekends. She was to come in after he left for work every weekday morning, and be gone by the time he arrived home, which often wasn't until quite late. Producing and hosting *Australia at Noon* consumed every minute of every weekday from morning until late afternoon.

So it shouldn't really matter whether he liked his housekeeper or not.

But he couldn't stomach the thought of someone he didn't like in his personal space when he wasn't there.

The main problem was that every woman he'd interviewed so far had been a big fan of his show. Not a crime, admittedly. But irritating. They had all been way too gushy. And way too eager.

Jake was suspicious of eager, especially when it came to women. A flaw, he supposed, common with confirmed bachelors. Still, he kept picturing them putting things about their *wonderful* new job and their *wonderful* new boss on all the social media sites they would invariably be on, complete with photos.

The upshot was he hadn't hired any of them, and was instead waiting for another candidate to arrive, sent out by Housewives For Hire, a newish employment agency, the owner of which had fortuitously appeared on a segment of his show a few days ago.

Her agency promised to provide exactly the sort of employee he was looking for. Apparently, the women on their books were mostly housewives themselves, wanting to earn extra money whilst their children were at school.

He'd rung the lady who owned the agency the other night—her name was Barbara—explaining what kind of housekeeper he needed. He'd asked her to find him someone suitable, preferably a woman who didn't obsessively watch his show and think he was God's gift to women.

She'd promised to find him the right person.

So here he was, sitting in his study at five to two on a Saturday afternoon, waiting to interview Barbara's top recommendation, but thinking to himself he was possibly wasting his time again.

This woman Barbara was sending him was way too young for starters. Only twenty-six. And a widow no less. How on earth had that happened?

Barbara hadn't said and he hadn't liked to ask.

Jake sighed. A car accident, he supposed. Or an illness of some kind.

At least she didn't have children. Nothing sadder than a young widow trying to raise children alone. Nothing tougher, either.

This young woman—her name was Abby Jenkins—was apparently looking for work and wasn't qualified for much, her very short CV showing she had left high school at seventeen to work in a fish and chip shop till she'd married at twenty, shortly after which she'd left to become a stay-at-home housewife.

A strange choice for a modern young woman. Rather old-fashioned, in Jake's opinion. Made her sound a little odd. He didn't fancy employing odd.

But he would give her a chance. Everyone deserved a chance.

He heard a car pull up outside. A glance at his watch showed it was right on two. She was punctual at least.

Jake stood up and made his way from the study to the front door, arriving in time to unlock the deadbolt just as the doorbell rang. He took a deep breath and opened the door, not sure what to expect.

His breath caught at the sight of a very pretty blonde whose lovely green eyes were looking up at him with a decidedly worried expression. No, not worried. Nervous. The girl was terribly nervous, chewing at her bottom lip and clutching the strap of her black shoulder bag as if it were a lifeline.

He supposed it was only natural that she'd be nervous. Barbara had mentioned that this was the girl's first job interview for her agency. Possibly it was her first job interview ever.

Jake's eyes flicked over the rest of her appearance.

She was wearing dark blue jeans and a cream crocheted top, their snug fit showing a very good figure. Her honey-blonde hair was long and straight, pulled back into a low ponytail. She wasn't wearing make-up, not even lipstick. It pleased Jake that she hadn't dolled herself up like some of the other women he'd interviewed.

'Mr Sanderson?' she asked hesitantly.

Jake's eyebrows rose at the realisation that she didn't recognise him. Which meant she hadn't ever watched his show, or any of the documentaries he'd made over the years.

He didn't know whether to be happy or hurt, which was ironic.

Either way, it was still a positive factor. He definitely didn't want a housekeeper who was a fan.

'Yes, that's me,' he replied, willing now to overlook the fact that she was not only way too young but way too pretty. Jake reasoned that if he hired her, he wouldn't be around her on a daily basis so he wouldn't be in danger of being tempted by her very attractive package. Because, to be honest, it would be seriously hard to ignore those eyes. And that mouth.

Jake dragged his gaze away from it before his mind wandered into R-rated territory.

'And you must be Abby,' he said, smiling a little stiffly.

She smiled back. Not a big smile. A small one. But it showed lovely white teeth behind those luscious lips.

'Yes,' she said simply, then added in a rush, 'it's very good of you to give me an interview.'

'Barbara recommended you highly,' he said.

She seemed startled. 'She did?'

'Indeed, she did. Said she'd dropped in unexpectedly at your home before she signed you up and it was immaculate.'

A soft blush pinked her cheeks. Lord, but she was sweet as well as pretty. Jake liked pretty women, but he wasn't usually attracted to sweet.

Till now...

'I like to keep things nice and neat,' she said.

'Same here,' he said rather brusquely. 'Come in and we'll talk some more.'

'Oh. Right. Yes.' But she didn't move, her lovely eyes wide and unblinking.

Maybe he'd frightened her with his brusqueness. Jake could be very charming, when he chose to be. But he could also be intimidating.

Very charming was definitely not on. But intimidating was not nice either. Best stick to businesslike.

'Perhaps I should give you a tour of the house first,' Jake suggested matter-of-factly, stepping back and waving her inside. 'Show you what you'll be letting yourself in for. You might not want the job, even if I offer it to you.'

'I'm sure I will, Mr Sanderson,' she said and made her way past him into the hallway, where she stopped and stared down. 'Oh, what a lovely floor. I love polished wooden floors.'

'They're hard work to keep clean,' came Jake's blunt comment as he shut the front door behind her.

'I'm not afraid of hard work,' she said, turning to look up at him.

Jake admired the flash of feistiness in her eyes.

It came to him then that he liked this girl. Really *liked* her.

'Excellent,' he said, knowing that he had found his house-keeper at last.

And if it bothered Jake that he also found Abby very desirable, then he determined to ignore it. But he also determined to put things in place so that he would hardly ever see her.

Out of sight was out of mind, after all!

CHAPTER ONE

Twelve months later...

ABBY WAS HUMMING happily as she locked up her neat little weatherboard cottage and headed off to work. She never suffered from Monday-itis. She liked her job. Liked looking after Jake Sanderson's very beautiful house. And looking after Jake Sanderson himself, despite not liking *him* all that much.

Still, Abby would always be grateful to the man for hiring her when she had no current work experience or references.

Frankly, she still could not believe her luck at getting such a cushy position. Aside from the convenience of getting to work—East Balmain wasn't too long a drive from Seven Hills—she was her own boss since Jake was never there when she was. She could do as she pleased; have breaks whenever she wanted; work at her own pace.

Not that she was a slacker. Abby was somewhat of a perfectionist when it came to keeping house. You could eat food off the floors in her own home. And off Jake's by the time she left each day.

Admittedly, when she first arrived on Monday mornings, things could be on the extra messy side. Abby always knew when Jake had had company over the weekend, the kind who stayed the night and didn't bother to lift a finger to pick up dirty wine glasses or load the dishwasher or do anything other than whatever it was his playmates did. The man who'd been voted most popular television personality earlier this year was reputed never to be short of female company.

Abby's sister, Megan, who was addicted to Twitter and gossip magazines, kept Abby well informed about who her boss was currently dating. His latest squeeze was a newsreader from the same television channel that Jake's show aired on. Her name was Olivia, a stunning brunette with big brown eyes and a figure to die for. A smile to die for as well.

There had been a time when Abby would have felt jealous of that smile.

But not any more.

Abby stopped humming abruptly as her tongue ran over her top teeth, still amazed at how fantastic they felt. Her bottom teeth too.

Of course, porcelain veneers came at a huge cost. Abby still hadn't finished paying off the personal loan she'd taken out to have them done. But really, it had been a case of necessity rather than vanity.

'You need confidence to go back into the workforce after all this time, hon,' her sister had advised. 'Which means you need to do something about your teeth!'

And Megan had been so right. Imagine showing up for an interview with Jake Sanderson the way she'd been. She suffered from fluorosis, a condition which involved an excess of fluoride, caused perhaps by eating fluoride laced toothpaste as a child. She'd loved the taste. Her fluorosis had worsened over the years, the brown stains darkening, pitting her teeth, especially the top ones. Wayne had said she was beautiful the way she was. But Abby had never believed him. So finally, when there'd been no Wayne to object, she'd taken Megan's advice and gone to the dentist.

It had been the best thing she'd ever done, despite putting her into debt.

Not for much longer, though. Each week she saved every penny she could from her wages, not spending a cent on female fripperies like having her hair and nails done, or even clothes. She just made do with what she had. She also rarely ate out, or went out. If there were no further unexpected expenses—like having to pay for Timmy to have his tonsils out—she would be debt free by Christmas and able to finally start up her travel fund.

Abby had always wanted to see the world, dreams of one day travelling overseas sustaining her when she'd been an unhappy teenager. Okay, so those dreams had been replaced by other dreams when she'd married Wayne, her focus changing to creating a happy family life, the sort of family life that neither she nor Wayne had ever had.

But those dreams had failed to eventuate...

Abby swallowed hard for a few moments, pushing the awful memories aside and forcing herself to focus on dreams which were achievable. And which might make her forget. They did say time healed all wounds. Time, and hopefully travel.

Her dream holiday would encompass at least six months, seeing Europe, Asia and the Americas. There were so many places on her USA bucket list. Niagara Falls. The Grand Canyon. New York.

Which meant of course that one day she'd have to quit her job as Jake's housekeeper.

Megan thought she was crazy to contemplate giving up her cushy job to go tripping around the world.

But Abby didn't agree. She needed to have a dream which looked forward and not back. If she wanted to travel, then she would travel. And to hell with her job as Jake Sanderson's housekeeper. He'd survive without her, and she'd certainly survive without him.

Shortly before nine-thirty, Abby turned into the street which led to Jake's house. The road sloped gently down to the water, and the ferry terminal, most of the houses two-storey terraces which dated back to the early twentieth century. All of them had been renovated at some stage, Balmain being a very desirable address these days, a far cry from its working-class roots.

Jake's house had once been a large corner shop which

someone had bought and turned into a house, extending it up and out. Jake had bought it a few years ago. It had come fully furnished in the Balinese style and with everything else he wanted, including a no-lawn backyard, a lap pool with a relaxing water feature and an en suite guest bedroom downstairs.

Apparently, at the time of his purchase, he'd been suffering from some leg injury incurred whilst working overseas and hadn't been capable of climbing stairs for a while. He'd told her all this on the day he'd given her the job, when he'd shown her through the place and explained what he expected her to do. Frankly, he'd spoken to her more that day than in the subsequent twelve months.

Megan was always asking Abby questions about her *oh, so famous and handsome* bachelor boss, not quite believing her sister when Abby said she still knew next to nothing about him other than the basics, which was that he'd once been a famous documentary maker and was now an equally famous television show host. She had recently learnt that he had a favourite uncle named Craig who was a fairly famous foreign correspondent. Abby only knew this because the man himself had recently come to stay for a while after he'd suffered a skiing mishap.

Megan probably knew a lot more about Abby's boss since she avidly watched his programme every day. It was called *Australia at Noon*, a live one-and-a-half-hour programme which focused on celebrity interviews and current affairs, with a bit of variety thrown in—a tried and true formula whose success depended on the popularity of its host. Which Jake Sanderson was. *Very.*

Abby did turn his show on occasionally during her lunch break but found she wasn't as entranced by it—or by its handsome host—as her sister. She found it hard to match his charming television persona with the rather abrupt man who rarely said more than two words to her on the rare occasions their paths crossed.

Not that she cared, as long as he kept on employing her and paying her till her travel fund was full.

This last thought popped into Abby's mind shortly after she let herself into the house and saw what was written in capital letters on the whiteboard in the utility room, where her boss wrote down things he wanted her to do, or buy. He never texted her, seeming to prefer this rather impersonal method of communication.

Will be home around three.
Need to talk to you about something.
Jake

Abby's stomach flipped over, her immediate thought being that she'd done something wrong and he was going to fire her. But then common sense kicked in, Abby reasoning it might be nothing more important than his wanting to show her something which needed doing.

Yes, that was probably it. No need to panic.

But a sense of panic still hovered as time ticked slowly away that day. Meanwhile, Abby worked like a demon so that by the time three o'clock came around every room and surface in Jake's house was clean and shining. All the pictures and side tables had been dusted. The washing had been done and dried, the master bed remade with clean sheets and fresh towels hung in the main bathroom. Even the courtyard had been swept, and a few of the pavers scrubbed where some red wine had been spilled. She hadn't had a break, eating her lunch on the go.

At ten to three Abby removed her cleaning gloves and tidied her hair, brushing it before putting it back up into her usual ponytail. She always wore jeans and trainers to work, with a T-shirt in the warm weather and a sweater in the cold. Today's jeans were old and faded and a bit loose. Her black T-shirt was slightly too big for her as well. She'd lost weight lately, courtesy of her banning chocolate and ice cream from her diet.

Abby sighed at her reflection in the laundry mirror. She wished she looked better. She would have taken more trouble with her appearance this morning if she'd known she was going to have a meeting with her boss. But how could she have known? She hadn't seen him for weeks. Still, she really should go out and buy herself a few new things. Jeans and T-shirts didn't cost much at Kmart.

Three o'clock came and went without any sign of Jake. After ten minutes she wondered if she should text him. She did have his phone number but he'd made it clear from the start that she wasn't to bother him that way, except in an emergency.

Him being late was hardly an emergency. Still, if he hadn't arrived by three-thirty she would text him. Meanwhile, she hurried to the kitchen and put on the kettle.

CHAPTER TWO

JAKE STEPPED OUT onto the deck of the ferry and scooped in several deep breaths. His stomach was still tied up in knots. He'd done his best with his show today, but his mind hadn't been on the job. Not that he cared. Frankly, he wouldn't care if he never did another show. Andrew had stood in for him as host last Friday and the ratings were just fine. No one was indispensable in the entertainment game.

Jake contemplated letting Andrew take over for a week or two whilst he took a well-needed break. He'd jump at the chance, ambitious young buck that he was. Alternately, he might sell the show lock, stock and barrel and do something else with his life. Harvest Productions had been sniffing around for ages. If he could talk Sebastian into making him a half decent offer, he just might take him up on it.

Though maybe not…

Jake ran his fingers through his hair in total frustration. Damn it. He hadn't felt this indecisive in years. Of course he knew the reason. He just didn't like facing it. Sighing, he made his way over to the railing and stood there, staring out at the water.

Sydney Harbour on a clear calm day in spring was a sight to behold. But Jake wasn't in the mood for admiring his surroundings. Or even noticing them.

Closing his eyes, he surrendered to the grief which he'd had to put on hold today whilst he did the show, and which he'd been struggling to contain for several days.

Jake still could not believe that his uncle was actually dead. Not even the funeral last Friday had made it real. He could not picture Craig in that coffin. Could not conceive of the fact that he would never see the man again. Would not talk to him again. Or drink with him. Or anything at all with him.

Craig had been much more than an uncle to Jake. He'd been his mentor and his friend. His idol, too. Even as a boy, Jake had admired the way his uncle lived his life.

Craig hadn't gone down the traditional route, getting a nine-to-five job then marrying and having children. He'd become a foreign correspondent, travelling the world to all the wildly exotic and sometimes dangerous places which fired Jake's imagination. He'd also stayed single, explaining once to a teenage Jake that for him to marry would be cruel to the woman, and to any children they had because he would neglect them shamelessly.

There'd been women, of course. Lots of women. Beautiful, exciting women who'd graced the dashingly handsome Craig Sanderson's bed but who knew never to expect any more than his highly stimulating company.

Jake had decided long before he left university with his communications degree that that was the life for him. No way was he going to follow in his father's footsteps. Craig's only brother had married before he was twenty, when his even younger girlfriend fell pregnant, then worked himself to death—literally—to support his ever-increasing brood.

Jake couldn't think of anything worse. He could not recall his father—when he was alive—having any time to himself. Everything he'd done had been for his family.

When his dad died of a coronary at the age of forty-seven, Jake had been heartbroken but more determined than ever to embrace bachelorhood as well as a job which he loved and not one he was compelled to do just to pay the bills and put food on the table.

Jake had been true to his resolve. He'd spent his twenties making documentaries in far-flung corners of the world, earning a small fortune at the same time. He'd still be overseas, living that life, if a run-in with a group of rebels in war-torn Africa hadn't forced his life into a different direction.

Working in television was tame by comparison, but it had its moments. Jake couldn't really complain.

Admittedly, since he'd stopped flitting from country to country and city to city, Jake had given up one-night stands and fleeting flings in favour of longer relationships. If you could call a few months long, that was. His current girlfriend was a career-orientated and highly independent woman who was great company, great in bed and knew better than to pressure him for marriage or, God forbid, a baby. Olivia had assured him on their first date that she wouldn't get bitten by the biological clock bug like his last girlfriend. The only responsibility Jake wanted in life was paying his own personal bills.

Which was exactly the way things had been…till the solicitor for Craig's estate had dropped his bombshell at the wake.

Jake already knew he'd been left the bulk of his uncle's estate, Craig having given him a copy of his will for safe-keeping. What he hadn't known was that Craig had summoned his solicitor to his bedside a few days before his death and given him a letter for Jake, to be delivered after his funeral.

Jake pulled the letter out of his pocket, unfolded it and read it for the umpteenth time.

Dear Jake
Hope you aren't angry with me for not telling you about my illness, but there was nothing anyone could do and I do so hate pity. I had a good life, my only re-gret being that I didn't go out with more style. A bullet or a bomb would have been much more me.

But on to the reason for this letter. Jake, there's something I want you to do for me. Last July, when I stayed at your place after I bunged up my knee, I got to know your very nice housekeeper quite well. Abby was extra kind to me and went over and above the call of duty to make my stay both comfortable and enjoyable. And, no, nothing untoward happened between us. She's not that sort of girl.

Anyway, on to my request. I didn't want to add a codicil to my will. Too much trouble at this stage. Still, what I would like, Jake, is for you to buy Abby a new car to replace that appalling bomb she drives. Something small and stylish but with a long warranty.

I also want you to give her twenty-five thousand dollars out of your considerable inheritance to go towards her travel fund. Please insist that she not use it for any other purpose. Don't let her give it away to any of those free-loading relatives of hers.

I have every confidence that you will do this for me. You're a good man. And not a greedy one. Give Abby my love and tell her not to wait too long to see the world. Life is meant to be lived.

The same goes for you, my boy. I'll be watching over you from above.
Your Uncle Craig

Jake closed his eyes as he folded the letter, a huge lump having formed in his throat.

'Damn it, Craig,' he ground out, his heart squeezing tight with grief. 'You should have told me you were ill. I could have been there for you the way you always were for me. You shouldn't have had to die alone.'

And you should have just put a damned codicil in your will, came the added thought, grief finally giving way to exasperation.

It was impossible not to do what Craig asked, Jake accepted as he shoved the letter back in his pocket. But it annoyed him all the same.

It wasn't a question of money. He had plenty of money. It was the fact that fulfilling his uncle's deathbed wishes would force him into Abby's personal space—and company—something he'd been careful to avoid ever since he'd hired her.

Because let's face it, Jake, you fancy her even more now than ever.

But he could see no way out. He would just have to gird his loins and endure!

CHAPTER THREE

AT TWENTY PAST THREE Abby's boss finally showed up, looking slightly harassed but still very handsome in a smart grey suit and a crisp white shirt which highlighted his dark hair, olive complexion and deep blue eyes.

Even Abby had to admit that in the flesh her boss was a hunk. But she'd never been blindly attracted to a man on looks alone. Handsome is as handsome does, in her opinion. What attracted her most in the opposite sex was kindness and gentleness, qualities which Wayne had had in spades.

'Sorry I'm late,' Jake said as he strode into the kitchen, where Abby was making herself coffee. 'Damned ferry was running late. Could I trouble you for some coffee? Black, with no sugar,' he ordered as he slid on to one of the kitchen stools, reefing off his tie at the same time.

Abby wanted to scream at him. Didn't he know how stressed out she was? But she held her tongue and made him the darned coffee.

'So what did you want to talk to me about?' she asked as soon as she'd placed his mug in front of him. She stayed standing on the other side of the breakfast bar, not daring to pick up her own coffee yet for fear of spilling it.

His forehead bunched in a frown, which only added to her discomfort.

'You're going to fire me, aren't you?' she blurted out.

His head shot up, his dark brows arching. 'What? No. No, of course not! Good God, is that what you thought this was about?'

She just shook her head at him. 'I didn't know what to think.'

'Why on earth would I want to fire you? You are the best housekeeper a man could have. I'm sorry if you thought that.'

Abby found herself flushing at his compliment. And his apology. Relief swamped her as well. She didn't want to lose this job. Not for a good while yet.

'It's to do with Craig's will,' Jake said abruptly.

'Craig's *will*?' she repeated, feeling somewhat confused. 'Are you talking about your uncle Craig, the man who stayed here for a while during the winter?'

It had been back in July, she recalled, about four months ago.

'Yes. The thing is, Abby, he's left you something in his will.'

Abby just stared at Jake, shock joining her confusion. 'Are you saying that he's *dead*?'

'What? Oh. Yes. Yes, he died last week. Incurable cancer,' he finished up with a heavy sigh.

'But…but that's impossible! I mean, he was so *alive* not that long ago.'

'Tell me about it,' Jake said as he swept an agitated hand through his hair. 'It came as a shock to me as well. I gather he found out during an MRI for his busted knee about the cancer. But he never told anyone, not even me. And we were very close. I knew nothing about his illness till his solicitor rang and told me he'd passed away.'

Abby found it hard to understand what he was saying. 'You mean you weren't with him when he died?'

'No. No one was, other than the palliative care nurse. He'd booked himself into a hospice without telling anyone.'

'But that's terrible!' Abby declared heatedly, upset that anyone would choose to die like that.

Jake's shrug carried a weary resignation. 'It was what he wanted. I'm surprised you didn't hear about his death. It was all over the news at the weekend. He was quite famous.'

'I… I don't often watch the news.'

'I see.'

She wanted to ask him why he hadn't told her himself, but of course why would he? She wasn't a relative, or a friend. He wouldn't have known how much she'd enjoyed the time she'd spent with his uncle whilst he'd stayed here.

Craig had been a fascinating individual, highly intelligent, widely travelled and very well read. He'd been incredibly nice to her, showing an interest in her as a person and not just some kind of maid. The day before he'd left, he'd given her a list of ten books which he said everybody—especially young women—should read. She was still slowly working her way through them. They were the reason she didn't watch the news much any more, and why she hadn't seen the report of his death.

Tears flooded her eyes at the realisation that this very nice man was actually dead.

'He…he said he was going away to have a holiday.' Abby's voice caught at the memory.

'He told me the same thing,' Jake said.

'Instead he went away to die,' she choked out. 'Alone…'

Abby couldn't think of anything sadder than dying alone. It was the main thing which haunted her about Wayne's death. That he'd been all alone, out there in the ocean, with the storm raging around him and little chance of being rescued. Had he lost all hope in the end? Had despair engulfed him in the moments before he drowned?

Suddenly, a huge wave of grief overwhelmed her, emotional distress welling up in Abby till it could not be contained. Tears filled her eyes so quickly they spilled over and ran down her cheeks.

When a sob escaped her throat, Jake stared at her with a look of horror.

Embarrassment flooded in but there was no stopping her now. When more sobs racked her body, all Abby could do was bury her face in her hands. She simply couldn't bear to witness her boss watching her whilst she wept her heart out. No doubt she was making a fool of herself. No doubt he thought she was a typically sentimental female to cry over a man she hardly knew.

The feel of strong male arms suddenly pulling her into a comforting embrace shocked Abby rigid. She certainly hadn't expected a hug. Not from her very aloof boss. Unfortunately, his uncharacteristic kindness only made her weep all the more.

'There, there,' he said, patting her back as she clasped the lapels of his suit jacket and sobbed into his shirt. 'No need to cry. Craig had a good life, with no regrets. He wouldn't want you crying over him. Craig wasn't one for tears.'

Abby could hardly explain that it wasn't just Craig's death which had set her off, but the *way* he'd died. All alone.

Oh, God...

Abby was gritting her teeth and doing her best to pull herself together when Jake stopped patting her back and slid his arms right around her, holding her quite close. No doubt he was still just trying to comfort her but for some reason Abby no longer felt comforted. She felt very *dis*-comforted. Because she *liked* him hugging her like that. She liked it a lot. The urge to slide her own arms around his back was acute. She wanted to hug him back, wanted to bury herself in the solid warmth of his very male body and...and...

And what, Abby? Make an even bigger fool of yourself? For pity's sake, get a grip, girl.

Taking a deep gathering breath, Abby lurched backwards, releasing the lapels of Jake's jacket as she gulped down a sob of shame.

'I'm so sorry,' she choked out, her face flushing as she spun away from him and grabbed a handful of tissues from the box on the kitchen counter, not saying another word till she'd blown her nose and composed herself. She did note rather ruefully, however, that Jake didn't wait long to hurry back to the other side of the breakfast bar.

Her groan carried more shame. 'I've embarrassed you, I can see. It's just that... Oh, never mind.' Her fisted right hand came up to rub agitatedly at her mouth. For a moment she was tempted to confide in Jake about Wayne's tragic death. But only for a moment. Maybe, if he'd been any other kind of man she might have explained why she'd been so upset at the news of his uncle dying alone like that. But Jake didn't invite confidences. Why, he'd never even asked her how her husband had died!

Despite his hug just now, Jake didn't really care about her. She was just his employee, hired to look after his house. His housekeeper. A glorified cleaner, if truth be told.

Craig hadn't treated her like that. He'd been genuinely interested in her life. Not that she'd told Jake's uncle the total truth. Abby had become masterful at blotting out the really painful parts in her past. Talking about them wouldn't have achieved anything, anyway.

'The thing is,' she went on, compelled to make some excuse for her emotional display, 'I really liked your uncle a lot.'

'He must have liked you a lot too,' Jake replied.

'Well, yes,' she said slowly. 'He seemed to.'

'You haven't asked me what he left you,' Jake went on, his eyes on her.

'What? Oh... Some books, I suppose.'

Jake frowned at her. 'No, no books,' he said. 'Nothing as mundane as that.'

'Then what?' she asked, perplexed.

'To be honest, he didn't leave you anything directly. He left a letter for me with instructions of what he wants you to have.'

She blinked, then frowned. 'That sounds...weird.'

'Yes, I thought so too,' he agreed drily. 'But Craig was never a conventional man. Look, why don't we both drink our coffee before it gets cold? Then, afterwards, I'll fill you in on everything.'

When Jake picked up his coffee mug, Abby did likewise, sipping slowly and thoughtfully. A hot drink always calmed her. And brother, she needed calming after that crazy moment when she'd almost hugged her boss back.

'I would have liked to go to his funeral,' she said after a suitably calming minute or two. 'Was he buried or cremated?'

'Buried,' he said.

'Where?' she asked.

Jake's face looked grim as he put down his coffee. 'Rookwood Cemetery.'

She wasn't sure where that was. She didn't have a GPS in the ute and often got lost. 'I'd like to go and visit his grave some time. Pay my respects. Say a prayer or two. Would you take me?' she asked him before she could think better of it.

Jake's sigh suggested that was the last thing he wanted to do.

'Okay,' he said with a resigned shrug. 'But I can't go till next Saturday. In the meantime, wouldn't you like to hear about what Craig wanted me to give you?'

'Oh, yes. What is it?'

'Well, first of all he wants me to buy you a new car. Something small and stylish, with a decent warranty.'

Shock at this news was swiftly followed by confusion.

'But that doesn't seem right,' she said. 'As much as I would love a new car, why should he ask *you* to pay for such a thing?'

'It's basically Craig's money, Abby. He left most of his estate to me. Trust me when I say that my inheritance was considerable. So it's no hardship on me to spend a seriously small portion of it on you.'

'But why didn't he just leave some money to me in his will to buy my own car?'

'I have no idea. It might have been simpler all round if he'd done that. Apparently, he was worried that you might not spend it on yourself—that you might give it away to relatives.'

'Oh, dear,' she said, embarrassed. 'I suppose it's because I told him about paying for Timmy's operation.'

'No. He didn't mention anything specific. Who's Timmy?'

'My sister's little boy. She's a single mum and doesn't have any private health insurance. Timmy needed his tonsils out but would have had to wait eighteen months to have it done. She couldn't afford the operation so I paid for it to be done privately.'

'I see,' he said, his tone sceptical.

A degree of anger pushed aside Abby's embarrassment. 'Please don't think my sister's a user because she's not. She's doing the best she can under the circumstances. Megan didn't ask me to pay for Timmy's operation. That was *my* idea. She won't come and live with me, even though I said she wouldn't have to pay any rent. Your uncle got the wrong idea.'

'Possibly, but that's irrelevant now. I have no alternative but to follow through with Craig's dying wishes. He was most specific in his letter about what he wanted me to buy for you. A new car is the first cab off the rank. Then he wants me to give you twenty-five thousand dollars. For your travel fund, he said.'

Abby's mouth dropped open. 'Twenty-five thousand! But…but that's way too much. What will people think?'

'Who cares what they think?' came his arrogantly dismissive comment. 'And who are *they*?'

'My sister for starters. She'll think I've done something I shouldn't have with your uncle to get him to leave me all that money.'

'Really. Such as what?'

'You know what,' Abby shot back.

'True,' he said drily. 'In that case I suggest you don't tell her about your unexpected windfall.'

Abby gave a snorting laugh. 'Hard to hide a brand-new car.'

'True again. So what do you want me to do, Abby? Go against my uncle's wishes? Forget everything?'

She looked at him with pained eyes. 'I couldn't do that. I don't care so much about the new car, but I couldn't turn down the travel fund money. It's my dearest wish to go overseas and see the world. And I'd like to go before I get too old.'

Jake laughed. 'You're hardly ancient, Abby.'

'I might be by the time I save up twenty-five thousand dollars.'

He seemed startled by this statement. 'Do I pay you that poorly?'

'No. But I have a house and a lot of bills.' And the remainder of a debt for porcelain veneers.

Jake frowned. 'You have a mortgage?'

'No. My husband's life insurance paid that off. But I still have a lot of bills. Maintaining a house is expensive.'

'Tell me about it,' he said with the first hint of a smile that day. He really wasn't much of a smiler. Not with her, anyway. He smiled on television a lot though. Abby wished he would smile more. It really transformed his face from cardboard handsome into a likeable human being.

Unfortunately, his smile also did things to Abby which she was finding hard to process. Her stomach curled over and she found herself staring at his mouth and thinking totally unacceptable things. Like what would it be like to be kissed by him? And not just on her mouth.

Lord, but this wasn't like her. She didn't even enjoy sex that much, unlike her sister, who couldn't live without it. Sex with Wayne had been okay, but nothing to write home about. She'd done it whenever he wanted, more for him than herself, because she'd loved him so much. In her mind, making love was a natural part of loving. Of marriage. She'd never been into sex for sex's sake.

Why then was she looking at her boss and thinking that here was a man who just might change her mind on that subject?

Not that she'd ever have the chance to find out. Not only did he have a gorgeous girlfriend but he was totally off-limits. He was her boss, for heaven's sake! On top of that, he clearly didn't fancy her. A girl knew when a man fancied her and Jake definitely didn't.

Her eyes dropped from his to her near empty coffee cup.

'I'm still finding it hard to believe all this,' she said, glancing up again once she had her wayward thoughts under control. 'In one way it's like a dream come true. But I still can't get over your uncle dying like that. And all alone.'

'Indeed,' Jake said, that hint of a smile disappearing as quickly as it had come. 'I've been thinking,' he went on, his face very businesslike again. 'I'll put next Saturday aside so that I can take you to visit Craig's grave in the morning, then we'll go on and buy you a car afterwards. It's not far from Rookwood Cemetery out to the major dealerships at Parramatta. Do you trust me to pick out a car for you, or do you want to choose one yourself?'

'Well, I… I don't know,' she stammered, startled by how quickly he wanted to organise everything. 'I'm not much of a car buff. But if it's going to be mine I think I would like to look up a few possibilities on the internet.'

'It's a good idea to buy something that is cheap to repair,' he advised firmly. 'I would suggest you look at the Japanese cars. Or the Korean ones.'

'All right,' she agreed. He seemed to know what he was talking about, whereas she was pretty ignorant when it came to cars.

'And what bank account would you like the twenty-five thousand put into? The same one your salary goes into, or do you want to start up a special travel fund account?'

Abby was taken by surprise when her chin began to quiver. But really today had all been a bit much.

'Don't you dare start crying again,' he commanded.

Abby bit her bottom lip and blinked madly.

'Sorry,' she muttered through gritted teeth. 'I'm not usually a cry baby.' Which was true. Nowadays, Abby kept her emotions under tight control. There had been a time when she'd cried too much. And too often. But no longer.

Lifting her chin, she speared her boss with a dry-eyed and rather rebellious glare.

'Good,' Jake snapped, making Abby want to hit him. How on earth she could have been sexually attracted to this man—even for a moment—was beyond her.

'You should go home,' he went on in that same brusque manner. 'You look tired. Ring me when you've decided on the brand of car and we'll make arrangements for Saturday. You can tell me then what account you want the money put into.'

'All right. Bye then,' Abby went on rather sharply, gathering up her things and taking off before she could say or do something which might jeopardise her job. Or Craig's remarkable legacies.

She almost slammed the front door, just getting control of her temper in time. She did slam the door on the ute and accelerated off faster than her usual sedate speed. But she soon slowed down, telling herself not to be so silly. No point risking her life because her boss was a pain in the butt.

Think about your new car, she told herself. *And all that lovely money.*

Abby sighed. Yes, it was sad that Craig was dead, but life went on, as she very well knew. You had to search for the positives in life or you would go mad.

Another thought suddenly came to Abby which made her wince. How much of this was she going to tell Megan? As she'd said to Jake, you couldn't hide a new car. But perhaps it would be best if she didn't tell her sister about the money. It might make her jealous and, yes, suspicious.

Abby pulled a face at herself in the rear-view mirror. She hated lying to Megan but she just might have to. Oh, dear. Even when things took a turn for the better, life wasn't easy.

CHAPTER FOUR

'YOU HANDLED THAT WELL,' Jake growled as he pulled a bottle of red at random out of his wine rack. 'I love the way you kept her at a distance.'

Still, what could he do when she started crying like that? Common sense demanded he do nothing. But common decency insisted that he comfort her.

Big mistake.

The moment he'd taken her in his arms, all those good intentions of his dissolved in the face of a desire so strong it took every ounce of willpower not to pull her even closer than he had. He didn't want to pat her damned back. Or utter soothing words. He wanted to tip up her chin and kiss the tears from her lovely face.

Thank God he hadn't given in to that desire. Because she would not have surrendered to him as she did in his darkest dreams. She would have slapped him, then resigned as his housekeeper.

Abby didn't particularly like him. That, he knew.

Which should have been a relief, given his resolve never to act on his secret desire for her. Instead he felt peeved by her indifference. And jealous of her obvious affection for Craig. Which was all perverse, given his own decision not to have anything to do with her on a personal level, a decision which fate—courtesy of his uncle—had now blown out of the water. Next Saturday morning he would be *personally* escorting Abby to Craig's graveside, then afterwards he would be *personally* buying her a car.

That was all pretty personal, in his opinion.

But there was no way out, Jake accepted bleakly as he gazed down at the label of the bottle he'd pulled out and saw it was one of his favourites. A Shiraz from the Clare Valley. Good. Because he needed to get drunk. And he might as well do so on a favourite tipple rather than rubbish.

Not that he ever bought rubbish, he admitted as he poured himself his first glass. Long gone were the days when he drank rough red from casks. Hell, he hadn't done that since his university days. And yet they had been good days. Happy days. Carefree days.

Nothing like today, Jake thought ruefully as he lifted the glass to his lips for a deep swallow. Today would not go down as good. Or happy. Or carefree. Today was…what?

He wasn't sure how to describe it.

Dangerous came to mind. And not in a good way. Jake had enjoyed danger in his life at times. But this was a different kind of danger. This wasn't physical danger. This involved his emotions. Intense, uncontrollable emotions.

Jake didn't like intense, uncontrollable emotions. They made you do things which never ended well.

Jake carried the glass and the bottle out to his courtyard, where he placed the bottle on the small circular glass table he liked best then sat down in the chair next to it.

When his phone rang, he saw that it was Olivia.

He didn't want to talk to Olivia just now. He didn't want to talk to anyone. So he just turned off the phone and went back to drinking his wine.

CHAPTER FIVE

WITHIN SECONDS OF arriving home Abby rang Megan, not wanting to procrastinate over the call. Megan would only be even more suspicious if she waited too long to give her the good news.

'Hi there, kiddo,' Megan answered, a term of endearment which often led people to think Megan was the older sister. And whilst there wasn't much between them, Abby was actually older by fifteen months.

Abby had already decided that the best way to play this was to sound very happy about it. And she *was* happy. Just a bit wary about her sister's reaction.

'You'll never guess what's happened,' Abby said brightly as she dumped her bag on the floor and plonked herself into a nearby armchair.

'Something good by the sound of things.'

'Unbelievably good!' And she launched into an explanation of the day's events. As planned, she left out the part about the travel fund money and only mentioned the new car. Naturally, she didn't include the bit about her bursting into tears and Jake hugging her.

Megan exclaimed a shocked, 'No!' at the news about the new car, but thankfully didn't make any sarcastic crack about what Abby might have done with Jake's uncle to deserve such an incredibly generous gift. Things might have been different, however, if she'd mentioned the twenty-five thousand dollars as well. Though possibly not. Maybe Megan instinctively knew that Abby would never do anything sexual with a man she didn't love. Wayne had been her first and only lover because he was the first and only man she'd ever loved.

'Aren't you a lucky duck?' Megan said without a trace of jealousy in her voice. 'A brand-new car! And you don't even have to wait for probate to come through, since your hunky boss is buying you the car himself. This Saturday, you said?'

'Yes. This Saturday.'

'It's a wonderful gift. Especially when you hardly knew his uncle. But perhaps not so much if he was filthy rich. Was he filthy rich?'

'He must have been. Jake said he'd inherited heaps. That's why he doesn't mind forking out the money for me for a car.'

'Oh, right. Still, it's nice of him to do that. He's not legally obliged to, I would imagine.'

'Probably not, but he said he would never go against his uncle's deathbed wishes.'

'Did you see this letter his uncle left him?'

'Well, no, but why would he lie about something like that?'

'Maybe he fancies you.'

'Oh, don't be ridiculous! Why would he fancy someone like me when he has that gorgeous girlfriend? I've been thinking, Megan, since I'm getting a new car, would you like the ute? I know it's done a good few miles but it goes really well. Wayne put a new engine in it not long before he died.'

'Oh, I'd *love* it. Thanks, Abby.'

'Jake is going to take me to see his uncle's grave as well,' she blurted out before she could think better of it.

The silence at the other end of the line was telling.

'Oh, is he?' Megan said at long last in one of her knowing voices. 'And why is he doing that?'

'Because I asked him to,' Abby said, angry with herself. 'And, before you jump to conclusions, we're just dropping in at the cemetery on the way to the car yards at Parramatta. It's hardly out of his way. And you are so wrong about his fancying me.'

Megan laughed. 'We'll see, hon. We'll see.'

'Oh, for pity's sake.'

'You've always underestimated your looks, Abby. Even when your teeth were not great, you were gorgeous. Now that you've had them fixed, you're a knockout. And your figure is to die for.'

'Oh, go on with you!'

'No, I mean it. Your fantastic figure was one of the reasons Wayne was so possessive of you. And why he didn't want you to work after you were married. Because he didn't want other men lusting after you.'

Abby's first reaction was to hotly deny what Megan said. But in her heart of hearts she knew it was true. Wayne had been very possessive of her. Right from the start, he'd wanted her all to himself. Which had suited Abby fine. All she'd wanted back then was to be Wayne's wife, plus the mother of his children. She'd been only too happy to stop work and not have to face the world every day with her horrible teeth. Not so happy, however, as the years had passed and the nursery remained empty.

'That's probably the reason he wouldn't pay for you to get your teeth fixed,' Megan continued. 'Because he was afraid you'd be too beautiful and he'd lose you to another man.'

'That's ridiculous!' Abby protested. 'The reason I didn't get my teeth fixed back then was because it's very expensive and we had a huge mortgage. Besides, Wayne already loved me, even with my horrid teeth. As for being too beautiful, please don't make me laugh. Even if by some miracle I'd become the most beautiful woman in the world, I would never have left Wayne, no matter what. I loved him.'

'Did you, Abby? Or did you just love that he loved you with the kind of crazy obsession which can be oh, so flattering?'

'I did so love Wayne,' she insisted. 'Very much. We would have been happy together if we'd had children.'

Megan sighed. 'If you say so, Abby.'

'I do say so. Now, I do not wish to discuss Wayne

any more, thank you. I didn't realise how much you disliked him.'

'I didn't dislike him. I just didn't think he was good enough for you. You deserved someone better.'

Abby didn't know whether to feel flattered or frustrated. 'Such as who, Megan? Prince Charming?'

'Yeah, why not? And let me tell you something else, kiddo. If you bought some new clothes and put on some make-up occasionally, you would be so hot that every man you met would be drooling. And that includes your handsome hunk of a boss.'

Abby didn't like to tell Megan that she was being delusional—about Jake at least—so she just laughed.

'Yeah, you can laugh if you like. Just you wait and see. Speaking of your boss, did you happen to watch his show today?'

'Hardly. I was too busy cleaning his house.'

'He interviewed Maddie Hanks. You know, the latest Aussie actress who's made it big in Hollywood?'

'I know who you mean. She was in that biblical epic. Played a slave girl.'

'Yeah, that's the one. Well, she was flirting with Jake big time. And brother, she is stunning. He seemed very taken with her. Couldn't keep his eyes off her cleavage. Though I don't think her boobs are real. Anyway, I wouldn't mind betting they get together in the near future.'

Abby rolled her eyes. Truly, her sister was so addicted to gossip that she saw scandalous behaviour everywhere. 'Jake already has a gorgeous girlfriend,' she pointed out. 'That newsreader. Remember?'

'Huh! That won't stop him getting into Miss Hanks's pants.'

'He's not like that,' Abby said sharply.

'Oh, really? And how would you know, Miss I-Know-Nothing-Personal-About-My-Hunk-of-a-Boss? Did something else happen today that you didn't tell me about?'

'No,' she denied, blanking the hug out of her mind. 'Look, I'm not overly fond of the man, but he's not some sleazebag.'

'Wow. He's sure got you fooled. All men can be sleaze-bags if the right temptation comes along.'

Abby just shook her head. 'Truly, Megan, you are such a cynic when it comes to men.'

'I have good reason to be.'

This *was* true. Timmy's father hadn't been the first man in Megan's life to treat her badly. She'd met a few since becoming a single mother who'd wined and dined her till they got what they wanted before dumping her as cruelly as the cowardly creep who'd got her pregnant then disappeared once he discovered fatherhood was too much commitment for him.

'I hope you're going to make yourself presentable when your boss takes you out on Saturday,' Megan said.

'It's not a date, Megan.'

'You still want to look a bit nicer than you do when you clean his house.'

'I will do my best.'

'Good. Gosh, wait till Jan hears all this. She's going to be green with envy.'

Jan was Megan's next-door neighbour, a single mother like Megan. She was one of the reasons Megan wouldn't come to live with Abby, because she didn't want to leave her best friend. Abby wasn't overly keen on Jan, but she'd been a good friend to Megan and had a similar personality. Both were very easy-going but extremely untidy. Abby had been somewhat relieved when Megan knocked back her offer for her and Timmy to come live with her. Their messy lifestyle would have driven her mad within a week.

'Jan's sure to think I did something suspect with Jake's uncle,' Abby said drily.

'Nah. Now if it was *me*.'

Abby smiled. 'Come on, Megan, you're not as bad as you pretend to be.'

'Yeah, I am. Not everyone is as saint-like as you, sweetie. Though, to give you credit, being a goody-two-shoes got you somewhere this time. I dare say you waited on that rich old bastard hand and foot. You probably even baked him those delicious peanut butter cookies of yours.'

Abby fell silent with guilty embarrassment. She *had* made a fuss of Jake's uncle. But, at the time, it had been ages since her nurturing side had had an opportunity to flourish. Looking after Jake's house was a rather impersonal job. It had been so satisfying to bake cookies for a real man and, yes, watch him eat them with relish. She'd enjoyed it all immensely.

'You did, didn't you?' Megan said with laughter in her voice. 'No wonder he thought of you when he was dying. Those cookies of yours are super-yummy. Though way too fattening. I refuse to let you make me any more. Though Timmy wouldn't mind some, when you have your next baking session. I have to go and get the little devil himself now. He's been playing next door. Ring me tomorrow night. Gotta go. Love ya.'

'You too.'

After Abby clicked off her phone she just sat there, thinking about some of the things Megan had said about her marriage to Wayne. It was true that her husband had loved her more than she'd loved him. But she *had* loved him. Okay, not with a grand passion. Her feelings for Wayne had been based more on a deep friendship and eternal gratitude rather than the kind of wild sexual yearnings which some people obviously experienced.

Abby supposed she *had* been flattered by Wayne's fiercely possessive love. And his insatiable desire for her. After her second miscarriage, she'd wanted to take her doctor's advice to go on the Pill and give her body a rest. But no, Wayne had refused to countenance that idea, saying he didn't like to interfere with nature. He'd promised instead to abstain from sex for a while but, of course, that hadn't lasted for long. He'd never been able to control his desire for her and she'd never felt good about refusing him, mostly because she knew how much he seemed to need it.

Abby liked the kissing and cuddling part of lovemaking—she'd loved being wrapped in Wayne's strong arms—but she'd never felt any urgent need for the sex act itself, unlike Megan, who claimed she couldn't live without it. It had never really bothered Abby that she didn't come during lovemaking. It had bothered Wayne, however, so after a while she had just faked it.

She hadn't had to fake falling pregnant, however, and a few months after her second miscarriage she'd been pregnant again. But, once again, she'd miscarried at the three months stage. After that, she'd gone on the Pill without discussing it with Wayne, and she was still taking it long after her husband was gone, mainly because she'd discovered it saved her from premenstrual tension.

It felt good, Abby realised, to finally be in control of her body and, yes, her life. She'd been gutted by Wayne's tragic death, had taken months to get over it. But in the end she'd picked herself up and moved on.

Now, because of Craig's wonderful kindness and generosity, she would be able to move on some more. And Jake would find another housekeeper easily enough.

Thinking of Jake reminded Abby of what Megan had said about him, and about men in general. Abby had to admit that *her* view of the opposite sex was possibly narrower than her sister's. But she wasn't stupid. She was sure she would recognise a sleazebag when she came across one. And Jake Sanderson was no sleazebag.

But that was possibly the only good point of his character. Abby could see that he had a tendency towards arrogance and self-absorption. Neither was he into commitment, hence his never-ending parade of beautiful girlfriends. But that didn't mean he would be a cheater. She couldn't imagine him having sex with some flashy, fly-by-night actress whilst he was dating that truly gorgeous newsreader.

Abby would be utterly disgusted if she ever found out he *had* done something like that. Not that it was any of her business what her boss did in his private and personal life. Still, it bothered her a bit, thinking that he could be, right at this moment, meeting up with Maddie Hanks somewhere in the city then bringing her back to his place for the night.

It occurred to Abby that she would know within a minute of arriving at his house tomorrow morning if he'd had a new woman stay overnight. Abby knew his current girlfriend's smell because she recognised the perfume. It was a heavy musky scent which didn't wear off easily. During the last few weeks Abby had smelled that perfume every couple of days, and almost always on a Monday after the weekend.

But not *this* Monday morning, she suddenly realised. Which led her to wonder if maybe they'd split up. Maybe that was why he'd been giving Maddie Hanks the eye on his show today. Men like Jake didn't go without sex for long. Because they didn't have to. Women threw themselves at famous men in droves—beautiful, sexy, successful women who knew everything there was to know about lovemaking and never had to fake a thing.

A very rude word burst from Abby's lips as she stood up abruptly then marched into her immaculate little kitchen, where she snapped on the kettle then yanked open the freezer, which was full of frozen meals for one.

Still feeling decidedly disgruntled, she grabbed a chilli con carne and shoved it into the microwave to reheat, telling herself all the while that her boss's sex life was definitely none of her business.

'He can sleep with whomever he damned well likes,' she said in a tone quite uncharacteristic of her usual serene self. 'Just so long as he delivers everything he promised me today!'

CHAPTER SIX

JAKE LEFT IT until nine that evening to ring Olivia back, having learnt from experience that it was never wise to ring her before she'd been home for a while after work. After reading the news from six till seven, Olivia usually went for a de-stressing drink down near the quay before catching the Manly ferry home.

Her phone rang several times before she picked up.

'Well, hello, stranger,' she answered waspishly. 'Why didn't you answer when I rang you earlier?'

'I didn't feel like talking,' he said with blunt honesty.

'Are you upset with me for not going to your uncle's funeral?'

'No,' he told her with equal honesty. 'I didn't expect you to cancel your arrangements when they'd been organised weeks before Craig died.'

Olivia and five of her girlfriends had driven up to a resort in the Blue Mountains on the Friday for a hen party for one of the girls, who was getting married shortly.

'I was home by eight last night,' Olivia pointed out tartly. 'Why didn't you ring? I was waiting for your call. Or your text. Or something.'

Jake was totally taken aback. They didn't have the kind of relationship where they called and texted each other all the time. They were lovers, but not in love.

'You told me you were turning off your phone for the weekend,' he reminded her. 'Nothing stopped you ringing me when you got home last night.'

'I was tired.'

'More likely hungover.'

'Yes,' she admitted grudgingly. 'That, too. But you still could have contacted me this morning.'

'Come now, Olivia. You know I'm busy on weekday mornings, getting ready for my show.'

'Ah, yes. Your show,' she said in a tone which had a decided edge to it. 'I happened to watch your show today...'

'And?' he prompted when she didn't go on.

'I saw the way you were ogling that actress's boobs. You do know they're fake, don't you?'

Jake could not believe what he was hearing. He sincerely hoped it wasn't the sounds of jealousy. Because jealousy meant only one thing.

'I dare say it was the cameraman doing the ogling,' he said coldly. 'Not me.'

'That's not the way I saw it. Just remember that if you're dating me, Jake darling, you can look, but you can't touch anyone else.'

'Don't start getting possessive on me, Olivia,' he warned, his tone darkly ominous.

There was a short silence before she suddenly laughed. 'Of course not. I was only kidding. Any red-blooded man would have to be blind not to ogle Maddie Hanks's boobs. That's why they pay her so much to take off her clothes. So when am I going to see you next? I was thinking we could meet up somewhere in the city for dinner tomorrow night. Café Sydney, perhaps?'

Jake knew if he did that then Olivia would want to come back to his place for the night. And he simply didn't want to have sex with her. Truth be told, he'd been glad she'd gone away the previous weekend. After Craig's wretched funeral and wake he'd just wanted to be alone.

'I don't think so, Olivia,' he told her, trying not to sound as cold and hard as he suddenly felt towards her. But in his head he kept comparing her to Abby, who had cried in his arms over a man she hardly knew. And that was before she knew what he'd left her. Olivia might look all woman but she didn't have a soft or compassionate bone in her body. She could read the most tragic news and shed not a single tear.

'But why not?' Olivia demanded to know in the stroppy tone she adopted when things weren't going her way.

'I just don't feel like going out at the moment,' he replied wearily. 'I'm still down about Craig's death.'

'Then the best thing for you is to get out and about!'

'I said no, Olivia.'

'But I've missed you,' she went on, changing her tone to wheedling. 'Okay, how about I come to your place and we can get some food delivered?'

'Olivia, you're not hearing me. I don't feel like company at the moment. Please don't make a fuss. I'll ring you later in the week. We'll go out somewhere Saturday night.'

'Why not Friday night?'

'I've an early engagement Saturday morning.'

'Doing what?'

Jake sighed. He was an expert at picking up when his girlfriends started wanting more from him than what they'd agreed to. He sensed that something had changed over the weekend. Possibly something to do with this friend of hers getting married.

'Olivia, look, I…'

'Gosh, but don't you sound serious,' Olivia broke in, her voice light and teasing. 'I thought we promised each other never to get serious.'

'*You* were the one who was starting to sound serious,' Jake pointed out.

'Yes, I know. Silly me, getting all jealous about that actress. But you can't blame me, Jake. I'm competitive by nature and I just didn't like the way she looked at you. Like she was going to have you for supper.'

'Olivia, I have no intention of having anything further to do with Maddie Hanks. It was an interview. End of story.'

'Yes, of course. I'm sorry. Am I forgiven?'

What could he possibly say to that?

'Don't be angry with me, Jake,' she went on before he could find the right words.

'I'm not angry,' he said. Just dismayed.

'Excellent,' she said. 'Because I'm in desperate need of sex. And you, lover boy, are just the man to deliver.'

A week ago, before Craig's death, Jake would have laughed. He'd always liked Olivia's slightly bawdy nature, plus her sometimes insatiable sex drive. Why, then, did he feel so disgruntled over her reducing him to the role of stud? He should have been pleased. And relieved. This was all he wanted from a woman, wasn't it?

An image suddenly popped into his mind, of another woman—one with lovely big eyes wet with tears—one who would never say things like that.

'I'm sorry, Olivia,' he said. 'But I'm not in the mood for sex right now.'

Her silence showed how much his rejection shocked her. Jake knew in his heart that this was the beginning of the end. Olivia was not going to be happy, but it was better to break up whilst they were still friends.

'Maybe you should find someone else,' he suggested quietly, hoping she would get the message without his having to spell it out.

'Like you have, you mean,' she threw at him. 'Who do you think you're kidding, Jake? You're always in the mood for sex. There's someone else, isn't there?'

Jake swallowed half a glass of wine before answering. 'No, Olivia,' he told her rather wearily. 'There's no one else.' It wasn't really a lie, even if Abby's face kept popping into his mind.

'Then who are you spending next Saturday morning with?' she demanded to know.

'If you must know, I'm taking Abby car shopping,' he said, well aware that it would cause trouble. But he no longer cared. He wanted Olivia out of his life.

'Abby who?' she screeched.

'Abby Jenkins,' he told her quite calmly. 'My house-keeper. Craig left me instructions in his will to buy her a car.'

'But...but...why would he do that?'

'Apparently she was nice to him when he stayed here a while back.'

'Nice to him in what way?' she said nastily.

How predictable she was. 'In her usual sweet way, I would imagine. Abby is a sweet girl.'

'*Girl!* I thought you said your housekeeper was a widow.'

'She is. Her husband died young.'

'I see. So how old is she, if I might ask?'

'Twenty-seven.'

'You never told me she was that young,' Olivia said, her tone accusing.

'Well, I'm telling you now.'

'Is she attractive?' she snapped.

'Olivia, I don't like the way this conversation is going.'

'Just answer the bloody question.'

'Abby's a very attractive girl.'

'I'll just bet she is. I dare say you wouldn't hire any other kind. So how long have you been sleeping with her?'

'I am not sleeping with her,' Jake denied. 'I hardly ever talk to her.'

'I don't believe you.'

Jake remained silent as his temper rose. If he spoke now, he'd say something he'd regret.

'You're not fooling me, Jake. You are sleeping with your housekeeper and nothing you say will make me believe otherwise.'

'In that case, I think we should call it quits, don't you?'

'Absolutely,' she said, and cut him off without another word.

Jake sighed. He preferred his relationships to end a lit-tle more civilly, and a lot more classily. But sometimes it just wasn't possible. A pity, though. Olivia had suited his lifestyle very well. Or she had, till Craig died and forced Jake to face what he had been secretly wanting for a long time: Abby.

No doubt Olivia would spread it around that she'd come home from her weekend away to discover that Jake was sleeping with his housekeeper. He could deny it, of course. But he'd always found that denial fuelled rumours to greater heights. It wasn't as though any of this would reach Abby's ears. If he ignored the whispers around the channel—the TV world had a gossip grapevine second to none—by next week it would be yesterday's news.

Meanwhile, he had a week of shows to do and a difficult Saturday to endure.

Shoving his phone into his pocket, he stood up and made his way to the kitchen to make himself some supper before retiring for the night. As he extracted two slices of raisin bread from the freezer then popped them in the toaster, his thoughts slid back to Olivia's accusation that he was sleeping with Abby.

He wished!

Okay, so he possibly could seduce Abby if he put his mind to it. Jake knew he hadn't exactly been Prince Charming around her up till now. But seducing a woman like Abby would be a double-edged sword. Because she was the kind of woman men fell in love with—the kind of woman who made men want to marry them. Maybe even have children with them.

His mind boggled at this last thought!

Nope. Seducing Abby was one big no-no in Jake's head.

Now, if only he could convince his body to agree with him…

The toast popped up but Jake didn't notice. He was remembering how Abby's breasts had felt pressed hard against his chest. They were full and feminine and very soft. He wondered what kind of nipples she had. Would they be small and pink, or large and dusky? He didn't mind either way, as long as they were responsive.

Jake sucked in sharply once he realised where his thoughts were taking him.

'This is not good,' Jake muttered as he turned his attention to the rapidly cooling toast. He didn't want to be tempted to seduce Abby. It was a powerful temptation, though a dangerous one. Because, even if he managed to keep it to just an affair and not let his emotions get involved, Jake knew Abby didn't have the experience to handle an affair with a man like him. In the end, he would break her heart.

And it wasn't a hard-boiled heart like Olivia's. Abby's heart was soft and sweet. To risk breaking such a heart would be wicked. And Jake wasn't wicked. At the same time, he wasn't a saint. Best to keep physical contact with Abby to a minimum, came his firm lecture to himself. Be especially careful when you take her to that cemetery on Saturday, for starters. Whisk her away before she starts crying again. No more hugging. And not too much chit-chat.

Jake supposed he couldn't get out of helping her buy a new car, since she'd want to trade in that old ute and was sure to be taken advantage of by some slick salesman. But once he knew what kind of car she liked, he'd do a lot of the groundwork over the phone before Saturday then direct her straight to his chosen dealer, who would have her choice all registered and ready to go. That way there would be no dithering around. Before you could say Jack Robinson, she'd be driving off home in her new car, leaving him to watch her go with a clear conscience.

Humph! And who was he kidding? Jake suspected that by the end of Saturday his conscience—as well as his male hormones—would have been sorely tried. Hopefully, he would win the battle and not do anything stupid!

Crunching into a piece of cold raisin toast, he ripped off a large mouthful with a savagery which matched his mood.

Jake hadn't felt this frustrated since he'd been laid up in hospital with a useless leg.

Life as a confirmed bachelor, he decided, wasn't all it was cracked up to be!

CHAPTER SEVEN

AFTER AN UNCHARACTERISTICALLY restless night, Abby woke with butterflies in her stomach. She didn't want to care what Jake might have done with that actress the night before. She didn't want to rush into the master bedroom as soon as she arrived at his house this morning. She certainly didn't want to be compelled to inspect the bed for evidence of a female visitor the night before.

But Abby knew that was exactly what she was going to do.

There was no use pretending differently. Her curiosity had been aroused by Megan's insistence that Jake would not be able to resist Maddie Hanks. It was all she'd thought about the evening before. She'd tried to read. She was on to the last of the list of ten books Craig had given her, Daphne du Maurier's *Rebecca*, which she was thoroughly enjoying. But even that hadn't distracted her from thinking about what Jake might be up to. She'd tossed and turned until well after midnight.

Strangely, despite less sleep than usual, she didn't feel tired. Just annoyed. With herself. Even more so when she started dithering over what to wear to work.

'As if it matters what you look like,' she flung at herself, reaching for another pair of old jeans and an equally ancient T-shirt which had once been white and was now an unflattering shade of grey. 'He's not going to come home again while you're there today. Now stop all this nonsense about Jake Sanderson. Who he sleeps with is none of your business!'

Famous last words. For what did Abby do as soon as she let herself into his house? She dropped her bag in the hallway then dashed upstairs to the master bedroom, her heart going as fast as her feet.

It was a large room, dominated by a huge bed which could easily accommodate its long-limbed owner and whatever playmate—or playmates—he so desired.

Abby blinked.

Had Jake ever entertained more than one woman at a time in that bed?

It looked messy enough this morning to have hosted a whole harem in there last night. Maybe he'd had the newsreader *and* the actress.

With some trepidation Abby approached the bed. Gingerly, she picked up one corner of the snow-white duvet and threw it back off the end of the bed. That was followed by the top sheet, revealing nothing but a rather crumpled bottom sheet. No female perfume wafted up to her nostrils, the only smell being Jake's, which was a mixture of man and the sandalwood scent belonging to his aftershave.

Still not certain that he hadn't had company, Abby bolted into the en suite bathroom to see how many towels had been used since yesterday. Only two, she noted, flung carelessly over the bath as was Jake's habit. If he'd had someone to stay then she hadn't showered in here, or used a fresh towel.

Abby let out a deep sigh of satisfaction.

'I told you he's not a sleazebag, Megan,' she said aloud.

Feeling much better, Abby went downstairs, collected her bag from the hallstand and made her way to the kitchen. There, she put on the kettle before proceeding into the utility room to inspect Jake's whiteboard, which was empty. She'd returned to the kitchen and just poured herself some coffee when her phone rang, her heart jumping when she saw the identity of her caller.

'Hello,' she said, unable to hide the surprise in her voice. 'What's up?'

'Nothing's up,' her boss answered after a moment's hesitation. 'I just wondered if you'd decided what kind of car you wanted yet. And what colour.'

'I... I haven't got around to that yet. Sorry,' she added.

'No need to apologise. But could you decide by tomorrow? That way I can have it ready for you by Saturday. Perhaps give me two choices of colours though, to be on the safe side. White is always a good pick. It's cooler and holds its value better.'

'Yes, yes, I know you're right. But I rather like blue.'

He sighed. 'What colour blue?'

'Not pale blue. Or turquoise. A royal blue.'

'Right. A royal blue. I know the Hyundai i30 comes in a nice royal blue. One of my assistants on the show has one and she loves it. Look, check it out on the internet and give me a ring tonight with your decision. Also, work out what bank account you want your money put into.'

'Okay,' she said, thinking to herself that he really was in a hurry to have done with all this, a thought which was a bit of a downer. It came to Abby that, against all logic and common sense, she was beginning to have feelings for Jake which were not only unwise but pointless.

It was all Megan's fault, she decided irritably, for putting silly ideas in her head.

'Make sure you have your old car looking as good as you can on Saturday so you can get the best trade-in possible.'

'Oh, but I'm not going to trade in the ute,' she told him. 'I'm going to give it to my sister. She doesn't have a car.'

'Right,' he said slowly.

'Is that a problem?'

'No, no, I suppose not.'

His attitude once again betrayed a degree of annoyance. No doubt he would prefer to spend this Saturday doing anything but chauffeuring her around to cemeteries and car yards. But really, there was no other solution if he wanted this all done and dusted as quickly as possible.

'Okay,' he went on after a longish hesitation. 'Ring me

tonight and tell me if you're happy with that Hyundai and I'll get the ball rolling. But if they don't have any royal blues on the lot then it might have to be white.'

'That's all right. It doesn't really matter. What time should I ring?' She didn't want to ring him whilst he was out with his girlfriend. Or anyone else who would remain nameless.

'Any time after six. I'm not going out tonight.'

Why did she have to like the sound of that so much?

'Okay. Thanks, Jake. For everything.'

'No sweat. Bye.'

Abby just stood there for a while after they'd both clicked off, her head in a bit of a whirl. Pointless it might be, but she was definitely going to buy herself some new clothes before next Saturday. No way could she go car shopping with Jake looking anything but her best.

Thursday night was late-night shopping. Perhaps she would take Megan with her. Then again perhaps she wouldn't. Not only would her sister ask awkward questions about why she was buying new clothes all of a sudden, but Megan would also steer Abby into buying clothes which were to *her* taste, which meant tight and tarty.

Feminine pride demanded she look nice for Jake on Saturday, but not tarty.

No, she would go shopping by herself and buy a few mix and match things which weren't too expensive but which fitted properly and made her feel good. She might also indulge herself with a trip to the hairdresser. Get her hair trimmed and a treatment put in. Maybe have her nails done at the same time.

No, not her nails. That was going too far. She didn't want Jake to think she was trying to doll herself up for him. She just wanted to look as good as she could. She'd felt ashamed of herself yesterday in those daggy old clothes with her hair scraped back and not a scrap of make-up on. If she was really going to move on with her life, it was high time she started looking after herself.

She'd really let herself go since Wayne died. Abby vowed she would turn over a new leaf tonight by having a long relaxing bath and giving her whole body some well needed attention.

Once she had a firm plan of action, Abby got started on the house. On Tuesday afternoons she always popped down to the supermarket to restock Jake's cupboards and fridge. When she'd started this job, Jake had given her a long list of food items that he didn't like to run out of.

He occasionally cooked meals for himself, though not often. Abby suspected he ordered takeaway a fair bit. Mostly Asian food. She'd seen the many and varied brochures on top of his fridge, plus the empty cartons in the bin. Abby had never seen the signs of a proper dinner party, despite the house having a lovely dining room with a beautiful big table and eight chairs. He probably took people out to dinner instead. Or maybe his current girlfriend gave dinner parties for him at her place.

Abby was wondering if this Olivia was as good a cook as *she* was, when she pulled herself up with a jolt.

You have to stop this, Abby Jenkins, she lectured herself. *Jake Sanderson is your boss and that's all he'll ever be. There is no point thinking about him, or his sex life, or what his girlfriends do or don't do. It's just as well you'll be leaving this job soon and going overseas before the man becomes some kind of sick obsession. You're lonely, that's all. So go get that shopping done then get yourself home, and around seven ring Jake and, for pity's sake, just keep the conversation businesslike.*

She wished she hadn't asked him to take her to the cemetery to visit his uncle's grave but it was too late now. He'd think she was loopy if she kept changing her mind. She'd just have to be careful not to cry. Because she didn't want him hugging her again. Gracious, no. No more hugging!

By the time Abby arrived home, a degree of depression had taken hold, this sudden unexpected attraction towards Jake making her acutely aware of just how lonely her life was. Really, she had no close friends other than her sister. Most of her neighbours worked in the city and were gone all day. Then at the weekends their lives were taken up with their children and their houses. Occasionally she was invited to a barbecue, but not often.

There was only one neighbour she would classify as a friend, an elderly widow who'd been very kind to her when Wayne died, but who, unfortunately, was also a terrible gossip. Abby hadn't told Harriet that her boss was the celebrity host of *Australia at Noon*, knowing that if she let that little gem drop she would be bombarded with questions about Jake. She'd just said her boss was called Mr Sanderson—which was a common enough name—and was a bachelor businessman who worked long hours in the city and needed someone to look after the house for him. When Harriet assumed he was a middle-aged workaholic who was married to his job, Abby let her.

Abby had been relieved to see that her next-door neighbour Harriet's car wasn't in her driveway, which meant she was out and therefore wouldn't be dropping in for a cuppa as she sometimes did when Abby arrived home from work. Abby wasn't in the mood for gossip.

There was no doubt that life hadn't been very kind to her. Firstly there was her teeth, which had been a huge problem in her eyes but which her parents had dismissed as nothing. Probably because it would have cost money to fix and they'd spent all their spare cash on alcohol. Then, shortly after her father had been killed in a drunken pub brawl, her mother had also died, succumbing to too many sleeping tablets downed with too much gin.

The coroner had called it an accidental death as opposed to suicide, but what did it really matter in the end? There'd been no life insurance to consider.

Abby had only been seventeen at the time, just entering her last year in high school. It had been impossible to do well at her studies while living in a refuge. She'd left school in the end to work full-time at the local fish and chip shop, earning enough by working seven days a week to rent the small flat above the shop for herself and Megan. At twenty she'd married Wayne but she'd been unable to carry a baby full term.

That was the cruellest cut of all, even crueller, in a way, than Wayne's tragic drowning. Because, more than anything in the world, Abby wanted to have children, wanted to create a happy family, wanted to be the best mother in the world. Instead, she hadn't even had the chance.

When tears dripped from her nose into her tea, Abby shook her head quite violently, determined not to dwell on the past any more, or on anything negative.

'Time to run a bath and start looking after yourself, kiddo,' she said aloud, smiling at how much like Megan she sounded.

Her mood was still up when she picked up her phone to ring Jake at seven. Okay, so she found the man attractive. Most of the women in Australia did. There was no need to get into a twist over it. Nothing would come of it, and soon she'd be off overseas on the holiday of a lifetime.

Given all her common sense reasoning, it annoyed Abby that her hand still shook as she lifted her phone to her ear and waited for Jake to answer.

'Hi, Abby,' Jake answered in his usual businesslike voice. So why did the sound of it suddenly have her stomach curling over and her heart beating faster? 'Made up your mind about the car?'

In truth, Abby didn't really give a hoot about the make and model of the car. She was thrilled just to be getting a brand-new one. Not so thrilled that she was acting like some schoolgirl with a crush on her teacher.

'I like the look of that Hyundai you mentioned. And it doesn't have to be royal blue. A white one would be fine.'

'Good. I'll pick you up at ten on Saturday morning. Is that too early for you?'

'No, no. Ten will be fine.' She'd be ready at dawn if he wanted.

'See you Saturday morning.'

He was gone before she could say another word, leaving her with a dry mouth and the sure knowledge that the next few days were going to be the longest in her life.

CHAPTER EIGHT

BY FRIDAY JAKE found it difficult to concentrate on the preparations for his show. Or care. He hadn't been sleeping well and, quite frankly, doing this damned show every day was beginning to bore him silly.

There was no doubt now that he would sell it and do something else with his life, something more challenging, preferably overseas and well away from a certain girl who he couldn't get out of his mind. Instead of going over his notes for the show like he usually did, he kept thinking about tomorrow.

The door to his dressing room suddenly opened.

'Five minutes, Jake,' Kerrie said.

'Yeah, yeah, I'm ready.' Though he wasn't.

He did the show on autopilot that day, no one guessing that his mind was elsewhere. Or so he'd imagined. Afterwards, the director pulled him aside and asked him if there was anything wrong.

'No,' Jake said. 'Why?'

'A little birdie told me you've been having girl trouble.'

Jake smiled a wry smile. He'd known Olivia would become vicious and vengeful.

'Not me, Victor. I never have girl trouble.'

Victor didn't look convinced. 'Not telling, eh? Fair enough. But it's never wise to let your private life affect your professional life. The lights were on today, Jake, but nobody was home.'

Jake shrugged. 'Just a bit tired, that's all.'

'No sweat. No one else would have noticed. Only old eagle-eye here. But it might be an idea to get some shut-eye tonight. Man does not live by sex alone.'

Jake laughed drily. 'I wish.'

'So the rumours were right? Olivia's been dumped in favour of your sexy young housekeeper?'

Jake rolled his eyes. 'I didn't *dump* Olivia. We broke up because she jumped to the wrong conclusion about my housekeeper, who's a very nice, *sweet* girl and definitely *not* my lover.'

Again, Victor didn't look convinced.

When Jake's phone rang he stared at the identity of the caller, his emotions suddenly a-jangle. He hoped nothing had happened to prevent them getting together tomorrow. The truth was he couldn't wait to see her. 'I have to take this call,' he said sharply, then strode off down the corridor.

'Yes, Abby?' Jake said, an attack of anxiety making his stomach swirl. 'What is it?' He didn't mean to sound so abrupt but he was shocked by his nervous reaction to the possibility that he might not be seeing her the next day after all. 'I hope you're not going to change tomorrow's arrangements,' he snapped before he could stop himself.

'What? No, no. I just wanted to ask you if I could go home early today. I was going to do some late-night shopping last night but my sister wasn't well and she needed me to look after Timmy for her.'

Relief swamped Jake, as did remorse over his snapping at her like that.

'Of course you can go home early.'

'I've done everything I had to do.'

'I'm sure the place is perfect,' Jake said. 'It always is. What do you need to buy?' he added, hoping to redeem himself by showing an interest in her life for once.

'Just some new clothes so that I don't embarrass you tomorrow by looking like your cleaning lady. Even if I am,' she added with a sweet laugh.

'You are much more than my cleaning lady,' Jake said, the devil's voice whispering in his ear that he would like her to be a hell of a lot more. 'As I said the other day, you are the best housekeeper a man could have.'

Her sudden silence brought a tension to Jake which was wickedly sexual. Heat licked through his loins, giving him an inkling of how it would feel if she ever surrendered to him.

He had no idea what she was thinking but he hoped she might be softening towards him a little. Or was he just fantasising? Abby had been making him fantasise a lot lately, all of it rather R-rated. How many times this week had he pictured going home early and sweeping her up into his arms, kissing her senseless and having her then and there? His favourite fantasy scenario was to hoist her up on to the kitchen bench-top where he would spread her legs—she'd be somehow naked, of course—and sink into her as she wrapped her arms around his neck and urged him on and on. Then there was the polished floor scenario. And the one against the wall. In the lap pool. Across the dining table.

His raunchy fantasies were multiplying.

Deplorable, really.

And very dangerous.

Because they were oh, so exciting.

'So everything's still right for tomorrow?' he asked, his cool voice belying the heat in his body.

'What? Oh, yes...yes. I'll be ready. Ten o'clock, you said, didn't you?'

'Yes. Oh, and Abby, what account do you want the twenty-five thousand put into?'

'Just put it in the one my salary goes in.'

'Very well. I'll do that this afternoon.'

'I... I don't know what to say except thank you.'

'It's Craig you should be thanking.'

'I will, when I visit his grave tomorrow.'

'You do that. See you tomorrow then.'

'But you don't know my address.'

'Of course I do. It was on your CV, which is still in my computer. You haven't moved, have you?'

'No.'

'Then I'll see you at your place at ten on the dot. Have to go. Bye.'

Jake sighed heavily as he clicked off his phone.

It was always an intimate situation, driving a woman somewhere, especially in a car which had once been described by a motoring magazine as sex on wheels. Jake figured Abby had never seen his red Ferrari. During the week he kept it locked away in the garage. He always used the ferry to get to and from work, and took taxis if he was socialising in and around the city. The Ferrari was only brought out at weekends for drives either up or down the coast. Jake liked nothing better than to zoom along one of the freeways with the top down and a beautiful woman by his side, one who was as responsive as his car.

Jake suddenly recalled his thoughts the other day about Abby's breasts, and how responsive they might be. If he closed his eyes he could still feel how they had felt, pressed up against him.

He cursed and jumped to his feet. This was all getting beyond a joke. Anyone would think he didn't have any self-control. He needed to stop all this nonsense immediately and just act naturally with her. He would not, he resolved, do or say anything provocative or seductive or, God forbid, charming.

An affair with Abby was out of the question.

Still, as Jake headed out of the dressing room, he resolved not to tempt fate by putting the top down on the Ferrari on Saturday. Better to be safe than sorry.

CHAPTER NINE

FOR THE UMPTEENTH time that morning, Abby smiled at herself in her large bathroom mirror, which was, actually, the only mirror she had in her house. All those years of having horrible teeth had made her allergic to mirrors. She still wasn't entirely used to her new appearance. Still didn't smile as much as other people.

But Megan was right. Her face did look much better now that her teeth were lovely and even and white. Her face looked a lot better with some make-up on as well, and with her hair all shiny and blow-dried properly.

Deciding that she'd admired herself long enough, Abby returned to her bedroom, where she'd laid out all the clothes she'd bought after her trip to the hairdresser. Abby hadn't splurged out on too much—a couple of pairs of stretchy jeans and a few tops and T-shirts, all of them cheap but in fashion. She'd also bought a lightweight blazer, a pair of trendy sandals and a new handbag. Finally, she'd splurged on a delicate gold necklace which went with everything, along with some new make-up, nail polish and a small bottle of perfume.

All in all she'd only spent just over three hundred dollars, which she considered very reasonable. Really, you didn't have to spend a lot on clothes these days, and it was about time she made more of an effort with her appearance. With today promising to be warmer than yesterday, she selected the white jeans and a short-sleeved silky top that had a white background and little brown dots all over it. The slinky fabric hugged her curves and the scooped neckline was perfect for her new dainty gold chain.

A glance at the digital clock beside the bed made Abby

sigh. Only nine o'clock, excitement having got her up at the crack of dawn. She had a whole hour before Jake was due to arrive. That was, if he even arrived on time. People didn't seem to care about punctuality these days. She supposed it would take her a while to do her nails, but not an hour.

As the minutes ticked slowly away she became aware of her heart beating faster behind her ribs. Beside the excitement of a new car, she was nervous at the thought of being with Jake outside of a work environment. Would he think she looked pretty in her new clothes? Did she want him to think her pretty? Did she want him to...what?

Abby knew she was being foolish. He had a girlfriend. A gorgeous girlfriend. Why would he look at her twice? Why would she even want him to?

He's your boss, she reminded herself firmly. *And he's only doing all this because his uncle asked him to. He doesn't want to spend time with you. He doesn't want to buy you a new car or take you to a cemetery. Not really. He's honouring his beloved uncle's deathbed wishes. Get a grip, girl.*

The sight of a bright red sports car careering down her street was not a sight designed to make a girl get a grip.

Abby wasn't surprised when the sleek red car with the prancing horse logo on it slid into the kerb outside her house. For who else would drive a Ferrari but a man who'd been voted not only the most popular television personality but also Sydney's most eligible bachelor?

Megan kept her well informed about all aspects of her boss's professional and private life.

'Oh, *my*,' Abby murmured when Jake emerged from the driver's side, looking even sexier than his car, if that were possible. Up till now Abby had only ever seen her boss dressed in a business suit. Today, he was wearing a pair of chinos and a black polo shirt which hugged the contours of his upper body, showing off his naturally broad shoulders and nicely flat stomach. As he strode around the low-slung bonnet of the car, a lock of his dark brown hair fell across his forehead. Jake lifted his hand and impatiently combed it back with his fingers. The action brought Abby's attention to his face. It wasn't the face of a pretty boy but very handsome all the same, with a strong straight nose and a ruggedly squared jawline. His blue eyes—possibly his best feature—were hidden by a pair of expensive-looking sunglasses.

For a split second, Abby wondered what her neighbours would think when Jake walked up to her front door. It was a lovely spring day so quite a few of them were out in their gardens, mowing lawns and tending to their flowerbeds. Not that they would recognise him. He could be anyone in those glasses. Anyone handsome and very rich, that was.

Abby took a backwards step from the window when Jake stopped on the pavement to stare at her house, her hackles rising as he continued to stare at it for some time. What was he staring at? she wondered.

Abby wasn't in any way ashamed of her home. Okay, so it was small and old, built not long after the war. But it was nicely painted and neat, with well kept gardens, front and back. Inside, each of the rooms was equally well painted, the wooden floors shiny and polished. The furniture *was* on the cheap side but it had been bought new and looked quite stylish, like the clothes she was wearing.

He finally opened the gate and strode up the path to the small front porch, Abby using those few precious seconds to get a handle on her suddenly defensive mood.

It wasn't like her to be sensitive about criticism; it was a survival habit she'd acquired over her school years when her supposed friends had made bitchy comments about her teeth. But Abby suspected she would be very hurt if Jake made her feel small, especially today when she felt so good about herself. Hopefully, he wouldn't. He didn't seem an unkind person. But then, she didn't really know him all that well, did she?

The doorbell ringing made her heart jump, then race like mad. Lord, but she was getting herself into a right state. Gathering herself, Abby hurried to the front door, her head held high.

CHAPTER TEN

JAKE THOUGHT HE'D steeled himself sufficiently by the time he'd rung the doorbell, having given himself a firm lecture during the drive over. He'd told himself in no uncertain terms that he had to stop fantasising about what Abby might be like in bed and concentrate on the job his uncle had entrusted him with.

Craig certainly hadn't included seduction in his dying wishes.

Even after he'd arrived, Jake had lingered outside for another minute or so, harnessing all his willpower for the mental and physical battle he had ahead of him.

Jake thought he was well prepared until Abby opened the door.

His startled gaze raked over her from top to toe before returning to her face. He'd found her attractive before. Today she looked downright stunning, and so desirable it was criminal.

Thank goodness he was wearing sunglasses, the kind you couldn't see through.

What to say? Nothing personal. Nothing too complimentary. She might think he was coming on to her.

'Don't you look nice,' he said.

If only she hadn't smiled at him. Such a beautiful smile.

'I went on a bit of a shopping splurge last night,' she said a little sheepishly. 'I hope Craig would approve. I didn't spend too much.'

'I'm sure he wouldn't mind,' Jake said. But *he* did. That outfit she had on was extremely sexy, those tight white jeans contrasting with the silky top which skimmed her hips and left her full breasts oh, so accessible. In his mind's eye, Jake immediately saw himself pressed up behind her, their lower halves glued together whilst his hands slid up underneath, cupping her breasts. In his fantasy she moaned softly, her head tipping back against his shoulder. She moaned again when he unclipped her bra and took her erect nipples between his thumbs and forefingers and squeezed them.

Hard.

It was impossible to think such wickedly erotic thoughts and not have his body respond. Alarmed that Abby might notice, Jake did the only thing he could think of.

'Would you mind if I used your bathroom before we get going?' he asked with some urgency.

'It's the second door on the right,' Abby directed him.

Abby smiled as she watched Jake head for the bathroom, thrilled to pieces with his compliment on her appearance. And whilst she was flattered and pleased—she was a female after all—she was quite confident that Jake was not about to pounce on her the way Megan had said he might. She'd sent her sister pictures of her new clothes last night, and been subjected to renewed warnings over the male species and their lack of conscience and morals where pretty girls were concerned.

'Playboys like your Jake are the worst,' Megan had pointed out. 'They think they can't be resisted and, unfortunately, that's often true. Hard to resist a good-looking man with charm and money.'

When Abby argued that she'd never found Jake all that charming, Megan had just laughed.

'That's because you haven't been a target before. Once he gets a look at you in your new things he'll go into charm mode in no time flat. First will come the compliments, then the accidental touches, followed by flirtatious remarks, finishing up with a drinks or dinner invitation. You mark my words, kiddo.'

At this point, Abby had decided not to tell Megan that

she would be the one extending a dinner invitation. As a thank you gesture. Truly, sometimes it was best not to tell Megan things.

Still, she had to confess that she'd got a real buzz when he'd said how nice she looked.

Whilst Jake was in the bathroom, Abby collected her new bag from the lounge, then picked up the house keys from the hall table so she'd be ready to lock up when Jake was finished. She understood that he didn't want to waste the whole of his precious Saturday with her when he could be with his girlfriend. His attitude to this whole business had been one of impatience from the start.

Jake took his time, however, Abby's gaze travelling back to his car whilst she waited.

Now that was another thing she'd definitely not be telling Megan. Abby hadn't known till today what kind of car Jake drove so she would invent a nice safe sedan, if need be. She could just imagine what Megan would say if she found out her sister had spent Saturday afternoon swanning around in Jake's sexy red Ferrari.

By the time Jake left the bathroom he'd gathered himself, ready to face his tormentor with his body almost under control and his sunglasses firmly in place.

Jake wondered again what was making her so irresistible to him. Was it her relative innocence? Her lack of experience?

It wasn't just her beauty. He'd had lots of beautiful women in his life, and in his bed. No, it was something else. Something intangible. Something very sweet and very special.

It made him afraid for her.

He'd been right to be fearful, he decided as he watched Abby turn to lock up, her rear view as tasty as her front. He suppressed a groan and willed his own body to behave.

It ignored him and Jake swore at himself in his head.

'How long will it take to get to the cemetery?' she asked innocently as she turned back to face him.

'Not long,' he said a bit abruptly. 'I've also already contacted the dealership in Parramatta,' he went on, masking his inner torment behind his best businesslike voice. 'I spoke to a salesman there at length yesterday and they have a car on their lot which should suit you admirably. If you like it, you could drive it away today. It's all registered and ready to go.'

'Really?' She sounded pleased. 'What colour is it?'

'White. Sorry. No blue ones available. But really, it's the most sensible colour for our climate and city. Never gets too hot or looks too dirty.'

She laughed, bringing a sparkle to her eyes and some added colour to her cheeks. She was making things awfully hard for him.

And wasn't that an understatement? came the wry thought. Thank goodness he wasn't wearing tight jeans.

'I can't imagine me ever letting any car of mine get too dirty,' she said, 'especially a new one. Megan calls me a neat freak.'

'A good quality in a housekeeper,' he said through gritted teeth. And in a lover, came the pesky thought.

Jake liked his women well groomed. All over. Liked their clothes to be just so, especially their underwear. When he started wondering what Abby had on underneath that top and jeans he knew it was time to get this show on the road. 'Come on, let's get going.'

Quite automatically, he went to reach out and take her elbow, a habit he had when escorting a woman. He pulled his hand back just in time, instead waving her on ahead of him.

Damn, he thought wearily as he trudged after her. It was going to be a long morning.

CHAPTER ELEVEN

A VERY HAPPY Abby was striding along her front path towards the gate when Harriet, her elderly neighbour, suddenly popped her head up over the hedge which separated their two houses.

'Hello, dear,' she said. 'My, but don't you look extra nice today. Going somewhere special?' Her curious eyes zoomed from Abby to Jake to the Ferrari then back to Abby again.

Abby suppressed a sigh as she reluctantly ground to a halt and turned towards her neighbour. 'Just going car shopping,' she replied truthfully. 'Got a windfall from a long-lost uncle. My friend here's going to help me find the right one,' she said, casting a rueful glance over her shoulder at Jake. 'He's a car nut, as you can see. Can't stop and chat,' she hurried on, not wanting to have to get into awkward introductions.

'We're already running late,' she added, and headed for the Ferrari. 'Bye.'

'Drop in for a cuppa tomorrow,' Harriet called after her.

'Will do,' she called back.

Jake didn't say a word as he swiftly opened the passenger door for her. Neither did he help her, despite it not being the easiest car to get into. But Abby had always been an agile sort of girl, with long slender legs and sure hands, so by the time Jake closed the door and walked around to the driver's side she was all buckled up and ready to go, her new handbag settled in her lap.

'A car nut, am I?' Jake said wryly after he climbed in and gunned the engine.

Abby shrugged. 'I had to say something.'

'Will you really go in for a cuppa tomorrow?' he asked as he accelerated away.

'Probably,' Abby admitted. 'Harriet was very good to me when Wayne died. I wouldn't hurt her for the world. I just didn't want to have to introduce you.'

'Why's that?'

'Well, mostly because I don't want her to find out that you're the businessman I clean house for. She'd immediately think that there was something going on between us and, before I knew it, the whole street would think the same thing, which would be very embarrassing. Gosh, but this car is amazing,' she rattled on, happy to change the subject from their hypothetical affair. 'It must have cost you a small fortune.'

'There are more expensive cars but it wasn't cheap. I only drive it at weekends and when I'm on holiday.'

'It's not a convertible though, is it?'

'Actually, it is. The top retracts.'

'That's incredible!'

He said nothing for a few seconds, though he did glance over at her with a bit of a frown. But then he smiled a strange little smile as though he was secretly amused about something.

'I'll show you, if you like,' he said.

His offer startled her. 'Oh, no. No, please don't. Not today. My hair will get all messed up and it took me ages to do it.'

'Fair enough. Some other time then.' And he smiled another strange smile.

Abby could not envisage there would ever be such a time, which was a shame really. It would be wonderful whizzing along an open country road on a fine summer's day with the top down and her hair blowing in the breeze. Even better if she were driving.

She almost laughed. Imagine her driving a Ferrari. She wasn't a Ferrari kind of girl.

Jake was right. The cemetery wasn't far away but it was a depressing place. Abby didn't like the long rows of gravestones.

She hadn't buried Wayne. He'd been cremated with his ashes sprinkled in the ocean at his favourite fishing spot. Which was ironic given it was the sea which had killed him. But it was what he had once told her he wanted, if anything ever happened to him. Perhaps, however, he'd imagined being killed in a car accident, not what had actually happened.

'This way,' Jake said after they both climbed out. He set off at a brisk walk, not looking back to see if she was behind him. Which was so typical of her boss.

No charm yet, Megan, she said silently to her sister. One little compliment was as much as he could manage.

Abby followed Jake down a long row of well tended graves, some of which had fresh flowers in vases on them. She hadn't thought to bring flowers, her mind being on nothing but looking her very best this morning, a realisation which upset her a little. Stupid, Abby. Get your priorities straight!

Still, Jake might have thought it was overdoing things if she'd brought flowers.

He stopped suddenly in front of a freshly dug grave which was covered with a large green felt blanket topped with a huge arrangement of native flowers which didn't look at all bedraggled, although they had to have been there over a week.

'That's Craig's grave,' he pointed out, his rough voice betraying a depth of emotion which moved Abby.

Clearly, he had loved his uncle. A lot. Craig's death must have upset Jake terribly, his grief heightened by not having been able to be with the man when he'd died. It had been a cruel thing for his uncle to do. He'd probably thought he was being kind, and brave. But it had been selfish of him, really. Selfish and insensitive.

Abby opened her mouth to say something sympathetic, but when she looked up at Jake she found him staring down, not at his uncle's grave but at the grave on the left of it. The name on the gravestone was Clive Sanderson, beloved husband of Grace, much loved father of Roland, Peter, Jake, Sophie, Cleo and Fiona.

It didn't take a genius to realise this had to be Jake's father, the dates revealing he'd died at the age of forty-seven. How sad. What to say?

Nothing, Abby decided. She understood enough about her boss to know that he wouldn't want to talk about it. So she returned her attention to Craig's grave, closed her eyes and said a prayer of thanks to him, at the same time adding that he really should have told his family that he was dying.

But it was too late to change anything now, she accepted. Death was very final. It took no prisoners, as the saying went. When Abby felt tears prick at her eyes she blinked them away then looked over at Jake.

'I've said my thanks,' she said matter-of-factly. 'I think I'd like to go now.'

'Good,' he said, and stalked off in the direction of the car, not saying another word till they were both back in their seats. Only then did he speak.

'I'm sorry,' he apologised. 'I still can't get over his death.'

'Your uncle's, or your father's?' she asked gently.

'Ah. You saw.' He loosened his grip on the wheel and turned to face her. 'Both really. But Craig's is still very raw.'

'It gets easier with time,' was all she could offer. Though, down deep, Abby knew some deaths stayed with you for ever.

He sighed, leant back against the car seat, took off his sunglasses then glanced over at her. 'How did your husband die, Abby?'

'He drowned,' came her rather stark reply. But there was little point in not telling him the truth. 'He went out fishing in a small dinghy not suitable for the open sea. A storm came up and he was tipped into the water. He wasn't wearing a life belt. His body was washed up on Maroubra Beach a couple of days later.'

'You must have been devastated,' he said quietly, his eyes sad for her.

'I was.'

He nodded at the obvious sincerity in her statement. 'You are a lovely young woman,' he went on with a sigh. 'You'll find someone else eventually, get married again and have lots of equally lovely children.'

She laughed. She couldn't help it. 'I don't think so, Jake. I don't want to get married again.'

'You loved him that much?'

It was one thing to tell her boss the brutal truth about Wayne's death, but everything else was her own private business. She would not share it with him.

'It's not a question of love, Jake, but what I want to do with the rest of my life. I thought I wanted marriage and children when I was younger, but my priorities have changed. I want to travel whilst I'm still young. I want to see another side of life than just what's here in Australia. I want to see the world.'

He looked over at her for a long time. 'I see,' he said at last.

Probably not, she thought.

'We'd better get going again,' he went on gruffly. 'We have a car to buy.'

CHAPTER TWELVE

'OH, JAKE, I simply adore it!' Abby exclaimed when she climbed in behind the wheel of the sporty white hatchback. 'Thank you so much.'

Jake just smiled and let the salesman, Raoul, continue showing Abby all the features of her new car. After he'd run through everything, Raoul suggested Abby take it for a test spin round the block. Jake declined her invitation to accompany her, which in hindsight was not a good move, since Raoul was only too happy to go in his place. The salesman was about Abby's age, an immigrant from South America, tall, dark and handsome with a sexy accent and charm by the bucketload. Jake wished within seconds of them disappearing down the street that he'd gone with Abby.

He was damned if he did and damned if he didn't! When she'd confessed her wish to spurn marriage and see the world, he'd been momentarily overcome with joy that now he could seduce her and not feel guilty about it. But Jake knew in his heart of hearts that a girl like Abby would want marriage and children again one day. And then there was the unpalatable added fact that whilst she was grateful to him, she clearly wasn't at all enamoured with his character.

Was it too late to turn on the charm?

He rather suspected that it was.

Jake paced the car lot until Abby returned, doing his best to calm down whilst inside he was churning with regret and, yes, jealousy, an emotion he despised. But it was no use. He was jealous. As soon as the white hatchback turned into the driveway he strode towards it, anxiously searching for evidence that the couple inside were in any way attracted to each other.

Raoul, it seemed, was doing all the talking whilst Abby was just nodding. When Abby climbed out and smiled over at *him*, Jake was so relieved that he smiled back.

'So how was it?' he asked as she walked towards him.

'Brilliant!' she exclaimed. 'And so easy to drive.'

'It certainly is,' Raoul said on joining them. 'But then, you are also a very good driver, Abby.'

She smiled over at him.

Jake's gut tightened. He didn't want her smiling at other men, especially this one. What was the point in controlling his own desire for the girl if she fell into the clutches of some slick-talking salesman?

Jake decided it was time to go.

'You're happy with that particular car then, Abby?' he directed at her.

'Oh, yes. Very happy.'

'Then we'll take it,' he told Raoul. 'I presume I can pay for it with my credit card.'

'But of course, Mr Sanderson. Come with me into my office and I'll fix up everything for you.'

'Lucky you,' Raoul said when he finally handed over the registration papers and keys, 'to have such a generous employer as Mr Sanderson.'

'He's a wonderful boss,' Abby agreed.

Jake winced inside. He'd explained to Raoul on the phone yesterday that Abby was a valued employee of his and the car was her Christmas bonus. Jake had informed Abby of his little white lie just before they'd arrived at the dealership, but he'd forgotten that the male mind often thought the worst when it came to an attractive female. Clearly, Raoul had jumped to the conclusion that Abby was getting this car as payment for services rendered outside work hours. Fortunately, Abby didn't seem aware of this. He just hoped that he could get her out of here before she twigged to the situation.

'Thank you for your assistance,' Jake said, standing up and extending his hand over the desk.

The salesman stood up and took his hand. 'My pleasure, Mr Sanderson,' he returned in a rather unctuous manner.

'Now, if you have any trouble, Abby,' Raoul went on, smiling over at Abby, who had also risen to her feet, 'any trouble at all, you just ring me. Here's my card.'

Abby took it, of course. Which irked Jake considerably. Couldn't she see he just wanted to get into her pants? Surely she wasn't *that* naïve?

'If you have any trouble with your car, Abby,' Jake bit out as he walked her over to it, 'you ring me first, not that sleazebag.'

Abby lifted startled eyes to his. 'You think Raoul's a sleazebag?'

'Yes, I do.'

Takes one to know one, Jake, came the brutally honest thought.

Abby's face fell. 'And there I was, thinking he was just being extra nice. Because of you being famous, you know?'

Jake could see he'd upset her, which was the last thing he'd wanted to do. He'd loved seeing her so happy about the car.

'You could be right,' he said. 'Take no notice of me, Abby. I'm a cynical bastard at times.'

Abby frowned. 'No, you're probably right. Megan says I'm too trusting where men are concerned.' She glanced up at him and smiled. 'But I know a truly good one when I meet him. Which reminds me. I want to do something special for you, Jake, to thank you for everything.'

Jake tried not to let his mind trail over all the things he'd like her to do for him. But it went there all the same. She'd called him 'truly good', but he wasn't. Not at all.

He swallowed before he spoke, lest a thickened voice betray him. 'You don't have to do anything, Abby. It was my pleasure to follow through with Craig's wishes. He obviously liked and admired you a lot.'

She flushed prettily. 'Not as much as he liked and admired you. Look, I thought that perhaps I could cook you dinner one night. I know that's not much in the way of a thank you present, but I'm actually a very good cook.'

'I'm sure you are, Abby, but truly, it's not necessary.'

Her face fell again, which made him feel dreadful. After all, she didn't know the battle that was going on inside him. It was obvious she wanted to do this. A thought suddenly occurred which would hopefully save his sanity.

'Very well,' he agreed. 'Dinner it is. But not just for me,' he added. 'For my sister as well.'

Abby blinked her confusion. 'Your sister?'

'Yeah, my sister, Sophie. I promised to take her out to dinner next Friday night. She's the only one in my family who knows about Craig's letter and she was saying the other day that she'd love to meet you. We could kill two birds with one stone. What do you say, Abby? Would you mind cooking for her as well?'

'I wouldn't mind at all. But maybe your sister would mind.'

'Good heavens, no. She'd love it.'

'Well, if you're sure…'

'I'm very sure.'

'Your place or mine?'

Jake almost choked on the spot. 'What?'

'Do you want me to cook the dinner at my place or yours?'

What *had* he been thinking? About sex, of course. What else?

'I don't mind either way, Abby, but then I don't have a problem with neighbours. Perhaps we should have this dinner at my place?'

'Yes, I think that would be best.'

He looked at her and thought none of this was for the best. But Sophie's presence would at least stop him from doing something stupid—like piling on the charm and plying Abby with wine before carrying her up to bed and having his wicked way with her all night long.

'I presume you'll be okay to drive home alone in your new car,' he said. 'You won't be nervous, will you?'

'Maybe a little. But only because it's new. I really am a good driver. And the car has GPS. Even if it didn't, I know the roads around here like the back of my hand. I used to live out this way. The fish and chip shop I worked in for years is just around the corner.'

Jake was suddenly overwhelmed with curiosity about her life before coming to work for him, especially about her marriage and, yes, her drowned husband. The temptation to invite her to go for coffee with him somewhere was acute, but he resisted it.

Just.

'In that case I won't worry about you,' he said instead. 'Off you go then.'

Abby sighed. 'What a shame. I would have *loved* another ride in that gorgeous car of yours.'

Don't say a single word, his conscience insisted firmly.

Suddenly, Abby beamed up at him. 'But I'm going to enjoy driving my own gorgeous little car even more. Bye, Jake. And thanks again.'

'My pleasure,' he returned. And, despite everything else, it had been. How perverse was that?

He shook his head as he watched her drive off with surprising confidence, not hesitating before joining the traffic and changing lanes quite assertively. Naïve and vulnerable Abby might be in some ways, but in practical life skills she seemed experienced and assured.

Once again, he wondered about her life before she'd been widowed, and even before that. What kind of child had she been? What were her parents like? Had she been good at school? Possibly not, if she'd ended up working in a fish and chip shop. But she certainly wasn't dumb. When Raoul had been showing her all the features of the car, she'd been very quick on the uptake. She also claimed to be a good cook and Jake came to the conclusion that Abby would be good at anything she set her mind to.

Inevitably, his own mind shifted to other areas at which Abby might excel. She'd been married for quite a few years, after all. And she hadn't gone to work during all that time. Clearly, she'd been content to stay home and be the kind of old-fashioned housewife a lot of men craved, always being there when hubby came home. He could see her now, waiting on the man she loved hand and foot, giving him everything he desired, in bed and out. As much as Jake didn't want that kind of life—or wife—for himself, he could see its appeal. He could see Abby's appeal. He could feel it, right now. He didn't want to marry her, but he did want her.

'Damn and blast,' Jake growled to himself as he marched off to where he'd parked his own car. He virtually threw himself behind the wheel, slamming it with both fists in a burst of frustration unlike any he'd ever felt before.

When he eventually calmed down, he just sat there, thinking.

Jake decided he should never have broken up with Olivia. He wasn't the sort of man who liked to sleep alone for too long. And she would be a good distraction from Abby. But there was no going back now. And if he was honest he didn't really want to.

Maybe he should give Maddie Hanks a call. She was still in Sydney, he knew. Okay, so her charms were rather obvious but, on the plus side, she wasn't interested in becoming Mrs Jake Sanderson. She just wanted some fun and games whilst she was here. A man would have to be a fool to knock that back, especially one who was climbing the walls with frustration. She'd given him her number after the show and he'd politely put it in his phone, even though at the time he'd had no intention of acting on her none too subtle invitation.

But lots of water had gone under the bridge since then.

Jake pulled out his phone and brought up her number, his lips pursing as his finger hovered. Did he really want to go to bed with someone like that?

Jake could not believe it when he abruptly deleted Maddie Hanks's number and rang his sister instead.

Sophie answered quickly. 'Hi, Jake, darling. How are you bearing up? You know, I watched you yesterday on that silly show you do, and I thought you looked a bit down.'

'What do you mean, calling my show silly?'

'Perhaps silly is not the right word. Lightweight, then.'

'Still, hardly a compliment.' But she was right. It was lightweight. No wonder he was bored. He'd meant it to be a hard-hitting current affairs show when he'd conceived it, but it hadn't turned out that way.

'If the cap fits, wear it, Jake. Now, to what do I owe the pleasure of this call? You're not going to call off our dinner date next Friday, are you?'

'Not at all. But I have a favour to ask you…'

And he told her everything.

CHAPTER THIRTEEN

ABBY FELT SATISFIED as she surveyed the dinner table in Jake's formal dining room. She had copied the exquisite setting from one of her sister's magazines, having known straight away it would suit the polished wooden floors and white walls of Jake's dining room. She'd used Jake's cutlery and glassware, but she'd bought the snow-white tablecloth and white napkins, along with the red and black table mats and matching coasters from the magazine, which Abby had found in a city store.

Since Jake's dining table could seat eight she'd only set one end of it, with Jake at the head, his sister to his right and herself to his left. That way she was nearer the door and the kitchen. Abby had also bought a crystal candlestick as a centrepiece, which held one red candle. A vase of fresh flowers from her own garden sat on the carved wooden sideboard, along with a vanilla-scented candle which she hoped would mask any smell which might waft from the kitchen once she started cooking the prawns and scallops.

It had taken ages for Abby to settle on a menu for the dinner party. She didn't want to be dashing in and out to the kitchen all the time but, having been reassured by Jake over the phone that neither he nor Sophie were fussy eaters, she'd chosen a seafood platter entrée, rack of lamb for the main and a passionfruit-topped cheesecake which she'd cooked in advance and which she knew from experience tasted better after spending a day in the fridge. The various wines had come courtesy of recommendations from the man who owned her local wine shop.

A quick glance at her watch warned her that she only had twelve minutes before Jake and Sophie were due to arrive. Abby had told Jake over the phone that she didn't want him around whilst she was cooking, which hadn't seemed to bother him. Jake had said he'd go to his sister's place after work and they would drive to Balmain together.

Abby had had another reason for wanting Jake to be absent during her preparations for the evening. She'd wanted to surprise him with the table setting, not to mention the fact she was actually wearing a dress. When Jake had let slip that his sister was a professional stylist, Abby had gone shopping again, knowing instinctively that jeans were not the right sort of thing to wear for the dinner.

She did feel some guilt that she'd gone and bought some more clothes, but there was no denying the pleasure she got every time she looked at herself in the large mirror in Jake's hallway, which was what she was doing at this very moment, staring at herself and hoping Jake would like what he saw.

In one way, Abby wished it was just the two of them tonight. Though, really, that was all so much pie in the sky, hoping that he would suddenly fancy her the way Megan said he would. Abby knew how men acted when they fancied a woman and it certainly wasn't to organise a third person to be present when they could easily have been alone. On top of that, she wasn't at her best making conversation with strangers. And Jake's sister was a stranger.

No sooner had this wimpy thought entered Abby's head than it was banished.

'No more negative thoughts!' came her firm lecture as she stared at her reflection in the mirror and put on an assertive face. 'So you're a bit nervous about meeting Sophie. That's only natural. She's a professional stylist—a sophisticated career woman who's no doubt as good-looking as her brother. But you'll be fine. You look darned good yourself. And you're no dumb blonde. You're smart. You know you are. Jake's uncle thought so too.'

Whirling on her new high heels, Abby marched back into the kitchen determined to be more confident.

'You're not very talkative,' Sophie said after she parked her car outside Jake's place right on seven. 'If I didn't know you better, I'd think you were nervous.'

'Don't be ridiculous,' Jake snapped. 'I don't get nervous.' Which was true. He was, however, apprehensive about the evening ahead.

Despite having physically avoided Abby during the week, they'd talked a couple of times over the phone. Nothing personal, just Abby asking him about what foods he and his sister liked. But even her voice did wicked things to him. How was he going to cope with the real thing tonight? During one phone call he'd been so turned on, he'd been seriously tempted to tell her Sophie couldn't make it and it would just be the two of them.

If only Abby wasn't so darned sweet he might have done exactly that.

'Then what *is* your problem?' Sophie persisted as they walked up to the front door together. 'The girl said she didn't want to get married again. What's to stop you from dating her, if that's what you want?'

Jake threw his sister a convincingly exasperated look. 'Come on, sis. Abby only *thinks* she doesn't want marriage and children, but she'll change her mind about that eventually. Besides,' he added, 'she doesn't fancy me.'

Sophie laughed. 'Not only nervous but delusional. You've got it so bad your brain is addled. Of *course* she fancies you. That's why she offered to cook you dinner, you fool. You're not very good at reading between the lines, are you? And I thought you were a smart guy where women were concerned.'

'You don't understand,' Jake muttered as he inserted his key in the front door. 'I'm trying to do the right thing here.'

'Mmm… The road to hell is paved with good intentions, you know.'

'Yeah, I know. I'm already there.' And he pushed open the door.

'Something smells nice,' Sophie said on entering the hallway. 'Oh, look, it's a scented candle,' she added after peeking into the dining room. 'My, doesn't the table look lovely. Your Abby's gone to a *lot* of trouble.'

Jake heard the innuendo in Sophie's voice. 'Please don't start reading anything into this evening's dinner, sister dear. Abby has no romantic feelings for me whatsoever. She's just a very nice woman. This is gratitude, not lust.' *He* was the one in lust.

'Abby, we're here!' he called out as he took Sophie's arm and steered her down the hallway into the kitchen.

'My goodness!' he exclaimed. 'You're wearing a dress.' Or almost wearing one. His eyes clamped onto her cleavage and didn't budge.

Sophie winced at Jake's tone. Heavens, he made it sound as if wearing a dress was a crime.

Sophie watched the dismay on the girl's face quickly change to defiance.

'I am indeed,' she said as she came closer and twirled around for him to see her better.

Sophie tried not to smile at the look on her brother's face. Truly, the poor idiot was more than just smitten. If she didn't know him better, she might have thought he'd fallen in love. And she could see why.

Abby was one seriously attractive girl, with a delicately featured face with lovely greenish eyes, perfect skin and the most dazzling smile. There was nothing wrong with her figure either, which was most eye-catching, its hourglass shape shown to advantage in a floral wrap-around dress, the bodice crossing over her bust before tying into a bow on her left hip.

Of course, if Sophie had dressed her, she would have

chosen a block colour rather than floral, and the V neckline would have been much lower. Why have great boobs if you didn't flaunt them, especially when you were young?

But all that was beside the point. The point at this precise moment was the way her brother was acting. Which was totally unacceptable.

Sophie decided to step in and smooth things over till Jake could get control of his hormones.

'I'm Sophie,' she introduced herself brightly, coming forward to give Abby a brief hug and a kiss on the cheek. 'That's a fab dress you're wearing. You'll have to tell me where you bought it. Did Jake mention that I'm in the fashion industry?'

Abby knew she would never give Sophie *that* information. The little black dress Jake's sister had on screamed luxury designer whereas Abby's dress had been cheap as. But Sophie's kind compliments did make her feel better in the face of Jake's obvious disapproval. She did, however, feel somewhat comforted by the fact that Sophie wasn't drop dead gorgeous like her brother.

'Jake,' Sophie said sharply, 'stop glaring at Abby and tell her how lovely she looks.'

'She looks very nice,' he bit out. 'It was just a shock, that's all. I've never seen her in a dress before. How's the food going, Abby? I'm so hungry I could eat a horse.'

CHAPTER FOURTEEN

ABBY CONTROLLED HER temper with difficulty. 'Sorry. Horse isn't on the menu for tonight. You'll have to make do with lamb. Now, if you'd like to follow me into the dining room, I'll show you where you're both sitting.'

Jake winced when she swept past him with a hurt look cast his way. He knew he was behaving badly but he couldn't seem to find that much vaunted charm he was famous for. His social skills had completely deserted him in the face of a sexual attraction which was as cruel as it was powerful. Thank heavens he'd put his suit jacket back on before leaving Sophie's place. And thank heavens he would soon be sitting down.

Sophie came to his rescue, saying all the right things about the table setting, plus Abby's choice of wine. Jake finally opened his mouth to agree with his sister about the wine, which brought another cool look from Abby.

He fancied her even more when she was like this!

Jake tried not to stare when she poured Sophie some wine, but the action required her to bend forward, making the neckline of her dress gape a little. When she moved around to pour his wine, he kept his eyes firmly on the tablecloth. He knew his *thank you* sounded forced. He didn't want to thank her. He wanted to have sex with her, right here, on this table.

Jake sighed with relief when she left the room to cook the entree. Picking up his wine, he downed half the glass; he needed to do something to calm the storm raging within him, because if he didn't he might do something he'd bitterly regret in the morning.

'You've really got it bad, haven't you?' Sophie said quietly. 'You implied as much over the phone but seeing it is worth a thousand words.'

Jake glanced over at his sister, who was studying him over the rim of her glass with an intuitive gaze.

'I'll survive,' he returned before swallowing another large gulp of wine.

Sophie smiled knowingly. 'We'll see, Jake. Like I said before, your Abby's gone to a lot of trouble tonight.'

'She's not my Abby. She's still in love with her dead husband.'

'Maybe. But he's dead, Jake. And you're one handsome man.'

Jake sighed. 'Could we stop this conversation right now, please?'

Sophie did stop, but only because Abby entered the dining room carrying with her two plates which exuded the most delicious smell. When she placed his in front of him, Jake saw that it contained a mixture of prawns and scallops over which had been drizzled the source of that tantalising aroma.

'If this tastes as good as it looks,' he said, unable to restrain his admiration for her cooking, 'then we're in for an amazing treat.'

When Jake looked up and saw Abby's delighted face he was consumed with guilt over his earlier bad manners. He hadn't meant to hurt her.

'And, for what it's worth at this late stage,' he added, 'I think that dress you're wearing is stunning. If you ever wear it outside of this house, you'll be fighting the men off with sticks.'

CHAPTER FIFTEEN

ABBY SHOULD HAVE been thrilled with this last compliment. But she wasn't. And the reason was mortifying. Because it was *him* she wanted the chance to fight off, not other men.

Not that she would fight Jake off. Abby knew if he ever made the slightest pass at her, she would be a goner. But he wasn't about to do that, was he? For pity's sake, when was she going to get it through her silly female head that he was just her boss, plus the rather reluctant trustee of his uncle's dying wishes?

If she was brutally honest, it had always been painfully obvious that Jake hadn't wanted to do any of it. Not the car or the money. Or taking her to the grave. But he had, out of a sense of duty, and decency. She meant nothing to him on a personal basis. She was just the person who looked after his house who'd been lucky enough to score a generous legacy from his very kind and thoughtful uncle.

The hurt this realisation brought was very telling, reminding Abby of the various warnings Megan had given her about Jake. But Megan had been wrong. It wasn't Jake she had to worry about but her own silly self. Somewhere along the line she'd started caring about what he thought of her. Started caring for *him*. Which was a total waste of time.

It annoyed Abby that she'd turned into some kind of infatuated fool who fantasised about a man who was way out of her league. As a teenager she'd never had crushes on movie stars or rock stars, and she wasn't about to start now with a television star.

'I'll go get my entree,' she said, and hurried from the room, returning to find that her two guests had waited for her.

The dish was a success, as was the main course, judging by the many compliments she received, plus the evidence of empty plates. Hers weren't quite so empty, her appetite deserting her, as it did when she was emotionally upset over something. She tried not to look at Jake too much or too often, lest he see her feelings for him in her eyes. In the main, she looked at and talked to Sophie, who was quite the conversationalist, one of those women who liked to ask questions, mostly about Abby's likes and dislikes where fashion was concerned. During dessert, however, their conversation turned more personal.

'Jake told me about your husband's death,' Sophie said. 'How tragic for you. He must have been quite young. After all, you're only—what? Mid-twenties?'

'I'm twenty-seven. And, yes, Wayne was only twenty-five when he died. We were the same age.'

'How dreadful for you. And how long had you been married at the time?'

'Four years.'

Sophie's eyebrows arched. 'But no children?'

It was a question which used to cause Abby unbearable pain. It still hurt, but she'd grown to accept that she would never become a mother.

'We were trying,' she said. 'But it just didn't happen.' No way was she going to talk about her three miscarriages. That was way too private. And, yes, way too painful.

'Perhaps it was all for the best,' Sophie said, 'under the circumstances.'

'Perhaps,' Abby choked out.

Jake frowned, having picked up on the raw emotion vibrating in Abby's reply. He recalled he'd said something similar when he'd interviewed her. Suddenly, he saw that it was a tactless remark. He tried to catch Sophie's eye, but she was oblivious to his attempt to put a stop to her queries.

'So, Abby, Jake tells me you want to travel,' his sister continued in her usual blunt fashion.

'Yes. I do.'

'Alone? Or with a friend?'

'Sophie, for pity's sake,' Jake jumped in. 'Stop giving Abby the third degree.'

Sophie gave him a mock innocent look. 'I'm just talking. Okay, change of subject. Jake, how about letting me live in Craig's apartment for a while? Or are you going to sell it?'

'No,' Jake replied slowly. 'I'm not going to sell it. Not yet, anyway. Why do you want to stay there?'

Sophie sighed. 'My flatmate wants to move her boyfriend in and I can't stand him.'

'I see. Well, of course you can stay in Craig's place. I'll give you the keys before you leave.'

'I'll pay you rent,' she offered.

'I don't want any rent. Just pay the electricity bill when it comes in. And don't sublet it to anyone else.'

'I won't. I'm like you, Jake. I like my own space. I should never have shared a flat in the first place. I should have bought one. But I'm just too extravagant to save the deposit. All my money goes on clothes,' she directed at Abby. 'And hair,' she added, patting the chic red bob which flattered her square face.

Jake frowned. 'Craig left you enough for a deposit on a flat, I would have thought.'

'Yes, well, I know he did. But I have other plans for that money. Business plans. So, Abby, you do realise that my brother is going to be shattered when you leave him? He thinks you're the most incredible housekeeper. He never stops raving about you.'

'Really?'

'Really.'

'I'm sure he won't have any trouble finding someone else,' she said.

When her head turned his way, Jake had to use all of his willpower to douse the surge of desire which threatened to unravel him. But he was doomed to failure. He could not stop his eyes from dropping to her mouth, her extremely delicious mouth. How he wanted that mouth; how he wanted *her*!

Abby frowned. Why was Jake staring at her mouth like that? Perhaps she had some food on her lips. When she lifted her napkin from her lap to dab at them, he continued to stare, Abby glimpsing something in his glittering blue eyes which shocked her to the core. It was the way Wayne used to look at her when he wanted sex.

But what shocked Abby the most—aside from the fact that this was Jake lusting after her—was the intensity of her own physical response. Instantly her heart began to race, her belly and nipples tightening in a manner which was both perturbing and insidiously exciting. There was another tightening as well, deep inside her.

When an embarrassing heat threatened to turn her face and neck bright red, Abby quickly stood up.

'I'll go and put the coffee on,' she said, and fled the room.

'Well, well…' Sophie murmured. 'Those weren't the actions of a girl who doesn't fancy you. She's got the hots for you almost as much as you have for her.'

Jake didn't say a word, having been rendered speechless. Because if Sophie was right about Abby then nothing would stop him now. Not his conscience, or anything.

But maybe Sophie was wrong. Maybe Abby had seen the lust in his eyes just now and fled the room in panic.

'I have to get going soon,' Sophie said suddenly. 'I have an early start in the morning.'

Jake gave his sister a narrow-eyed look. 'Doing what?'

'Spending two hours in the gym working off the calories I've consumed tonight. Overweight stylists don't get much work, you know. And don't make a fuss. I'm leaving the path clear for you to finish the evening the way you've been living it in your head for hours. Not that I blame you. She's utterly gorgeous. But possibly a bit fragile after her husband's death. So be careful, Jake. Abby's not your usual type.'

'You think I don't know that?' he snapped. 'Why do you think I've been giving her a wide berth?'

Sophie tipped her head on one side. 'You really care about her, don't you?'

Did he? Jake supposed he did, otherwise he wouldn't have controlled himself this long. But the main reason for that control no longer existed and the dogs of desire he'd been trying to rein in had finally been let loose.

'Do me a favour, will you?' he said abruptly.

'Anything, within reason.'

'Go and tell Abby that you don't want coffee because you have to go home. Tell her you suffer from migraines and you can feel one coming on.'

Sophie shook her head at him as she stood up. 'I suppose there's a slim chance she might knock you back. But I doubt it,' she added laughingly, then went to do as he'd asked.

CHAPTER SIXTEEN

BY THE TIME Jake walked into the kitchen after seeing Sophie off, Abby had achieved a measure of control over her wayward body, mostly by busying herself clearing the table and stacking the dishwasher. Unfortunately, as soon as she glanced up at him, things started tipping out of control again.

If only he would stop looking at her like that!

Okay, so Megan had warned her that Jake might fancy her if she dolled herself up. But she hadn't really believed her. Until now.

For a long moment Abby just stood there next to the dishwasher, staring at Jake and thinking that if she let him seduce her—she could see in his eyes that was what he meant to do—she would be thrown into a world she was not equipped to handle. She wasn't like Megan. She'd never slept with a guy just for the sex. She'd never wanted to. That was what worried her the most. How much she wanted to sleep with Jake.

For pity's sake, at least be honest, she castigated herself. You don't want to do any *sleeping* with Jake. You want to have sex with him. But only after you've explored his naked body first, then kissed him all over. You want to do all the things you've read about but never experienced, or even wanted before.

When some shockingly wanton images filled her mind, panic wasn't far behind.

'I... I think I should go home,' she stammered, her cheeks burning with shame.

He shook his head then began walking slowly towards her, closing the dishwasher on the way.

'You can't,' he returned, his voice cool but his eyes still hot. 'You're over the limit.'

He was close now, close enough to reach out and touch her. He softly traced down her nose with one fingertip before slowly encircling her mouth. For a few fraught seconds, Abby held her breath, wide eyes clinging to his, pleading with him not to do this. Or that was what she thought her eyes were doing.

All Jake saw was the dilation of excitement. When her lips finally gasped apart, he smiled. It was a wicked smile, full of satisfaction and arrogance and erotic intent. He meant to have her tonight, and he knew she didn't want to say no.

'Abby, Abby...' he murmured, his voice husky. 'Do you have any idea how much I want you?'

Abby wondered dazedly if he said that to all his women. She had to admit that it was very effective. She shuddered when he pulled her into his arms, squeezing her eyes tightly shut as his head started to descend. The feel of his lips on hers brought a low moan from deep in her throat. When he stopped kissing her, her eyelids fluttered open to find his narrowed eyes scanning hers with concern.

'Tell me you want this too, Abby,' he said. 'Don't go along with me because of gratitude, or because you think you might lose your job if you don't.'

Such thoughts had never entered her head. Nothing much was entering her head at this moment. Nothing but the urgent desire for him to continue. Her lips remained parted as she struggled for breath, her body flushing with a heat which might have been embarrassing if it hadn't been so exciting.

'Tell me you want me to make love to you,' he repeated harshly. '*Say* it.'

Abby swallowed, then licked her lips in an effort to get some moisture into her mouth.

'Yes,' she croaked out.

'Yes, *what*?' he persisted.

'Yes, I… I want you to make love to me.'

He groaned then pulled her even tighter against him, his mouth crashing down on hers with a wild passion which surpassed anything she'd experienced in her marriage. Where Wayne had been gentle and tentative, Jake simply took, invading her mouth with his tongue whilst his hands roved hungrily up and down her spine, one slipping under her hair to capture the back of her neck whilst the other splayed over her bottom. She moaned at the feel of his erection pressing into the soft swell of her stomach, how hard it felt, and her insides contracted in anticipation. She wanted him, not gently, but roughly. Demandingly. She wanted him to fill her. She wanted to come with him inside her.

With a cry of naked need, Abby reefed her mouth from under his, her eyes wide and wild.

'What's wrong?' a stunned Jake asked her.

'Nothing. Everything. Oh, just don't stop, Jake. Please, I… I can't wait.'

Jake didn't need telling twice. He hoisted her up on to the stone counter, ignoring her startled gasp as he reached up under her skirt to remove her panties.

'Lie back,' he commanded as he drew her skirt up and eased her legs apart.

Abby's face flamed with a mad mixture of shame and arousal, sucking in sharply when she felt his hands slide up under her dress to take a firm grasp of her hips, gasping when he slid her forward so that she was right on the edge. She didn't dare look at him, keeping her dilated eyes firmly on the ceiling. But she could feel him, pushing against her hot wet flesh, searching for entry into her oh, so needy body. And then he was there, taking her breath away as yes, he filled her totally. Her head swam when he started up a powerful rhythm, each forward surge of his body bringing her both pleasure and even more frustration. She closed her eyes but nothing could shut out the sounds she started making, moans and pants. Just as she thought she could not bear another moment of such exquisite torment, Abby came, her flesh contracting around his with an electric pleasure that was as stunning as it was violent. Spasm followed spasm, evoking a raw cry from Jake. Then he came too, flooding her for an incredibly long time.

Jake shut his eyes as he wallowed in his glorious release, but it wasn't long before the heat of the moment cooled, and the reality of what he'd just done sunk in, along with the possible consequences.

Jake groaned at his stupidity. After all, the last thing he wanted to be confronted with was an unwanted pregnancy. Which was possible, given he hadn't used a condom.

He really didn't want children, even with a girl like Abby. He enjoyed being free to do as he pleased whenever he pleased. Even one child would put an end to that. Okay, so it was probably selfish of him, but better to be selfish than miserable. He wanted his uncle's lifestyle, not his father's.

When Jake finally opened his eyes, he encountered Abby staring up at him with glazed eyes. Her arms were flopped out wide in the form of a T, her breathing now slow and steady. He did note, however, that her lips remained softly parted as if they were waiting for him to kiss her some more.

He wished he could. But there was no getting away from what he had to do first.

With a sigh he scooped her up and held her close, his face buried into her hair. 'I'm so sorry, Abby,' he murmured with true regret in his voice.

She pulled back a little and blinked up at him. 'For what?'

'I didn't use a condom. But let me assure you,' he raced on when her eyes widened, 'that I'm no risk to you, health-wise. I've always practised safe sex. Till tonight, that is,' he confessed ruefully.

'It's all right, Jake,' she said. 'I can't get pregnant. I'm on the Pill.'

'You are?' He was genuinely surprised. Then relieved. Then curious.

'Don't think I'm not happy about that, but why?' he asked.

She shrugged. 'It gives me control over my body. I don't suffer PMT when I'm on the Pill.'

'So it's not just a birth control thing?'

'No. Though it's as well I am taking it, under the circumstances.'

'I'll say.'

A frown formed on her pretty forehead. 'Can I ask you why you didn't use a condom this time when you say you always practise safe sex?'

Jake didn't want to tell her the truth: that he'd been so crazy with desire for her for so long that stopping to put a condom on would have been impossible, even if he'd thought of it.

He produced a wry little smile as he wrapped her legs around his waist.

'Acute frustration,' he said instead. 'You can blame yourself. You looked so delicious in that dress that I've thought of nothing else but sex all night.'

'Oh…'

Gently, he cupped the back of her head and pulled it down against his chest. His hands stroked up and down her back as they had that day in this very kitchen. But this was hardly the same. Once again, she pulled back and lifted puzzled eyes to his.

'Is…is it always like that for your women?' she asked him.

Jake was somewhat taken aback. What exactly did she mean? Did his lovers always come? Did they come the way she'd just come? Like a woman who hadn't had a climax in years.

'Not always,' he said. 'Not all people click, sexually.'

She nodded at his answer. 'But we do. Click sexually, I mean.'

He smiled again. 'Very much so. We're going to have a great time together.'

'But…what about your girlfriend?' She needed to be sure he wasn't cheating with her.

'I broke up with Olivia some time ago.'

'I see,' she said thoughtfully. 'Yes, I see.'

Jake wasn't sure what she saw. He wasn't all that keen on the way women liked to analyse everything. He didn't want to have a post-mortem of why the sex between them was so good. He wanted to get back to some serious love-making. In bed next time. He just wanted Abby naked in his bed where he could make slow love to her for hours.

He didn't withdraw. He just scooped her up from the breakfast bar, holding her tightly as he headed for the stairs, their fused and very wet flesh reminding Jake once more that he hadn't used a condom. Walking up stairs while still inside her was doing things to him which should have been impossible, given he'd just had the most satisfying climax.

And wow it felt good. *She* felt good. Maybe he'd just forget the condoms for tonight. After all, they'd already done it once. Might as well be hanged for a sheep as a lamb, as they said. From tomorrow he'd go back to being super careful. Tonight, however, he would indulge himself to the full.

CHAPTER SEVENTEEN

ABBY HAD BEEN right about not wanting to actually *sleep* with Jake. She didn't. She couldn't. Every nerve-ending in her body was still electrified. *He'd* finally fallen asleep, however. It wasn't surprising after two hours of almost constant sexual activity. Abby had lost count of how many times she'd come, Jake showing her that a woman's capacity for orgasms far surpassed a man's, especially when said woman was being made love to by a man of his experience. He knew exactly where to touch. What to touch. How to touch.

Abby closed her eyes as she relived all that he'd done to her. First there had been that incredible episode on the kitchen counter. That had been amazing enough. But not as sensational as once they were both naked in bed together. After another incredible orgasm, just when she'd thought she couldn't bear any more, he'd carried her into the shower and revived her under some cool jets of water. After drying her off, he'd carried her back to bed, where some more kissing and caressing had soon had her trembling with desire again. His own flesh had been solidly re-aroused also, the size of him astonishing her at times. But always bringing her the most exquisite pleasure.

Such thinking sent Abby's eyes over to Jake, who was lying face down on the bed, sound asleep. She stared at his back, which had several red tracks where her nails had raked over his skin. She shook her head at the savagery of her passion for Jake. Not to mention her stupidity. What had possessed her to admit she was on the Pill? Her brain knew it was a risk to have sex without a condom, despite his reassurances. But her body hadn't cared. In truth, she would have let him continue even if she *hadn't* been on the

Pill. Which was insane! Just the thought of falling pregnant made her feel ill. She could not go there again. Not now. Not ever. It had hurt too much each time a baby had been wrenched from her body. More so because she'd wanted a child so much. Or she had, back then when she'd been married to Wayne. No way did she want Jake Sanderson's child. He didn't want a child, either. Or did he think he would simply pay her to have an abortion if the Pill failed and she got pregnant? Which it might. The Pill wasn't one hundred per cent safe.

A ghastly thought suddenly crossed her mind, propelling her from the bed. With a groan she hurried into the bathroom, where she wrapped a bath sheet around herself, intent on getting downstairs as quickly as possible to make sure she'd taken her Pill for the evening. Now that she thought about it, she couldn't actually remember taking it. *Oh, God!*

Abby didn't make it past the foot of the bed before Jake stirred.

'Abby?' came his slurred voice.

She froze as his right arm stretched out, feeling for her. Finding the bed empty, he rolled over and sat up.

'Where do you think you're going?' he asked.

'Downstairs,' she answered in an astonishingly calm voice. 'I… I have to check on something.'

He frowned. 'What?'

'I suddenly had this awful feeling I might have forgotten to take my Pill earlier. But if I have, please don't worry. I'll get the morning-after pill. I don't want to have a baby any more than you do. But from now we should use condoms. The Pill I take is a good one but no Pill is one hundred per cent safe.'

He nodded. 'Very true. Okay, from now on, we'll use condoms. After all, we don't want any unfortunate accidents, do we?'

Abby swallowed. 'No,' she said, thinking that surely fate wouldn't be that cruel to her. She always took her Pill around six-thirty. She glanced at the digital clock sitting on her side of the bed. Ten to one.

But she was getting ahead of herself, Abby realised. What she needed to do was get herself downstairs and check.

'I won't be long,' she said, and bolted for the door and the stairs, heading for the kitchen where she'd left her new bag on the counter-top next to the microwave. Ten seconds later she was almost sobbing with relief, as she saw the punched through dome where the day's Pill had sat. Thank heavens, she thought, though her heart was still racing. What she needed, she realised, was something to calm her down. Not coffee. Some wine perhaps.

A minute later, Abby hurried back up the stairs, carrying with her the bottle of dessert wine they'd hardly touched at dinner, along with two glasses. Hopefully, she didn't look as horrified at herself as she suddenly felt. In a matter of hours Jake had turned her into…what? A woman with needs— needs which this man could obviously satisfy.

The bed was empty when she entered the bedroom, Jake simultaneously walking back into the room from the bathroom. But where she had a towel wrapped modestly around her, he was stark naked.

Abby liked that she now felt free to ogle him. For he was a man worth ogling: magnificently built with broad shoulders, flat stomach, slim hips and long strong legs. His skin was naturally olive, his body hair dark but not overly abundant. It was thickest in the middle of his chest, arrowing down to his groin. Abby gazed at that part of him which she admired and desired the most. She hadn't kissed him there yet. But she wanted to.

'It's all right,' she said straight away. 'Pill all safely taken.'

'Fantastic. Now, why don't you dispense with that towel, wench?' he said as he climbed back on to the bed, sitting up with pillows stuffed behind his back.

'Can't,' Abby replied rather breathlessly. How easy it was for him to turn her on. 'My hands are full.'

'Then come closer and I'll do it for you,' he said, his smile quite wicked.

Her head spun as she approached his side of the bed, waiting there like a good little wench till he reached out and peeled the towel from her body. His gaze was hot and hungry as it travelled over her, lingering on her breasts till she could actually feel her erect nipples tingling with anticipation.

'Give the bottle to me,' he commanded.

She did so. He placed it on the bedside table.

'Now the glasses,' he added.

She handed them over and he filled each one halfway, handing one back to her.

'Drink,' he ordered, and she did, downing all of it.

He didn't drink any of his, putting the glass down next to the bottle. Abby stared when he dipped his finger in the chilled wine then reached out to dab it over her nearest nipple.

She gasped.

'You like that?' he asked throatily and she nodded, her tongue feeling thick in her throat.

'Come,' he said, taking the empty glass out of her hand and putting it down before drawing her back on to the bed. Not on her side, but on his, sitting her down first then tipping her back across his thighs.

When Abby stared up at him with stunned eyes, Jake knew then that she was as innocent as he'd always feared. Up until this point he hadn't been absolutely sure. The way she'd insisted on a quickie down on the kitchen counter hadn't smacked of innocence.

But it was obvious that no one had ever dabbed wine on her nipples before, let alone her clitoris. Her surprise delighted and excited him. He dabbed some wine on her other nipple before pulling her on to the bed so that he could bend his mouth to her very beautiful breasts. He loved the way she moaned when he sucked her nipples deep into his mouth. Loved the way she couldn't seem to stop him from doing whatever he wanted. He liked her lack of experience, but at the same time it worried him. If he wasn't careful she might fall in love with him, which was the last thing he wanted.

CHAPTER EIGHTEEN

ABBY LOVED THE feel of his mouth on her breast. Loved it when he lapped gently at her nipple. Loved it even more when he nipped it with his teeth. She groaned when his head lifted abruptly, not wanting him to stop.

'What's wrong?' she said when she saw his frown.

His intense gaze grew quite frustrated. 'I don't know why I'm going to say this but I am. You won't be silly and fall in love with me, will you, Abby?'

Abby could not have been more taken aback, her focus tonight having been all on her sexual feelings, not romantic ones. Still, once she thought about it, she could see that it would be easy for her to become seriously infatuated with Jake. But love? It was difficult to fall in love with a man who'd shown no interest in her till circumstance had thrown them into each other's company, coincidentally at the same time he'd broken up with his current girlfriend.

Abby wasn't a fool. She could see that his suddenly fancying her was very convenient to Jake, that was all. He wanted her, but only because she was there. And pretty enough to interest him. Wayne, however, had wanted her from the first moment he'd clapped eyes on her, stained teeth and all. Her husband might not have set her heart racing the way Jake could, but he'd been a man worth loving. Abby could never truly love a man who was only sexually attracted to her. That kind of man would never capture her heart and soul.

'I'm not interested in marriage and children,' he told her, cementing any possible doubts she might have about loving him.

'I know that, Jake,' she replied a little coolly. 'You don't have to spell it out for me. Your reputation precedes you. I'm not interested in marriage and children, either. I don't want anything from you but sex, so you don't have to worry.'

He blinked his surprise at her.

'It's true,' she said, nodding as she thought about what her sister would say to her.

You've discovered the pleasures of the flesh at last, hon. Enjoy it whilst it's on offer. Because a man like Jake will move on after a while.

Thinking of her sister's probable advice confirmed in Abby's mind what she was feeling for Jake. This was sex, not love.

'I assure you I won't fall in love with you.' In lust maybe, but never in love.

His laugh was dry. 'I guess I asked for that. But you don't have to sound so sure. That's not very flattering.'

'Sorry.'

He smiled wryly. 'No need to apologise. I appreciate honesty. Now, where was I?'

Before he could bend his mouth once more to her breast, Abby sat up. She no longer wanted him to do that. She wanted to do things to *him*.

'Jake,' she said sharply, her eyes a bit nervous as they met his.

He frowned again. 'What now?'

'Since you like honesty, can I be honest with you about something else?'

'Be my guest,' he said, leaning back against the pillows.

Abby swallowed then gathered her courage to get out what she wanted to say. 'The thing is, I've…um…only been with one man before you. My husband. I loved Wayne dearly but I…we…well, I don't think I clicked sexually with him the way I do with you. I've never come before, during sex. I mean I've come but not during actual intercourse. I've also never done some other things that I've read about and which I feel I…um…would like to do with you.'

It hadn't been easy admitting all that, especially with Jake's eyes on her all the while, mainly because she couldn't read his expression. Surely he couldn't be *pleased* with her confession. She would have thought he liked his women very experienced.

'I see,' he said rather cryptically. 'What kind of things?'

She tried not to blush. She couldn't imagine Jake liking women who blushed. Gritting her teeth, Abby resolved to continue telling him the truth without surrendering to silly schoolgirl nerves.

'Well, oral sex, for starters. That's one thing I'd like to do. But I want to do it properly. I was hoping you might show me how.'

CHAPTER NINETEEN

ABBY WOKE SLOWLY, awareness of her physical well-being seeping into her brain before she remembered whose bed she was in, plus everything she had done in it the night before.

'Oh,' she cried, sitting up abruptly in what proved to be a blessedly empty bed. Lord knew how she would have coped if Jake had been lying there beside her, bearing witness to her very fierce embarrassment.

What had seemed so natural—so *right*—last night, now seemed very wrong. And very decadent. It blew Abby's mind that she had told Jake she'd never come during sex before. As for her telling him she wanted him to teach her how to go down on him…

She might have sat there, castigating herself for ages if the man himself hadn't walked back into the room, holding two mugs of steaming coffee and smiling at her with genuine warmth in his eyes. He wasn't naked, thank heavens, though he was only wearing jeans, his chest still bare.

As was hers, she realised, snatching up the sheet to cover her breasts.

'Now, now,' Jake chided with dancing blue eyes as he approached her side of the bed. 'None of that false modesty this morning, thank you. I've already seen your beautiful breasts at close quarters. Not to mention the rest of your very lovely body.'

His compliments went some way to soothing her embarrassment, as did his totally natural manner. Abby realised that if she wanted to continue having sex with Jake—and she very definitely did—then she had to get her head around the way he expected his women to act. At the same time, she wasn't about to turn into some kind of exhibitionist.

'Well, that was last night,' she returned, keeping the sheet where it was. 'I don't like swanning around with no clothes on in the daytime.'

'How do you know?' he said, placing one of the mugs on the bedside table next to her. 'Maybe you should try it some time.'

Abby wondered if it had been a mistake telling him so much about her past sex life. It worried her that Jake might think he had a licence to do anything and everything with her.

He frowned at her as he sat down on her side of the bed. 'I have a feeling that you're suffering from a severe case of the morning afters.'

Abby shrugged, then carefully picked up the very hot mug with one hand whilst keeping the sheet in place with her other hand.

'Probably,' she admitted after taking a small sip.

'What's worrying you?'

She took another sip of coffee, mulling over what to say.

'I guess I just don't know how to act this morning,' she said at last. 'I mean…it's an awkward situation, with me being your housekeeper.'

'I think it's anything but awkward,' he said, smiling a wickedly sexy smile. 'It's very convenient that you're already here, in my house, every day.'

'I'm not going to be your secret mistress, Jake,' she warned him, despite suspecting that she would be whatever he wanted her to be. Provided he kept having sex with her.

'You can't be my secret mistress,' he said, the corners of his mouth twitching. 'I'm not married.'

She glowered up at him. 'Secret lover, then!'

'Okay,' he said. 'Fair enough. How about you just become my girlfriend? Nothing secretive. All above board. If you like, I'll tell the world on next Monday's show. Or, better still, I'll put it on Twitter this very day. *My gorgeous young housekeeper and I are now an item.*'

Abby looked horrified. 'Don't you dare!'

Jake's eyebrows lifted. 'Is there any reason why I shouldn't?'

'My sister is addicted to Twitter. *And* your show.'

Now his brows beetled together. 'You don't want your sister to know we're an item?'

'No!'

'Why not? Will she be shocked?'

Hardly, Abby thought, since Megan had warned her that this might happen.

Abby sighed. 'Probably not,' she admitted. 'But she'll go on and on about it. She'll want to know the ins and outs of everything, and I'm just not ready to answer all her questions at this stage.'

'So I'm to be *your* secret lover, am I?'

Only then did Abby realise that that was exactly what she wanted him to be. She simply wasn't ready to share this incredible experience with anyone else. She didn't want to risk spoiling anything. She didn't want a cynical Megan telling her not to expect their relationship to last. Not that it was a *relationship*. It was just sex.

'Would you mind?' she asked him, shocked by her own boldness.

Jake actually did mind. Quite a bit. He didn't like the thought that Abby wanted to treat him as a sexual object rather than a proper boyfriend. Which was ironic, considering that was what he'd done in reverse for years—treated women more as sexual objects rather than proper girlfriends.

But he could see no pluses in arguing with her just now.

'If that's what you want,' he said with a nonchalant shrug of his shoulders.

She stared at him. 'You're very easy-going, aren't you?'

'Very,' he lied, deciding this was the way to play the game for a while. Give her what she wanted. Though he had no intention of being her secret lover for long. That was not what *he* wanted. 'Now, how about I take you away somewhere for the weekend? In the Ferrari. You can do some of the driving,' he offered with a devilish grin.

'I'd love to,' she said excitedly. 'But won't you be recognised if we go anywhere in public together?'

'Maybe. Maybe not. Sunglasses and a baseball cap go a long way to disguising one's identity. But I'll certainly be recognised once I book us into a place for the night. The name on my credit card will give the game away. But *your* identity can be kept a secret. For a while. But only for a while, I suspect. The truth will out in the end, Abby. Your sister will find out eventually, even if you don't tell her. The media has long and very tenacious tentacles. So I would suggest that when we get back on Sunday evening, you give her a call.'

'We'll see,' she said, still not happy at the thought of telling Megan about them.

Abby couldn't deny she was flattered that Jake actually *wanted* her to be his girlfriend. But, if truth be told, she didn't feel adequate for such a role. She wasn't well educated, or well travelled. Hardly a woman of the world in the bedroom, either. Still, maybe that was what he liked about her, the way Max de Winter liked the heroine in *Rebecca*— because she was the total opposite of his dead but highly decadent wife. Maybe it was Abby's own ordinariness that appealed to Jake after having a string of over-achieving, super-glamorous girlfriends.

Of course, he wasn't about to propose, as the hero did in *Rebecca*. Aside from the fact that Jake was anti-marriage, men these days didn't have to marry to enjoy the pleasures of the flesh. Neither did women, Abby conceded, a highly erotic shiver running down her spine as she looked at Jake's beautiful male body. She could hardly wait to have it all to herself again. There was so much more she had to learn. So many more things she had yet to try.

'Keep looking at me like that, sweetheart,' Jake said drily, 'and we won't even get out of this house today.'

CHAPTER TWENTY

WHEN ABBY BLUSHED, Jake stood up abruptly before he gave in to temptation and made his last words come true. As exciting as sex with Abby was, he didn't want to confine their relationship to a strictly sexual one. He wanted her company out of the bedroom as well. He wanted to show her all the places she'd never been before. Wanted to share with her all the wonders the world had to offer.

This last thought jolted him a bit. He'd never travelled overseas with a female companion before. Nothing beyond a few days in some fancy South Seas resort, that was. But he wanted to with Abby. And he was done with that silly show of his. It actually annoyed him that he couldn't go anywhere these days without being recognised. He pretended he didn't mind to Abby but the truth was it irritated him to death.

So the decision was made. He would sell the show ASAP and do something more exciting and fulfilling with his life. But first things first.

'I'll go fix us both some breakfast while you get showered and dressed,' he said. 'Then we're heading north. Port Macquarie, maybe. That's a decent drive. Have you ever been there before?'

She shook her head. 'I've never been out of Sydney. No, that's not true. I went on a school excursion to Canberra once when I was twelve.'

'And what did you think of our capital?'

'Can't remember it much. I was only there for two days and I froze to death the whole time.'

'It's much nicer at this time of year. Would you like to go there instead?'

'I don't really mind where we go,' she said. 'You decide.'

'Canberra it is, then.'

'You'll have to take me home first,' Abby told him hurriedly. 'I'll need to change and get some more clothes. I only have the dress with me that I wore last night. And I'll have to get some overnight things.'

'Fair enough. We won't get waylaid by your next-door neighbour, will we?'

'Harriet doesn't get up till lunchtime on a Saturday.'

'We should be long gone by then. Now, hop to it, Abby. Patience is not one of my virtues.'

'What are your virtues?' she asked, her eyes sparkling with uncharacteristic mischief.

Jake shrugged. 'Not sure. Honesty, I suppose. And integrity. Now, no more chit-chat. Up!' he ordered as he strode purposefully from the room.

Abby sat there a few seconds longer, thinking that there was more to Jake's virtues than honesty and integrity. He was also generous and caring. She liked that he'd loved his uncle as much as he had. Liked the way he'd fulfilled his uncle's dying wishes, even though he'd obviously found her a nuisance at first.

Not so much a nuisance now, she thought, a rather naughty smile pulling at her lips.

'I can't hear the shower running!' Jake called up the stairs, his voice echoing in the quiet house.

'Just going now,' Abby called back, putting the mug down and throwing back the doona.

Abby never sang in the shower. But she did that day, feeling even happier than when she'd got her porcelain veneers. Nothing could compare with the delicious lightness of spirit which was surging through her veins at that moment. She could not recall ever feeling so exhilarated. Or so excited. It did cross her mind for a split second that she might be falling in love with Jake, but she immediately dismissed the idea as fanciful. She liked him very much. And lusted after him a lot. But that was the sum total of her feelings at this stage.

She did concede later, as she ate the fantastic breakfast Jake had cooked, that her feelings for him might deepen if he kept on spoiling her this way.

But she would not worry about that today. Today was to be devoted to having the kind of carefree fun she'd never had before. She might even get to drive a Ferrari. How incredible was that?

'You're quite a good cook,' Abby complimented him.

'I can do the basics like steak and salad, and bacon and eggs. But I could never cook anything like you did last night. That meal was marvellous, Abby.'

'It wasn't all that special,' she said, trying to be modest.

'I thought it was. And so did Sophie.'

'I liked your sister, Jake. You're very close, aren't you?'

'Yes. Much closer than my other siblings. Sophie are I are the loners in the family. The rest are all married with children.'

'Goodness. That must make for a big group at Christmas. Do they all live here in Sydney?'

'Yep. And you're right about Christmas. I've already hired a boat for a cruise on the harbour this year. No one's house can accommodate everyone, except when some of them go to the in-laws. Which apparently isn't happening this year. What about you, Abby? How many in your family?'

'Just me and Megan. And little Timmy, of course.'

'What about your parents?' Jake asked, curious about Abby's family now.

'They're dead. Dad got killed in a fight when I was seventeen. Mum died of an accidental overdose a few months later.'

Jake was taken aback by Abby's matter-of-fact relaying of what must have affected her badly at the time. 'That's very sad, Abby.'

'I suppose so. But truly, they were terrible parents. Always down at the pub. There was never enough money for me and Megan. All they loved was alcohol.'

Jake tried not to look too shocked at Abby's truly ghastly background. Poor thing. She'd had it really tough. No wonder she'd got married young. Probably wanted some man to look after her and love her. Which obviously this Wayne had before he'd died too.

Abby didn't like Jake's silence. No doubt he thought she came from a low-life family. He was probably regretting asking a girl like her to be his girlfriend. 'It's not a pretty story, is it?' she said, a bit defiantly.

'I admire the way you survived it with the lovely nature that you have,' he said gently.

Abby blinked rapidly as moisture suddenly pooled in her eyes.

'You're not going to cry, are you?' Jake asked, alarm in his voice.

Abby almost laughed. Clearly, he didn't like his girlfriends to cry. Which was perverse since she was sure every one of them cried buckets when he broke up with them. Which he always did. Eventually.

It was a sobering thought, and one which she vowed never to forget.

'No,' she said with creditable calm. 'I'm not going to cry. Now, why don't I clear up here whilst you go and get ready? Oh, and Jake…'

'Yes?'

'Um…don't forget to pack some condoms.'

Was he startled by her very practical request? Or annoyed?

Abby imagined that he didn't want to use condoms. Neither did she, if she were honest. But she refused to lose her head totally over Jake.

'How many should I pack?' he asked, his tone as provocative as his glittering blue eyes.

'How many do you have in the house?' she countered, constantly surprised at her boldness. Surprised but not displeased. Abby suspected she was going to like her new bolder self.

'Not sure,' Jake replied thoughtfully. 'There's one unopened box in the bathroom upstairs, as well as a few loose ones in the top drawers of both bedside tables. There's a couple more in the glovebox of my car and two more in my wallet. So a rough estimate would be about two dozen. How many do you think we might need?'

Abby kept a straight face with difficulty. The man was a wicked devil all right.

'Don't ask me,' she said, brilliantly po-faced. 'I only have last night to go by and that might have been a one-off for you. I would imagine a man can get it up quite a bit with a woman during their first night together. But after that, things might very well go downhill. It's not as though you're a teenager, Jake, or even in your twenties. Which reminds me, how old *are* you? Late thirties? Early forties?'

Jake glowered at her for a long moment before shaking his head then smiling a drily amused smile.

'You're teasing me, aren't you?'

'No more than you teased me.'

'Fair enough. And, since you asked, I'm thirty-four. Which makes me still in my prime. So watch yourself tonight. You might find yourself begging me to stop before I'm finished.'

Abby feigned a disappointed face. 'You mean I have to wait till tonight?'

Jake wagged a finger at her. 'I should call your bluff. But I won't. Now, let's get going.'

CHAPTER TWENTY-ONE

'YOU'RE RIGHT,' ABBY said, closing her eyes as she leant back, her hair flying free. 'Riding in this car with the top down is amazing. I would do this every day if I could.'

'Sorry. Weekend treat only. Next time we *will* head north to Port Macquarie.'

Abby opened her eyes as her head turned towards Jake. 'I wouldn't mind where I go,' she said. 'As long as it's in this gorgeous car.'

And as long as I'm with you.

'Great. Now, do you want to stop somewhere for lunch or just go straight to Canberra?'

'No,' Abby said straight away. 'I don't want to stop. Not unless you do. I'm not hungry at all. We can have something to eat when we get to Canberra.'

'A girl after my own heart,' he said with a warm smile thrown her way.

Abby's own heart twisted with his remark, because there was no point in her being after his heart. All Jake wanted from a woman was her body in bed, and her company when out of bed. He obviously liked having a steady girlfriend. Much more convenient for his lifestyle. What he didn't want was for his girlfriends to want more from him than he was prepared to give. Clearly, whenever a girlfriend started looking for more they were out of the door.

Abby realised she would only have herself to blame if she started wanting more. Forewarned was forearmed.

To give Jake credit, he'd been honest with her about his intentions. Or lack of them. She recalled he'd listed honesty as one of his virtues. Integrity as well. Which meant he wouldn't have lied to her about not being a risk to her health when he didn't use a condom.

Thinking of condoms brought Abby's mind back to the incredible climaxes she'd had with Jake last night. She hadn't known till then that such pleasure existed. Whenever Megan raved on about how much she enjoyed sex—how much she actually *needed* it at times—Abby had thought her some kind of nymphomaniac. Now, she appreciated where her sister was coming from. Abby felt sure that by tonight she would very definitely be needing sex with Jake. Already she could feel herself responding to just the thought of being with him, desire invading her body from her curling toes right up to her spinning head. Waiting till tonight was almost beyond bearing. But she *would* wait. No way was she going to humiliate herself by throwing herself at him any earlier.

Abby turned her head just enough so that she could at least have the pleasure of looking at him.

He was wearing stonewashed grey jeans and a white polo top, along with sunglasses and a black baseball cap which did, thankfully, make him more difficult to identify as Jake Sanderson, famed television host and one of Sydney's most recognisable personalities.

Abby didn't want to share him with his adoring public today. Or any other day, for that matter. She couldn't think of anything worse than having strangers come up to them all the time, asking Jake for his autograph. She certainly didn't like the thought of people looking at *her* and wondering what on earth Jake was doing with such a nobody.

Not that she wasn't attractive, especially now that she was dressing better and wearing make-up. Jake, however, was the type of man who dated movie stars and supermodels, or at the very least glamorous newsreaders who were instantly recognisable. They were also women who didn't wear clothes from bargain basement stores. When she'd put on the same outfit this morning that she'd worn when Jake had taken her car shopping last week, Abby had been happy enough with the way she looked. She'd thought—possibly mistakenly—that her tight white pants and spotty top looked quite classy and not cheap. But maybe she'd been deluding herself.

Abby jerked her head round to stare out of the passenger window, not liking that she was suddenly losing confidence in herself. I *do* look good, she told herself firmly. Stop with the worrying.

But the worries continued. Not with her appearance but with what Megan would say when she rang her sister on Sunday night and confessed all. As much as she would like to keep Jake as her secret lover, she could see he wasn't going to allow that to happen.

No doubt Megan would say 'I told you so' in the most irritatingly smug way. She wouldn't be shocked. Well, not about the sex part. She would, however, be shocked that Jake wanted her to be his girlfriend. Abby could just imagine Megan's reaction to that. It would be pure cynicism.

Abby wasn't looking forward to that conversation one little bit. She wanted to enjoy her time with Jake. The last thing she needed was her cynical sister telling her it was only a temporary role. For heaven's sake, she already knew that. She might not be a genius, but she wasn't stupid. Okay, so it was inevitable that one day she would get her marching orders. Abby resolved that she would face that moment when it came. Meanwhile, she aimed to live for the moment. Wasn't that what those lifestyle gurus were always advocating? Not to worry about the past or the future but to seize the moment. Well, at the moment she was in this gorgeous car with a gorgeous man and she wasn't going to let anybody or anything spoil things for her.

Famous last words, Abby thought, and heaved a huge sigh.

'Would you like me to put on some music?' Jake offered, perhaps thinking that her sigh meant she was bored.

'No, thanks,' she replied with a quick smile his way. 'I just want to relax and enjoy the scenery.' Plus try very hard to just live in the moment.

'Actually, the scenery's not that good. That's the trouble with motorways. They bypass the interesting bits.'

'I don't really care about the scenery. I'm just enjoying the ride. And the company,' she added smilingly.

CHAPTER TWENTY-TWO

ME TOO, JAKE THOUGHT, confirming his earlier idea about taking Abby overseas with him. Not that he would mention it to her just yet. It was too soon. Not for him. For her.

'Would you mind if I asked you something?' he said.

'That depends, I guess, on what it is.'

'Nothing too personal. While I was waiting for you at your place this morning, I saw a big pile of books on your coffee table in the living room. I couldn't help noticing that they included some of my uncle's favourite novels, which reminded me that you asked me if he'd left you books in his will. Am I right in presuming he gave you those books?'

'Actually, no, he didn't. But he did give me a list of books which he said any self-respecting female should read. I bought them myself from a secondhand book shop.'

'I see. And have you read them all yet?'

'I'm on the last one now. *Rebecca*.'

'And which ones are your favourites?'

'Goodness, that's a hard question. I liked them all. But I guess not equally. I'd already read three of them at school. *Pride and Prejudice* and *Wuthering Heights* and *Jane Eyre*. Oh, and I've seen about three movie versions of *Great Expectations*, so I knew what was going to happen, which half spoils a story, doesn't it? Though I can see now how brilliantly written they all were. Difficult to pick out just one. Hmm… I adored *Shōgun*. What a fantastic story with a fantastic hero! *The Fountainhead* was riveting stuff too, though the main characters were a bit OTT, in my opinion.'

'I couldn't agree more,' Jake said. 'What did you think of *To Kill a Mockingbird*?'

'Oh, that was a wonderful story. It made me cry buckets. So did *Anna Karenina*. That poor sad lady.'

'So you don't have an all-time favourite?'

'Not really. Though it might be *Rebecca*, as long as it finishes well.'

'What part are you up to?'

'She's about to come down the stairs dressed in that same outfit Rebecca wore, and I just *know* Max is not going to be very happy.'

Jake had to smile. 'You can say that again. Actually, you've quite a bit more to go. And a few more surprises to come.'

'Don't you dare tell me anything!'

'Obviously you haven't seen the movie version.'

'No. I didn't know there was one.'

'Yes, it was made in nineteen forty, only two years after the book was published. Alfred Hitchcock directed it. Laurence Olivier played Max and Joan Fontaine was the unnamed heroine. I'll get a copy for you after you've finished the book.'

Her face carried a touching mixture of disbelief and excitement. 'Would you really?'

'Of course.'

'But where would you get a copy from?'

'You can get just about everything over the internet these days.'

Happiness radiated from her truly lovely green eyes. 'Would you watch it with me?'

'It would be my pleasure. It's a great film. Craig loved it, though not as much as the book.'

'Your uncle was an incredibly well-read man, wasn't he?'

'Yes. And he read books right across the spectrum from literary works to popular fiction. He was the same with music. He absolutely adored the classical composers, but he loved all music, from Country and Western to rock and even rap. There wasn't a snobbish bone in his body.'

'You loved him a lot, didn't you?'

Jake's heart squeezed tight in his chest. He scooped in a deep breath then let it out slowly. 'I'm still angry with him for not telling me he was terminally ill.'

Abby nodded. 'You're right. He should have told you.'

Jake shrugged, not wanting to spoil their weekend together by talking about sad things. Thinking of Craig, however, had reminded Jake of what his uncle had told him in that last letter, about living life to the full. Suddenly, he didn't want to wait to take Abby overseas with him. Time to seize the day!

'Do you have a passport, Abby?' he asked.

'What?'

'A passport. Do you have a passport?'

'No. Why?'

'You're going to need one when we go to Hawaii in January.'

She blinked over at him. 'Are you serious? You want me to go to Hawaii with you?'

'Not just Hawaii. I also want to take you to mainland America. California first, and possibly Vegas, then later over to New York. After New York, we'll go on to Europe, but only after the weather turns kinder. Europe in the winter is not for a girl who's never been out of Australia.'

'But...but...don't you have to be here in Sydney to do your show?'

'No. I don't want to do it any more. I'm going to sell it. I have a buyer who's been after the show for ages. You're going to love Europe, Abby,' he swept on, feeling the excitement already building. 'And Asia. Especially Japan.'

When he glanced over at her, she was shaking her head at him, her expression troubled. 'Maybe by January you won't want to take me anywhere.'

Jake could not have been more startled. 'And why would that be?'

'You might grow bored with me.'

He smiled over at her. 'I find that highly unlikely. What's the matter, Abby? Don't you want to go?'

'Yes,' she said after a heart-stopping space of time. 'Of course I do. It's just that…'

'Just that what?'

'What if you grow bored with me when we're overseas? You won't dump me in some strange city, will you?'

Jake was so shocked he almost ran off the road. As it was, he hit the shoulder, sending gravel spurting out behind them.

'Hell, Abby, what kind of man do you think I am?' he threw at her once he'd righted the car. 'I would never do anything like that. And I won't grow bored with you. Where on earth is all this talk of boredom coming from?'

'According to Megan your girlfriends don't last very long.'

Jake rolled his eyes, inwardly cursing the tabloids for reporting every time one of his relationships broke up, even the ones that never really got off the ground. They made him sound like a playboy of the worst kind. He realised Abby would take some convincing that he wasn't that bad.

'Firstly, let me say that it's not always me who ends the relationships. The women I've dated always claim they don't want marriage, but in the end they do. That's a deal breaker for me, Abby. You sounded very sure last night when you said you didn't want to get married again and I believed you. Was I right to believe you?'

'Absolutely,' she said with a little shudder.

Jake still couldn't make up his mind whether her aversion to marrying again was because she'd loved her husband too much to contemplate marriage to another man, or because her dead husband had done something to turn her off the institution.

He decided to find out.

'But why *is* that, Abby?' he asked. 'What happened to turn you off the idea of remarrying?'

CHAPTER TWENTY-THREE

ABBY STIFFENED. SHE hadn't expected their conversation to take this path. She hadn't expected Jake to offer to take her overseas, either. She certainly hadn't expected him to ask her to explain why she didn't want to get married again.

Clearly, she would have to tell him something, or he might rescind his offer. The thought of travelling to all those exciting places with Jake was way too tempting. But what to say? Not the truth, that was for sure. Just when she was getting desperate, Abby remembered something she'd recently read.

'If you must know, my reason is like what Scarlet told Rhett in *Gone with the Wind*, when he asked her to marry him.'

Jake frowned. 'Sorry. I can't remember what she said. Enlighten me.'

'She said she didn't *like* being married.'

'Ah, yes, I remember now. But Abby, that reason was about her not enjoying sex. Maybe you didn't enjoy sex with your husband but you sure as hell enjoy it with me.'

Which means, Jake thought, that she might change her mind at some future date and want to marry him.

'No, no, you've got the wrong end of the stick,' Abby said firmly before he could explore that rather worrying thought. 'It's not the sex part of marriage that disappointed me. Not really. I quite liked sex with Wayne, even if I didn't come the way I do with you. What I didn't like was my loss of independence, plus my total loss of freedom. In the beginning, I thought I wanted to be an old-fashioned housewife, but the truth is I was just running away from life because I had no self-esteem. I thought I would be happy staying at home twenty-four-seven and being a good little wife and mother. Wayne was a very nice man and he loved me to death, bad teeth and all. But in the end I wasn't happy.'

Which was a huge understatement, Abby thought as she swallowed the lump in her throat then gritted her teeth so she wouldn't cry.

'I'm glad now that we didn't have children,' she lied. 'Once I got over my grief I decided I had to get out there and get myself a job. But first I had to get my teeth fixed or I simply wouldn't have the confidence to go for an interview. Not that I was all that confident when I first showed up at your house,' she added with a rueful little laugh.

'You were a bit nervous,' Jake admitted.

'I was surprised when you gave me the job. Surprised and grateful. It did wonders for my self-esteem. But it was meeting your uncle, Jake, which changed me the most, not just on the outside but on the inside. He made me see myself as an intelligent woman with a lot of potential. He made me braver. It was wonderful of him to give me a new car and some travel money, but his legacy is much more than that. The old Abby would never have dared go to bed with you last night or come away with you this weekend, let alone contemplate going overseas with you. The new more adventurous Abby, however, simply can't say no. I want to do all the things I've never done before—to go places I've never been before. I want to be carefree, not committed. I want to have fun. Is that terribly selfish of me?'

'Hardly, since it's the credo I live by. Why do you think I don't want marriage and children? During my growing up years I witnessed two ways of life with my father and my uncle. When my father died at forty-seven, a worn-out shell of a man, I knew which one I would choose. I was only a teenager when I made a conscious decision to live the life of a bachelor and I've been very happy doing that.'

Up till now, came a sudden and rather perturbing thought.

He eased off the accelerator as he brought his attention back to the road.

'If ever there was a car designed to corrupt it's this little baby,' he said ruefully.

'Same as its owner then,' Abby quipped.

Jake's eyebrows shot upwards. 'You think I've corrupted you?'

Abby smiled. 'Don't sound so shocked, Jake. Of course you've corrupted me. And I dare say you haven't finished yet. But not to worry, I'm enjoying every single moment.'

Their eyes locked, Abby finding it difficult to maintain her saucy attitude in the face of Jake's intense gaze. She could talk big all she liked but underneath her bold facade the old Abby still lurked. Even the new Abby had trouble accepting the strength of Jake's sexual interest in her. She was glad when his eyes swung back on to the road.

'No more talk now,' he said abruptly. 'I have to concentrate or I really will lose my licence.'

Abby didn't mind not talking. That way she could get back to living in the moment. She certainly didn't want to discuss her marriage any more, because inevitably it made her remember her miscarriages and the pain associated with them.

Maybe Wayne's death was a blessing in disguise, Abby decided. Because she knew she could not bear to ever lose another baby. That was why she didn't want to marry again. That was why she couldn't. But of course she could never tell Jake that. He would think she was emotionally damaged. Which, admittedly, she was. She'd always wanted children—wanted to give them the kind of secure and loving upbringing which she'd never had.

Failing to fulfil this most basic human need had been devastating for her. Her last miscarriage had nearly broken her, as had Wayne's tragic death. She'd been dreadfully depressed for months. But eventually she'd begun to recover, finding a resilience and a courage which surprised her.

Signing up with the Housewives For Hire agency had just been the first step in her plan to embrace a different life than that of marriage and children. As soon as she'd got her job with Jake, she'd begun putting that plan in action by saving every cent she could. Even if Jake's wonderful uncle hadn't left her all that money in his will, she would eventually have saved up enough to travel. In the meantime, she would have done a course to help her with her finances. Something in hospitality. A barista course perhaps, and a bar course. There was always work for an attractive girl in pubs and cafés.

And she *was* attractive, Abby conceded, as she smiled at herself in the side mirror of the car. Attractive enough for Jake to consider her girlfriend material. In truth, he seemed well and truly smitten now, enough to consider taking her away on a grand tour with him. Her mind still boggled a bit at that one. Obviously, he genuinely enjoyed her company. It came to Abby that Jake was somewhat jaded with life at the moment, hence his desire to sell his television show and travel overseas. And who better to go with but a female companion for whom he currently had the hots and who would be oh, so impressed by all the places he took her? Which, no doubt, she would be. No use pretending she wouldn't.

But how long before her lack of worldly experience and serious lack of education wasn't quite so appealing? Would it irk him when he couldn't have the same kind of intellectual conversations which he'd had with his very clever uncle and that last newsreader girlfriend who probably had a degree in journalism or communication or whatever degree newsreaders had to have? Female newsreaders weren't just pretty faces these days. They were also smart. Super smart.

Abby realised all of a sudden that silence wasn't good for her. It led to too much negative thinking. She'd come a long way lately in feeling good about herself and she didn't aim to go backwards.

After glancing around, Abby was surprised to realise

she actually recognised where she was. On the long ave-
nue which led to the centre of Canberra. She felt sure that
soon they would go over a bridge and then past lots of famous buildings before ending up in front of a grassy hill on
which stood the houses of parliament—both old and new.

'I remember more of this than I thought I did,' she said
as they approached the bridge which crossed Lake Burley
Griffin, named after the man who'd designed the city of
Canberra. Abby recalled vaguely that he was an American
architect who had won some sort of competition to have
the honour, but she didn't say so in case she was wrong.

'Well, the layout of Canberra is very memorable,' Jake
remarked. 'And quite beautiful.'

'Yes, it is,' Abby said as she gazed at the expanse of
lovely blue water they were crossing. 'It was a marvellous
idea to put a lake in the middle of the city.'

'Did you know you can go for a balloon ride over the
city?'

'No, I didn't. But no, thank you. A balloon ride would
scare the life out of me.'

'You only live once, Abby.'

'I'd still prefer to keep my feet on the ground, thank you
very much.'

He threw her a questioning glance. 'Does that attitude
apply to planes as well? Because, if it does, it's going to be
a slow boat ride around the world next year.'

'No. I'm prepared to fly, but only on a very reliable air-
line, one with an impeccable record for safety.'

Jake smiled. 'I wouldn't dream of letting you fly any
other way. You're too precious to me for that. Now, I think
we'll whip into this car park over here. It's only a short walk
to the National Gallery, where there is a very nice café.'

Less than one minute later, Jake had zapped into an
empty space in the underground car park, a dumbstruck
Abby still not having recovered from his remark about her
being too precious to him. She wondered if he really meant

it or if he said that kind of thing to all his girlfriends. Whatever, it had done things to her insides which were perturbing. She didn't want to fall in love with Jake, but it seemed a futile wish if just a few words could send her into such a whirl.

'Don't do that,' he said when she went to open her own door. 'Let me do it for you.'

He jumped out from behind the wheel and strode round the bonnet of the Ferrari with a few long strides, opening the passenger door with a masterful flourish and holding out his hand to her.

Abby almost told him that he didn't have to play the gentleman with her. He hadn't done this when he'd taken her car shopping. Or at any other time today. Though she hadn't exactly given him the opportunity, had she? This morning she'd driven her own car home, with Jake following in the Ferrari. Then, after she'd changed outfits, she'd hurried out of the house and practically dived into the passenger seat before any of the neighbours saw her. Jake had rolled his eyes at her at the time but she hadn't twigged to why.

'Do you treat all your girlfriends like this?' she asked him as she placed her hand in his.

His fingers closed tightly around hers as he helped her out of the low-slung seat. 'Only when the woman deserves it. Which you do, my lovely Abby. You deserve the best of everything.'

'Wow,' she said. 'But really, Jake, you don't have to overdo the compliments. Trust me when I say I'm already a sure thing tonight.'

He laughed, then pulled her into his arms. 'Goodness, but I adore you!'

Abby stared up into his glittering blue eyes and thought that maybe he did. For the moment. But the moment was all that she could rely on. History invariably repeated itself and Jake's history with women was not good.

Abby pushed aside this painful thought, telling herself

firmly that she wasn't going to worry about the future. She was going to live for the moment. And this moment felt quite wonderful.

'As much as I would like you to kiss me right now,' she said, 'I am in desperate need of the ladies' room. And then something to eat.'

CHAPTER TWENTY-FOUR

As Jake took the last swallow of his coffee he began wondering how best to spend the afternoon. He had no intention of arriving at the hotel he'd booked till after five, well aware that he wouldn't be able to keep his hands off Abby once they were alone. He didn't want this weekend to be nothing but a sex-fest. He wanted to *show* Abby that he enjoyed her company out of bed as well as in. Hopefully, that would allay her fears that he would quickly get bored with her.

'Did you visit this place when you came down with your school?' he asked. 'Not this café. The National Gallery itself.'

'No, I don't think so. We weren't here all that long. Only two days. We drove down one morning and had lunch in a park somewhere. Then in the afternoon we visited both parliament houses. Then they drove us out to a kind of tourist park for the night. The next day they brought us back in here to visit a science centre. Can't remember what it was called. It started with a Q.'

'Questacon,' he said. 'It's not far from here. I went there once. Great place.'

Abby rolled her eyes. 'For you maybe. I found it boring.'

'Well, you won't find the National Gallery boring. The art in here is fabulous. Not just paintings either, but sculptures as well.'

Abby looked a bit worried. 'I don't know all that much about art.'

'That's probably better then. You won't have any preconceived ideas. Promise me you won't say you like something just because it's in here, okay? Some of the purchases have been very controversial over the years. Have you ever heard of *Blue Poles*?'

'It rings a vague bell,' she replied, frowning.

'It's a very famous painting by an American artist, Jackson Pollock. It was bought by this gallery in 1972 for one point three million. They had to get special permission from the Prime Minister at the time to spend that much money. Caused a massive stir. Still, it's reputed to be worth up to twenty million now so I guess it was a good investment after all. Come on. I'll take you to see it,' he said, standing up and reaching for her hand.

'It's huge!' was Abby's first comment when she stood in front of the painting, which measured approximately two by five metres.

'It certainly is.'

'The artist must have had to stand on a ladder to paint the top bits.'

'Actually, he did it whilst it was lying flat on the floor. But that's all beside the point. Do you *like* it?'

Abby scrunched up her face as she stepped back and stared at it for a long moment. 'I can't make up my mind if it's brilliant or an Emperor's New Clothes piece of rubbish.'

Jake had to smile. Only Abby would dare to question what was considered to be Jackson Pollock's best work.

'No, no, I take that back,' she said after a few more seconds of narrow-eyed scrutiny. 'It's definitely one of those paintings that grows on you. But you could hardly hang it in your living room, could you?'

'True,' Jake said, trying not to laugh. But she was such a delight. And so natural, her opinions untainted by the one-eyed opinions of art critics and pseudo intellectuals.

'I certainly wouldn't pay twenty million for it,' she added.

'Me neither,' a male voice said from just behind them.

Jake recognised that voice. Instantly.

He spun round. 'Tony Green, you old devil! Fancy running into you here.'

Abby was astonished when Jake enfolded a tall, skinny, darkly bearded man in a big bear hug.

'I thought you weren't ever coming back to Australia,' Jake added as the man hugged him back. When at last they pulled apart they both had boyish grins on their happy faces.

'Neither were you, if I recall,' the bearded man said. 'Till a bullet changed your mind.'

Abby sucked in sharply at this news, but Jake just shrugged. 'I was about ready to come home, Tony. I'd had enough. Now, before we go and have a drink together and catch up on old times, I think I should make some introductions.' He turned back to Abby and took her by the hand again. 'Abby, this is Tony Green, the most fearless cameraman money can buy. But also just a tad dangerous to work with.'

Tony laughed. '*You* ought to talk. This man's a maniac. I told him he was crazy to go into that particular village that day, but he wouldn't take any notice. Said he'd come to help rescue some girls who'd been kidnapped by a gang of rebels and he was going to free them, come hell or high water. He just wouldn't listen to reason. And guess what? The girls did get rescued but our boy here almost lost his life in the process.'

'Goodness!' Abby exclaimed. 'I had no idea…'

Tony grinned. 'Modest as well as brave. That's our Jake. But also stubborn. Once Jake makes his mind up to do something, nothing will change his mind. But then you probably already know that, since I gather you two are an item.'

'We are,' Jake said, giving Abby's hand a squeeze. 'And I'll have you know I'm not a maniac any longer.'

'Possibly true. I couldn't believe it when I got back to Australia last month and saw you hosting that chat show. I mean, that's not you, mate.'

'It suited me at the time, Tony. And it's my own production. But I've decided to sell it before Christmas. Abby and

I are going on a world tour together next year. *Not* to the places *we* went to. To the nice places.'

'Wow. So you two are pretty serious about each other then?'

'You could say that,' Jake replied, and gave Abby's hand another squeeze.

'You *have* changed. Look, as much as I'd like to get a drink and catch up on old times, I can't. I'm meeting someone up at Parliament House in about fifteen minutes. I just popped in here to fill in time till she gets off work.'

'Someone special?' Jake asked.

'Very. We met over the internet. She's the reason I came back to Australia.'

'I see. Well, I hope it works out for you.'

'You too. We should stay in touch.'

'I'm on Facebook,' Jake told him.

'Me too. Have to go, mate. It's been great seeing you again.'

They hugged once more and Tony was gone.

'Well,' said Jake with a sigh, 'fancy that. I honestly never expected to see him again.'

There was so much Abby wanted to ask Jake, the many questions in her head underlining how much she didn't know about him and the job he used to do. But right now, here in this gallery, with people milling around, didn't seem the right place to have such a conversation.

'I don't really want to walk around looking at art, Jake,' she said truthfully. 'Can't we just go to that hotel you booked? Or is it too early?'

Their eyes met, the desire which they'd both put on hold earlier flaring between them.

'And you accused me of corrupting you,' he murmured wryly, then glanced at his watch. 'It's only half past two. Check-in time isn't till three. But I suppose I could call them and play the celebrity card.'

He played the celebrity card, Abby wishing for a few

excruciating minutes in Reception that he hadn't. The behaviour of the attractive brunette behind the desk was more
than embarrassing. She gushed all over Jake, half flirting
with him whilst totally ignoring Abby's presence. By the
time Jake steered Abby over to the bank of lifts in the corner, she wasn't sure who she felt sorrier for, herself or Jake.

She sighed as they entered a blessedly empty lift.

'Yes, I know,' he said ruefully. 'But it won't be like that
when we're booking into hotels overseas. Over there, I'll
be a nobody.'

'I suspect you'll always get special treatment from female staff, Jake,' Abby said a bit tartly. 'You're way too
handsome for your own good.'

He smiled at her. 'That's the pot calling the kettle black.
I haven't forgotten the way dear old Raoul came on to you,
beautiful.'

Abby blinked up at him. 'Are you saying you were jealous of Raoul?'

'Painfully so.'

'Good,' she said, and he laughed.

'I like it when you get stroppy with me. And when you're
jealous.'

The lift doors opened on the tenth floor, Jake wasting no
time steering Abby along the corridor to their room. Their
overnight bags were waiting for them inside, as was a bottle of chilled champagne and a fruit basket, courtesy of the
management. The room was what was called superior, with
views over the lake, a separate sitting area, a king-sized bed
and a spa bath.

Although impressed, Abby wasn't all that interested in
any of it. All she wanted by then was for Jake to take her
in his arms and kiss her.

'Care for a glass of champagne?' he asked her as he lifted
the bottle out of the ice bucket and set about opening it.

Abby winced. How did you tell a man that all you wanted
was him?

He glanced over at her then and laughed. 'You should see the look on your face.'

Now she blushed.

'I take it you don't want the champagne just yet,' he said as he walked slowly across the room to where she was standing beside the bed.

'Do you?' she asked him.

'The only thing I want at the moment, my darling girl,' he said, 'is you.'

He undressed her quickly, without so much as a kiss, not stopping till she was totally naked. Then he left her standing there like that whilst he undressed, his eyes on her all the while. Her own gaze was hot and hungry as she watched him strip off, her need intense before he'd even laid a finger on her. She closed her eyes when he scooped her up and laid her on the bed, gasping when he started stroking her body, first her breasts then her stomach, her thighs, her calves.

'No, no...' she moaned when he spread her legs and used his mouth on her.

But protesting was useless and she splintered apart under his tongue within seconds. Her climax hadn't abated when he rolled her over on to her stomach and started stroking her again. Her back this time, then her buttocks. And between. She writhed beneath his knowing hands, and his wickedly probing fingers. In no time her desire for release became desperate again. Her legs moved invitingly apart, her hips moving restlessly in a circular fashion.

'Not that way, my darling,' he growled, and flipped her back over. 'Not this time. I want to see your eyes when you come. Just give me a sec.'

She groaned at the time he took to don the condom, crying out when he entered her at last, penetrating her with a forceful surge which filled her to the hilt. His own eyes, she noted, were wildly glittering, his breathing ragged. He groaned when she wrapped her legs high around his back, pressing her hips hard up against his.

'Hell on earth, woman,' he ground out. 'Be still or I'll come.'

'I want you to come,' she told him in a wickedly wanton voice as she moved her hips in a slow sensual circle, squeezing him at the same time.

A decidedly crude four-letter word punched from his throat.

Abby didn't swear much herself, but somehow, today, at this moment, it turned her on. 'Yes,' she said with a low moan. 'That's what I want, too. Just do it, Jake. I don't care if I come or not.'

'Bloody hell,' he muttered, then started to move, the veins in his throat standing out as he set up a steady rhythm.

Abby was touched by his efforts to last, but she would have none of it, certain that she would come if he came. She kept squeezing him mercilessly, and rotating her hips, watching with increasing frustration as he tried desperately to maintain control. Desperate herself now, she removed her hands from where they'd been gripping the sheet on either side of her, clamping them onto his buttocks and digging her nails in as she pulled him even deeper into her.

It was the final straw for Jake, tipping him over the edge with a speed and power which Abby found thrilling. He didn't watch her come because his eyes were shut at the time. But come she did, exulting in the way her body matched his, spasm for spasm. They shuddered together for ages till finally they were done, Jake rolling from her and collapsing on to the bed, still gasping and panting. Abby just lay where she was, a very deep languor seeping through her sated body as her breathing calmed and her muscles relaxed. She didn't want to go to sleep, but her mind had other ideas. Five minutes later she was out like a light.

CHAPTER TWENTY-FIVE

JAKE WAS BEYOND words for some considerable time. Frankly, he was somewhat stunned at how he'd lost control of the lovemaking. There he'd been, thinking he would show Abby this weekend what a great lover he was and bingo, he'd come with the speed of a randy teenager. For a girl of limited experience, she seemed to know exactly what to do to drive a man wild.

Jake sighed. So much for not wanting this weekend to be a sex-fest. Suddenly, that was all he could think about. His head turned to where Abby was lying on the bed, her naked body splayed out in the most provocative pose. Unfortunately, she was also sound asleep. But that didn't stop Jake from looking.

Naked, Abby had the sort of body a man could look at for hours, with its delicious combination of slenderness and curves. Her breasts were just the right size. Full but not heavy, her nipples surprisingly large and yes, very responsive. Not pink, they were a dusky brown colour which made them stand out from her rather pale skin. Jake's stomach tightened at the urge to roll over right now and suck them. But he didn't. Though he would, after he'd been to the bathroom. She didn't need to sleep for long. Hell, it was only mid-afternoon. She could sleep later tonight, after he'd run out of steam. And condoms.

Climbing off the bed, Jake walked into the bathroom to attend to the condom. He wished he didn't have to use them.

'I really don't want to take *any* chances, Jake,' she'd reiterated at breakfast today. 'I went through a few nasty moments there last night when I thought I'd forgotten to take my Pill.'

It would have given him more than a *few* nasty moments if she'd become pregnant, Jake accepted. Which meant he would just have to keep on using condoms.

Not that it really mattered. Safe sex was a way of life for him. Still, perhaps after they'd been together for a while, she might tell him not to bother with the condoms any more. He trusted her to take the Pill every day. After all, she seemed just as paranoid about falling pregnant as he was. Meanwhile, he still had almost a dozen condoms left for this weekend, which seemed overly ambitious…but then he walked back into the bedroom and saw that Abby had rolled over and curled up into a foetal position.

Just looking at Abby's peachy bottom started doing things to him which would have been impossible a few minutes earlier.

Jake climbed back on to the bed with a rueful smile on his face.

'Abby, darling,' he crooned, running a single finger up and down her spine. 'You can't go to sleep yet. It's only four o'clock.'

'Go away,' she mumbled. 'Tired.'

Jake smiled as he rose and went back into the bathroom, where he poured some of the provided bath salts into the spa bath he'd noted earlier. After that, he turned on the water, adjusted the temperature, then went to collect the champagne and the fruit basket, the bath fortunately having ledges large enough in each corner to accommodate the ice bucket and two glasses. Once the water was at the right height, he switched off the taps, hid a couple of condoms amongst the fruit then joined Abby on the bed, this time bending his lips to her shoulder.

'Jake calling Abby,' he murmured between kisses. 'Do you hear me, Abby?'

Her eyes fluttered open as her head turned and gazed up at him with heavy lids. 'You can't possibly want to do it again this soon,' she said sleepily.

'Not right away,' he said. 'I've run us a spa bath. There's room enough for two.'

She blinked, then sat up abruptly, her messy hair falling across her forehead and one eye. 'But I haven't... I've never...'

'What happened to the girl who told me she wanted to experience everything?' he said as he gently pushed her hair back from her eyes. 'Trust me, okay?'

She rolled her eyes at this.

'I've taken some refreshments in there for us to enjoy,' he went on. 'I thought you might be hungry. We can eat and talk at the same time.'

'You want to talk? I thought you wanted sex.'

'Not until you wake up properly.'

Jake kept a straight face as he said this.

But, perversely, Abby took him at his word.

'So what are we going to talk about?' she said even before she'd lowered herself into the warm water.

'Whatever you'd like to talk about,' he replied, temporarily settling back into the opposite end of the bath. 'But first I'll pour us both some champagne.'

Abby wondered as she watched Jake pour the bubbly just how often he'd done this. She wasn't jealous, but she did rather envy his know-how. Did he have any idea how awkward she felt at the moment? How...ignorant?

Not a total fool, however. He hadn't brought her in here to talk. And whilst she did want him to make love to her some more in whatever exotic ways he wanted, there *was* something she wanted to talk to him about whilst she had the chance.

'That man in the gallery, Jake,' she said as he handed her a glass of champagne. 'Tony,' she added after taking a sip.

'What about him?' Jake asked.

'He said you were shot. And I was wondering where.' She hadn't seen any scars on him.

'Africa. Sierra Leone.'

'No, no, I mean where on your body.'

He laughed. 'Here,' he said, and showed her a scar on his inner thigh which was more towards the back than the front. No wonder she hadn't seen it.

'Heavens. You were very lucky.'

'Sure was. A couple of inches either way and I would have lost the family jewels.'

'Which would have been a dreadful shame.'

'My feelings exactly.'

'Still, it was very brave of you to do what you did that day.'

'More stupid than brave.'

'I don't agree. So I suppose that was when you stopped making documentaries?'

'Yep. I had to come home to get proper medical treatment. Then, once I was home, I decided I'd had enough of traipsing around the world. Craig said I'd get tired of it one day and he was right.'

'Then why do you want to go back overseas?'

'Travelling as a tourist is very different from what I was doing, Abby. Have you seen any of the documentaries I made?'

'No.'

'Then don't. They're grim viewing.'

'Then why did you make them?'

He shrugged. 'Initially, I thought it would be great fun, following Craig around and filming the places he went and the things he witnessed. But after a few years I found myself becoming emotionally involved in the injustices I saw. I naively thought that if the problems of the Third World were shoved in the face of the Western World, they might do something to solve at least some of those problems. That was when I became a crusader. But I was deluding myself. People liked watching my more hard-hitting documentaries. I made a lot of money out of them. But they didn't inspire much action. There's still war and poverty and abuse of the worst kind. Nothing ever changes.'

'But you tried,' Abby said gently. 'All you can do is try, Jake.'

'You *are* sweet,' he said. 'But could we possibly change the subject?'

Abby was touched by his sensitivity. Clearly, he wasn't as selfish and self-centred as he liked to pretend. But then, she'd already known that, hadn't she, even before she'd heard the good things Tony had said about him. Look at the way he'd followed through with his uncle's legacy to her, even though he hadn't wanted to at first.

A thought suddenly occurred to her.

'Were you telling the truth when you said you were jealous of Raoul?'

'Jealous? I wanted to tear him limb from limb.'

'But why? I mean…we weren't an item then.'

'Maybe not. But I already wanted you like crazy.'

She shook her head from side to side. 'I find that hard to believe.'

'Oh, Abby, Abby, you gorgeous thing, you.' He sighed and shook his head back at her. 'You don't understand men very well, do you? Now, drink up your champers, sweet thing. I have an urge to have my wicked way with you. All chit-chat is to cease as of this moment. That is, except for words like, *Yes, Jake. Please, Jake. Don't stop, Jake.*'

She couldn't help it. She laughed.

'Don't you dare laugh at me, you cheeky minx.'

She smiled instead and said, 'Yes, Jake.'

CHAPTER TWENTY-SIX

IT WAS LIGHT when Abby came to consciousness, turning over on to her back and stretching before glancing over at the sleeping male form next to her in the bed. Jake was lying on his side, his back to her, his breathing deep and heavy.

She smiled in memory of Jake's reluctance to let her go to sleep, even when it was obvious he'd exhausted himself making love to her. The only time they'd stopped was first at six-thirty so she could take her Pill and then when he'd ordered room service around eight, a huge seafood platter which they'd devoured together in record time before getting back to devouring each other.

Abby picked up her phone from the bedside table and checked the time, surprised to find that it was after nine. They'd finally gone to sleep around two, so both of them had had a good seven hours of sleep. Still, no need to wake Jake yet, she decided, rising quietly and going to the bathroom. Closing the door behind her, she turned on the light and took a good look at herself in the large mirror.

Not only was her hair a total mess—she really should have put it up before that last shower—but she had faint bruises on her breasts.

'Goodness, Abby,' she said, sounding slightly shocked. 'You look like a woman who's been well and truly ravaged.'

'And didn't you just love it,' she answered herself in a low sexy voice which wasn't at all shocked.

The new Abby realised there was no point in pretending. Given she was unlikely ever to come across a lover like Jake again, she aimed to take full advantage of his erotic skills—plus his gorgeous male body—whilst she had the chance. If she had to have her heart broken by him at some stage in the future, then she was going to enjoy herself in the meantime.

Though how long that meantime lasted was anybody's idea, she accepted with an inevitable lurching of her silly female heart. Okay, so he'd asked her to go overseas with him next year. And he *had* sounded as if he meant it. But that could just have been a wild impulse on his part. He could change his mind tomorrow. Or next week. Or next month. It was only mid November. All she could rely on was today. The present. This moment.

'That's it, kiddo,' she told herself firmly. 'Live for the moment. Now, go wake up old sleepyhead.'

With her body buzzing from wicked resolve, Abby returned to the bedroom and climbed in under the sheet next to a still unconscious Jake. She didn't hesitate, snuggling up to him with her naked front pressed up against his back, her left hand free to travel at will over his body, much the same way as he had done to her in the bath. He stirred slightly the moment her fingers brushed over his nipples, but shot awake with a raw gasp when her hand moved further south.

'You have a beautiful penis,' she murmured. 'Nice and long. And so silky up here.'

He made a strangled sound as she ran her thumb pad over the engorged tip.

'You like that, don't you?' she crooned, another echo of what he'd said to her when he'd teased her at length in the water. 'But you'd rather I do this with my tongue, wouldn't you?'

When he swore she laughed. 'No, not this time, Jake. This time you're going to let me have *my* wicked way with *you*.'

It surprised Abby how in control she felt, her own needs firmly in check as she set about making *him* lose control. She loved it when he called out her name as he came, blown away by the satisfaction she felt as his whole body shook.

But alongside the satisfaction lay the certainty that she

would not feel this way with any other man. The realisation hit suddenly that she loved Jake—loved him in the way she should have loved Wayne, but hadn't. The thought sent tears into her eyes, tears of guilt and regret and true sadness.

The old Abby might have fallen apart at that moment. The new Abby was a far tougher creature. She told herself firmly that she'd gone into this affair with her eyes open and it was a little late to start becoming maudlin. So she gathered her emotions, blinked away the tears and lifted her head.

It was impossible not to look at him. Impossible to stop her emotions suddenly getting the better of her. How awful it was to love someone the way she loved Jake without being able to tell him.

Jake was taken aback when he saw she was on the verge of tears.

'Abby! Darling! What is it? What's wrong?'

'Oh, God,' she cried, then burst into tears.

Stricken with remorse over he knew not what, Jake cuddled her close, searching his mind at the same time for the reason behind her tears.

'Tell me what's wrong,' he said as he cradled her face and rained kisses all over it.

She made a choking sound, closing her eyes at the same time.

'You wanted to do that, didn't you? I didn't ask you. You *wanted* to. And I loved it. Truly I did.'

Still, she said nothing, just buried her face into his shoulder and wept.

'Please don't cry, my darling.'

She opened her still wet eyes then and just stared at him. 'Don't call me that,' she blurted out. 'I'm not your darling.'

Jake didn't know how to respond. Had her husband called her his darling? Was that it?

'What do you want me to call you?'

She closed her eyes again as she shook her head. 'Oh, God. I'm so stupid.'

Jake sighed. He wished he knew what was going on in her head. But he'd never been good at reading women's minds. Females could be complex creatures. Maybe she was hormonal. Maybe her period was due. All he knew was that he hated seeing her upset, her tears calling to something deep inside himself which was impossible to control. His heart actually ached with the need to make her feel better.

'Abby… I hate seeing you like this. I wish you'd tell me what's wrong. I want to be your friend as well as your lover. I want you to feel that you can tell me anything.'

He waited and finally, when she opened her eyes, her expression was calmer. Or was it resigned?

'It's not you,' she said. 'It's me. You haven't done anything wrong. I love what kind of lover you are. I've had more fun with you this weekend than I've had in years.'

Jake pulled a face. Now she made it sound as if he was shallow. Yet he felt anything but shallow when he was making love to her. Perhaps because that was exactly what it was. Making love. Not just having sex. Jake could no longer pretend that he wasn't becoming seriously involved with Abby. He'd avoiding falling in love in the past because he didn't want marriage and children. What Jake hadn't realised was that true love could not be avoided. It just happened. If truth be told, he'd been half in love with Abby from the moment he'd hugged her that awful day, long before she'd stormed past his conscience less than two days ago. Now he was well and truly head over heels.

But of course he couldn't tell her any of that. Not yet. She didn't want him to love her. Not at the moment. Perhaps one day, when the time was right, when he was sure that she returned his feelings, he would declare his love and they would find a way to spend their lives together. Not marriage. Though perhaps a child eventually, if that was what she ever wanted. Jake still wasn't thrilled with the idea of becoming a father but one child might be manageable.

'So why were you crying just now?' he asked.

Abby shrugged. 'This will sound silly but I was feeling guilty that I couldn't give my husband the pleasure that I obviously give you. Wayne deserved better than a wife who didn't really love him.'

'You did love him, Abby,' he reassured her. 'I know you. You wouldn't have married him if you hadn't loved him. Maybe it wasn't a mad passion but it was love all the same. It wasn't your fault that the physical chemistry between you wasn't right. It wasn't his fault, either. But that's all in the past, Abby. You can't change what happened in your marriage and it's a waste of time to beat yourself up over it.'

'You're right,' she said, nodding. 'I can't change anything that's already happened. All we have is the present. I decided earlier today that I want to live in the moment from now on. That's what you do, isn't it?'

'To a degree,' he replied carefully. 'I do make some plans for the future when required.'

'You mean like when going overseas.'

'That's a good example. You can't just show up at the airport and take the first available flight. You need to do things first.'

'Like get a passport,' she said, her eyes looking marginally happier.

'Indeed,' he said, smiling.

'I'll get straight on to that first thing next week. And I might do some more clothes shopping at some stage. I don't want you ever feeling ashamed of me.'

Jake was truly taken aback. 'I would never be ashamed of you.' But it did occur to him that women thought differently to men on matters of fashion.

'You should go clothes shopping with Sophie. She would know exactly what you need. I tell you what; I'll ring and ask her to take you.'

'Oh, no, don't do that. I can't afford the sort of clothes your sister would show me.'

'Yes, you can. I'll give her my credit card. It doesn't have a limit.'

'I can't let you do that!' she exclaimed.

'Why not?'

'Because…because…'

'I'm a very rich man, Abby. I want to do this for you. Please don't say no.'

'I shouldn't let you.'

'Don't be silly. I'll ring her and tell her you need a new wardrobe to cover every occasion. Now, no more objections. I insist. And another thing, you have to ring your sister tonight and tell her about us.'

Abby groaned. 'I really don't want to, Jake.'

'And I don't want to keep on being your secret lover,' he growled. 'I certainly don't intend to spend every date with you wearing sunglasses and a baseball cap. The world is going to find out about us sooner or later, Abby, and there's nothing you can do about that.'

'I know,' she said with a sigh. 'But at least we have today before that happens.'

'Don't you believe it. That receptionist last night was probably on Instagram and Twitter within seconds of our booking in. You can't keep anything a secret these days, not if you're in the public eye. You just have to not care what people think or say. People that don't matter, that is. Family is different.'

'Are you going to tell your family about me?'

Jake smiled. 'I won't have to. Sophie will. But, speaking of family, I want you to join us for our harbour cruise on Christmas Day.'

Dismay filled Abby's face. 'I'm sorry, Jake, but I can't do that. I've already invited Megan and Timmy to spend Christmas Day with me and I would never disappoint them.'

'I see,' he said, thinking he should have known. Olivia

would have dumped her family like a shot if he'd asked her to be with him on Christmas Day. But Abby was not Olivia. She was unique. A woman in a million. 'Well, there's no reason why they can't both come on the harbour cruise with all of us,' he said. 'There'll be plenty of room, and plenty of food. And lots of other kids for Timmy to play with.'

'That's incredibly generous of you, Jake, but I'm not sure Megan will want to come.'

'Why's that? Is she shy?'

Abby laughed. 'Not exactly.'

'Look, when you ring her tonight, just ask her.'

'What if she says no?'

'Then I'll ring her and ask her myself. I've been told I can be very persuasive, when I want to be.'

Abby's expression was pained. 'As long as you don't flirt with her. If you do that, I won't be too happy. She already thinks you're God's gift to women.'

'In that case persuade her to come yourself. Because I don't intend to be without you on Christmas Day. I also want to show you off to my whole family, and that way we can do it all in one go. Far better than having to trot you around to everyone one at a time.'

'You won't tell them about my background, will you? And my teeth!'

'Sorry, sweetheart, they'll already know everything about you by then. Sophie is not renowned for keeping her mouth shut. And why wouldn't you want them to know about your teeth? They look fabulous!'

'I wasn't referring to my new teeth but my old ones.'

'There's nothing shameful about having had problem teeth.'

'Pardon me if I don't think so,' Abby said, rolling away from him on to the bed, her body language indicating she wasn't happy.

'Okay,' he said nonchalantly.

'What?' Stormy green eyes shot his way.

'I'll pardon you. For about ten seconds. You're the one who said you wanted to move on with your life. Well, the first thing for you to do is not be oversensitive about your past. I want to tell my family all about you because I'm serious about you, Abby. I don't want you for a fling. Okay, I might not want marriage but I want you in my life. If you must know, I was attracted to you from the first moment I saw you.'

'You *were*?'

'I certainly was. But I thought you were the sort of woman who would want marriage and children so I kept my distance. Regardless of what you think of me, I am not a compulsive womaniser. I would never target a woman who was emotionally vulnerable, which I thought you were, being a widow. But on Friday night you confirmed that you didn't want to get married again. After that, I decided to hell with resisting temptation any longer. I wanted you like mad by then and decided I was going to have you.'

Only then did Jake realise Abby was looking pole-axed by his confession. He wasn't sure if that meant she was pleased, or sceptical.

'That was why I was jealous of Raoul,' he went on. 'Now, no more of this nonsense. And no more regrets about the past. You're living for the moment, are you not? And the moment calls for two activities. Breakfast first. I don't know about you but I'm starving. Then once we're dressed, fed and out of here I'm going to do something really amazing.'

'And what's that?'

'I'm going to let you drive my car.'

CHAPTER TWENTY-SEVEN

'I CAN'T BELIEVE IT,' Megan said for the umpteenth time since Abby had called her that Sunday night.

Abby sighed. 'I don't know why you keep saying that. You were the one who warned me Jake might come on to me if I smartened myself up.'

'It's not that I don't believe he fancies you; it's all the sex! I always thought you were frigid.'

'Well, I'm obviously not.'

'Obviously. At least, not with lover boy. But then, he's had a lot of practice seducing women.'

'Jake did not seduce me, Megan. I was with him all the way.'

'Honestly?'

'Honestly.'

'Wow.'

'He's asked me to go overseas with him next year.'

'You have to be kidding me.'

'I kid you not. I'm applying for my passport this week. Apparently, it takes a few weeks to get it.'

'This is insane, Abby. You do know that, don't you? I mean…it won't last. Men like Jake…they don't do for ever.'

'I'm well aware of that, Megan. He was nothing if not brutally honest with me on that score. No marriage and no children. But he claims he does want a relationship with me, not just a fling. So I am going to go overseas with him and nothing you say is going to stop me.'

'Oh, God, you've fallen in love with the bastard, haven't you?'

Abby sighed again. 'Jake is not a bastard, Megan. He's a very nice man. A gentleman, in fact. And yes, I've fallen in love with him. But not to worry. I've already come to terms with my feelings. I know I'm going to be hurt at some time in the future but I've decided not to worry about the future for a while. Or the past. I'm living for the here and now. Jake likes me. A lot. And he wants me. A lot. I won't give that up just because it might end badly one day.'

'I've never heard you talk like this, Abby. You sound so sure. And so mature.'

'I've grown up a bit since Wayne died.'

'He wasn't right for you,' Megan said gently, bringing a lump to Abby's throat.

'I can see that now,' Abby agreed. 'I talked with Jake about my marriage and he said I had to let it go. That it was past history.'

'He's right. But surely you didn't tell Jake everything, did you? I mean I know how you hate talking about your miscarriages.'

Abby's heart immediately squeezed tight in her chest. 'No, I didn't tell him about them. He thinks we were trying for a baby but it just didn't happen. It was more my relationship with Wayne I talked about. I told Jake I didn't want to get married again.'

'When did you say that?'

'I'm not sure. Some time recently. It might have been the day he took me car shopping.'

'After which he decided it was safe to seduce you,' came Megan's dry remark.

Abby rolled her eyes. 'Whatever.' Abby hadn't told Megan about Jake's declaration that he'd had the hots for her from the day he hired her. Mostly because Megan was too cynical to believe that. But, surprisingly, Abby did. For she could find no reason for Jake to lie to her. Not that it would change the ultimate outcome of their relationship. It gave Abby a real thrill to think she'd captured his interest but he'd cared enough about her emotional well-being not to pursue her at the time.

'I bet you'd marry Jake in a shot if he asked you to.'

'He isn't going to, Megan. He has, however, asked me to spend Christmas Day with him and his extended family on a harbour cruise.'

'Wow. He must be pretty serious about you then, if he wants you to meet his mum and dad.'

'He's only got a mum. His dad's dead. But he also has two brothers and three sisters, four of whom are married with children.'

'Good grief, I hope it's a big boat.'

'Very big, he said. Which is why you and Timmy are invited as well.'

'What? You're kidding! This is just so out there. I'm going on a harbour cruise with Jake Sanderson and his family? Golly, I'll have to go on a diet straight away. And buy something new to wear.'

'Speaking of new clothes, I'm going clothes shopping with Jake's sister some time this week. Jake insisted on buying me a whole new wardrobe.'

'Seriously? A whole new wardrobe?'

'Yes. And before you make any smart cracks about me being a kept woman, how about I get her to pick out something for you at the same time? I know your size and she'll choose something really stylish, since she's a stylist.'

Megan laughed. 'You're worried I'm going to turn up in something cheap and trashy, aren't you?'

'Not at all!' Abby exclaimed.

'You're such a bad liar. But not bad at keeping secrets, it turns out. There I was, trying to ring you all weekend and getting really mad, thinking that you'd accidentally turned off your phone. And now I find out that you did it on purpose so that you and your boss could bonk away like a pair of bloody rabbits.'

'You have such a delicate turn of phrase.'

'Gee, Abby. Ever since you started reading all those fancy books you seem different.'

'Different? How?'

'Oh, you know. Like you had some toffee-nosed education. Don't forget your roots, girl. You're a Westie and there's nothing you can do to change that.'

'I'm not trying to change that. I know exactly where I came from. But there's nothing wrong with trying to better myself. Even if my affair with Jake hadn't happened, I would have been going to night school next year, as well as saving up to travel all by myself.'

'But Jake has happened, so now you'll drop all those plans. Just don't forget that when *he* drops *you* you're going to lose your job as well. Have you thought of that?'

'It's crossed my mind. But like I said, I'm not going to worry about the future too much, Megan. I'm going to live for the moment.'

'That's because you're madly in love at the moment.'

'You can't talk me out of this, Megan. Now, I'm getting off this phone and going to bed. I've had a very tiring weekend.'

'Yeah, so I heard. I still can't believe it. Did you two do anything else this weekend except have wild sex?'

'I never said it was wild.'

'Yeah, right. Pull the other leg. I'll bet lover boy did more to you in one weekend than Wayne did in five frigging years.'

'You could be right there.'

'Ooh, do tell!'

'Absolutely not. I'm off to bed. Goodnight, Megan.'

Abby shook her head as she terminated the call then turned off her phone. She didn't have a landline so her sister and her curiosity would have to wait. Megan might want her to give a blow-by-blow account of her various sexual escapades but Abby was not that kind of girl. She was a very private person. And so was Jake, in his own way. She could see he didn't overly like his celebrity status any more than she did.

Abby got herself ready for bed, since she actually was *very* tired. Which was just as well. She didn't want to lie in bed and start overthinking everything. There was a time for deep and meaningful thinking, and it wasn't now. Now was the time for sleep.

Abby was settling herself down into sleep mode when all of a sudden she remembered that Jake had asked her to call him and tell her how things went with Megan. Sitting up in bed abruptly, she reached for her phone, instantly energised by the thought of talking to Jake. He answered on the second ring.

'I was beginning to think you weren't going to call me,' he said.

'I'm sorry, Jake. I forgot.'

'That's not very flattering, I must say. A couple of hours out of my sight and you forget me.'

Abby knew he wasn't really angry. She could hear the teasing note in his voice. 'You're not going to be one of those boyfriends, are you?' she teased back.

'And what kind is that?'

'The obsessive kind.'

'That depends on whether you're going to be one of those girlfriends.'

'And what kind is that?'

'The ones who drive men insane because they don't ring when they say they're going to.'

'I said I was sorry.'

'You also said you forgot.'

'I dare say you're not used to being forgotten.'

'Not often. But all this is beside the point. Did you tell your sister about us?'

'Yes.'

'And?'

'She wasn't shocked that we're sleeping together, but she's worried that I'm going to lose my job when we eventually break up.'

'Who says we'll eventually break up?'

'It seems likely, given your history with women.'

'I'm not as fickle as the tabloids make out.'

'I know that. But, in any case, I'm not worried. I can always get another job, provided you give me a good reference.'

'I'm not sure I like that sister of yours. She sounds like trouble.'

'She's only looking after my best interests.'

'And I'm not?'

'Don't go getting all huffy, Jake. Why do you think I didn't want to ring her? But you insisted. Sometimes she rattles me with her cynicism but this time I didn't take notice of anything she said, which rather pleased me. I want to be with you, Jake, and nothing that Megan or anyone else says is going to change my mind.'

'You've no idea how glad I am to hear that. Because I want to be with you too. And not for just a few weeks, or a few months. I have a feeling this relationship might go the whole nine yards.'

Abby sucked in sharply. 'And what does that mean?'

'Now, don't *you* go getting all huffy. I'm not talking marriage. But I am talking about living together, as of tomorrow.'

'Tomorrow?'

'Too soon for you?'

Abby tried not to lose her head. She might be madly in love with Jake but she wasn't about to let him run every aspect of her life.

'A little,' she said. 'How about we wait till after Christmas?'

'But that's over five weeks away!'

'That's hardly a lifetime.'

'So you're knocking me back.'

'I'd like us to just date for a while before taking such a big step.'

'But you've already agreed to go away with me next year,' Jake argued.

'Yes, but that's just a holiday, not real life.'

'Not real life,' he echoed, clearly taken aback.

'Jake, could we not get into this right now? I'm tired and I want to go to sleep. We can talk about this tomorrow.'

Jake could not believe that Abby was giving him the brush-off. He hadn't been on the receiving end of that before. He almost blurted out that he loved her but he held his tongue just in time.

'Fair enough,' he said. 'Till tomorrow then. Goodnight.'

'Goodnight, Jake. And thank you again, for such a wonderful weekend.'

Jake kept the dead phone clamped to his ear for ages whilst he tried to work out exactly what he was feeling. Frustration, mainly. Not sexual frustration—frustration that for the first time in his life he wanted more from a relationship than the woman did. Not only did he want Abby to move in with him, he wanted her to love him the way he loved her. But she didn't want to fall in love. She wanted fun and games, with a fancy holiday overseas thrown in for good measure.

'Not real life,' he growled when he finally threw his phone down. He'd show her real life. He'd take her to places in Asia and Africa where real life meant crippling poverty and appalling cruelty, with no hope for the future.

But no sooner had these vengeful thoughts entered his head than Jake realised he would never do anything so contemptible. Abby deserved better than to be on the receiving end of that kind of behaviour. She deserved the very best this world had to offer. He would take her to large vibrant cities like London and Paris, Tokyo and New York. And then there were the magnificent rivers. He'd take her cruising down the Seine, and the Rhine, and the Danube. Maybe even the Nile, if Egypt got its act together.

Jake's good humour returned as he thought about their trip next year. It would be incredible. The trip of a lifetime, for both of them. And who knew, by the time they returned Abby might care about him enough to move in with him permanently. She might even love him.

He wasn't that unlovable, was he?

CHAPTER TWENTY-EIGHT

ABBY HAD ALWAYS liked Jake's house, sometimes fantasising in her head as she'd cleaned it that if she ever had a spare couple of million dollars she would buy herself such a house. She loved the white walls and the polished wooden floors, the high ceilings and the unfussy furniture. She especially loved the sparkling white kitchen and bathrooms.

But as she cleaned Jake's house that Monday morning it wasn't buying such a house she began fantasising about, but living here. Which of course was no longer a wild fantasy but a fact, *if* she changed her mind and moved in, the way Jake wanted her to.

She was tempted. She wouldn't have been human if she wasn't tempted. But as much as Abby had resolved to live in the moment, common sense demanded she not ignore what would happen if she gave in to Jake's suggestion. Before she knew it she would stop being a Housewife For Hire, but a housewife for real. She'd start thinking of this house as her home and Jake her de facto husband. She'd start cooking for him and caring for him and, yes, loving him with all her heart and soul. Inevitably, the day would come when she'd blurt out how much she loved him.

And that would be the beginning of the end.

Far better, she decided as she worked her way steadily through the upstairs rooms, that she stay strong and not do what Jake wanted. Except in the bedroom, that was. She was not foolish enough to think she wouldn't do whatever he wanted there. Already, she missed his lovemaking, waking this morning with a wave of desire so powerful that it had taken all of her willpower not to ring him on the spot and beg him to come home early from work.

Fortunately, she'd got a grip in time and plunged herself into the shower instead. But her heart had leapt when her phone rang as she exited the bathroom.

It was Jake.

'Hi,' he'd said in that lovely voice of his. 'Sleep well?'

'Like the dead. And you?'

'So-so. I would have slept better if you'd been with me. Which brings me to the point of this early morning call. I understand that you don't want to live with me twenty-four-seven, but most girlfriends sleep over occasionally.'

Abby resisted telling him that she *had* noticed that.

'I probably will,' she'd said carefully. 'But only after we've been out on a date.'

'I see. In that case I'll just have to ask you out every night.'

'I wouldn't want to go out every night, Jake. I do have other things I have to do, and a sister I like to visit.'

'Fair enough. What about tonight?'

She'd wanted to say yes. Desperately so. Abby knew, however, that she had to maintain some control over this relationship or she'd be lost for ever.

'I don't think so, Jake. I noticed this morning that my place needs some attention. If I don't water the garden soon, all my plants will die. We haven't had rain for ages.'

'The weather forecast predicts a storm this afternoon,' he'd pointed out, his voice on the stormy side itself.

'I never listen to weather forecasts.'

'Don't you watch morning television?'

'I don't watch much television these days.' She used to watch it non-stop when she was a stay-at-home wife with no children and nothing much to do. She still watched the occasional movie but on the whole Abby now preferred to read.

'Have you ever watched my show?'

'Once or twice.'

'And?'

'You're very good at what you do.'

'Sophie thinks it's lightweight. And it is. Which is also why it's so popular, and why I'm going to get oodles of money for it.'

'You're definitely going to sell?'

'I've already put the sale in motion. It will take a couple of weeks to finalise things, though. Meanwhile, I have to do the show and keep the ratings up.'

'Right. Maybe I'll watch it today. Tell you what I think of your performance.'

Jake laughed. 'While I've got you on the phone, Sophie is going to ring you today. I told her all about me wanting her to help you with your new wardrobe and she wants to line up a date.'

Abby sighed. 'Do I really have to buy a whole new wardrobe?'

'Why can't you be like other women, Abby? Most of them would be over the moon at getting a whole new wardrobe, especially one chosen by one of Sydney's top stylists.'

'I guess I would like it better if I could pay for it myself. I have the money. Twenty-five thousand dollars, remember?'

'That's not for clothes. That's for travel. Not that I expect you to pay for anything when you're with me. Think of that money as your emergency fund. For later in your life. Or for when you tire of me and want to go your own way.'

Abby knew she would never get tired of Jake. She loved the man. But she could hardly say so. 'If you insist.'

'I insist. I'll be home early so don't rush off till I get there. I have a surprise for you.'

'What kind of surprise?'

'If I told you that then it wouldn't be a surprise.'

'You're a terrible tease, Jake Sanderson.'

'Takes one to know one. See you around about three.'

It wasn't even close to three, Abby thought as she started cleaning Jake's kitchen later that morning. It was only eleven-thirty. But already her body was humming with anticipation. Not just because of his promised surprise but because she wanted to see him, wanted to kiss him, wanted to make love to him, and vice versa.

In the end, she turned on the television at noon and watched his show, just so that she could feast her eyes on his handsome face and those sexy blue eyes. After it was over, she could hardly remember the content, her mind filling with images of what they'd done together over the weekend and what they might do in the future. No, not the future. Today. This afternoon. As soon as he got home. She could not wait till they went on some stupid date; her need was too strong for that.

Abby was feverishly cleaning the kitchen counter tops when her phone rang again. But it wasn't Jake. It was his sister, Sophie, who was in a rush and quickly told Abby when and where to meet her the following day before apologising and then dashing off before Abby could object to anything.

Like sister like brother, she thought.

By five to three that afternoon, Abby was in quite a state, her body at war with her mind. To throw herself at Jake as soon as he walked in the door would undo all the groundwork she'd laid down to keep some control over her life. But oh, how she wanted him.

The sound of his key in the front door brought a cry to her lips followed by an abrupt stiffening of her spine. *Be strong, Abby! And, above all, be cool.*

He strode into the kitchen, still dressed in the superb suit he'd worn on his show.

'Hi there,' she said, her smile feeling a tad forced. 'Want me to put on some coffee for you?'

'Not particularly,' he replied as he swept across the kitchen and pulled her into his arms.

'Coffee is the last thing on my mind at the moment,' he ground out as his head descended.

'Could I tempt you into sleeping over tonight?' Jake asked when his mouth finally lifted from hers, his hands remaining clamped over her shoulders. 'After I take you out to dinner, of course.'

Abby took a couple of seconds to get her head together, which wasn't easy considering it was totally scrambled.

'I can't stay the whole night,' she said with dismay in her voice. 'Your sister rang and she's arranged to take me shopping all day tomorrow. Which means I have to go home some time tonight and do all sorts of girl things so that I look my best.'

'Fair enough,' Jake said, then kissed her some more.

'What about my surprise?' she asked when he finally gave her a breather.

Jake smiled. 'I almost forgot about that. Look, it's nothing sparkly or expensive. I suspect you don't want to be that kind of girlfriend. It's just a fun present.' And out of his suit pocket he brought a packet of condoms, each one with a different fruit flavour. 'I thought, since we have to use condoms, then we should at least make things interesting.'

Abby had to smile. 'Where on earth did you buy them? Over the internet?'

'Nope. I did a segment on condoms one day on my show and these were given to me as samples. I've had them in a drawer in my dressing room for months.'

Abby liked that he hadn't used them on any of his other girlfriends. 'Such interesting flavours,' she said as she read the list on the packet. 'I like the sound of pineapple and coconut. And, of course, passion fruit. Blood orange sounds dangerous.'

'In that case, we'll try that one first,' he said as he shoved the condom packet in his pocket then bent to scoop her up into his arms.

'Come on,' he said. 'Let's go have some fun.'

CHAPTER TWENTY-NINE

'NO, NOT THAT one,' Sophie said when Abby came out of the dressing room in a black and white spotted dress that she herself had chosen. 'It makes you look too busty. When a girl is as well endowed as you, Abby, she should never wear dresses which come right up to the neck. You should mainly stick to lower necklines, not to mention block colours. You can get away with some patterned materials but only if the design is delicate and not overpowering. That dress you wore last Friday night looked good on you because the pattern wasn't too big, or bright. And the dress had a V neckline, if you recall.'

Abby sighed. 'There's a lot more to choosing the right wardrobe than I ever imagined. It's also very tiring.' They'd been at it all day, only stopping for a light lunch. Admittedly, they'd bought heaps, Sophie waving aside any protest from Abby, claiming she'd been given instructions from Jake that there was to be no expense spared. Abby was to have a full wardrobe suitable for travelling, and which catered for every occasion and season.

Abby had stopped looking at the price tags after a while, but she knew the clothes had to be costing a small fortune, Sophie taking her into several expensive-looking boutiques as well as those floors in the big city department stores which carried the designer ranges. Jake's sister got special treatment everywhere she went, the sales people obviously knowing her well. They didn't even have to carry their purchases around, the various shops agreeing to deliver everything they bought—free of charge.

Whilst Abby felt somewhat overwhelmed by the experience, she suspected she could quickly get used to being treated with such consideration and deference. She could also get used to wearing the kind of clothes which fitted perfectly and looked fantastic. Ignoring any qualms that she was fast becoming a kept woman, Abby resolved to enjoy the experience. After all, Jake could afford it; Sophie told her over coffee just how much he'd inherited from his uncle. Not that she'd sounded jealous. Apparently, Sophie had received a substantial cash legacy, as had all her brothers and sisters; her mother as well.

'Come on,' she said to Abby. 'Get that dress off and we'll call it quits for today. Tomorrow I'll take you shopping for shoes and handbags and underwear.'

'Underwear?' Abby exclaimed.

'Got to have the right underwear, Abby. It can make all the difference to the way a garment looks. Same with the shoes. And then, of course, there's the jewellery.'

'No,' Abby protested at last. 'No jewellery.'

'But…'

'No buts. And no jewellery. I've gone along with this wardrobe business because I don't want to embarrass Jake by not being dressed correctly. But I am his girlfriend, Sophie, not his mistress. So I'd like to keep the underwear and the accessories to a minimum, if you don't mind. I'm not broke. Once I know what I should be buying I can get some of these things myself. I appreciate your help, I really do. But enough is enough!'

'Wow. You can be really forceful when you want to be.'

Abby realised with some surprise that that was true. But forcefulness was a fairly recent trait.

'I've had to learn to be forceful with Jake,' she said. 'He's way too used to getting his own way with women.'

Sophie grinned. 'You could be right there.'

'Did he tell you he asked me to move in with him?'

'No!' Sophie exclaimed, stunned. 'Now that's a first.'

'Oh, dear. Maybe I shouldn't have mentioned it.'

'Why not? Am I right in presuming you said no?'

'Yes, I did. For now, at least.'

'Good for you. Make the devil wait.'

'He might not ask me again,' Abby said with a frown.

Sophie smiled. 'I think he will. Now, why don't you put on those sexy blue jeans you had on earlier? I'll find you a white shirt to go with them, and some little black pumps. Then we'll go down to Café Sydney for some drinks before dinner. I'll text Jake to meet us there instead of going home.'

'No, please don't do that,' Abby said straight away. 'I got a text from Jake earlier today saying that he has a meeting with the man who's buying his show and he's sure to have to take him to dinner. Look, I honestly think I should just go home. I'm wrecked. I wouldn't mind a coffee first, though.'

She didn't want to tell Sophie that she could feel a headache coming on. She really needed to sit down for a while and take a couple of painkillers before it developed into a migraine.

Unfortunately, by the time they got out of the department store and into a café, Abby was seeing circles in front of her eyes. Fortunately, the table they were shown to had a bottle of water already on the table with two clean glasses. Abby poured herself a glass immediately then dived into the inner zipped section of her handbag where she kept her painkillers. It was also where she always put her Pills if she was going to be away from home in the evening, like last Friday night.

The sight of her strip of Pills made Abby catch her breath. There was one more than there should have been. *What on earth...?*

Instantly alarmed, she checked the strip again.

'What's the matter?' Sophie asked. 'What have you lost?'

Abby groaned. She hadn't lost anything, except perhaps her mind. For she knew immediately what must have happened. She'd forgotten to take the Pill on the night of the dinner party, just the way she'd feared. And then in the panic of the moment she had miscounted.

Her head spun at the thought of all the unsafe sex she'd had that same night. Just the *possibility* that she might have fallen pregnant sent her stomach swirling and her breathing haywire.

'Abby, what's wrong?' Sophie asked, alarmed.

'I think I'm going to be sick,' she choked out, leaping up and rushing for the Ladies, where she dry retched into the toilet. Afraid that she was going to faint, she sank down on to the tiled toilet floor, pale-faced and panting.

Sophie didn't know what to do. Abby looked dreadful. It reminded her of how her father had looked when he'd had his heart attack. Though surely Abby was too young to have a heart attack.

'Do you have any pains in your chest?' she asked frantically.

When Abby nodded, Sophie didn't hesitate. She called for an ambulance. Ten minutes later, paramedics were checking Abby over, taking her blood pressure and asking her questions. In the end, they declared that she wasn't having a heart attack but a panic attack, which sometimes had similar symptoms to a coronary. They administered a sedative, both for her nausea and her nerves, then suggested Sophie take her straight home. Before they left, one of the paramedics quietly told Sophie to encourage her friend to see a therapist to discover the cause of such a severe panic attack.

Within no time they were in a taxi heading for Balmain, Sophie overriding Abby's request to go to her own home, saying that she wasn't taking her anywhere she would be alone. Then she rang Jake and explained the situation. Not that she could really *explain* the situation.

'A *panic* attack?' Jake exclaimed, sounding both shocked and puzzled. 'What in hell happened to give her a panic attack?'

'Honestly, Jake, I don't know. She was looking for something in her handbag when she suddenly went a ghastly colour. Then she bolted for the Ladies. Look, I suggest you make your excuses and catch a ferry home. I dare say we'll be at your place before you are, even though this is the long way around. I'll put Abby to bed in the downstairs guest room. She's almost asleep now. The ambulance guys gave her something to calm her down.'

'I wish I knew what upset her in the first place.'

'Me too. We'll put our heads together when you get home.'

'I'm on my way.'

'Good.' She clicked off then dropped her phone in her own handbag.

'You shouldn't have called him,' Abby mumbled from where she was half sitting, half lying in the corner of the back seat.

'Are you kidding me? Jake would have had my guts for garters if I hadn't. He loves you, Abby,' Sophie said, not because Jake had confessed as much to her but because she knew her brother better than anyone. No way would he have asked Abby to live with him if he didn't love her.

Abby shook her head from side to side. 'No, he doesn't.'

'Oh, yes, he does,' Sophie insisted, wondering if this was part of Abby's problem—the fact that Jake was asking a lot of her without telling her that he loved her. She would have to speak to him about that.

'But let's not worry about that right now,' Sophie went on, and gently pulled Abby over towards her, putting an arm around her shoulders and cradling her head against her chest. 'All you need to do at the moment is rest.'

When a deeply emotional shudder rippled through Abby's body, Sophie wanted to weep. She wasn't the most empathetic of people, but there was something about Abby which touched her. Sophie could see that she'd touched Jake too, more than anyone else ever had. She had no doubt that he loved her. Of course, it was highly possible her anti-commitment bachelor brother didn't know that he'd fallen in love at long last. Maybe she should tell him. As soon as he got home—*before* he went in to talk to Abby.

His blue eyes stormed at her across the kitchen. 'You're not telling me anything I don't already know, Sophie. I realised over the weekend that I was in love with her.'

'Then why haven't you told her?'

'Perhaps because she doesn't want *any* man to love her at the moment, Miss Smarty-Pants. You heard what she said last Friday night. She doesn't want to get married again. If you don't mind, I would like to go in and talk to Abby and see if I can find out what upset her.'

'She might be asleep,' Sophie called after him as he strode from the room.

She wasn't. She was just lying there in the bed, on her back, her hands crossed over her chest, her eyes fixed on the ceiling. Jake watched her from the doorway for a long moment, his heart going out to her, his ego troubled by the thought that he might not be able to fix whatever it was that had distressed her so much. When he finally walked into the room, she turned her head to look at him, her face bleak but worryingly blank.

'Sophie shouldn't have interrupted your meeting,' she said in a dull voice. 'Or brought me here. I would have preferred to go home but she insisted and I was too weak to argue with her.'

Jake sat down on the side of the bed and picked up one of Abby's hands. It was alarmingly cold.

'She did the right thing,' he said as he gently rubbed her hand with both of his. 'You had a nasty turn, from what I've been told. A severe panic attack, according to the paramedics.'

'Yes,' was all Abby said before she turned her eyes away to stare up at the ceiling again.

Jake hated seeing her like this. So sad. *Too* sad.

'Do you know what caused it?' he asked softly.

'Oh, yes,' she said with a strange sigh.

Jake's hands stilled on her. 'What?'

'The Pill in my handbag,' she answered, still without looking at him. 'I miscounted, which means I didn't take my Pill last Friday night after all. Which also means that I could be pregnant.'

Jake tried to make sense of her rather confused confession but failed, so he just cut to the chase, which was that it *was* possible she'd fallen pregnant last Friday night since they'd had heaps of unsafe sex. He could understand that this would upset her, but not to the extent of having a panic attack. He was definitely missing a piece of the puzzle here.

'You'd have to be unlucky to fall pregnant on one slip-up, Abby,' he pointed out.

She laughed. A short dry laugh which worried the life out of him.

'That's me,' she said. 'Unlucky. Especially when it comes to babies.'

He recalled her saying that she'd tried for a baby during her marriage but it hadn't happened. Which should have reassured her, in a way. Obviously, she didn't fall pregnant easily.

'It's not the end of the world if you did have a baby, is it?'

Again that odd laugh.

'You don't *have* to have a baby these days, Abby,' Jake continued gently. 'Terminations are legal and not dangerous.' Yet even as the words came out of his mouth Jake knew he wouldn't want her to terminate *their* baby. It shocked Jake to discover that he wasn't unhappy with the idea of Abby having his child.

Not Abby, though. She obviously found the idea devastating.

Her eyes flashed his way, eyes full of sudden fury and hurt. 'I should have known that was what you'd suggest. But you don't have to worry about arranging a termination for me, Jake. I'm the original baby terminator. Put a baby in me and it's lucky to last three months. Do you know what it's like to lose three babies, Jake? No, how could you? You don't want children, anyway. But I did. Once upon a time. More than anything I wanted to make my own family where the mummy and daddy truly loved each other as well as their children. Wayne did, too. He'd been a foster child, did I mention that? My parents were pretty rotten but his were even worse. Oh, God,' she sobbed, her hands lifting to cover her face. 'I failed him on all counts, didn't I?'

When Jake saw the tears seeping out from under her fingers he felt like weeping himself. But at least he now knew why she'd had that panic attack. Abby was suffering from a type of Post Traumatic Stress Disorder, something he'd become acquainted with after several years of filming in war-torn countries. When he'd started not sleeping, then having flashbacks of the various horrors he'd witnessed, he'd gone to a doctor who'd diagnosed his problem and suggested he go home and do something less stressful. Of course he'd dismissed the doctor's diagnosis as rubbish and kept on filming the world's atrocities till one day a bullet had forced him to come home.

During his recovery he'd read up on PTSD and finally agreed he had been suffering from the condition. Apparently there were only so many rotten things you could see and experience before it affected your well-being. He imagined that for a woman who desperately wanted children even one miscarriage would be distressing. Three definitely qualified as traumatic! Where once Abby had longed to fall pregnant, now just the possibility of falling pregnant set off old hurts which were so full of pain and loss and grief that her whole nervous system had gone berserk.

Unfortunately, Jake didn't think she was in a fit state right now to listen to that kind of logic. What she needed at this moment was kindness and compassion.

'Abby…darling,' he said, holding both her hands tightly as he searched for the right words to say. 'I'm sure Wayne never thought of you as a failure. He obviously loved you very much. And if I know you, I'm sure you were very loving to him in return. As far as your miscarriages are concerned, things like that happen sometimes. One of my sisters-in-law had a couple of miscarriages before she carried a baby full term. There's no reason why this baby— if there is a baby—won't survive, and be born happy and healthy.'

'No, no,' Abby sobbed. 'It won't survive. And I won't be happy. Oh, God, you don't understand.'

'I understand more than you realise. You're crossing your bridges before you come to them, Abby. Why don't we wait and see if you are pregnant? I'll take you to the doctor tomorrow to have a test done. They've made great strides with pregnancy tests these days. They can tell if you are or not even after a few days.'

She snatched her hands away and looked at him then, her expression strangely wary. 'How come you know that?'

'Not for the reason you think. I did a segment on the subject on my show.'

'Oh...'

'And if you are pregnant, then I want you to know that I will stand by you, no matter what you decide to do. I promise I'll be there for you, Abby. Always.'

She stared at him, her eyes still sceptical. Which he supposed was better than sad.

'You won't want to take a pregnant lady overseas with you,' she said.

Jake smiled. 'How do you know?'

'I know.'

'Why don't we just wait and see what the doctor says?'

Abby groaned. 'I really don't want to be pregnant, Jake.'

Not with my baby, Jake thought with some dismay. The temptation to tell her he loved her was acute, but it still didn't feel like the right time.

'Why don't you close your eyes and go to sleep? Then

later, when you're feeling better, I'll cook you something for dinner.'

Her chin began to quiver.

'No more tears now,' he said, his voice thick with emotion. 'Everything will be all right, just you wait and see.'

When he returned to the kitchen Sophie was there, looking anxious.

'Did you find out what upset her?'

Jake nodded. 'I'll just get us a drink and then I'll tell you the whole wretched story.'

'Oh, the poor love,' Sophie said once she knew everything. 'No wonder she had a panic attack. So what are you going to do, Jake? I mean, if she *is* pregnant.'

'That rather depends on Abby, don't you think?'

'Would you marry her?'

'In a heartbeat.'

'Did you tell her that?'

'No.'

'Why not?'

'Because I honestly don't think it's what she wants. Not right now.'

'You could be right. There again, you could be wrong.'

Jake rolled his eyes. 'Thanks for the vote of confidence.'

'Sorry. But there are no certainties in life, Jake. Or guarantees. Sometimes you just have to take a risk.'

'That's very good advice,' Jake said thoughtfully, deciding then and there that as soon as the time was right, he would tell Abby that he loved her.

CHAPTER THIRTY

ABBY WAS UNABLE to get an appointment with her doctor until four o'clock the following Friday. Jake had wanted to take her to *his* doctor but Abby had insisted on her own, a very nice female doctor who was both understanding and kind.

In the meantime, Jake had tried to get her to stay at his place but she'd refused, saying she'd prefer to go home after work each day. He'd rung her several times, insisting that he go to the doctor with her. But Abby had refused this as well. She wanted to be alone when she heard the news. She didn't want him to confuse her any more. Bad enough that she was already half wishing that she *was* pregnant. Which was crazy. But it was hard to think straight when you were as deeply in love as she was with Jake.

'Abby Jenkins?' her doctor called out from across the waiting room.

Abby tried to smile as she rose from the chair. But there were no smiles left in her. 'Coming,' she said.

Jake drove into the surgery car park and parked next to Abby's car, having determined to be there for Abby as he'd said he would. He didn't go against her wishes and go inside, but no way was he going to let her leave this appointment without his love and support.

The wait felt interminable. He put some music on to distract his escalating tension, but it didn't work, his stomach doing a somersault when he finally spotted Abby emerging from the building shortly before five.

He was out of his car like a shot, his eyes searching her

face for signs of distress as she walked towards him, not finding any comfort in her frown.

'What are you doing here?' she demanded to know straight away. 'I told you not to come.'

'Sorry,' he said straight away. 'I simply had to. So what did the doctor say? Did he do one of the new tests?'

'She's a she and yes, she did a very new test, and no, I'm not pregnant.'

Jake didn't know if he was disappointed or not, though, of course, his main concern was how Abby felt.

'Well, that's good news, isn't it?' he said.

'Yes,' Abby bit out. 'Good news.'

Why, then, he wondered, didn't she *sound* happier?

'I see,' he said, wishing he knew what was going on in her head. 'So what are you going to do now?'

Her sigh was heavy. 'Go home, I suppose.'

'Don't do that. I'd like to take you somewhere for dinner.'

'To celebrate, you mean,' she said with a decided edge in her voice.

'In a way…' Jake thought of the diamond engagement ring he had in his pocket and which he hoped would convince Abby of his feelings for her.

Just then, some more people emerged from the surgery. When a woman started staring at him and pointing, Jake decided it was time for a quick getaway.

'Hop in, Abby,' he said quickly as he reefed open his passenger door. 'Before that woman gets on Twitter and the paparazzi arrive.'

'But what about my car?' she asked even as she did as she was told.

'We'll come back and get it later.' He quickly exited the car park and zoomed up the road.

Abby suddenly bursting into tears brought a groan to his lips, and a swift end to his idea of a romantic dinner. 'Oh, Abby. Darling. Please don't cry. Look, I'll take you home.'

'Yes, please,' she choked out, obviously doing her best to stop crying. But it was no use. The waterworks were open and she kept on weeping.

Jake took her not to her home, but to his. By the time they arrived she'd stopped crying but was looking totally worn out. He parked out front and led her inside, where he offered her either coffee or a glass of wine. She opted for the latter, sliding up on to one of the kitchen stools whilst he did the honours with a bottle of chilled Sauvignon Blanc.

'Can I ask you something, Jake?' she said when he'd poured two generous glasses.

'Of course.'

'What would you have done if the test had come back positive?'

He hesitated, though not for long. 'I was going to ask you to marry me.'

Her silence did not augur well. When Jake glanced over at her, she was staring at him with shock in her eyes.

'You don't mean that,' she said at last, sounding shaken. 'You don't do marriage and you definitely don't do children. You made that quite clear. You said it was a deal-breaker for you.'

'That was before,' he said.

'Before what?' she demanded, sounding angry now.

'Before I fell in love with you. Actually, I was going to ask you to marry me today, whether you were pregnant or not.'

She shook her head from side to side, her eyes disbelieving.

'But that's crazy, Jake. You're not thinking straight.'

'I had a feeling that might be your reaction,' he said. 'So I thought I had better have backup.'

'A backup?'

'Yep. A backup.'

Jake put down the bottle of wine, his whole body tensing up as he faced a startled Abby, though he tried not to show it.

'Sophie said you were averse to me buying you jewellery but I gather that was because you didn't want me treating you like a mistress. So I bought the one piece of jewellery which would never be given to a mistress.'

When he brought a small black box out of his pocket and flipped it open, revealing a diamond engagement ring set in yellow gold, Abby stared down at it, then up at him.

'Oh, my God,' she choked out. 'It…it's lovely, Jake. And so are you. I'm touched. Really I am. But I… I can't.'

Dismay made his heart turn over. 'Are you saying that you don't love me?'

The loving look in her eyes was some comfort. 'Of course I love you. Surely you must know that. But I can't marry you. Because marriage means children to me. And I just can't go there again. Not yet. Maybe not ever.'

Jake did his best to hide his hurt and disappointment.

'Can't we just stay as we are, Jake?' she pleaded. 'You know you don't really want marriage, anyway.'

Actually, I don't know any such thing, Jake thought, a great lump filling his throat. After Craig died, he'd realised that his way of life wasn't as great as he'd thought it was. Who wanted to die alone, with no one at their bedside, holding their hand and telling them that they were loved?

Abby's hands clasped the sides of her face, a face full of escalating panic.

'Oh, God, if only you could understand…'

When she looked as if she was about to burst into tears again, Jake knew she was thinking about the babies she had lost. It must have been truly terrible for her. He could see that. He could also see that he had rushed her with his proposal. She wasn't ready to face that kind of commitment.

But one day she would be. And when she was he would be right there by her side.

Slipping the ring box back into his pocket, he smiled over at her. 'It's all right, Abby,' he said gently. 'We'll do what you want and just go on as we are. But could you at least move in with me?'

She lifted adoring eyes to his. 'Oh. Yes. I'd love to.'

CHAPTER THIRTY-ONE

Twelve months later...

'IT WILL BE so good to see Megan and Timmy again,' Abby said excitedly as the plane started its descent into Mascot. 'And your family too.'

'We'll see them all on Christmas Day,' Jake told her. 'I booked the same boat we had last year.'

'Did you? You didn't tell me that.' Which surprised Abby. Because she and Jake told each other everything. During the last year, their love for each other had deepened to a true love. It wasn't just lust, as Abby had once feared. Travelling together, living together, twenty-four-seven had been marvellous. She'd loved every minute of it. Paris in the summer had been magnificent, even if she had picked up a tummy bug. But honestly, she was glad to be home.

'I wanted to surprise you,' Jake went on. 'I have another surprise for you as well.'

'What?'

'Tomorrow morning you have an appointment with one of Sydney's top fertility experts.'

Abby sucked in sharply, her stomach tightening as well. 'You...you shouldn't have done that without talking to me first.'

'Abby,' Jake said gently but firmly, 'it's time.'

And it was. He was right. During the last year, Jake had convinced Abby that he really would like to marry her. And one or two children would be all right by him. And whilst she'd remained on the Pill they had stopped using condoms. But there wasn't a single day that she forgot to take that Pill; she'd programmed her phone with a reminder.

The trouble was, Abby was still afraid. Afraid of hoping and wanting and having her dreams dashed one more time.

'If all else fails,' Jake said, 'we can adopt.'

Her eyes widened. 'Are you sure?'

'Absolutely. There are a lot of wretched orphans in this world who would love a wonderful woman like you as their mother.'

Abby's heart melted with love for this man. 'That's the nicest thing you've ever said to me.'

Jake smiled. 'So when we get home can I drag out that engagement ring which is still sitting in a drawer somewhere?'

'Oh, God, I still feel awful about that ring. Have you forgiven me for turning down your proposal that day?'

'There's nothing to forgive. You were right to turn me down. It was too soon. But it's not too soon now, Abby. It's time for us to face the future together.'

Jake watched Abby fiddling with her ring as they waited for their turn with the doctor. She was terribly nervous. But then so was Jake. He knew how much having children meant to Abby. He'd seen the look in her eyes every time they'd come across a happy family during their overseas travels. Becoming a father still wasn't an all-consuming dream of his but anything that made Abby happy would make him happy.

The door to the doctor's office opened and Dr Gard walked out. She was about fifty, tall and slim with a plain but kind face.

'Mr and Mrs Sanderson?' she asked, whereupon Abby threw Jake a wry smile.

They traipsed after the doctor into her rooms, where she waved them to two chairs in front of her desk. Clearly, she often saw couples together.

Jake listened to Abby bravely tell her whole medical history, even though her voice was shaking. The doctor listened intently, throwing in a question every now and then.

'I think, Abby,' she said at last, 'that I should examine you. Would you mind?'

Of course she didn't mind and was taken behind a curtain for what felt like an eternity to Jake. Finally, the two women emerged with the doctor's expression a rather puzzled one.

'Well,' she said once they were both seated again, 'I have to confess that this doesn't happen to me very often.'

'What?' Jake asked immediately, sensing that it wasn't all bad news.

Her eyes were directed at Abby. 'You said you were on the Pill?'

'Yes,' Abby replied.

'And you've been having regular periods?'

Abby flushed. 'Well, not exactly. We've been travelling and I've been skipping the white pills so that I didn't have to worry about periods.'

'I see,' the doctor said with a smile. 'Well, Abby, I am happy to inform you that you're actually pregnant.'

'Pregnant!' Abby gasped whilst Jake held his breath. His head was whirling.

'Yes. About four months, by the feel of your uterus. We'll know for sure when you have an ultrasound. I'll organise one for you straight away.'

Both Abby and Jake were in shock as they were taken into another room for the ultrasound. But underneath the shock lay the hope of happiness. If the doctor was right, then Abby was already past the three-month danger time, which was further than she'd ever got before.

Jake held her hand whilst the doctor moved the instrument over Abby's gelled-up stomach, which did indeed have a small baby bump. She'd complained only the other day that she'd put on weight, blaming all the restaurant food they'd been eating. But it hadn't been that. It had been a baby. *His* baby.

Jake's heart turned over as he stared at the screen and saw the outline of a living, breathing human being.

'A little more than four months, I would say,' the doctor told them. 'Do you want to know the sex?'

'Yes, please,' they both chorused.

'It's a girl. Small but beautifully formed.'

'Oh,' Abby said through her tears.

Jake lifted her hand to his lips. 'Just like her mother,' he said, his heart so full of love for this woman, and his child, he was almost in tears himself. He vowed then and there that he would be the best husband and father. Just like his own dad, who he saw now might not have had wealth, but had been rich with love.

'You…you think I'll be all right then?' Abby tentatively asked the doctor.

The woman smiled down at her. 'I'm sure you'll be fine. After all, you have a very good doctor. Don't you worry, dear. I'll look after you.'

EPILOGUE

THE DOCTOR WAS as good as her word. Jake and Abby's daughter went full term. She came into the world a very beautiful baby with a soft crown of fair hair, big blue eyes and the prettiest little face. The birth was a natural one but with enough drugs to make sure Abby wasn't in too much pain.

After the birth, Abby could not stop looking at her daughter, and cuddling her. Jake hardly got a look in. Not that he minded. He knew how much having this baby meant to Abby. Finally, after she'd had her fill, she handed the bundle over for him to hold.

Parental love squeezed Jake's heart as he rocked his daughter to and fro.

'Paris,' he murmured. It was the name they'd chosen once they worked out that that was where she'd been conceived, the doctor explaining that the gastric bug Abby had caught had probably rendered the Pill ineffective for a few days.

'Well, Mrs Sanderson,' he said with the fatuous smile of a besotted father, 'you've produced a real beauty here.'

'She is lovely, isn't she?'

'She's the spitting image of her mother.'

'Do you think so?'

He did, and so did everyone else who came in to visit them. Sometimes, there were so many people in Abby's room that the nurses would complain about the noise. The maternity ward breathed a sigh of relief when Jake took Abby and Paris home.

Sophie and Megan were asked to be godparents at the baby's christening three weeks later, both of them receiving very generous gifts from the happy parents. Abby gave an over-the-moon Megan her old house and Jake presented Sophie with the deed to Craig's apartment.

The following Christmas was an especially joyful one. Jake hired the same boat for another harbour cruise, amazed at how much he enjoyed the family gathering, perhaps because he could show off his very beautiful daughter. Abby revelled in everyone's compliments plus the knowledge that, at last, her dream of creating her own happy family had finally come true. Already she was planning a second baby, and Jake was happy to oblige. Truly, for a man who'd once claimed not to want marriage and children, he'd proved to be a wonderful husband and father.

'She was a big hit, wasn't she?' Jake said that night as they stood next to Paris's pretty pink cot and stared down at her sleeping form.

When he slipped a tender arm around Abby's waist, she leant her head against his and sighed. 'It was a wonderful Christmas Day. Even better than last year.'

Jake had to agree. Though last year's Christmas had been pretty special. It had been, after all, their wedding day as well. Which reminded him.

'I have a surprise present for you,' he said. And he produced another ring box, which contained an emerald and diamond eternity ring.

'Oh, Jake,' Abby choked out as he slipped it on her finger. 'It's beautiful.'

'Not as beautiful as you, my darling.'

'You say the loveliest things to me.'

'That's because I love you.'

'I'm still not sure why, but I'm glad that you do.'

Jake bent his head and kissed her. He could think of a thousand reasons why he loved Abby, not the least that she was the bravest, kindest, most genuine person he'd ever met. He thanked his uncle every day for the legacy which had set him on a path that showed him marriage and children need not be a grind; they could be a joy. He'd never been happier than during the last year. Of course, he was lucky that he didn't have to work if he didn't want to. But Jake knew he would not enjoy being idle for long. He was already thinking of creating a series of documentaries called the *Honeymoon Show*, highlighting places to go for a honeymoon, a feel-good show full of happy people who actually loved each other.

Now that would be different...

When Abby gave a small moan of desire, his head lifted.

'Time for bed, I think, my love.' And, taking Abby's hand in his, he walked off with her into the future.

* * * * *

DOUBLE THE ROMANCE WITH
MODERN 2-IN-1S

From January 2020, all Modern stories will be published in a 2-in-1 format.

MILLS & BOON
MODERN
Power and Passion

Eight Modern stories in four 2-in-1 books, published every month. Find them all at:

millsandboon.co.uk

COMING SOON!

We really hope you enjoyed reading this book. If you're looking for more romance, be sure to head to the shops when new books are available on

Thursday 12th December

To see which titles are coming soon, please visit

millsandboon.co.uk/nextmonth

MILLS & BOON

MILLS & BOON

Coming next month

BILLIONAIRE'S WIFE ON PAPER
Melanie Milburne

'But you don't want to get married.' It was a statement, not a question.

A shadow passed through his gaze like a background figure moving across a stage. He turned back to face the view from the windows; there might as well have been a 'Keep Away' sign printed on his back. It seemed a decade before he spoke. 'No.' His tone had a note of finality that made something in Layla's chest tighten.

The thought of him marrying someone one day had always niggled at her like mild toothache. She could ignore it mostly but now and again a sharp jab would catch her off guard. But how could he ever find someone as perfect for him as Susannah? No wonder he was a little reluctant to date seriously these days. If only Layla could find someone to love her with such lasting loyalty.

'What about a marriage of convenience? You could find someone who would agree to marry you just long enough to fulfil the terms of the will.'

One of his dark eyebrows rose in a cynical arc above his left eye. 'Are you volunteering for the role as my paper bride?'

Eek! Why had she even mentioned such a thing? Maybe it was time to stop reading paperback romances and start reading thriller or horror novels instead. Layla could feel a hot flush of colour flooding her cheeks and bent down to straighten the items in her basket to disguise it. 'No. Of course not.' Her voice was part laugh, part gasp and came out shamefully high and tight. Her? His bride of convenience? Ha-di-ha-ha-ha. She wouldn't be a convenient bride for anyone, much less Logan McLaughlin.

A strange silence crept from the far corners of the room, stealing oxygen particles, stilling dust motes, stirring possibilities…

Logan walked back to where she was hovering over her cleaning basket, his footsteps steady and sure. Step. Step. Step.

Step. Layla slowly raised her gaze to his inscrutable one, her heart doing a crazy tap dance in her chest. She drank in the landscape of his face—the ink-black prominent eyebrows over impossibly blue eyes, the patrician nose, the sensually sculpted mouth, the steely determined jaw. The lines of grief etched into his skin that made him seem older than he was. At thirty-three, he was in the prime of his life. Wealthy, talented, a world-renowned landscape architect—you could not find a more eligible bachelor...or one so determined to avoid commitment.

'Think about it, Layla.'

His tone was deep with a side note of roughness that made a faint shiver course through her body. A shiver of awareness. A shiver of longing that could no longer be restrained in its secret home.

Layla picked up her basket from the floor and held it in front of her body like a shield. Was he teasing her? Making fun of her? He must surely know she wasn't marriage material—certainly not for someone like him. She was about as far away from Susannah as you could get. 'Don't be ridiculous.'

His hand came down to touch her on the forearm, and even through two layers of clothing her skin tingled. She looked down at his long strong fingers and disguised a swallow. She could count on one hand the number of times he had touched her over the years and still have fingers left over. His touch was unfamiliar and strange, alien almost, and yet her body reacted like a crocus bulb to spring sunshine.

'I'm serious,' he said, looking at her with watchful intensity. 'I need a temporary wife to save Bellbrae from being sold or destroyed and who better than someone who loves this place as much as I do?'

Continue reading
BILLIONAIRE'S WIFE ON PAPER
Melanie Milburne

Available next month
www.millsandboon.co.uk

Copyright ©2019 by Melanie Milburne

LET'S TALK
Romance

For exclusive extracts, competitions
and special offers, find us online:

facebook.com/millsandboon

@MillsandBoon

@MillsandBoonUK

Get in touch on 01413 063232

For all the latest titles coming soon, visit
millsandboon.co.uk/nextmonth

MILLS & BOON
A ROMANCE FOR EVERY READER

- **FREE** delivery direct to your door

- **EXCLUSIVE** offers every month

- **SAVE** up to 25% on pre-paid subscriptions

SUBSCRIBE AND SAVE

millsandboon.co.uk/Subscribe

WANT EVEN MORE

ROMANCE?

SUBSCRIBE AND SAVE TODAY!

'Mills & Boon books, the perfect way to escape for an hour or so.'

MISS W. DYER

'Excellent service, promptly delivered and very good subscription choices.'

MISS A. PEARSON

'You get fantastic special offers and the chance to get books before they hit the shops.'

MRS V. HALL

Visit millsandboon.co.uk/Subscribe and save on brand new books.

MILLS & BOON
DARE

Sexy. Passionate. Bold.

Sensual love stories featuring smart, sassy heroines you'd want as a best friend, and compelling intense heroes who are worthy of them.

Four DARE stories published every month, find them all at

millsandboon.co.uk/DARE

MILLS & BOON

THE HEART OF ROMANCE

A ROMANCE FOR EVERY KIND OF READER

MODERN

Prepare to be swept off your feet by sophisticated, sexy and seductive heroes, in some of the world's most glamourous and romantic locations, where power and passion collide.
8 stories per month.

HISTORICAL

Escape with historical heroes from time gone by. Whether your passion is for wicked Regency Rakes, muscled Vikings or rugged Highlanders, awaken the romance of the past.
6 stories per month.

MEDICAL

Set your pulse racing with dedicated, delectable doctors in the high-pressure world of medicine, where emotions run high and passion, comfort and love are the best medicine.
6 stories per month.

True Love

Celebrate true love with tender stories of heartfelt romance, from the rush of falling in love to the joy a new baby can bring, and a focus on the emotional heart of a relationship.
8 stories per month.

Desire

Indulge in secrets and scandal, intense drama and plenty of sizzling hot action with powerful and passionate heroes who have it all: wealth, status, good looks…everything but the right woman.
6 stories per month.

HEROES

Experience all the excitement of a gripping thriller, with an intense romance at its heart. Resourceful, true-to-life women and strong, fearless men face danger and desire - a killer combination!
8 stories per month.

DARE

Sensual love stories featuring smart, sassy heroines you'd want as a best friend, and compelling intense heroes who are worthy of them.
4 stories per month.

To see which titles are coming soon, please visit

millsandboon.co.uk/nextmonth

GET YOUR ROMANCE FIX!

MILLS & BOON
— blog —

Get the latest romance news, exclusive author interviews, story extracts and much more!

blog.millsandboon.co.uk